World-Walker

World-Walker

Melisa Michaels

Five Star • Waterville, Maine

First Edition
First Printing: October 2004

Published in 2004 in conjunction with Tekno Books
and Ed Gorman.

Set in 11 pt. Plantin by Carleen Stearns.

Printed in the United States on permanent paper.

Library of Congress Cataloging-in-Publication Data

Michaels, Melisa C.
    World-walker / by Melisa Michaels.—1st ed.
      p. cm.
    ISBN 1-59414-215-7 (hc : alk. paper)
    1. Women—Fiction.   2. Life on other planets—Fiction.
I. Title.
PS3563.I2734W67 2004
  813'.54—dc22   2004053703

For Richard, who Walks with me
no matter how steep the path.

1
Suli

World-Walker First Class Suli Grail wondered how much her superior knew of her relationship with the man known to Central as the Other. According to Central, he had abandoned his name with the life it represented. He was at home in no world, though he tried to be at home in them all.

Suli saw little real difference between him and any other world-walker: they were essentially nothing more than a scattered society of the nameless and the homeless. She had not heard her name spoken more than three times since she joined, and she had lived in so many worlds now that she was not sure she would know hers if she saw it again. She was at home in no world, though she tried to be at home in them all.

"The difference is, you're legal."

She came to herself with a start: she was seated in an uncomfortable, straight-backed, ugly acrylic chair next to the massive and very battered black wooden desk of the most senior world-walker in the worlds, who despite his exalted position was as nameless and perhaps even as homeless as she. In the years since she'd first met him, she had never seen him outside this office, a featureless little bright box of a room decorated with the mismatched appurtenances of a dozen worlds, belonging to none.

It took her a moment to absorb the meaning of his remark, which had been the opening move of the interview and, as such, was intended to convince her either that he was psychic or at least that he had a comprehensive understanding of the workings of the average world-walker's mind. If he meant to unnerve her, he failed. Her response was distant and unimpressed. "Yes, sir."

Her superior eyed her with amused severity. "And you are sworn to uphold order, peace, and the integrity of worlds. You are trained in ways and means. The Other is not. He pleases himself, worlds be damned—and if we don't stop him, some of them will be damned, you know."

She nodded soberly, causing the dark curls that framed her face to bounce in an unintentionally and incongruously cheerful way. "Yes, sir."

He smiled: a grim tightening of ancient lips that did not light his faded yellow eyes. "You identify with him, don't you?"

Her expression remained bland. "Yes, sir."

"You believe he has been cruelly hounded into a life of crime by an unjust fate. Or perhaps, at least in part, by unduly harsh laws and rigid societies."

She lifted her chin. "Yes, sir."

He leaned forward across the desk, his narrow shoulders hunched, his paper-skinned hands folded over a rack of information chips, his watery eyes regarding her with startling intensity. "You've met with him."

"Yes, sir."

"More than once."

"Yes, sir."

"You believe you know him."

She hesitated, thinking it over. "Yes, sir."

He smiled again, still hunched toward her like a frail, de-

8

hydrated frog. "And the musician Jesse Farrell?"

If the name startled her, she concealed it well. "Yes, sir?" Neither her face, which was expressionless, nor her posture, which was faultlessly composed, altered in any way; but she could not prevent the spark of defiance that briefly lit her clear amber eyes.

Her superior unfolded his hands, gazed at them with apparent disapprobation, and folded them again. Without lifting his gaze to her he said gently, "The Other displaced him." He looked at her then, his expression unreadable. "The Other deliberately put him in Limbo."

"Yes, sir." Her voice was clear and controlled, her face serene.

"At best, that is against the law." He was looking at his hands again.

"Yes, sir." She betrayed no impatience, though he stated the obvious.

Leaning back in his chair, he let his folded hands fall into his lap, shifted his shoulders as though they pained him, and studied her with narrowed eyes. "I said, at best."

"Yes, sir." Her expression became remotely curious.

After a moment's thought he picked up an information chip from his desk and examined its label without interest. "Were you given a brief of this case?"

"Yes, sir."

His voice became sharp. "Did you read it?"

"Yes, sir."

With a degree of care that would have been appropriate to the handling of powerful explosives, he put the chip down again and aligned it very precisely with its neighbors. "Then you know that Jesse Farrell is pivotal."

She shifted neither her position nor her level gaze. "Yes, sir."

9

"If you say 'yes, sir' once more, I will put *you* in Limbo."

"Very well, sir."

For a timeless moment they gazed at each other, each of them utterly expressionless: then he shook his head slowly without removing his gaze from hers. "I was warned you had become a rebel." His tone implied that her present behavior confirmed the report.

"I was warned you had become a martinet." Her tone implied nothing.

He emitted an unexpected bark of amusement. "I admire honesty."

She permitted herself the faintest hint of an answering smile. "I have observed that, sir."

With a brief, impatient gesture he dismissed her observation. "We're wasting time."

"I agree, sir."

This time the twitch of his shoulders might as well have been produced by vexation as by physical discomfort. "Tell me what you learned from the brief."

"That the Other doppelgangered some musician in World V2G 5N8 slash three and was bounced from there into slash six, where his doppelganger had died in the auto accident that damaged the Other's leg in his home world; that he spent about five local months there, meddling with politics or religion, before something happened—no one seems to know what—that drove him into Limbo; that he moved from Limbo into World V4G 7N7 slash ten, was doppelgangered by another musician (I thought it odd that his doppelgangers in that district were all musicians, but the brief didn't comment on that); and that we lost him for a while after that until he bounced into slash four, this time managing to bump the musician into Limbo instead of getting bounced himself. Which means he's learning the ways."

Her superior nodded. "Yes? And?"

She shrugged almost imperceptibly. "That's about it. I know it's forbidden to jump time to stop a gatecrasher before he gets started, but—"

"You want to jump time to stop him?"

"I think it would work."

"Meaning, presumably, that you think legal means won't work."

She lifted her chin, staring him down. "That's right."

"Noted." His gaze was bland. "Anything else?"

She blinked. "I assumed the musician he bounced into Limbo must be pivotal, since the monitors are in such a bother."

He opened a drawer of his desk, withdrew a vial of pills, and popped one into his mouth. "The musician has a name."

Without expression she said promptly, "I guessed that particular Jesse Farrell was pivotal, since the monitors are in such a bother."

He replaced the vial of pills in the drawer and closed it gently, watching her. "In theory, the Other is Jesse Farrell."

"In practice as well, in his home world," she said. "And at this point, in World V4G 7N7 slash four, too."

He conceded the point with a curt nod. "And the Jesse Farrell from V4G 7N7 slash four has been temporarily relocated in slash three till the Other can be ousted from slash four."

"What happened to the one from slash three?"

Another grim smile tightened his lips. "You surprise me." He did not sound surprised.

"By my ignorance? It wasn't in the brief."

11

"By your curiosity," he said.

Something flickered in the shadows of her eyes. "Surely most world-walkers are curious."

He nodded thoughtfully. "Very curious."

She had used "curious" to mean "interested in learning"; he used it to mean "odd." A smile of acknowledgment tugged at her lips. She suppressed it.

After studying her a moment longer, he leaned back in his chair again and folded his hands over the flat frailty of his midsection. "The Jesse Farrell from V4G 7N7 slash three was on the point of death from what is referred to in his world as substance abuse, which is, as I understand it, a somewhat bizarre method of suicide. The monitors on duty decided to switch him with the Farrell from slash four. So you see, the Other has again betrayed the integrity of worlds; there should be no living Farrell in slash three now, but there is."

"He died in Limbo?"

Her superior looked at her. "The Other?"

"The Farrell from slash three."

"Oh. Of course. Yes."

"Alone?"

The old man's eyes glittered in the light from the window by his desk. "One might say the Other killed him."

"One might, sir." Her eyes were defiant, but her tone was bland.

"You would prefer to blame the monitors?"

"It's not my job to lay blame."

Scowling in sudden irritation, he said harshly, "No, it's not. Your job is to bring the Other to justice."

"The better to uphold order, peace, and the integrity of worlds," she said.

Nodding quite seriously, as though unaware of her intended sarcasm, he said in the tone of one imparting needed but uninteresting information, "Emotional identification can be a severe handicap in our work."

"Yet you hoped I would identify with this Jesse Farrell." It was neither a question nor a challenge, merely a piece of information to match his.

He shrugged, his irritation gone. "I do think it preferable to identifying with the Other."

After the briefest hesitation she said carefully, "The Other is more like me."

"Is he?"

"He walks worlds." She was explaining it to him earnestly, as to one who had no previous knowledge of the subject. "He has no name, no home—"

His pale eyes glittered. "No morals, no empathy, no conscience . . ."

Startled, she grinned at him inadvertently. "Point taken," she said. "All right, yes."

His expression remained severe. "Yes what?"

A spark of amusement danced in her eyes. "Yes, *sir*."

That surprised another bark of laughter from him. For a moment the tension between them was gone, replaced by a tenuous sense of camaraderie; they were both worldwalkers, and they knew what they knew. But the moment could not last. With a sigh, he returned to practicalities. "You said you have met the Other?"

Her eyes flickered. "I have, sir."

"In fact, you had a relationship with him?"

"I had, sir."

He was visibly pleased that she did not defend herself. "You know what will happen to him if you bring him back?"

"I know, sir."

"Exceptions have been made in the past." It was a comment, not an offer.

"Yes." She lifted her chin at him. "Sir."

He allowed himself the hint of a smile. "You do not expect an exception in this case."

She shrugged. "He won't ask."

"You might."

"You don't know him at all, if you think he would thank me for that."

"One is seldom thanked for saving a life. Would you deny him the chance you might give him?"

"Would you deny me mine?" The question was inadvertent and instantly regretted, but too late to recall the words. She met his gaze with a curiously stunned look, both vulnerable and fierce.

He did not hesitate. "Yes. I would. I will."

She studied him, unblinking. "How did you know what I meant?"

He sighed. "Child, do you think you are unique? But consider what your plans would mean. Would you really want to destroy whole worlds for him? You know it can come to nothing better than that. If you were to run away with him, where could you go? It would only mean two Others running from us, endangering worlds, instead of only the one; until we caught you both and brought you back."

"And sent us to Limbo."

"And sent you to Limbo."

"We'd get out."

"I think not." He turned half away from her to look out the window at his side. The view was of a square of blue sky, nothing more, yet he seemed fascinated by it. "It is possible to survive in Limbo," he said.

14

"Not for us," she said, and leaned forward. "He's a Natural, sir."

"Perhaps," he said.

"The New Worlders," she began.

He waved one hand dismissively, interrupting her. "Radical nonsense," he said. "Not worth discussion." He hesitated. "Does he know?"

She looked at him in surprise. "Does he know what?"

"Does he know that you love him?"

For the first time during the interview, she made an involuntarily revealing movement in reaction to his words: an ineffable little half-shrug, half-flinching movement that he saw only from the corner of his eye, and understood all too well. "I don't know," she said.

He nodded, as if to himself. "If you bring him back," he said, and hesitated. "If you bring him back before irreparable damage is done between worlds—" He turned his head again to face her. His faded yellow eyes seemed blinded, as though he had looked too long at the sky. "I cannot promise anything."

Her mouth twisted down at one corner. "I asked for nothing."

He nodded. "Not even for promises."

She did not respond.

"Not even from him." He was pressing too far, not certain himself what he wanted from her, and for one frozen instant he thought she would attack him, but she controlled her sudden rage with a visible effort and, again, made no response. He sighed. "There is always a price," he said.

Her mouth twisted again. "What's yours? Not that I'll pay it. Sir."

He shook his head and made an impatient gesture with one frail hand. "No, no, you misunderstand." He felt sud-

15

denly weary. "If the Board were to grant leniency in this case . . ." Lost in contemplation, he let his voice trail away.

She eyed him dubiously. "The only way would be to grant us a home."

After a moment he nodded. "Yes. One world."

Visibly struggling against hope, she said carefully, "Where we could stay."

His expression became unreadable. "Where you would have to stay." When her only response was a bemused frown, he sighed again. "You've walked worlds, both of you. He plays in them like a child in a sandbox, building and breaking and running away. You tramp across them with some heroic vision of yourself as an avenging angel or a cosmic cop. Both of you have known a kind of freedom few mortals even imagine. You've had all the worlds at your doorstep. Could you settle for one? Could he?"

She looked stubborn. "I don't know."

He turned away from her. "Bring him back, world-walker," he said wearily. "And if you cannot bring him back, then kill him." At her audible intake of breath, he smiled distantly. "He might prefer that to Limbo."

"I—" She hesitated, choosing her words. "Sir, why can't we jump time, just this once? If the alternative is to kill him? Surely it wouldn't . . . surely killing is just as bad. Just as disruptive."

"You are welcome to jump time all you like," he said, deliberately misunderstanding.

"Sir, to stop him. Before he started. I could . . . I could find the pivotal moment, couldn't I, and stop him there?"

"Simplicity itself, you think, to find that moment?" He did not quite smile, but there was a look of sympathetic amusement in his eyes.

"I could do it." She blushed, but kept her gaze steady.

"Perhaps you could." He shook his head. "Child, alter the past and you become what he is: a destroyer."

"I'm that, either way, it seems."

"I'm sorry, child." He meant it.

She made one last effort. "I'm trained for killing, certainly, and if I had to, to save someone, or in self defense . . . but not—not for policy. Not for orders. No." She shook her head. "I'm not a killer."

He looked at her. "It is your job," he said. "You may have to be."

2

Jesse

Jesse Farrell bounced back out into the white-hot light of center stage and grinned into the arena. The faces of the audience, like a sea of luminous, featureless ovals, floated motionless in the swimming shadows that darkened to bottomless black in the distance.

He grinned at the audience: an urchin's grin: a sweet blue-eyed smile like a small boy's, innocent and cheerfully shy. He blinked under the merciless spotlights, listening to the drawn-out, hissing moan of his name washing up across the shimmering heat of the stage like a storm wind rising, and tried not to think about the police waiting backstage.

His body reacted of its own volition to the time and place: he bounced, he danced, he shadow-boxed, forced into constant motion by that peculiar mixture of energy and exhaustion that was the result of stage fright, a long tour, a responsive audience, and a visceral love of performing. Ruth used to laugh at him for that. "Most guys have to psych themselves up for a gig," she said. "Jesse has to psych himself down for the rest of his life."

Ruth was dead. The police showed him hideous photographs, and seemed to believe he had killed her. True, they were unfairly biased because he was a long-haired rock 'n' roll singer, and they thought all rock musicians were drug-crazed punks. It made no difference to them that Jesse was known in the business, somewhat derisively, as Mr. Clean. As far as they were concerned, he was a rock star; therefore he must be drug-sodden scum.

But they wouldn't have arrested him for that alone. Much more damning were the hours last night that he could not account for. And the blood on his clothes. And the knife. . . .

He closed his eyes. The big lights beat down steadily, a tangible weight pressing against him. The air smelled of burnt insulation and sweat. The audience, which had howled and stomped for him when he was offstage and roared with approval when he finally came on, was growing restive again, rustling and muttering under the constant wash of his name moaned impatiently from a thousand adoring throats.

The concert was only half over, and he had been late in returning to the stage after the brief intermission. The band, already onstage when Jesse was delayed, had long since settled down to play, awaiting only a signal from him. Bob Lyle shifted uneasily behind his microphone to Jesse's left, looking a question at him; behind him one of Darla's drumsticks rattled inadvertently against the side of a drum. The sound was barely audible under the constant sibilant moan from the audience. "Jesse . . . Jesssseeee . . . Jessssseee . . ." If the music did not begin soon, the crowd would resume the half-wild foot-stomping, hand-clapping, and shouting that had convinced the stone-faced police lieutenant to let Jesse finish the show before they took him away. Jesse raised one arm straight over his head, fingers splayed. The fans roared their approval at the familiar signal, then by degrees fell silent in eager, obedient anticipation.

When the expectant stillness was complete, he let his

arm fall limp at his side and stood waiting with the audience, head bowed, face shadowed by hair that had, at the beginning of the concert, been a glittering golden halo but by now was only a mass of wet, tangled yellow curls. Behind him Mirabelle Kane touched the synthesizer keyboard with questing fingers, and a whisper of sound fell out of the air like the pure, clear tones of fairy trumpets sounding the break of day.

On cue, the lighting changed from glaring white to colored gels that swept stage and audience both with pools of crimson, lilac, and celestial blue. The fairy trumpets were joined by organ tones, as cold and as unearthly as starlight. The sobbing notes of Bob Lyle's careful bass guitar joined in, almost subliminal at first and swelling to a moan, a bleak wail of desolation, then dropping back into the sparkling darkness of a soft lament.

Darla Black's drums rustled like dried leaves. Jesse moved almost imperceptibly to finger a chord and the audience, rapt in the spell of the filigreed melody, shuddered visibly as his guitar squalled in sudden torment, shattering the magic. As quickly as he had destroyed it he rebuilt harmony out of discord, but that terrible sense of pain and loss remained, a poignant backdrop for stringed laughter that faded only when he began to sing.

His deep, rasping voice was so hoarse he sounded as though he should not be able to hit one right note, yet he invariably hit them all with heart-shaking clarity. Bob Lyle sang a harmonic echo, his voice as vulnerable as Jesse's was savage. The melody, all aching flats in the chorus, soared into a kind of mad ecstasy in the verse and Jesse leaned into it, clinging to the microphone, his voice clear and compelling.

Bancroft Averill's guitar picked up the theme and played with it, tangling the melody and unraveling it and weaving it up again into a thing of brilliant colors and unexpected flashes of light. Lyle's bass mourned unbearable losses, thrumming a plaintive lament that became a supporting understructure for the instrumental, as his sweet tenor supported the raw violence of Jesse's voice.

Darla's drums thundered into a passionate fury during each repeat of the chorus, then settled down in the verses to maintain an unrelenting rhythm as unassuming and as essential as a heartbeat.

> *All the hollow haunted memories . . .*
> *The lies you've been told . . .*
> *Will be something to hold . . .*
> *When the music's over . . .*

Jesse unhooked the mike to race across the stage as he sang, pausing to direct his words to new sections of the audience, working his way across the stage in a series of carelessly graceful leaps and bounds, wholly caught up in the power and fury of the song.

The air around him throbbed with the force of the music. The pure, clear tones of the synthesizer counterbalanced the brutal quality of his voice. Together they created an aching sense of longing that the other instruments picked up and augmented. Jesse moved against it in pure reflex, bobbing and weaving with the unconsciously fluid motions of a trained dancer.

> *Your weariness will follow you . . .*
> *And when you know what you're worth . . .*
> *Just tell the wind where it hurts . . .*
> *You ain't got nothing on earth . . .*
> *But forever . . .*

He was never to fully understand what happened then. He did not even perceive the change until a half-beat after it occurred, when the song caught in his throat and died: the stage floor had gone soft and mushy, tripping him. The music was gone. The band was gone. The audience, that vast sea of luminous faces fading into light-hazed emptiness before him, was gone.

He stood alone in an endless, featureless desert of red sand that shimmered with heat waves under the heavy vertical rays of an oddly orange noonday sun. An acrid odor, unfamiliar and unpleasant, as though the sand were not ordinary sand but some combination of bitter chemicals, burned in his nose. There was no sound but the harsh rasp of his labored breathing, no sign of any living thing but him, not even a breath of wind to break the sullen and oppressive stillness: just Jesse Farrell, drenched in sweat and blinded by the light, standing suddenly alone in an impossible, alien desert.

A voice, neither distant nor near, said clearly, "Try 101 slash A, why don't you?"

"He's pivotal, you idiot," said a second voice.

Shaken, Jesse turned unsteadily, his boots scraping unpleasantly in the gritty sand. There was no one and nothing in sight but sand like crushed glass gleaming under the sun. Nothing but flat, hot, blinding emptiness in every direction as far as the distant horizon, where shattered red melted in shimmering waves into a lowering green sky. No audience, no arena, no band, no music.

"Well, you can't leave him there, then," said the first voice, calmly impatient. "Put him back, why don't you?"

"I can't," said the second voice. "The Other is still there."

"Suppose you move him one over, would that work? He

could stay there till a world-walker clears this up."

"Move him one over from where he was? But he'd doppelganger the one there."

"That won't matter if the timing's right. Look at the condition that one's in. He can't survive the concert."

"Somebody there?" said Jesse, turning in circles, seeing only a wasteland of sand. He cleared his throat, swallowing panic. "Hello?" No answer. He stumbled in the deep sand under his boots where seconds before there had been the hard wood of a stage floor, staring in wild-eyed disbelief at a world gone suddenly mad. "What the hell?"

He meant to sound unruffled, but his voice cracked. The impossible was both obvious and inescapable: wherever he was, he was certainly not onstage in the arena anymore. Acrid dust burned his eyes and he closed them hard, swallowed past a tearing dryness in his throat, lifted his hands to rub the tears from his aching eyes . . .

. . . And the crowd shifted and rustled, with a growing sibilance of whispers and a nearly palpable sense of worried tension that brought his eyes open with a jerk. He stood alone in the center of the light-drenched stage again, with the band behind him shifting and fumbling as uncertainly as the audience before him.

A quick glance at the sides of the stage revealed no police; only the usual security guards, who stared back at Jesse with expressions as blandly bored as ever. Between them and Jesse, Bob Lyle stood motionless with his guitar at rest, giving Jesse a very odd look.

Jesse blinked dizzily and grasped the microphone stand to steady himself. The lights beat against him, as heavy and hot as that impossible orange sun had been. The stink of alien chemicals was gone, replaced by the familiar odors of floor wax, ancient arena dust, and sweat. As suddenly as it had come the waking nightmare was gone, the world normal and prosaic again, and the audience waiting for him to give them a concert.

He ignored the small voice at the back of his mind that said in bitter despair, "The cops are right; I am crazy." Even if he was, it wasn't the fault of the kids out front. He looked out at them and attempted a reassuring smile. He didn't feel reassuring. He felt dizzy and bewildered, and the smile was not a success. Swallowing hard, he said just audibly, "Sorry, I . . ." and let his voice trail into silence. What could he say? I what? I'm going crazy right here in front of God and everybody?

Releasing the microphone stand, he fingered a chord on his guitar, trying to find his way back into the schedule, and then realized he wasn't sure whether they had finished the last song. They were on the final chorus when he . . . There was no acceptable way to phrase, even to himself, what had happened.

He stared out at the blur of faces all staring steadily back at him and said again, helplessly, "Sorry." His voice sounded hollow to his own ears, electronically amplified so his merest whisper reached out across black distance like a demented ghost, purposeless and horrifying. *What is happening to me?*

He backed away from the microphone and glanced desperately at Bancroft Averill, ten paces away to his right. He hoped for some clue as to how to proceed, or what had happened, or at least whether they had finished the song, but Banny's sober gray eyes stared unhelpfully back at him across the hot wash of the lights without a trace of encouragement or even friendship. His long face looked taut, and the mobile mouth that was usually twisted in a comical grin was instead pressed into a thin, straight line, grim and un-familiar.

"Hey." Jesse's voice cracked. He backed farther from the microphone to keep the sound of his growing panic out of the amplifiers and shook his head briefly, still looking at Banny. "I dunno . . . where were we?" Banny just stared, his expression distantly hostile. Jesse turned helplessly toward Bob Lyle, urgently aware of the crowd's growing impatience. Lyle was no more helpful than Banny, though he didn't look quite as hostile.

In sudden, bewildered fury he turned away from the band, facing the crowd again. Anger sustained him, steadied him. He could handle any audience, any time, with or without the band's support. It was one of the things he did best. He could relate to people in thousands as easily as he did to people in tens or even twos, because he always remembered that the thousands were made up of tens and twos. He gazed out over the sea of blank faces and said, to a skinny kid in the tenth row who existed only in his imagination and who looked a lot like himself at the age of twelve, the first thing that came to mind to say: "A long time ago . . ."

It worked. It was a tag line the fans recognized, the opening of every story Jesse told onstage. They subsided, appeased by expectation. "A long time ago . . . a long time ago when I was a kid and . . . you know . . ." He paused, thinking fast. If he could get them started on a number, any number, he'd have time to get a look at somebody's schedule and figure out where they were. The safest thing was to cue a song he was sure he hadn't scheduled for to-night; that way, at least they wouldn't be repeating themselves.

He drew an unsteady breath and decided, forcing a grin and feeling his way: "There was this girl I knew, this Gypsy girl." He played the opening guitar riff. "She didn't go to school, couldn't read or write." He glanced at Mirabelle, a little behind Banny, who looked puzzled but willing. With an odd little shrug at him, she began the piano score that complemented his guitar on the "Gypsy" lead-in, threading the slow notes in and out of his melody, fussing with it like fingers worrying a piece of string. To her right, Darla was grinning at him from behind her drum kit, sticks at the ready.

That was reassuring. "But, man," he said, "could that girl *dance*," and Darla played the expected drum roll. Jesse leered at the audience. In response, the fans briefly drowned out the guitar and piano with their cheers and cat-calls and laughter.

"And what happened—" He looked at Bob Lyle. "We used to spend a lot of time together doing one thing and another." Lyle looked wary, oddly resigned, almost angry, but he slid his bass guitar heartbeat in under the other instruments and let it drift with them, steady as a deep, slow river. "You know, dancing and stuff like that." The audience snickered. Jesse, satisfied that the song had not already been played and that the band was with him, faced front and finished his story.

"I wasn't, well, you know, I wasn't having a real good time at home just then, and when my dad would start yelling and hitting—" He hesitated, not having meant to be quite so specifically honest. "And, um . . ." The slip disconcerted him. "And—and I'd go slamming out of the house with no place to go . . ." Bloody and battered and crying with rage and frustration as often as not, but he didn't say that. "Well, I'd call up my girl, and we'd get together, and . . . let's just say that her and me, we did some serious *dancing*."

26

He put enough emphasis on the word to make sure the fans would laugh. The story was true, including the dancing; it had taken place the summer before the accident that killed his dancing career forever. But it wasn't funny that way.

"So anyway, what happened is—I told you she was a Gypsy, right? They don't usually stay in one place too long, Gypsies don't. And I guess her and her family just up and moved out of town and she didn't even have time to say goodbye. And so that's what this next song is about." The tangled background repetition swelled into the opening chords and Jesse launched into the song with a sense of coming home.

This time he tried to stay outside the music enough to keep an eye on his fans. He might have calmed them somewhat with his rambling preface to the song, but they had been disturbed, and he wasn't sure of them yet.

> *Let midnight take these haunted streets,*
> *This hollow desperation . . .*
> *Let morning gather up the dark*
> *Beyond our separation . . .*

He wooed them with his attention, his smiles, his gestures and expressions, and the raggedly sweet caresses of his voice, till he knew the disturbance was forgiven. And when he was sure of that, he cavorted and clowned and whooped and grinned with the music till the disturbance was entirely forgotten and the fans were shouting and singing with him when he asked for it, as they always did.

The musty odor of too many humans crowded into a stuffy arena gradually replaced the stink of desert sand in Jesse's nostrils, and the white heat of the lights dulled the shocking memory of a hard orange sun. Whatever that brief, unsettling experience had been, it was over, and he was safely onstage, in his element again.

> *Let midnight take the shattered glass*
> *Of torment we've been through.*
> *Let angels sing let silence ring*
> *Gypsy, I love you. . . .*

There were a few awkward moments after that, when the band began numbers they were not scheduled to play tonight, or mixed up the schedule; but Jesse followed their lead without much trouble and kept the fans largely unaware of the confusion.

Bob Lyle surprised him more than once with bass improvisations beyond his usual capacity, and Banny seemed subdued during what were usually his best numbers. Darla's drums were even more compelling than usual. Mirabelle Kane's swift fingers sang like magic on the synthesizer keyboard, pulling sounds out of it that Jesse would not have believed it could make: not just fairy trumpets, but crystal chimes clearer than starlight, and singing winds through the hollows of the Earth like nothing Jesse had ever heard before.

Altogether, their performance was brilliant. They had never played so well. The music swirled and tumbled in a glistening maelstrom that constantly threatened to wrench loose from Jesse's control and hurl itself into chaos, but never quite did.

They were halfway through the final number before he realized that the arena in which they were playing was not the same one in which they had begun.

3

Jud

Suli Grail had been gone from her superior's office less than thirty seconds when another woman entered, not by the door. She simply appeared in mid-stride in the center of the room and moved without hesitation to the same ugly, straight-backed acrylic chair Suli Grail had occupied. "Got everything in motion to save the universe, have you, Jud?" she said.

The old man behind the massive black wooden desk had been staring absently out the window at his patch of blue sky. At the sound of her voice, he turned without surprise and studied her expressionlessly. She was an old woman, at least as old as he, and her appearance would have suited many worlds' definitions of the word "witch," even to the pointy black hat. The only thing she lacked was a broomstick.

"Ariel," he said, acknowledging her presence.

"Jud," she said, nodding as expressionlessly as he.

"Why do you wear that absurd costume?" he asked.

"I've just come from my home world." She eyed his purple velvet suit. "What's your excuse?"

He moved his frail shoulders uncomfortably. "Don't start," he said wearily.

"I didn't," she said. When he made no response she said finally, "I don't have all day, you know. Your Lord High

Monitor will be here to see you in less than ten minutes. I don't expect you want him to see me."

"No." He reached for an information chip that lay separate from the others on his desk. "I recorded the interview," he said, holding it out to her.

She leaned forward to accept it. The heavy rust-black fabric of her shapeless and enveloping garment rustled like dried leaves. "Well?" she said impatiently. "Did it go as you expected?"

He shook his head in exasperation. "The world-walker," he began.

"Suli Grail," she said.

"Suli Grail," he said patiently, "has gone after the Other. He will evade her without difficulty."

"You've given her orders to kill him?"

"Naturally."

"You still insist that was wise?"

"It still seems the best way to be sure she'll get him on the run. He's got to be forced through as many gates as possible if he's ever to guess what he is." He glared at her with the injured innocence of a child. "I could hardly tell her it didn't matter whether she caught him or not."

Ariel nodded judiciously. "True. Too true. But Suli Grail is one of your best, and you're betting the fate of the worlds on the chance she'll fail this assignment. Suppose she doesn't oblige you? Suppose she succeeds?"

He shrugged helplessly. "Then we lose."

"A mild way of putting it," she said. "And Suli? Never mind the rest of you; insular atrophy is a slow death, even for worlds. She'll have the rest of her natural life to get through. What do you propose she do with it, in that case? Having killed her lover, does she just carry on as though nothing had happened?"

"Ariel," he said, and paused, obviously at a loss.

Ariel emitted a piercing, witch-like cackle meant for laughter, but devoid of amusement. "At least she won't know what she's really killed," she said.

"There was nothing else I could do," he said.

"You could have taken my advice, and informed her—"

"Don't say it. Not here, not now. Ariel," he said primly, "you must learn discretion."

"Or what?" she said, laughing at him.

"Or we may lose what small hope we have."

She studied him soberly for a long moment. He returned her gaze steadily. "It took me a long time to find Jesse Farrell," she said finally.

"The Other," he said.

She shrugged, robes rustling. "The Other. He may be unique. He is certainly rare. It would be a shame to waste him."

"Indeed," said Jud.

"Jud, I can't even get into the worlds much beyond your time. The atrophy has begun there already. This Other may well be our only chance," she said earnestly.

"I know," he said.

"I think you underestimate Suli Grail," she said.

"I think you underestimate love," he said.

She snorted. "Is that what this is about? You're counting on Suli's love to save the Other?"

He shook his head slowly. "No. Not that." He studied her. "Ariel, it is simply not possible to explain to you, in a way that you can understand—"

She smiled at him very sweetly. "Try."

He looked at the neat row of information chips his fingers had aligned on his desk. "I understand," he said slowly, "that Suli's sense of loyalty to her job and to the worlds will provoke her to kill her lover if she can see no other way to stop him. And it may be that she will see no other way to stop him."

Spurious sweetness forgotten, she scowled at him in honest bewilderment. "So where's the love you say I'm underestimating?"

"Perhaps I used the wrong word. I should have said empathy."

"She's going to empathize with him while she kills him?" Ariel's ancient face with its hooked nose and protruding chin was a mask of distaste. "How, exactly, is that expected to save the universe? Seems to me all that will do is destroy the girl."

"Ariel, you are a bad-tempered old witch and you're making no effort to understand what's going on here."

"I understand well enough," she said. "I understand I devoted most of my life to finding a key you're determined to throw away."

"I don't want to throw it away," he said. "I want to temper it."

"Oh, in the fires of love," she said, simpering, her gnarled hands clasped before her in feigned emotion.

"There are more people involved here than Suli Grail and the Other," he said wearily. "And the Other is not the only key. There are more things to unlock than gates. You know that. You know enough about worlds and the people who live in them. Now go away."

She disappeared in mid-cackle and he was left alone in the bright little boxlike room with its mismatched appurtenances of a dozen worlds, none of them his. But the grating screech of her laughter echoed, and when he turned back to gaze out the window again, his eyes were blind with uncertainty he could not afford and pain he could neither express nor escape.

4
Ruth

"What happened out there?" Ruth Sutton was a small woman with a gentle face and a fierce voice, whose reluctant fondness for Jesse Farrell fed her irrational anger with him now. She had little use for rock musicians in general and none whatever for people she termed substance abusers; but although the Jesse she knew fit into both categories, she had in the years she had known him fallen unwilling victim to the charm of his urchin smiles and to his naively affectionate nature. She thought of him as a younger brother, difficult and often disagreeable, but inescapably dear.

Apparently stunned by the sight of her as he came offstage after the final encore, Jesse stumbled in the middle of a bounding leap and nearly fell, managed to right himself, and then stood frozen in the half-dark beside the stage, still partially visible to the audience and blocking the other band members from exiting, looking at her as though she were risen from the dead.

Bancroft Averill pushed past him, scowling. Bob Lyle came after Banny, apparently indifferent though he looked hard at Jesse in passing; then Mirabelle Kane, openly curious; and finally Darla Black, who grinned amiably at Ruth and patted Jesse on the back in passing. "Good recovery," she said, and went on by without waiting for a response.

Aside from his expression of dumb astonishment, Jesse looked better than Ruth thought she had any right to expect. He was too pale, the skin of his face drawn too taut over the bones and his sandy-lashed eyes curiously haunted, but aside from that he looked positively robust. That, in the face of the worry he had put her through, made her furious. "Good recovery or not, that was the worst foul-up you've pulled yet," she said grimly. "What happened?"

He tried to speak, but produced only a harsh croaking sound. The husky quality that he could use to such good effect when he sang was a disadvantage in speaking, where his voice often cracked or failed him entirely. Ruth reached impatiently to pull him through the door into the backstage area before the house lights came up and he got mobbed. His skin was hot and slick, which she expected; he worked damned hard and sweated buckets under those blazing lights onstage. But it also felt shockingly unfamiliar. Unnerved, she jerked her hand away as from a flame, and was immediately perplexed at her own reaction.

Fortunately, her touch had mobilized him; he stumbled through the door with her, still staring as though she were a ghost. Her brief confusion was forgotten in the dismal worry as to what drug he had managed to get hold of this time. She had no way of knowing that the Jesse she was confronting had never done recreational drugs in his life.

"You know the crowd damn near rioted," she said. "One of these days you're going to go too far; even your fans won't put up with that kind of shit forever. Come on, let's get out of here."

But Jesse stood stock-still in the harsh fluorescent light of the broad corridor and stared at her, his mouth working. He tried twice to say something before any sound came out, and then his voice cracked. "Ruth?" His face was utterly white and as vulnerable as a baby's. He reached a trembling hand to touch her face, and there were tears in his eyes as he said softly, wonderingly, "You're all right. You're okay. You're alive." A roadie brushed past them, her arms full of equipment. They ignored her.

"Oh, for heaven's sake, Jesse." Embarrassed, both by his emotion and by her own puzzling diffidence in response to his touch, Ruth pushed away his hand. "What in hell have you taken this time?"

He started to say something, but again his voice failed him. He cleared his throat and then didn't speak after all. Instead he looked beyond her, then to each side and behind him: an oddly nervous, almost furtive glance. "Where . . . ?" He cleared his throat again, shook his head, and closed his eyes briefly. "I don't understand."

"Oh, you understand, all right." But she frowned at him, puzzled, uneasily aware of a subtle change in him that could not be accounted for by any drugs of which she was aware. His sweet, boyish face looked eerily unfamiliar, as though he were suddenly a stranger in Jesse's body.

He tilted his head, a tentative smile pulling at the corners of his mouth, and said gently, "Were we that bad?"

"Jesse, I thought you were dying!" She scowled at him, clinging to her anger to combat confusion. For some reason she was, on a subconscious level, actually responding to him as to a stranger. An attractive stranger. It unnerved her. "You know perfectly well that Dr. Zelig gave you about half a chance, at best, of making it through this concert alive."

She did not notice the almost imperceptible widening of his eyes; she was too shaken by her reaction to him as well as by residual fear from his apparent near-collapse during the concert to pay much real attention to him at all. "But old macho Farrell had to go on anyway, apparently stoned silly as usual," she said, exasperated. "I don't know why you're surprised I'm alive; you're the one bent on suicide. Maybe I should be congratulating you now for failing one more time, but damned if I feel like it. You scared me, damn you! You want to tell me what happened?"

He might not have heard her. He pushed his wet hair out of his face and looked around again, curiously, as though their surroundings were wholly new to him. "Ruth, where are we?" He sounded anxious, almost urgent. But his eyes, though certainly haunted, and bruised with weariness, were neither glazed nor crazed.

She shrugged irritably. "What do you mean, where are we? Good God, how stoned are you?" Suddenly aware of the technicians and roadies around them, and of the diminishing roar of the slowly departing audience out front, she started to take his arm to lead him away. At the last second she thought better of it, though she couldn't have said why, and gestured instead. "Come on, let's get out of here. We'll talk in the van. Can you walk?"

"Sure I can walk." But he stood still, staring at her in nearly comical bewilderment. "Why wouldn't I be able to walk? And since when do I get stoned on anything but music? You know I don't use drugs. You . . ." His eyes widened, perceptibly this time. "Oh, Jesus. You aren't . . . this isn't . . . Jesus." She hadn't thought his face could go any paler, but it did.

"Now what is it?" she asked wearily.

For a long moment he stood motionless, staring at her with wild, frightened eyes. Then, with obvious reluctance, he lifted one foot and looked at it, wiped the side of its sole with his fingers, and looked at them. "Red sand." He held the fingers out to her in an oddly childlike gesture. "Red sand. On my boots. Oh, Jesus. Ruth, there's red sand on my boots." He sounded as though it signaled the end of the world.

"Okay, so there's red sand on your boots. That's all right; it won't hurt you." She reached again for his arm, hesitated, frowned, and let her hand drop. "Come on, let's go," she said.

"But you don't understand. It means I—I went . . ." His voice trailed off. "I dunno what it means. I think I'm—I think it means I'm—"

"Never mind," she said, meaning to sound soothing and instead sounding weary. "Dr. Zelig's waiting in the van. If he can figure out what you've taken, he'll give you something to bring you down. You'll feel better. Come on."

"I'm . . . stoned?" His smoky blue eyes, half-shadowed by the pale, damp curls that framed his face, studied her with a curious intensity, the whites of them gleaming in a brief shaft of reflected light.

"Yes, babe, you're stoned," she said, amused. This, at least, was a familiar dialogue. "Big surprise. Now will you pull yourself together long enough to come out to the van with me? Come on, you can do it." She spoke to him as to a recalcitrant child; the Jesse she knew had often behaved as one.

"This isn't Blaisdell." He fell into step with her, not limping. That puzzled her; he never bothered not to limp when there was nobody but her to see.

"No, it's not. It's Smith-Painter. I've never heard of Blaisdell."

"But we always—" He broke off and shook his head, looking disoriented. He had regained some of his color, but the blue eyes still looked bruised. "Maybe we don't. I guess you'd know."

"That's right. I know. Watch out for that cable."

"I can see," he said irritably.

She shrugged. "How could I know? You can't always."

He looked at her, his expression unreadable. " 'Cause I take drugs." It was not quite a question, but almost.

"Yes. Because you take drugs." She sighed. "And I wish to God I knew what you'd taken tonight. And where you got it!"

He wasn't listening. "The band played better tonight than I've ever heard them." He sounded thoughtful, as though there were some hidden meaning in the fact of the band's good performance. "But only after the interval."

Someone dropped a microphone stand and the crash of it, magnified by the cavernous concrete-bounded space of the corridor, made Ruth jump. Jesse seemed wholly unaware of it. She glared in the direction of the noise and said, in answer to Jesse's comment, "I wouldn't know. I don't like rock music."

He grinned; his urchin grin, sweet and innocent and stunningly beautiful. "Well, that's one thing the same, anyhow," he said, diverted.

"The same as what?" she asked sourly. It always unsettled her that someone as suicidally demented as he could also be so beautiful. It seemed unreasonable. And unjust.

"The same as . . . ." His grin faded. "I don't know."

She sighed. "Oh, Jesse!" Looking up into his boyish and bewildered face, she felt again that inner shock of nonrecognition, of unfamiliarity, but she held onto her mild amusement with him and shook her head. "Whatever will we do with you?"

But she had lost his attention again. She assumed he was lost somewhere in the drugged corridors of his mind: his eyes looked at her, but he did not appear to see her. "The whole band played different."

38

"Sounded the same to me," she said, uninterested. "Too loud. You'll go deaf by the time you're thirty."

"But I'm already—" He stopped in mid-sentence and mid-step, put a hand to the wall next to him to catch his balance, and said slowly, not looking at her, "Ruth, what date is this?" His face was hidden behind the veil of his hair, and his voice was utterly expressionless.

"July fifth, Jesse." Her tone was deliberately, falsely patient.

He pulled her to a stop, the force of his grip bruising her arm. "The year, Ruth! What year is it?"

"Jesse, you're hurting me." She pulled away from him, frightened not so much by his words or actions as by the inexplicable strangeness of him, felt with shocking intensity under his touch. It was as though she were dealing not with a friend made unfamiliar by drugs, but with an attractive stranger made familiar by—what? Appearance? Circumstance?

"Sorry," he said, releasing her. "Please, what year is it?" His voice was the same, raspy and unexpectedly melodic. His face was the same, and yet it wasn't. It was different, unfamiliar, and she didn't know why.

"For heaven's sake," she said, impatient with her own perceptions. "It's 53. What is the matter with you?"

"It's what?" His face had gone gray again, with the eyes sunk deep in shadows. "It's what year?"

"Jesse, you look terrible. Here, lean on me." She looked up at him and saw only the dear, troubled boy she knew. "You're shaking. Can you make it? I could get help; I'm not big enough to be a very good support. I should've told Dr. Zelig to meet us. Jesse, can you hear me? Are you okay? Here's a chair. Maybe you should sit down and I'll go get Dr. Zelig. Or I'll call somebody—"

But he shook his head, looking absurdly fierce, his chin jutting defiantly. "I'm all right," he said, rejecting her support. "Just . . . I'm—I'll be all right." He hesitated. "You said—you said the year is—you said 53?" He sounded incredulous, almost embarrassed, as though the year were an absurdity.

"That's right, 53."

"1953? 2053? What?"

"No," she said patiently, "just 53. You sure you're okay, Jesse? You're still shaking."

"I'm okay." He used the back of one hand to wipe sweat from his forehead. It was an uncharacteristic gesture, but she did not consciously notice that at the time; what she noticed was that he used the same hand with which he had earlier wiped sand from his boot, and it left a dark smear above his right eyebrow.

"Now you've got your face dirty," she said critically. "Where did that sand come from, anyway?"

He laughed: a brief sound, almost a sob. "You wouldn't believe me if I told you." He swallowed audibly. "I'm not sure I believe me. Oops. Sorry." He had stumbled against the door she held open for him, letting in the smoggy night air from outside. "Um . . . what happened in the year One?"

She stared. "Nothing, why?"

"Well, just, I, um, I can't remember why we, you know. Started counting again."

"Oh, you mean why we don't still use the old calendar? Jesse—" She paused, took a steadying breath, and said carefully, "It's Post-Atomic, Jesse. We count from the limited nuclear exchange that ended World War Two. Now come on, before you fall down. I can't carry you."

"Limited nuclear—?" Mercifully he let that go and stumbled after her, looking very frail and frightened. "Is it far, this van?"

This was more like the Jesse Farrell Ruth knew: punchy, clumsy, stoned, and frequently half-hysterical offstage. On-stage he could usually pull himself together to present a strong, sane, competent, and incongruously healthy appearance for his audience, and this evening for once he had held onto a part of that act for a little while when he came off-stage, that was all. Now he had lost it, and he wasn't a stranger after all. "It's not far," she said, soothing him. "Here, lean on me if you need to."

He ignored that. "There's a doctor," he said. It sounded like a statement, but the look that accompanied it made it clearly a question.

"That's right. Dr. Zelig," she said, wondering how he could possibly have forgotten someone who had been a part of his life for so long. Whatever drug he had gotten his hands on tonight, it must really have turned his brain to mush.

He had preceded her through the door: now he stopped and looked back at her, his expression unreadable. "And I take drugs." That was a question, too.

She nearly laughed. "Yes, babe. You take drugs."

He nodded in a bemused way and started across the concrete parking area outside, then stopped again so suddenly that she nearly collided with him. "This doctor. He doesn't give me drugs?"

She could not help grinning at that. "You're really into wishful thinking tonight, aren't you? I'm afraid the only drug Dr. Zelig will give you is whatever it takes to bring you down from what you're already on. Assuming he can tell what that is, which I sure as hell can't. And I thought that after all these years with you I must've seen everything by now."

To her surprise, he was visibly relieved. After a moment's silence he said, almost absently, "It's no drug." It was just a comment, and not even one that interested him very much, apparently. She had heard the same thing from him any number of times, but usually in a much more defensive tone.

"Sure, babe." She tilted her head, studying him, and saw only the familiar lines and planes of his face and those startlingly clear blue eyes staring back at her. She shrugged. "Whatever you say. The van's this way."

He began to walk again without argument, and without a limp. He had his chin lifted at an even more defiant angle than usual, so that the bright lights of the parking area showed her his face in clear profile. She studied it curiously. Now that she thought of it, surely the line of his jaw was sharper, and his cheeks less puffy, than she remembered them from earlier in the evening. But then, she seldom really looked at him anymore. She did not like to see the inevitable deterioration brought about by his self-destructive life-style.

She slowed her pace, watching him. That deterioration was exactly what seemed missing from his appearance tonight. He looked leaner, tougher, and his eyes were clear, and he didn't limp, and his words weren't slurred, and his movements had again that peculiar fluidity they had in the early years when he was still fit.

He glanced back at her. "You coming?"

"Oh. Yes, of course." She caught up with him and matched her step to his. If he had taken a pain-killer strong enough to ease the discomfort of that leg, it should have made him clumsy. He was definitely not clumsy.

"That it?" He gestured toward the trailer-sized camper in their path.

"Don't you know?" How could he be this confused mentally without great physical impairment? Had he finally done himself some terrible, permanent brain damage? Was she going to be, from now on, tending a—

He turned the full force of those haunted blue eyes on her, his expression quizzical and intelligent and unequivocally sane. "No, I don't know. Is it?"

She had always known he was handsome, of course, but it had been an intellectual awareness only. Now suddenly she saw him as his fans saw him: the broad, high cheekbones; the square, defiant jaw; the hooded quality of his deep blue eyes; the lithe sensuality of that graceful, athletic body, sleek as a cat's. . . .

She blushed and looked away, unwilling to see him this way, and unable to regain her previous vision of him, blinded as she had been by familiarity and contempt. He was watching her. She had no idea what he saw, but whatever it was, it prompted him to produce one of his silly, impish grins and then roll his eyes and contort his mouth in a comical expression perfectly contrived to dispel the sexual tension between them almost before she realized it was there. "You okay?" He asked it with surprising gentleness.

"Sure." It was a lie. She was not okay, at all: she was uncomfortably aware of his proximity as they turned and walked on, and she held herself stiffly away from the possibility of accidental physical contact with him as though to touch him might cause pain. Perhaps it would.

The night air settled silently over them, heavy with the chlorine odor of city smog. Neither of them spoke. He was a stranger again; and she, who had always been very much in charge of their interactions and had tended to lead, direct, and even push him around as she might a child, felt strangely shy with him now, and too aware of the smoothly muscled curve of his shoulder, the sheen of moisture still visible on his skin, the blue line of a blood vessel on his forearm, and even the musky scent of his sweat in the still summer night.

It was a distinct relief to arrive at the van and be able to step forward to open the door for him. A bright yellow parallelogram of light from inside spilled out across the pavement, illuminating Jesse and laying down a loose-limbed darkness behind him, ridiculously long and thin, like a cartoon figure unexpectedly animated and inexpertly drawn. Unaware of this phenomenon, he moved slowly past her up the two metal steps and into the van while she stared at the pavement behind him, fascinated and oddly frightened by a shadow.

His hand inadvertently brushed hers as he passed her. The contact broke her concentration and dispelled the irrational uneasiness provoked by an accident of lighting. She glanced up at him and nearly smiled to see the grim set of his jaw and the determined way he squared his shoulders before he went in to face the doctor he claimed he did not remember. A moth blundered between them into the van, a sudden blue flutter of velvet wings. Ruth closed the door softly, shutting out the dark.

5

Jesse

Jesse knew perfectly well that Ruth was dead. Yet here she was walking and talking with him, and telling him improbable things she apparently expected him to believe. Worse: she expected him to already know. He was not yet thirty. The year was 53—it sounded more like someone's age than a year. She had never heard of Blaisdell arena, in which he thought he had begun the evening. And she said he was known to take recreational drugs.

If he had thought that being unable to remember a few hours from last evening was a sign of insanity, then surely this bizarre transformation of reality was proof of it.

Climbing up into the van without visibly favoring his leg took his mind off all that for the moment; the leg was more than usually painful and showed an annoying tendency to collapse at the knee that made climbing stairs extremely awkward. Ruth looked as though she expected him to fall. That made him all the more determined not even to stumble. Bad enough that she had already seen how confused he was mentally; he had no desire to look like a physical cripple, as well.

She also looked as though she very much regretted that moment of near-intimacy with him in the parking lot. That had taken them both by surprise, and she had not liked it. It was just as well that he had so automatically backed off, as

45

he always did from anyone who unexpectedly got too close. That was a habit he had often in past despised in himself, but not this time.

"Ah, Jesse! And how was the concert going tonight?"

Jesse stared. He did not know what he had expected the much-mentioned Dr. Zelig to be like, but the cheerful little man with a round face dominated by sparkling brown eyes who greeted him when he got inside the van was not it. He nearly betrayed himself by glancing uncertainly at Ruth, but stopped himself in time.

"He's stoned, as usual, Dr. Zelig." Ruth spoke as though Jesse weren't there.

"Is he?" said Dr. Zelig, interested. "Well, well. What are you supposing he's tried this time?"

Ruth shook her head. "He hasn't said, and I sure can't guess. It's like nothing I've seen him on before."

Cross at being discussed in the third person, but unable to think of a suitably cutting objection, Jesse ignored them as they were ignoring him. He glanced around the interior of the van, selected a comfortable-looking seat, and lowered himself into it with as much grace as his aching leg would permit.

For the first time since the concert he became aware, as all his major muscles throbbed with the pain of overdue relaxation, just how exhausted he really was. He was also badly in need of a shower, but had no idea whether the van would provide facilities for that, and did not feel inclined to ask. He should probably know without asking. His belief that he customarily used the showers at the arena, then did his duty with the local press in the back rooms there, was obviously faulty.

"He is looking surprisingly well," Dr. Zelig told Ruth confidingly. "As you are knowing, I had little hope of seeing him upright again after the exertions of a concert in his condition, yet behold! If one was not knowing, one would think him a healthy man."

"He does look well, doesn't he?" Ruth studied Jesse with clinical detachment.

"Feels pretty good, too," said Jesse.

Dr. Zelig chuckled. "Always the entertainer," he said, much pleased. "So tell me, young man, what is it with which you are altering your consciousness on this occasion?" He bent suddenly and lifted one of Jesse's eyelids, staring intently into Jesse's eye. "Hmmm," he said. "Hmmm. Interesting."

Jesse, whose first inclination had been to jerk away from Zelig's unexpected manipulation, instead forced himself to sit still and meet Zelig's gaze. An impish grin tugged at the corners of his mouth. "Think the other one's blue, too," he said helpfully. "Maybe you should check."

Dr. Zelig straightened, then bent slightly backward at the hips and tilted his head, studying Jesse soberly. "Odd. Very odd."

"Blue eyes aren't all that odd," said Jesse.

"Indeed not. It is not their color that is surprising me, but their clarity." Dr. Zelig glanced at Ruth and back at Jesse, shook his head briefly, and said, "No sign of drug abuse in them at all." He turned away, then turned back again suddenly, frowning. "Disrobe at once," he said severely.

Startled, Jesse looked at Ruth. "Is this customary?"

Ruth sighed heavily. "Just do what he tells you for once, babe, will you?"

Jesse considered it. "No."

Ruth looked at Zelig. "Shall I call for help?"

Zelig frowned at Jesse. "Not just yet." He turned away

again and busied himself at a small built-in hotplate on the wall opposite Jesse, putting a kettle on the burner and lighting it with a paper match. Ruth watched him for a moment, then pulled a wooden chair out from the wall next to the door and straddled it, sitting with her arms folded across its back and her chin resting on her arms, eyes closed.

Momentarily unobserved, Jesse took the opportunity to study the interior of the van. It was wholly unfamiliar to him. The door by which they had entered was just opposite and behind the driver's seat. There were three wooden chairs there, with clips to hold them against the wall when the van was in motion. The more comfortable chair in which Jesse sat was next against that wall, directly opposite a small kitchen area where Dr. Zelig was now fussing with cups, spoons, and a jar of instant coffee. Toward the front, opposite the door and behind the driver's seat, was a fold-out table around which, presumably, the wooden chairs were meant to be arranged for meals.

The back of the van was curtained off from the front, but the curtains were pulled back so that Jesse could see a set of built-in bunk beds, the upper of which could apparently be folded back so the lower one could serve as a couch. A narrow aisle separated the beds from a more normal-looking couch on the opposite wall, with a big window above it. That couch, too, seemed to function as a bed, since it was covered by a rumpled sheet with a plump pillow tossed at one end.

Beyond the sleeping area was a narrow corridor with closet space on both sides, and beyond that another door, presumably to whatever bathroom facilities the van boasted. Jesse wondered almost wistfully whether they included a shower, and wondered why he could not remember that or

48

anything else about this place.

As well as why the rest of the world confused him. Either the red sand on his boots meant he really had been somehow thrust into that orange desert and from there into some world that was not his, or he was crazy. The latter seemed by far the more probable; people went crazy. They didn't go bouncing into and out of alternate worlds. "I'm hungry," he said abruptly.

"You're what?" Ruth stared at him as though that were as clear an indication of insanity as he had yet provided.

He looked at her. "Hungry," he said, and was embarrassed at the childlike note of appeal in his voice. "For Christ sake," he said, suddenly angry, "I'm always hungry after a gig. What's so damned weird about that?"

Ruth frowned, confused. "After a what?"

Dr. Zelig said at the same moment, in an unnaturally hearty voice, "Quite reasonable! Quite reasonable to be hungry after work, my boy. I was going to suggest a meal. What would you like?"

Jesse made a wry face, and was too aware that it must look more muddled than amused. "I get the impression I'm not usually hungry after a gig, right?"

"After a what?" asked Ruth, at the same time as Dr. Zelig said, "But my boy, you just said that you were always hungry after work, yes, yes?"

"Oh, hell." Jesse looked helplessly at the two of them. "I dunno if I usually am," he said bleakly, giving in, "but I'm hungry now, okay?"

"We'll just take your blood pressure first." Dr. Zelig bustled importantly, getting out the equipment. "And your temperature, yes? You won't mind that much of an examination, will you? And then we'll eat." He was rapidly unrolling the blood pressure cuff and reaching for Jesse's arm, his expression indicating that he did expect Jesse to object but hoped to move quickly enough to foil any efforts at resistance.

Jesse meekly held out his arm, his expression half amused and half resigned. Zelig looked startled, but was quick to wrap the cuff around Jesse's arm and thrust a thermometer into his mouth. Jesse obediently closed his mouth on it and waited. Zelig took his pulse, as well.

The results of the tests seemed to confound Zelig even more than Jesse's compliance with them had done. He scowled at his instruments and looked dubiously at Jesse, as though suspecting him of having in some way tampered with the equipment.

Jesse, uncertain what was expected of him, furtively rubbed his aching leg and said brightly, "So. Am I alive, doctor?"

Zelig looked at him seriously. "You have taken what drug, please?"

"Oh, hell." This was getting old fast.

"You must telling me, yes?" Zelig nodded earnestly, trying to convince.

Jesse sighed. "I don't know."

"You are forgetting what drug it is?"

"Guess so." He ran splayed fingers through his hair in a fruitless effort to untangle the ends. "Yeah."

"Where did you get it, please?"

Jesse scowled at him mulishly. "Thought we were gonna eat now."

"You must tell me this, please. I must know."

"Steak." The hint of a grin tugged at the corners of Jesse's mouth. "Prime rib. Meat," he said.

"Jesse, for God's sake, tell Dr. Zelig what he wants to know," Ruth said sourly.

Jesse's grin died unborn. His hands curled into fists as he stared helplessly from one to the other of them. "I can't," he said, his voice rising.

"Is it that you are forgetting this, too? You must try to remember, Jesse. It is necessary that you remember."

"*Damn* it!" Driven beyond endurance, Jesse surged to his feet in blind fury and struck futilely at the nearest object, which happened to be a metal cabinet a good deal harder than his hand. "Ouch." He shook his hand, looked at it, and hit the cabinet again, with the heel of his hand this time. It did not help.

Zelig and Ruth seemed wholly unmoved by this outburst. Jesse could not bring himself to face them. He hurled himself back into his chair and scowled his frustration at the floor. "I don't know, damn it!" After a moment he glanced up at them. They were watching him with detached interest, neither helpful nor hostile.

"Look, far as I'm concerned, I don't even take drugs," he said desperately. "Don't like them. Don't like having my consciousness altered. Got enough trouble with reality as it is." That struck him funny, under the circumstances, and he grinned helplessly, his rage abating. "If you know how much trouble . . . oh, hell."

He contrived to look as earnest as Dr. Zelig had done earlier. "Look, Doc, if I knew, I'd tell you, okay? You say I do drugs. Fine. I believe you. I even believe I'm on one now; what the hell, if I take 'em, I take 'em. That might explain a few things. But I can't tell you what I took or where I got it, 'cause I plain don't know."

"Let me look at your hand," said Zelig.

"Leave my damn hand out of it. Oh, hell. Here." He held out his hand, and was surprised to see that the knuckles were swelling. "Jeez." He glanced toward the cabinets. "Did I break what I hit?" The cabinet was dented. "Sorry. I've never done that before. I dunno why I did that."

"You were angry," Ruth said dryly.

He shrugged. " 'S no excuse. Don't usually—" he said, and paused, watching Zelig fuss over his hand. "Guess I dunno what I usually do, do I?"

Zelig glanced up at his face. "Are you still hungry?"

"Yes."

"Then we will eat. This will keep. You have broken nothing. It is meat you want? Beef? Ruth, perhaps you would see to it." He glanced at Jesse's face again. "Or shall we try a restaurant? There may be one nearby. Ruth would know, yes?"

"There's a Victoria Station," Ruth said dubiously. "I saw it when we drove in."

"Good, good," said Zelig. "I find I, too, am hungry now. Come along, children. You will drive us, please, Ruth? You are all right now, Jesse? This Victoria Station, it is satisfactory? I do not know, you understand. You must tell us what you prefer."

Jesse looked at him quizzically. "I won't hit anything again, if that's what you're worried about."

"Yes, yes, of course. Come along."

"Well, hell, I can't go out like this. I need a shower, and street clothes, for Christ sake."

"You what?" said Ruth.

"Never mind," Zelig told her. To Jesse he said earnestly, "Of course, yes, you are wanting cleanliness and a lack of rhinestones, certainly, naturally. Come along, I will see to it."

Jesse backed off, startled. "I can dress myself."

"And shower?" asked Ruth. "Alone?" She looked incredulous.

"You saying I usually need help?"

"Never mind," said Zelig, gesturing toward the back of the van. "Go, Jesse. Cleanse yourself."

He went. The bathroom was behind the last door, as he had guessed, and the fixtures therein conformed nearly enough to his expectations that he could figure them out without assistance. He never did understand where the water came from for the long, hot shower that eased his aching muscles. There was no visible cold water storage or hot water heater in or on the van.

It was a minor puzzle, to be filed with all the other minor puzzles; he had enough to worry about without questioning all the little details that set his nerves on edge with their inexplicable alienness. He could not find out what had happened to him by studying bathroom fixtures.

When he went in to shower, Zelig and Ruth had settled outside to watch the bathroom door. They hadn't moved when he peered out ten minutes later, clean and very much more comfortable physically if not emotionally, to ask sheepishly where his street clothes were kept. As he had known she would, Ruth responded to the question with a meaningful look at Zelig. He made a shushing gesture at her and very kindly showed Jesse where to find his clothes.

When he emerged at last, dressed sedately in blue jeans and a comfortably frayed sweatshirt, still towel-drying his long blond curls, Zelig rose and bustled them quickly out of the van and into a car that was parked alongside. "Your hair is able to dry itself as we go along," he assured Jesse. "You have the keys, Ruth? Yes?" He nodded eagerly. "Good, good. We are on our way, then, isn't it?" He had seated himself in front, beside Ruth, with Jesse in the back seat alone. Now he turned to face Jesse across the back of his seat and said with nearly demented cheerfulness, "This is better, not?"

"Doc, I *promise* I won't hit anything."

"Of course, of course." Zelig turned to face frontward and settled himself comfortably while Ruth started the car and pulled away from the van. Then, apparently struck by a thought, he turned to face Jesse again, squirming his whole body around in the seat despite the restraining efforts of his seat belt, and studied Jesse for a moment before he said carefully, "You understand, I am not concerning myself with that. With the hitting. I am having no interest in whether you hit something, yes?"

Jesse grinned. "Okay, I give up. What is it you are interested in?"

Zelig turned around again and resettled himself fussily. "We are speaking of it later. After we have eating. One thinks best on a full stomach, yes? It is so." He thought about that. "For me, it is so." He nodded several times in agreement with himself. "Yes. And there is thinking to be done, one is seeing that. Because there is a strangeness. No?"

Jesse emitted an involuntary bark of laughter. "There is a strangeness," he said. "There is, sure as hell, a very strangeness." He managed to choke off the laughter before it turned hysterical. On top of everything else, hysteria would have been the last straw. He might be crazy, but he still had some pride.

Zelig nodded agreeably. "Yes. A strangeness. Therefore, we are eating."

6

Suli

World-walkers did not simply step from one world to another without any preparation unless they were very much pressed for time. World-walker Suli Grail saw no reason at all to rush into World V4G 7N7/4 without taking time to get properly outfitted and supplied for the hunt. She was, in a way, not even anxious to catch up with the Other, though she longed to see him again; she really knew that she could not, in the words of her superior, "destroy whole worlds for him." But she wished that she could.

He would not come docilely to Central to be judged and found wanting and imprisoned for all eternity in Limbo. "Bring him back, or kill him," her superior had said; and they both knew which she would have to do. She tried not to think of the mountain-lake blue of his eyes, the boyishly defiant jut of his chin when he had smiled at her and told her he had to leave her. He had always been such a strange mix of child and man, full of power and vulnerability at once, clinging to her and pushing her away. He loved her. She knew that. But she also knew that he loved power more.

The supply officer at the gatehouse asked the number of her destination world, looked it up on the charts, and produced a suitable costume at once, so she could change clothes while he researched and supplied her additional needs. She retired to a private cubicle to change; workers at Central came from worlds with varying codes of modesty, many of which considered the naked human body to be offensive.

When she returned, feeling awkward in unfamiliar clothing, the supply officer showed her a heavy silver bracelet set with roughly cut and polished ovals of turquoise. "Primitive art," he said. "Very popular where you're going, apparently."

She stared at it with a curiously blind look, heart in her throat. She had seen it before. Until the moment he showed it to her, she had half-hoped . . . but here it was, with its center setting empty, awaiting the addition of her gatestone. Aside from that, it looked just as it had when she first saw it. It probably hadn't yet been made, then. The Other had drawn it out of time, to use against her.

She should have asked for a different design, or even withdrawn from the entire assignment when she saw that bracelet. Instead she drew her gatestone out of the small silver mesh bag in which she carried her few cherished possessions and gave it to the supply officer.

It wouldn't matter, in the end. If her gatestone never went in that bracelet, the best result she could hope for was that the Other would learn sooner the one thing Central didn't seem to know about him, and that she hoped he would never learn about himself: that he was a Natural. He needn't carry a gatestone, because in effect he was a gatestone. (And what the gods had meant by doing that to him, on top of everything else, she could not understand.)

While the supply officer dropped the stone into the open mounting on the bracelet and closed the metal bevel around it, she fastened the mesh bag around her neck by a slender chain and hid it under her bodice. "Do they have any weird habits I ought to know about?" she asked.

"Nothing listed." He handed her the bracelet. "Slip this on and see how it feels. Fit okay? The circuitry shouldn't give you any trouble. It's only a backup for the basics set in your stone. I've matched it to a monitor here and at Central Station, and this time you get two-way communication; you're going to a technology-oriented world where two-way long-distance communication is taken for granted. They'll just assume it's something of theirs."

"That's convenient," she said, eyeing the thing with dislike. "But—can the communicator be separated from the bracelet? I—I'd feel more secure if—if I didn't have all my chicks in the same nest." She hated the note of apology in her voice.

"Hadn't thought of it that way," said the supply officer, studying the bracelet without expression. "This nubbin on the back is what you want. Unscrews, see? So you could carry it separate. But it's small, easy to lose, by itself."

"Thanks." She watched him fasten the communicator back on the bracelet. "What's its range? Away from the bracelet, I mean?"

"Oh, it'll reach as well without the stone as with it." He looked sympathetic. "Difficult assignment?"

She looked at the bracelet. "How did they ever figure out to use these, anyway?"

He accepted her change of subject with a shrug. World-walkers seldom discussed their work. "All I know is what's in the history stones. World-walker Ariel Greef found a gatestone and used it, and that got everybody excited, but not many people could walk worlds with them till the circuitry was invented to go with, because there aren't that many near-Naturals like Ariel."

"Yes, but how did they know what circuitry to invent?"

"It was a technology-oriented world where they did it. How do they know what circuitry to invent for any of their technology? I don't know. I'm low-tech, myself." He shrugged ineffably. "Maybe they just experiment with everything till they find something that works, and use it. They found it, that's all I know."

"And started the Ages of Chaos," said the world-walker.

"Just so. You want to discuss history, or you want to get ready for work?" He leaned against the supply counter, awaiting her decision without impatience.

She sighed. "Sorry. What else do I need?"

He eyed her costume, a short dress with fitted bodice and flared skirt, made of a wispy, flower-patterned fabric that looked quite fragile but was not. On her legs she wore sheer, clinging, pastel tights with just a hint of glitter in the weave. "There are additional leg coverings here," he said. "A pair of sheer, skin-colored tights to wear with the dress on formal occasions, and a pair of long pants with color-coordinated shirt meant for inclement weather. Also a jacket-like affair to match the pants, in case you hit a really cold climate. That's all the garments. The fabrics are all self-repairing shake and wear, of course."

"And bless the technology that invented that!" She put a hand on the pile of extra clothing he had produced and pressed it downward against the counter, trying to diminish its mass. "It packs small, but this garment doesn't have any pockets. Where am I supposed to carry all this?"

"Ah, yes," he said. "Let me introduce . . . the purse." Grinning, he produced a large plastic pouchlike object that he presented to her with a flourish. "It comes in many sizes and shapes, this one having been selected to both match and accommodate your wardrobe. The females in nearly all the V4G worlds carry these with them everywhere. You

58

hang it from your shoulder by means of this strap, thus. You see? Of course, ours comes with a portable mass-compacter not available in the V4G worlds; it comes from an A7Q world originally."

"I've heard of those. You can put half the universe in a package the size of an information chip."

The officer smiled. "That's an exaggeration, but you've got the right idea. This will hold more than you can carry. The mass is compacted, not eliminated. Its weight is the limiting factor for you." The purse was a flat pouch about twenty centimeters square and two centimeters thick. He packed it with the spare pieces of her wardrobe without increasing its thickness. "Don't ask me how it works. I know how to use it, that's all. You find things by feel. It's set up so that what you see when you look inside is just a few ordinary trinkets that a woman on a V4G world might carry. Those are accessible, too, by the way, and fully functional. But anything you add is invisible till you pull it out again."

"It won't compact my hand?"

"No, nor any other living thing, so you can't stuff it with cats or anything, in case you wanted to."

"Not really. Just curious. That's living things, not organic? So it will compact food?"

"Yes, but there's no reason for you to take any beyond standard emergency rations. You can eat whatever the residents eat in the V4Gs."

She looked at the purse. "I'll need a weapon." Her voice sounded strange. She cleared her throat. "Something unobtrusive." She hesitated. "And lethal."

"What's the matter with your hands?"

"Nothing. But I might need backup."

He shrugged. "Well, you're cleared for it. They use

blades or projectiles. Or do you want it to look like an accident?"

She pushed aside a sudden image of accusing blue eyes.
"I don't think it matters. I'm after a gate crasher. The idea
is to put his doppelganger back where he belongs, so I can't
leave any spare bodies lying around, no matter how they
die." She closed her eyes, opened them again, and met the
supply officer's sympathetic gaze. "He knows me, so I may
not be able to get close enough to hand-kill him."

The officer nodded. "Blades are out, then. You need a
distance weapon. If you don't mind, you're safer carrying
something that fits the world, just in case you lose it."

She nodded. "Sure."

"You know that projectiles aren't very reliable."

"If that's what they use, I'll take my chances. Maybe I
won't have to use it, anyway."

He reached under the counter again and pulled out what
looked like a Smith & Wesson .38 snub-nosed revolver. "I
happen to have this on hand," he said. "Will it do?"

She shrugged. "I guess so. How does it work?"

He showed her. "You'll need something to make it legal.
Not everyone is allowed to carry a projectile weapon where
you're going. The last guy that used this was masquerading
as a local police officer. You think that would fit your
needs?"

"No reason not. Why, I have to carry personal identification, or something?"

"Yes, and I have police identification handy. We'll just
change the information on the card. Here, you get this flat
thing to carry it in. Called a wallet. This pin is called a
badge, and the card on the other side is your identification.
Step over to the camera and we'll take the photo now. It's
two-dimensional stuff, easy to work with. Hold still. There.

While that's developing, I'll change the description and add a name. Any preference?"

"For the name? No. Just leave it as it is, why don't you?"

"The previous user was a man." He was working with the card, smoothing the old lettering off with a moistened fingertip, then using an electronic stylus to put in the new. "Their names are sex-differentiated."

"Well, if you have to change it anyway, you might as well make it as near mine as you can. It's Suli Grail." The unfamiliar sounds had a guilty taste, though there was nothing wrong with saying her name in such a circumstance.

"I'll look it up." He did. "Susy Grey is as close as I can find, will that do?" She shrugged, and he altered the card. "If you have to show this to anybody official, you may be in trouble. I think their police forces are pretty regional. There, now I'll just slip it into the molecular binder to keep it from smearing, and it'll be as good as new." He did that, then handed it to her.

After a momentary pause during which she examined the card without interest, he said hesitantly, "I'm proud of my handiwork, but all the same . . . don't use it if you don't have to, will you? Those V4G worlds have a lot of rules. We're used to a certain amount of benevolence in government here, and that can lead to some pretty bad mistakes out there."

Her look told him what she thought of their benevolent government, but all she said was, "I know the rules."

"Not their rules. It's a positive wilderness of rules in every one of those worlds. I took my last holiday in V4G 7N8/6, which isn't far from where you're going. Do you know, they have people whose sole job is to keep track of the rules and decide whether they've been broken? And they

61

don't have access to Limbo, of course, so they frequently kill offenders."

"They wouldn't kill someone for using a wrong identification card, surely?" She looked amused.

He shrugged helplessly. "I don't know. You can't tell. Of course you'll have your gatestone, so you can get away if you have to, but just don't underestimate the hazard. Even with a gatestone you can't outrun the projectile from one of these things." He indicated the .38 with an apologetic half-smile.

"I'll be careful. But I always am. I spend more time out in the worlds than I do in Central, though I haven't been to any of the V4Gs lately."

He nodded. "I suppose they won't be as much of a shock to you as they were to me," he conceded. "I hadn't been out for a while. You get used to thinking about the universe of worlds, and you forget what it's like to be right out in one, where they don't even know the others exist." He looked at her. "You said you're after a gate crasher?"

"Yes."

"I heard something from the monitors about some pivotal musician getting doppelgangered into Limbo."

"That's the case I'm working on."

"They put him in a neighbor world for safe-keeping, didn't they?"

She nodded. "Slash three, when he belongs in slash four. But it's all right so far. The one from slash three died in Limbo, but he would've died anyway. I gather the monitors switched the two of them at the moment of death, or close to it. So it's just the timing that's been messed up, because there shouldn't be a live one in slash three by now. I don't think that'll matter much, if I'm quick."

"But how could it happen? Is there a gatestone loose?"

"I have no idea." She hadn't known the lie would be so easy. "That wasn't covered in the brief." She glanced inadvertently at her stone, newly locked in the bracelet that the Other was already wearing in some other world, and avoided the supply officer's eyes.

"He must've got ahold of one somehow. Lord, Lord." In extremity, he reverted to his home world's curses. "Where did he come from? Doesn't he know that's how the Ages of Chaos got started? From people indiscriminately walking worlds? Doesn't he care?"

"I think he would," she said slowly, "if he could see it. But he's . . . he was hurt, he was badly hurt, when he was just a child, and it's done something to him. It's as though he can't believe that other people are real, somehow. I mean he knows we are, of course, but—but it's an intellectual understanding. Emotionally, he's all alone. The only human being in the whole universe of worlds."

"You've been close to him." It was a kind of condolence, not a question.

"Yes. Yes, I have." She had been close to him, and she understood how he felt, but even if she had been willing to try, she could not have put it into words. She knew he was in pain. She knew he was blinded by suppressed rage that even he did not fully understand. She knew he had lost more than he could bear to lose, been hurt more deeply than he could endure, and that it made him need to strike out against the universe.

He was so absorbed in his own anguished need that he simply could not see beyond it to understand, or even to recognize, the humanity of those around him. It was like blindness, or deafness; a sensory lack. One could not explain color to a blind person. One could not explain humanity to the Other. He was too isolated. He was not a part of humanity. He did not and would not understand.

But she could say none of that to a stranger, so she looked at the officer and waited for him to introduce a new topic, or to end the conversation, or to die. At that moment, with the reproachful memory of the Other's eyes in her mind, she did not care which of those things he did.

7

Jud

The man who entered Jud's office a few minutes after the witch-like figure of Ariel Greef had disappeared came by more normal means, through the door. There was very little else normal about him. He was half Jud's apparent age, but his body was as frail as an old man's, the bones gnarled and the flesh stringy and loose. His face was narrow and pinched, the eyes protuberant, their irises an odd, dark color that glinted red in the light. His costume was as outlandish in its way as Ariel's witch-robes: he wore the white canvas skirts and broad-shouldered embroidered vest of his home world, and his wide fur belt glittered with tiny mirrors.

He seated himself, wordlessly, in the same acrylic chair both Suli and Ariel had occupied before him. His long, knobby-kneed legs protruded pinkly between the hem of his skirts and the tops of his tall fur boots. His bony arms, exposed from narrow shoulders to manicured fingertips, seemed too long for his body. The elbows jutted and the big, bruised-looking wrists seemed stiff and awkward, as if the weight of the twisted hands were burdensome.

Jud selected an information chip from the tidy row on his desk and pushed it toward the Lord High Monitor. "I recorded my conversation with the world-walker," he said, "as you requested, my lord."

"That's good." The Lord High Monitor made no move to pick up the chip. "Did you instruct her as I told you?"

"Yes, lord," Jud said wearily.

The Lord High Monitor nodded: a gesture that reminded Jud of storks. "Can you trust her?"

"She's the best world-walker on the rolls."

"But will she take care of this?" insisted the Lord High Monitor.

"You mean will she kill him," said Jud. "I don't know, my lord. I believe she will if she feels she must."

"It was your job to see to it that she would feel she must." The Lord High Monitor's expression didn't change, but his eyes seemed to glow with a dangerous ruddy light.

Jud nodded. "I have done what I could."

The Lord High Monitor looked suddenly around the room, still expressionless, but giving a clear impression of suspicion. "Someone else has been here," he said.

"No one since Suli Grail," said Jud, his voice and manner indifferent.

"Since whom?" The Lord High Monitor's expression changed at last, from severe distaste to something approaching astonishment.

"Since the world-walker," said Jud, obediently correcting himself, but without interest. "My lord, I sent you the demarcation impact report. Have you—"

"Oh, is that what it was?" the Lord High Monitor asked negligently. "I discarded it."

Jud stared. "My lord—"

"Yes?" The Lord High Monitor scarcely moved, but his posture seemed suddenly regal and surprisingly imposing, his gaze quelling.

Jud blinked. "I," he said, and hesitated, and shook his head. "I think . . ."

"These scientists get overexcited," said the Lord High Monitor. "The worlds' boundaries are as they have always been."

Jud nodded. "Yes, lord. But—"

"This business of studying the potential demarcation impact of a world-walker's assignment is repugnant to me. Our ancestors resolved those problems when they established Central and the corps of world-walkers. It is arrogance to imagine we can second-guess their work." That was a direct quote from one of his recent political speeches. "And in this instance we must not be delayed by nervous namby-pambies no matter how much spurious so-called science they throw at us. The emergence of a Natural cannot be left untended."

"We're not altogether certain—"

"The subject is closed."

"Yes, my lord." Jud's long fingers were rearranging the information chips on his desk again.

The Lord High Monitor sighed heavily, as one confronted with the repetition of an extremely tedious task. "I've explained it to you repeatedly," he said, his voice thin with impatience. "I don't know why you can't grasp a simple concept." He impaled Jud with his fiery gaze. "Or have you sided with the New Worlders?"

They were a small religious-political group who held that the gods would create a Natural to save the universe from annihilation. They were not far wrong. Jud stifled a sigh of his own and said politely, "No, my lord."

"They're insane," said the Lord High Monitor, stating what he regarded as an unequivocal truth. "The very idea that if a Natural should emerge, he should be allowed, not only to escape his world with impunity, but then to run rampant through as many worlds as he chooses without hindrance, is unthinkable. They must not be allowed to learn of this Other. And he must not be allowed to run rampant. Is that clear?"

"Yes, my lord. But he might not be—"

"The worst is that these idiot New Worlders actually imagine the boundaries could benefit from his . . . talent." He spat the word out with an expression of loathing. "We, or at least our forebears, went through all that in the Ages of Chaos. There can be no chances taken, no breaking of the rules that were set forth in those days, no leniency to those who threaten the worlds."

Or who threaten your career, thought Jud, but all he said aloud was a subdued, "Yes, lord."

"My career," began the Lord High Monitor, and for one frozen instant Jud imagined the man had read his mind. "My career has been based on dependability. Security. Safety. I have promised my constituents in both the knowing and the unknowing worlds that I will maintain their integrity, their safety. In other words, their purity. Their security from unwanted gate crashers, if you will." He was beginning to sound both pompous and wooden, as though repeating words written for him that he neither believed nor fully understood. "I will keep my promise," he said with artful force. "I will keep the worlds pure. I will not allow some noisy so-called musician's doppelganger to undermine what I have dedicated my career and my life to maintaining."

Jud nodded heavily. His shoulders hurt. "Yes, my lord. I understand, my lord. No one—"

But the Lord High Monitor wasn't listening. "You see that he's killed," he said with sudden venom. "Destroyed, do you understand me? Exterminated. Got rid of, finally and completely. Is that understood?"

"Yes, my lord. I understand, my lord."

The Lord High Monitor nodded, head bobbing absurdly on a too-long, stringy neck. "Good," he said. "That's good. I'm glad we've had this little chat." He smiled perfunctorily, rose, took the information chip he had been offered at the beginning of the interview, and glared balefully down at Jud. "You'll keep me posted as to the world-walker's progress?"

"Certainly, my lord." Jud's fingers closed convulsively on an information chip. "I'll let you know the instant her reports come in."

8
Zelig

In World V4G 7N7/3, the Jesse Farrell from World V4G 7N7/4 was devoting all his attention to a thick piece of prime rib and a steaming baked potato. Much to Dr. Zelig's fascination, he had already put away a healthy portion of salad and several pieces of bread while waiting for the meat to arrive. The Jesse Farrell Zelig knew had never had such a healthy appetite.

Jesse glanced up from his meal, noticed Zelig's undivided attention, and hesitated with the fork lifted halfway to his mouth. With an oddly diffident smile he looked slowly from Zelig to Ruth, who was also staring, looked at the fork in his hand that was obviously the source of their fascination, looked up at the two of them again, shrugged, and silently continued eating. The whole little routine was deliberately comical, and wholly atypical of the Jesse Farrell they knew.

Ruth glanced at Zelig. "Whatever drug he took, it can't be all bad. I've never seen him eat like this."

Jesse looked at her, his expression unreadable.

Dr. Zelig looked at Jesse for a moment longer, then back at his own meal, which he had been eating mechanically, barely tasting it. "I do not know what he can have taken," he said. "It is most odd."

"He doesn't think he took anything," said Jesse.

"He doesn't like drugs."

Ruth glanced at him, her expression impatient. "That's new, too," she said.

"The insistence that he does not like drugs?" asked Zelig.

"No, of course not. That business of talking about himself in the third person."

"Ah." Zelig nodded. "So it is, yes?" He smiled. "Just as you or I might do if the other two were to discuss us as though we were not present."

Ruth frowned at him, confused. "What other two?"

Jesse, visibly cheered by Zelig's understanding, grinned at Ruth. "You an' me. Or the doc an' me."

Ruth looked at him. "What?"

The grin died. He looked at his plate and shrugged sullenly, his face hidden behind a tumble of golden curls. "Guess I'm not a person to you at all. Never mind. You wouldn't understand."

"To us it is an odd concept," Zelig told him earnestly. "You are not often—" He hesitated, searching for a word. "Rational," he said experimentally, and thought about it, and looked pleased with himself. "Yes, rational enough, to do such a thing."

Jesse looked up, still sullen. "Do what? Talk?"

"Just so," said Zelig.

Jesse's face paled visibly. "Oh." His expression turned to stone. "I see."

"You must have known that," said Ruth, looking at him oddly. "You can't be so far gone that you don't even know what you're doing to yourself."

Jesse stared at his plate for a moment, then pushed it away and rubbed the back of one hand hard across one eye and up across his forehead, turned it over to run his fingers through his hair, paused for a moment with his fist tangled in curls and his eyes closed hard, then dropped his arm and shook his head in weary resignation. "Jeez," he said. "Jesus."

Ruth made an impatient gesture. "I keep getting sucked in: I keep trying to talk to him, like he'd know what I was saying."

"I am thinking he does," said Zelig.

"You think he's rational?"

Zelig shrugged. "He is seeming rational, isn't it? Tell me, Jesse. You did not favor your leg as we walked. Is it well? It is not hurting?"

Jesse scowled at him and said nothing.

"He always tries not to limp when he wants to convince us he's okay," said Ruth. "That doesn't mean anything."

"And how often, in recent times," said Zelig, "has he been successful in his effort not to limp, except onstage? He has been too ill, too weak, too what you call out of shape. It is too much. He cannot. Only when the adrenaline is there, you understand, of the performance. Then he is succeeding. Not offstage." He stopped, aware that Jesse was staring at him. "I am saying something disturbing?"

"You've," said Jesse, and swallowed. "You've been with us for years?"

"You see?" said Ruth. "He's so totally out of it he doesn't know what's going on. When he first came offstage he acted like he'd never heard of you before."

"Did he." Zelig looked at Jesse with renewed interest. "And had you, Jesse?"

"Had I what?"

"Heard of me before?"

Jesse looked at him for a moment, looked away, sighed heavily, and closed his eyes. "I'm tired. I wanta sleep. It's been a long, hard day."

Zelig nodded. "Of course. We will return to the van."

"Not to a hotel?" Jesse looked stricken as soon as he said it. "I mean—" He closed his mouth sharply, clearly wishing he had not spoken.

"You expected we would spend the night in a hotel?" asked Zelig. "That seems usual, to you? That we are staying in hotels?"

"Oh, for heaven's sake," said Ruth. "If you can't give him something to bring him down, why don't you just ignore him? What's the use of talking to him like he understood what was going on? Obviously he's regressed about a million years and doesn't know his head from a layer cake. Let's just take him back to the van and put him to bed. He'll sober up by tomorrow."

"Perhaps not," said Zelig.

Ruth stared. "You don't think the effects are permanent!"

"Perhaps," said Zelig.

"But . . . oh, God." She looked at him, then at Jesse. "But how will we—how will he—are you saying he's insane? Permanently?"

Jesse looked at neither of them and kept his face expressionless, apparently uninterested in Zelig's response, but the stillness with which he tried to conceal his tension had the opposite effect. Zelig, watching him, phrased his response quite carefully. "I am not saying just that."

"What, then?" asked Ruth. "Do you know what he took? Is that it? How can you know it's permanent if you don't know what it is?"

Zelig shook his head, still watching Jesse. "I am not prepared to put a name to the strangeness," he said. "If I say what I am thinking, you will perhaps believe it is I who am losing sanity." He started to say something more, thought better of it, and smiled encouragingly at Jesse.

"Are you joking?" said Ruth. "What do you mean?"

Zelig ignored her. "You are well, Jesse? You feel well, yes?"

"Yeah, sure."

"But something troubles you?"

Jesse's eyes were dark with ghosts. "Don't remember you." His voice was hoarse. "You been with us for years, and I don't remember you." He looked at Ruth. "And . . . what I do remember . . ." He shook his head. "It's crazy. Jesus. It's—" His voice broke, and he cleared his throat. "She's right, Doc. I must be crazy. Nothing else makes sense."

"Sometimes sense is too much to ask of the universe," said Zelig. "What is it you remember? Something about Ruth, yes?"

Jesse shook his head. "I don't wanta talk about it. I wanta sleep. Let's find a hotel."

"We don't have time for a hotel, Jesse," Ruth said patiently. "We'll be traveling all night."

"We don't fly between gigs?" When Ruth and Zelig stared, he shook his head wearily. "Never mind. Ruth's right, Doc. I'm mad as a hatter. Take me home and put me to bed, will you? Tomorrow's soon enough to sort out just how flipped I am."

"He is speaking oddly, yes?" Zelig looked thoughtful.

Ruth shrugged. "He's hallucinating or something. I don't understand half the words he uses. But he's got one good idea. Let's get him out of here before he decides he doesn't want to go. Strong as he seems tonight, I don't want to have to try to persuade him to do anything he doesn't want to do."

"Believe me, I'm not gonna change my mind about a bed," said Jesse. "I'm tired, okay?" He looked bone-weary and wretched.

"Get up, Jesse. Dr. Zelig, can you get him out to the car while I pay?"

"He can walk to the car all by himself," said Jesse.

"Yes," said Zelig. He might as easily have been responding to Jesse's comment as to Ruth's question; there was nothing in his tone or expression to indicate which he meant.

Ruth seemed satisfied. "Good. I'll meet you outside." She turned away, leaving Zelig and Jesse alone at the table.

Zelig looked quizzically at Jesse. "Shall we go?"

"She didn't leave a tip." Jesse rose and reached for his wallet, then remembered he hadn't been able to find one when he got fresh clothes in the van.

"She didn't leave a what?" asked Zelig.

"A tip," said Jesse. "For the waiter."

Zelig, having risen to stand beside Jesse, tilted his head to study Jesse's face. "This is a customary activity?"

"Sure it—" Jesse paused, stared at the doctor for a moment, and shook his head in defeat. "I dunno."

Zelig realized suddenly what he meant. "Ah, the gratuity, is it not?" He nodded happily. "She will be paying that with the check."

But Jesse had lost interest. "It doesn't matter. Let's go." He turned too abruptly, twisting his bad leg, and it nearly folded under his weight. His face contorted briefly and he swung his head in an automatic little gesture that concealed his features behind the veil of his hair; the pain, Zelig knew, would be debilitating. But Jesse controlled his face, straightened, and tried to keep walking without a break in his stride.

"It looks worse when you try not to limp," said Zelig. Jesse hesitated. "Huh?"

"The leg," said Zelig. "You twisted it. There is no one to see if you favor it, yes? These tables are empty, and Ruth is gone. I am saying that I know of your pain, so clearly there is no purpose to conceal it from me. Why do you try not to limp?"

Jesse looked at him, his face drawn, but his eyes clearly amused. "I dunno. It's just what I do." He studied Zelig's face. "You don't think I'm stoned, or at least you aren't as sure of it as Ruth is. Why?"

"By 'stoned' you mean intoxicated by a drug?" At Jesse's nod, Zelig tilted his head to one side. "I am not quite sure. There is undeniably a strangeness." He frowned, thinking about it. "Ordinarily, for instance, you do limp." He shrugged. "In many ways you are different. In ways not likely to be changed in minutes by a drug of any kind. I have no explanation. But I think you are not what you call stoned, yes?"

"Am I crazy, then?" Jesse asked steadily.

Zelig shook his head. "I am not knowing. Except insofar as we are all crazy, my friend. Come, let us go. We will solve nothing, standing here, yes?"

Jesse studied him a moment longer, shrugged, and turned away. Zelig followed him, his expression thoughtful. He felt as puzzled as Jesse looked, and only slightly less alarmed. Earlier this evening, a self-indulgent and quite un-pleasant overgrown boy had stumbled out of the van on Ruth's arm, ill in body and mind from years of drugs and dissipation. Zelig had known Jesse could not survive the concert, and he had not: in his place, this new young man had returned, bewildered and occasionally sullen, but friendly and in apparently excellent physical health, sanely

76

uncertain of his sanity in what was, if Zelig's reluctant surmise proved correct, an insane situation.

The clichéd phrase "he was a different man" had begun to echo in Zelig's mind. This was a different man. The thought was preposterous, but inescapable. The physical characteristics were the same, right down to the partially crippled leg; but this Jesse was older, stronger, healthier, pleasanter. Even his mannerisms were different: the way he moved his body, the expressions that altered the no-longer-bloated face, the underlying confidence in his eyes.

He called Zelig "Doc," after years of calling him "Zelly," and did not remember him at all. He looked at Ruth with wonder and affection, after years of regarding her with impatient contempt. The million-dollar voice was the same, and apparently the musical talent was unaffected, but all the personal characteristics were oddly askew—and vastly improved.

His language, containing many odd words and usages, was the most telling clue, and the one Zelig was most reluctant to consider. The doctor was a practical man, not given to flights of fancy. The explanation that seemed both probable and impossible, that Jesse actually was a different man, was one from which Zelig shied like a horse from moving shadows, but he could think of no other.

They reached the car ahead of Ruth. Jesse climbed wordlessly into the back seat and leaned his head against the headrest, eyes closed, shoulders slumped, absently rubbing his bad leg. Zelig climbed thoughtfully into the front seat and said without looking back, "Jesse?"

The almost inaudible whisper of Jesse's palm against his pant leg stopped. "Yeah?" His tone was wary.

"Tell me, were you noticing anything—strange—about tonight's concert?"

There was a brief silence during which Zelig could almost see Jesse considering and discarding possible responses. "Like what?" he asked suspiciously.

Zelig shrugged helplessly. "I cannot guess. Anything odd. Unusual. Unexpected or unexplained. Anything that might, perhaps, seem odd." He shrugged again, ineffably. "You do agree there is a strangeness, is it not?"

"Oh yes, there is a strangeness!"

"Then you can tell me the beginning of it, not?"

"Not." On that point Jesse's voice revealed no uncertainty at all.

"Ah, but you do know the beginning of it, yes?"

"Doc, I may be crazy, but I'm not stupid, and I don't much wanta end up in a funny farm somewhere, so I'm not gonna start describing my hallucinations to you."

"And would that be what it was? Hallucination, you think? Not the strangeness of an unusual reality?"

"Don't have the faintest idea what you're getting at. There aren't different kinds of reality. There's real, and there's crazy. And I don't much like being crazy, so I don't wanta talk about it, okay?"

"I am not convinced that you are crazy, Jesse."

Jesse snorted. "Neither am I, but I don't see any other explanation for . . ." His voice trailed off and the faint sound of his hand against his leg began again. "For stuff," he finished inadequately.

"Nor do I," said Zelig. "Yet there must be one."

"I'd like to think so."

"But you are not thinking so, yes?"

"Well, what the hell would it be?"

"You are a different man?" asked Zelig.

There was a pause. Jesse's voice, when he spoke again, was infinitely weary. "Jesus. I'm crazy, Doc, or you are."

He chuckled, as at a very feeble joke. "One of us has gotta be. Let's leave it at that, okay? I'm tired."

"Of course," said Zelig.

After a moment's silence Jesse said cautiously, "Doc?"

"Yes?"

"You've been real . . ." He shifted uneasily. "Um, 'specially if I'm a, uh, a druggie, I wouldn't be surprised if you'd be as impatient with me as Ruth is. You haven't been. Thanks."

"You're welcome," said Zelig. After a moment he added quietly, "Don't despair too much of your sanity, yes?" He looked over the back of his seat in time to see Jesse shrug wearily. It was the only response he made.

9

Jesse

Neither Ruth nor Zelig spoke again to Jesse during the trip back to the parked van, which meant he didn't have to answer awkward questions, but it also meant he had more time to think. His thoughts were not happy. Ruth's death, and in particular the grisly manner of it, had stunned him; but now it seemed that the manner of her resurrection was not much better for his peace of mind.

He did not know what to believe. Grateful as he was to find Ruth alive, he resented the havoc it inflicted on his concept of reality. Childhood abuse had left him wary and distrustful of the universe, but in recent years he had begun to find his way out of that morass of anxiety and self-doubt. Now all the gains were turned to losses and he was more confused and alone than he had ever been.

His instinctive reaction was the careful and entirely unconscious reconstruction of protective barriers: he would believe nothing. He would trust no one. He would watch, and wait, and nothing would catch him unawares again. He became, in the dark silence in the back of the car that night, the adult reflection of the battered child he had been: a soldier in a war zone, prepared at any instant to defend his life against a hostile universe.

A major part of the defense was a masquerade. He must at all costs appear normal, take on the protective coloration of his surroundings, and seem to be at his ease even in a state of siege. Any deviation from whatever was expected of him could be used against him. He must determine what a normal human would do in every situation, and mimic that reaction. It was all the more important because he realized, still on an unconscious level but with a deep sense of loss and isolation that was fully conscious, that just as his father had always told him, he was not normal. Perhaps he was not even human.

But he had years of practice at pretending to be human. And the small boy who was making these decisions in the back of his mind knew, with a tiny spark of defiant pride almost lost in the darkness of desolate alienation, that he could perform that masquerade to nearly flawless perfection. He was too young and too frightened to realize that meant the masquerade was no masquerade at all. And Jesse, unaware of the troubled adolescent portion of himself who guarded his survival, was in no position to enlighten him.

When they arrived back at the van, Zelig provided him with an odd pullover terrycloth robe in which he was acutely conscious of the fact that his legs were exposed below the knees. Ruth quickly settled herself in the top bunk bed and watched without interest as Zelig seated Jesse on the edge of the couch bed and rubbed a strongly-scented ointment onto his scarred leg. Jesse, embarrassed, wanted to protest. But both Ruth and Zelig behaved as though it were the most usual thing in the world, and the ointment so soothed the pain that once it had begun to take effect he was glad he had not had the courage to refuse it.

"No other strains? No pulled muscles, damaged tendons?" asked Zelig.

Jesse felt himself blush, and hoped they wouldn't notice. "I'm fine."

Zelig smiled. "You would have said your leg was fine, but it was not, yes?"

Jesse scowled at him and tugged at the hem of the robe, trying to pull it below his knees. "This where I sleep, on the couch here?" he asked desperately.

"You are finding it satisfactory?" asked Zelig.

Jesse shrugged. "Hey, I can sleep anywhere."

"Then this is where you sleep."

"Good. Okay." Jesse lay back and pulled the sheet up over his body. He preferred to sleep in the nude, but not in the same room with Ruth. Aware of Zelig's amused gaze, he turned over, wadding the covers more tightly about him. "Night." His voice was muffled.

"Good night, changeling," said Zelig. "May your sleep be well."

Startled, Jesse lifted his head to look at Zelig. "Uh, thanks," he said awkwardly.

"You're welcome," said Zelig. Looking at Ruth, he prompted gently, "Say good night, Ruth."

"Good night, Ruth," said Jesse. It was an ancient joke, but to his profound relief it produced a startled snort of laughter from Ruth and a broad smile from Zelig.

"Do not be alarmed when the van is beginning to move," said Zelig. "The driver will be here soon and we will be on our way, you understand."

"He knows that," said Ruth.

"Right. But thanks, Doc," said Jesse.

Despite what he had said, he had not expected sleep to come easily that night, but he was so exhausted, and the ointment had so soothed his leg, that he was asleep almost the moment he put his head down; asleep, and dreaming.

He could not afterward recall more than a jumbled series of images, primary among which were audiences that jeered his concerts, guitars that came to pieces in his hands, and the police photographs of Ruth's mutilated body shown over and over again relentlessly, endlessly, inexorably.

Only her sweet face was left untouched in the grisly chaos of splattered blood and mangled limbs. He could not move, could not look away, could not even close his eyes. He wanted to scream, or to run, or to vomit, or to die, but all he could do was look into the black-and-white glossy images of her terrified eyes while something small and insane within him gibbered in useless protest, "She's alive. She's alive. She's alive."

She was alive: suddenly, horribly, the photographed corpse was animated. The eyes in that blood-smeared face blinked at him, and the mouth opened to speak, and one mangled hand reached out to him.

In that petrified instant of abject horror and sickened hope the world twisted, the living photograph was extinguished like a candle snuffed, and he was standing again in that eerie red-sand desert under an orange sun.

This time there were no disembodied voices. There was something much more unnerving to Jesse Farrell: there was another Jesse Farrell.

He was dressed exactly as Jesse had been dressed on-stage last night. For one startled instant, Jesse thought he was actually seeing himself as he had been last night. Then the Other smiled, and Jesse knew he was not looking at himself. There were emotions in that smile that Jesse Farrell had never felt, and could not understand. There was a look in the Other's eyes so alien that its presence, in eyes that otherwise mirrored his, shook Jesse to the core of his being. If he had been asked at that moment what evil looked like, he would unhesitatingly have pointed to the Other.

And yet, the Other wore Jesse's face. Aside from his expression, and that look in his eyes, and the fact that the image was not reversed, the Other was the man Jesse had seen in mirrors all his adult life. Even the clothes were Jesse's working clothes. This was Jesse as he could have been, as he would have been if time and circumstance had been altered only slightly, or if his reactions to events had been just a little different.

This was not a good dream.

The Other laughed aloud. "It's not a dream." His voice was Jesse's voice, husky and vulnerable and startlingly familiar.

"What are you?"

The Other's smile widened. "You scared, rock star?"

Perhaps he should have been, but he was not: it was only a dream, after all. "What is this place? I've been here before. Where are we?"

"Shut up." The Other managed to look menacing without making a move. Had Jesse ever looked like that in real life? The man who looked like that might murder. Was this the way his subconscious chose to tell him what he had done? "You're here to answer questions, not ask them," said the Other. "Tell me about Ruth."

The image of those photographs danced crazily through his mind and he forced down a wave of nausea. "What about her?" Why had his subconscious created this unwholesome counterfeit to talk to himself about Ruth?

"Did you kill her?"

"She's not dead." He forced away the memory of that mangled body, the bloody hand reaching, the eyes imploring. Memory? Was it memory, the memory of reality? Or only the aftermath of his earlier dream?

The Other looked thoughtful. "Not dead. Yes, that's an

idea." Only half his attention was on the questions and answers. The rest he devoted to studying Jesse's gestures and postures and carefully substituting them for his own. "I'll use that if I have to. But let's see if there isn't an easier way." He watched Jesse closely. "In slash four she's dead. How did she die?"

"Dunno what you're talking about."

"The world you came from last night," the Other said almost patiently. "Where the cops were waiting for you. She was dead, there. They said you killed her. Did you?"

"She's not dead." The repetition was robbing the words of their meaning.

"What did the cops tell you when they came for you at the concert? Did they say you killed her?"

"They didn't come for me." To his chagrin he sounded defensive, a small boy wrongly accused. He cleared his throat. "That was all nothing. A bad dream. It didn't happen. She's alive."

"Yes, yes, she's alive there." The Other was losing patience. "Understand: that's a different world. Where I'm living, where you were before, Ruth's dead, and the cops did come for you. Only they got me instead. Now I want to know whether you killed her."

Jesse shrugged. It couldn't really matter what he said in a dream. "Dunno. Don't think so."

"How can you not know?"

"Don't remember. Don't remember what happened, that whole night. Doesn't matter. Nothing happened. Ruth's all right." But if that was so, why had his subconscious devised this unpleasant dream?

"You forgot what happened the night she was killed?" insisted the Other.

"You know I did: you're me, or at least I made you up."

But he was not really quite certain of that. Despite his first impression, the Other was not so alien that Jesse couldn't have imagined him: he felt he could, in fact, understand the Other only too well, with his bristling overlay of menace meant to conceal the half-healed scars of terrible abuse. But instead of seeing that as proof that the Other was only an aspect of himself, he recognized it as affirmation of the Other's essential otherness. That was scary. "Why can't I wake up?" he demanded irritably, very much afraid he knew the answer.

"Because you're not asleep." The Other grinned suddenly, in real amusement, and it transformed his face: he looked more human, and unnervingly more like Jesse. "This is real. I'm real. Get it through your head, rock star: you're facing the genuine article, your very own doppelganger." He looked thoughtful. "Though naturally I prefer to think of it the other way around, with you as my doppelganger." He shrugged, dismissing the notion. "All the same, I suppose. The point is, I don't know what you know, because I'm not you, and you didn't make me up. If you can get that simple fact lodged in your tiny brain we'll get along better. Now come on, did you kill Ruth or not?"

Jesse shook his head, bewildered by yet another impossible reality. He didn't know what a doppelganger was, but he knew the man before him, if not a dream, could be deadly. "Jesus," he said, "I'm telling you, Ruth isn't dead." The Other's face fascinated him. It was his, and not his. Jesse had never guessed what his own pain might look like from the outside. Or had this Other suffered even worse indignities than he?

"All right," said the Other, humoring him. "But remember when you thought she was dead?"

"Yeah," he said, wishing again that he would wake up.

This had to be a dream. But he did not wake up.

"Good. What did the cops tell you? When you thought they came for you. When you thought she was dead. How did she die?"

Jesse shook his head. "No." If he couldn't wake up, he would end this dream another way. He turned around, staring at the miles of desert around them. His movement stirred up red dust in an acrid cloud that burned his nose and throat and made his eyes water. "No," he said sharply. "Go away. Leave me alone." It was his dream; he ought to be able to control it. He started walking at an angle away from the Other. Before he had gone twenty paces, the Other was before him. He turned, and the same thing happened again. The Other was some hateful aspect of himself that he could not escape by ignoring it. "What do you want?"

The Other's smile was implacable, his eyes cold: a child with power. A bully. A dangerous adversary, but to Jesse he seemed as much damaged as deadly. "I want information. Tell me about Ruth's murder."

Jesse shook his head doggedly. "She wasn't murdered. She isn't dead." There was nowhere to go; only miles of featureless sand in every direction, and the Other ready to reappear in his path wherever he turned.

The Other's expression was unreadable. "You think she isn't dead. You made that up because you couldn't face the truth. Now tell me the truth. How did you kill her?"

Jesse tried not to remember the photographs the police had shown him. He remembered them anyway. "I didn't—I don't think I killed her."

"You're not sure?" The Other was still mimicking Jesse's expressions, copying his posture.

"I'm sure. I wouldn't hurt her." Jesse stood very still, annoyed by the mimicry, but the Other only mimicked his stillness. It shouldn't matter. It was foolish to be irritated at a character in a dream.

"Then why were you arrested?"

Jesse brushed one hand through his hair, absently pulling at tangles. " 'Cause my fingerprints were on the goddamn knife, okay? And there was blood on my clothes. They found it the next day. But I didn't kill her. Now leave me alone."

"I will, soon enough. Tell me more." The Other brushed one hand through his hair, pulling at tangles.

Jesse dropped his hand to his side and tried to keep his expression bland, blank, empty. "Tell you more what, damn it?"

The Other's expression went bland, blank, empty: but his eyes were lit by cold, calculating, oddly aimless fury. "More details," he said. "Where did she die? How, exactly? If you didn't kill her, where were you? Why did the police think you did it? What evidence did they have? What else, besides the fingerprints? Blood on your clothes, you said?"

"Yeah." Jesse could hear the defeat in his own voice; the remembered despair. But Ruth was alive . . . wasn't she? Or was that the point of this dream? Was he trying to tell himself Ruth wasn't alive, and that the world in which he'd seen her with Dr. Zelig had been only a sort of wish-fulfillment hallucination?

"Well?"

"My clothes were bloody. They had her blood on them. But I didn't do it. Damn it, nobody did it. She isn't dead!" The repetition didn't make it true.

"Yes," said the Other, as though answering an unspoken question. He thought about it. "Yes, I think she'll have to be alive. It's the only easy answer."

Jesse stared at him. "She is, or she isn't." He shifted,

looking for firmer ground. "You said she's alive in one world and dead in another. But there's only one world. Isn't there? How could there be more?"

"Don't worry about it." The Other studied him and squared his shoulders, the better to match Jesse's posture. His hair was shorter than Jesse's, and wouldn't stay back out of his face even when he held still.

Jesse felt oddly comforted by that observation: it convinced him, suddenly, that this was not a dream. The Other was real; why would he dream himself with shorter hair? He persisted, encouraged: "How can she be alive and dead at the same time?"

The Other shrugged. "There are worlds, okay? A lot of worlds, with Ruths and Jesses and everybody else duplicated in every one. I've taken your place in the one you belong in, where Ruth was murdered. You remember the jump, don't you? You must. It happened in the middle of a concert, when I stepped into your world. You can't stay in the same world with your doppelganger once one of you has seen the other. So when I jumped into your world, you landed here, in Limbo."

Disappointed, Jesse pointed out his error in logic. "We're both here now."

"There are different rules for Limbo." The Other was unconcerned with logic.

"Sure. There would be." That was what he got for arguing with what must, after all, be a dream-creature.

The Other smiled almost sympathetically. "Limbo isn't exactly a world, you see. It's more like a, sort of a between-worlds place, I guess you'd say. Or a place beyond worlds." He shrugged. "Never mind. You wouldn't understand. I'm going back to your world soon. Tell you what: just as a friendly gesture, when I go I'll bounce you back to the new world the monitors gave you. They aren't watching here to-night, and stuck in Limbo's no fate for somebody who looks so much like me." His expression sobered. "But that's all I'll do for you. And don't count on having Ruth there with you for long. I need her to get rid of the police. If I bring them a live Ruth, they won't hold me for the dead one's murder."

Jesse stiffened. "You leave Ruth alone."

The Other tilted his head in a posture so familiar to Jesse that he automatically tilted his head in response, as though trying to match an unruly reflection in a mirror. "I thought you didn't believe any of this," said the Other.

Jesse frowned at him, confused again. "I don't know what to believe. Nothing, maybe. This's gotta be a dream."

"That's right," the Other said gently. "It's just a dream. So what are you worried about? Nothing a dream person does to Ruth can hurt her."

"Maybe not, but you leave her alone." He scowled, aware that he sounded as defenseless as he felt.

"Or what, rock star?" The Other laughed without humor. "Don't you see? You're helpless against me. I have all the power." He sounded as though power were some-thing tangible, and more precious than gold. "I can do whatever I want, to Ruth or to anybody, and there's nothing you or anyone else can do to stop me."

That was pitiable, really. It was the boastful defiance of a frightened child. But child or adult, the Other was dan-gerous, and it was Ruth he meant to harm. Jesse stared at him, controlling sudden, murderous rage. He would not tolerate threats against Ruth. The Other, or anyone else, could do what he liked to Jesse, and while Jesse would natu-rally defend himself as he must, he would also do his best to understand and excuse his attacker. He had been taught to value himself too little and peace too much to do otherwise. But a threat against Ruth was beyond understanding or excusing. It came too near some inner core of transcendent, unrecognized need: it woke the boy soldier in charge of survival.

The Other mistook Jesse's sudden pallor for a sign of fear, and laughed aloud in triumph. At that, the last traces of Jesse's rigid self-control broke. He moved suddenly and silently, intent on murder. Which, in retrospect, surprised him almost as much as it surprised the Other; he was not ordinarily given to violence as a means of solving problems. He had not been involved in a fist fight since grade school.

But then, this was only a dream. One did not always behave sensibly in a dream.

What surprised him even more than his impulsive action was that, when his fist connected with the Other's jaw, it hurt. Dream injuries don't hurt. He was staring in surprise at his bruised knuckles when the Other hit him back. That hurt, too.

10

The Other

It was a mistake to doppel that Jesse out of his rock concert, but I didn't have time to look where I leaped; I'd made a mess in a neighboring world and got out by the skin of my teeth, with the bracelet set to doppel the nearest Jesse and damn the consequences. Story of my life.

I had some background from doppeling other Jesses here and there, including a couple of rock musicians (seemed like they were all to do with music one way or another). Given a little time to settle in, I could've played his concert better than he could; but I couldn't play it cold. I didn't have the schedule, didn't know all the songs, and the guitar I'd brought with me wasn't tuned with the band.

They probably wouldn't've even noticed that, of course, but I'm a goddamned (in more ways than one) musical genius (everybody has to be good at something, I guess), and one of the things that means is that it pains me, literally, to play discord that normal people can't even hear.

If I'd had time to check out the timing, I'd've jumped in after the concert. Or maybe I would've waited till I saw what came of the murder investigation, which wasn't something I'd foreseen. Once stuck with the cops who were waiting for the Jesse, I figured I could deal with them, but I didn't much like having to. If I'd realized they were there before I jumped I might've aimed for some other world entirely.

"If" is the biggest word in the universe, and the most useless. I jumped into the Jesse's concert, and I tried to finish the damn thing for him, and I confused the hell out of the band in the process, but I guess the fans got what they wanted. Then the cops arrested me, which was when I found out I'd doppeled a murderer. If it isn't one thing, it's another.

Getting arrested, in any world, is not my idea of fun. In this world it was really a bummer because they had it in for this Jesse in a big way. They were pretty rough about it. I've been handled rougher, but hell, I was going along with them, so there was no call for it, and I resented it.

There's never any sense fighting the authorities if you can avoid it, though. I took what they dealt me and kept quiet about it. I was too tired to do much else. In the world I'd jumped out of—well, I'd tried something, and it had backfired, and I'd had to do some serious running.

And then in this world I'd taken up where the Jesse left off, which I'd figured meant a pretty active concert if I knew my Jesses. So I'd danced (as well as a goddamn cripple can) and leaped around and sung my Jesse-style heart out (with the band an annoying quarter-beat behind me the whole way, it seemed like). By the time the cops got to me I was about ready to thank them if they'd just lead me to a bed.

It wasn't that easy, of course, and it ended up taking hours. I had to sign the Jesse's name to half a dozen pieces of paper certifying or swearing to one thing and another for what seemed half the night. And that's another thing. I hate signing for the Jesses. They have no right to my name. Time was, that was damn near all I had. I don't like sharing.

What a lifestyle. Maybe I should've taken up some kind

of honest work. I could've been a garbage collector. Or a salesman, or something. Something simple, with no messing with time (am I going to do that, or did I do it already?) and identity (am I Jesse, or is he me?) and world-walkers (poor Suli Grail. She never quite understood, but God knows she sure as hell tried. You gotta give her marks for that).

I had to throw a real snit fit to keep the bracelet with me in jail. I damn near foamed at the mouth. And the cops damn near took my arm off, trying to get it away from me. But some mental-health type finally spoke up in my favor and got them to bend the rules. I s'pose it seemed more than a little weird for me to be that attached to a hunk of silver and turquoise, but hey, I needed it. Or I thought I did, which comes to the same thing.

I needed some sleep more than anything, and I didn't want to do it in their world. I couldn't spare the time. Go to sleep in that cage and I might just wake up stuck in it for life. Which I could jump out of, but that'd be another world down and who knew how many left to go? I wanted to give each one my best shot. No sense wasting.

Where I went, instead, was the world where Suli and I had holed up for a few months right after we met. My home world. The one that should've been named Hell.

One night back then I'd stolen her gatestone and made a run into a few neighbor worlds just to check them out, and since I hadn't yet learned to jump time as well as worlds I hadn't got back till nearly morning. (She never even noticed.) That left a hole a good six hours long that I could jump into now and get some rest. (Hell, maybe that's why she never noticed.)

It felt even better than I remembered to curl up against her back, spoon-style, in the big brass bed we'd shared back then. She was warm and soft and sleepy, and smelled of soap. She muttered something and cuddled into the curve of my body like a little animal, sweet and trusting.

That trust of hers was a killer. Back when I lived there, I had damn near trusted her too, she was so good. Not quite (I did know better), but it was a close thing. Just as well I finally had to leave her. Well, didn't have to, but might as well: I'd gotten what I wanted from her. What I hooked up with her for in the first place. She called it a gatestone. I called it freedom.

I wasn't even supposed to know what world-walkers were, or that there were worlds to walk. But I'd seen Suli step into Hell, and I figured if that wasn't proof I'd finally lost my mind then it was proof of something else. I wanted to know what. So I got close to her.

It didn't take long to figure out that the thing she carried in that little bag around her neck must be the key. It took a little longer, and a lot of sweet talk, to find out what it was the key to. Like I said, she trusted me. She let it slip about the worlds, and I pumped her real carefully and found out about world-walkers.

She probably thought it was safe enough, as long as I didn't have a gatestone. At that time she'd never even mentioned gatestones. She never said anything about how to walk worlds, though once she got started she said plenty about the worlds themselves, and about the goddamn terminal importance of keeping them safe and separate and all that business.

Of course it was all right for her to go skipping around the universe like God. She was just doing her job, keeping the worlds safe for democracy or something. But we mustn't have any goddamn crippled musicians getting out of Hell just for the sake of it, oh my, no. I mean, I *asked* her, you know?

I figured it was a waste of time, but time was one thing I had plenty of. So I asked her, and I got this goddamn lecture about weakening barriers and letting trolls loose in civilized societies, or some such shit. You'd think I'd asked her to open the gates to everybody, the way she carried on.

I tried to let it drop, but she wouldn't shut up about it. She went on and on about the horrors of careless world-walking, and something called the Ages of Chaos, and how the whole point of world-walkers was to prevent that ever happening again. I told her I didn't want to start any goddamn Ages of Chaos, I just wanted out of Hell; she hardly even heard me. She just kept on about chaos.

Well, I couldn't really blame her. She'd just swallowed the party line whole and was spitting it back out at me page and paragraph because that was what she was supposed to do. Most people are like that. They've never been taught to think for themselves, and nothing ever happens to make them learn how, so they go around swallowing things whole and burping them back up again whenever it seems like the right time for it. They never even know how ignorant they are.

I didn't blame her, but I did figure she'd had her chance. I didn't owe her more than that. So I took her stone again, and I held it and wanted it and jumped, figuring that'd be my best bet for jumping to one of my own. I didn't want to keep hers if I could get my own, because that'd leave her trapped in Hell. Which maybe she deserved for wanting to keep me trapped there, but it would also set the monitors to looking for her. (She'd told me more than she knew, both before and during her rant about chaos.) That would be a really bad plan, because next thing you knew they'd be looking for me. There was a good chance Suli, handled right, would let me go if I got my own stone. There was no chance the monitors would.

That was my first experience with jumping time, and I wasn't ready for it. At first I didn't even know what had happened. I left a world where Suli was sleeping in our big brass bed, curled up naked in the tangled covers like a cat. I arrived in a world where Suli was still sleeping, but not in the big brass bed, and not naked. She was wearing an odd little dress I'd never seen before, fast asleep on a big wood-framed bed in a strange room. Her gatestone was beside her, worked into a big silver bracelet. And beside that were a bunch of cassette tapes with my name and my face on their covers.

Up until that moment, all I'd wanted out of this was a way out of Hell. I didn't know or care what I'd do once I was out; I figured I could work that out later. I had jumped into maybe three or four worlds, looked around just long enough to be sure they weren't too weird to live in, and got out again. I hadn't run into any doppelgangers, and that was one thing Suli never did talk about. So it threw me for a loop when I saw those tapes.

It also gave me a hell of an idea for what I was going to do with myself once I got out of Hell. I took time to study those covers, found out most of the songs were ones I'd written, and stared at my photographed face long enough to figure out it wasn't mine. There were little differences. Not just the difference between a photograph and a mirror. The hair was wrong, for instance. I hadn't worn my hair that long since high school; my father didn't like long hair, and it wasn't worth fighting for. And the guy in the photograph had weird eyes. Or maybe not weird, exactly, but anyway they weren't mine.

It wasn't a big jump from seeing those tapes to figuring there must be a Jesse Farrell in every one of those worlds

I'd visited, and that this guy in the photos was one of them. This hotshot with his guitar and his band and his peaceful, stupid eyes was what I might have been if I'd grown up in his world. And either he wasn't a cripple (but in that case, if he was like me inside as well as out, why wouldn't he be dancing?) or he'd found a way to live without the only thing I'd ever really wanted.

What I wanted to do, of course, was jump straight into his world and find out the answers to the half a million questions I thought of, looking at his tapes. But I wasn't as dumb as he looked. I knew you don't trust anybody, not even if he's wearing your face. And if you really want something so bad you can taste it, you make damn sure nobody can find out what it is you want and take it away from you before you even get it.

I'd have to plan and explore and do some fancy footwork to keep Suli and the monitors off my ass before I went after that Jesse's life. So I left the tapes and jumped back into Hell carrying Suli's gatestone-of-the-"future" in its silver bracelet in one hand, and her gatestone-of-the-"present" naked in the other. I would give Suli back the naked one and with any luck she'd never know what happened to the one in the bracelet.

What I didn't count on was how a world-walker's sort of connected to her stone. I knew enough to jump time, so I arrived about a minute after I left, and Suli was still sleeping. I put the one gatestone back in her little mesh bag and hid the other one in my jacket, which had big pockets. But when she woke up, she knew right away something was wrong. She checked the little mesh bag, found her gatestone, and gave me the weirdest look.

"You've got my stone," she said. "I don't know how, but you've got it."

"Don't be dumb. You've got it right there."

"You must've jumped time," she said, looking thoughtful. "But even so, how could you carry both of them at once, uninsulated? They should've canceled each other out. You should be stuck in the future someplace." She looked up at me. "But you're not. Oh, Jesse. You can't do this. You have to give it back, Jesse. It's for your own good."

That tore it. Any other phrase I might've stuck around to see what she had to say, but "for your own good" is a killer. As far as I was concerned, you hear those words and you like living, it's "fight or flight" time. You either kill or you get the hell out while you can. Because otherwise you're dead.

That was a holdover from childhood, and I knew it was an overreaction. I mean, we're talking one sweet, small woman here. That didn't stop me. Reason doesn't enter into it. I didn't want to kill her, and I didn't want to die, so I got the hell out. Fight or flight. Story of my life.

I guess I'll never forget the way she looked at me. That was my first panic jump, and my instincts were slower than they are now. I had plenty of time to see the look in her eyes, and to know that from her point of view I had just done about the worst I could do.

She probably could've cut me off if she'd chased me then, but she didn't. Maybe I'd caught her too much by surprise. Maybe I'd hurt her too much. Hell, maybe even she was being generous: she could've known how close to the edge I was, and chose not to risk pushing me over. Anyway she let me go, and I the hell *went*, I'll tell you.

I've been through a lot of worlds since then. At first I just looked around for the hell of it, getting a feel for the freedom. Then I met my first doppelgangers. They doppeled me into Limbo, and that just about scared the pants off me. So I studied the problem, and I worked out the quirk of concentration that would keep me in their worlds and doppel them into Limbo instead of me, and I practiced till I could do it every time. And there I'd be, with a life already set up waiting for me to live it.

Most of 'em weren't worth much. There were even a couple that rivaled Hell for how much fun they were. I got out of those in a hurry. But I stayed in some of the others for a while, living the Jesse's life and learning some stuff along the way. Mostly music.

All the Jesses were cripples, which was good; if I ran into one that wasn't, I wouldn't be able to live his life for him. Like I said before, they were all involved with music one way or another, too. I could pick up the instruments easy enough, and our voices matched, so that didn't give me any trouble.

I was still hung up on that first Jesse whose tapes I'd seen, but at that point I'd made only one small recon into his world, mostly to make sure I could find it. I got out before we could see each other; I wasn't ready to doppel him, and getting doppeled is too damn much trouble to put up with if you don't have to. Besides, it was too big a risk; I didn't want to get noticed anywhere near that world. Because somewhere in the back of my mind I had decided, don't ask me why, that his world would be the one I'd settle down in.

I'd known from the start what I really wanted in a world. I wanted power. I wanted the kind of power that Jesse had, and more. I craved power the way a junkie craves his drug. At the time it didn't occur to me to wonder why, though I guess I know: if you get enough power, nobody can hurt you. The powerful are not vulnerable.

Looking for more power led me into a couple of blind alleys. Music is good, but religion is better, and I spent some time in a couple of worlds trying to combine the two and to keep the power of them both for myself, under the Jesses' name. It's a long story, what went wrong. But the end was that I'd had to jump out of those worlds in a right quick hurry.

The second time that happened, I knew the religion thing was a dead end. What I found out, the most powerful religions were based on martyrs. I wanted power, not dead. So I guess I decided when I wasn't looking that I was ready for the tape-Jesse's world, since that's where that panic jump took me. Which is why I doppeled him in the middle of a concert and ended up doing his time in jail.

I spent the night with Suli in the past, then jumped back to the jail cell just after I left it, to get my bearings. Then I focused on the Jesse who belonged there, and jumped the two of us into Limbo. I figured he could tell me what the hell was going on, and I'd figure out how to get "him" (me) out of jail.

Plus I could look him over in the process, because I meant to stay in his world a while, maybe forever. It would be a good plan to copy his mannerisms and whatnot, in case anybody was paying attention. It's easier to take over somebody's life real smoothly if you know how to act like them most of the time.

He didn't tell me much. He was stupid and pissed and hard to handle. But I could see why I'd been drawn to his world. It wasn't just the world I wanted, or the luck he'd had in it. It was him. I liked him. I wanted to be like him. I didn't just want to take over his life and pretend to be him. I wanted to be him.

Which was crazy. In the first place, you can step into somebody's life all you want and it isn't going to turn you into him no matter how much you might wish it would. And in the second place, he was a turkey. He was stupid. He believed in things that you just don't believe in. He was totally, terminally naive.

I'd known that before we met in Limbo. It was in his eyes on those tape covers, it was in his music, it was in the way he acted in Limbo. You can tell a lot about a man just by what he takes for granted, and what that Jesse took for granted was that people are okay folks. He didn't even know how to hate, which if he had my background was pretty damn strange. He cared about people, God knows why. He had empathy for them. He understood them. Swear to Hell, he probably understood his father. He probably forgave the son of a bitch.

And I, well, despite knowing what a damn fool that made me, I admired him for that. I wanted to have what he had. That's what it came down to. He had something that I knew I might never find, no matter how much power I gathered to me: he was at peace with himself.

That pissed me off. So when he started a fight, I finished it. I finished it good.

11

Jesse

The movement of the van during the night had not awakened Jesse, but the silence when it stopped in the morning did. He sat up, stared at his unfamiliar surroundings for a moment, then pushed aside the curtains over the window beside his bed to look out at the world. There was nothing to see but an empty parking lot, foggy and bleak in the gray morning light. Still dazed with sleep, he watched the driver of the van climb down onto the cracked concrete outside, pulling his jacket shut against a chill wind as he called a greeting to someone out of Jesse's view and hurried away, out of sight.

The hand with which Jesse held back the curtain ached when he moved it. Groggy and irritable after a night of troubled sleep, he let the curtain drop and stared without comprehension at the bloodied knuckles of both hands. Memory returned slowly, in sleep-befuddled bits and pieces. The first and most shocking recollection was that last night, during the concert, something bizarre and inexplicable had happened: something eerie and improbable, like an episode of "The Twilight Zone." He had fallen into an alternate universe.

Or he had gone suddenly and completely mad. Unfortunately that was a more likely explanation, since insanity was a demonstrable reality and alternate universes were not.

The fact that he did not believe it, and did not feel insane, was hardly proof against it; he did not know, but thought it possible that even a raving lunatic might feel perfectly sane, so one's feelings about it probably meant nothing at all. And he might well qualify as a raving lunatic if he started talking about alternate universes. Bad enough to believe in them, but at least he could keep his mouth shut about it.

It would be different if he had any hope of proving that he came from a different universe, but the absence of proof was complete. All he had brought with him into this universe were his guitar and the clothes he wore, and if they were in any way wrong here, Ruth or Dr. Zelig would surely have noticed.

The fact that he had never met Dr. Zelig before was of no use as proof, because as far as Dr. Zelig was concerned, they had known each other for years. Which was an interesting point; that would mean that before he came to this universe, there was another Jesse here already, who was a duplicate of himself, at least in appearance.

That could explain a great many things, beginning with Ruth's expectations about his behavior and Zelig's about his health. But the explanation, in that case, was at least as confusing as the situation it explained. Quite aside from all other considerations, where would that Jesse have gone to make room for his arrival?

The thought of such a self-duplicate reminded him, with a sinking sense of despair, of the nightmare last night in which he had fought that mysterious identical-twin Other. That shot down the alternate worlds theory; he was just remembering the mumbo-jumbo his alternate self had thrown at him in his dream.

Until that moment, he had not realized how much he

wanted to believe in multiple worlds and multiples of himself to dwell in them. It would have been a rational explanation for the fact that he did not remember a doctor he had apparently known for years, and for the fact that Ruth was convinced he habitually used drugs recreationally, while he was convinced he never did. And multiple Ruths would have explained the confusion over her murder. One Ruth was killed, one was not. It would not have explained away the missing hours in his life on the night Ruth died, but it would explain how he could find her still alive and well after the concert, when during the concert the police had shown him those grisly photos.

He sighed heavily. Very likely Ruth was right and he did use drugs recreationally. That was a much more sensible explanation for everything. From what he had seen of drug abuse, it was easy to imagine that drugs might make one crazy enough to believe almost anything. Obviously, alternate universes were impossible. Therefore the dream was just a dream, and the fight with his imagined double never happened. He was, at best, confused; at worst, crazy.

And he had bruised knuckles on both hands, though he had hit a cabinet last night with only one hand. He stared at his hands, hopeful and dismayed at once. For the first time, it occurred to him that proof of alternate universes would be almost as alarming as proof of his own insanity. He had no wish to be insane, but he was not much more comfortable with the idea that the universe was insane. A reality in which one could fall without warning from one world to another would be insane almost by definition.

He chose to ignore his knuckles, bruised and bloody and aching from a fight that could not have happened. They made sense only if he believed that during the night he had been transported from this world to another and back. He put his hands under the bed clothes and tried not to think of them.

His hallucinations were not even consistent. When he had imagined himself transported from his old world to this new one, he had hallucinated an interim period in that red desert world that the Other in his dream had called Limbo. But that time, the desert world had been a sort of stopping place between worlds. This time, he had ended afterward in the same world from which he had started. And it was the wrong world. Or he was crazy.

He gazed bleakly around in the half-dark stillness of the curtained van, trying to recognize surroundings that were wholly unfamiliar to him. He knew the band had never traveled by surface vehicles, not since their earliest days together. Yet according to Ruth and Dr. Zelig, they seldom traveled by air. The van should probably seem almost like home to him. They must have spent months living in it on tour. He could not convince himself he had ever seen it before last night.

Last night, when Ruth was suddenly alive again—! A fit of panic made him try to rise to see whether she was still in the bed she had occupied last night, the upper of the two bunk beds opposite his. The abrupt movement sent daggers of blinding pain through his ribs. He stifled a groan and moved more carefully, swinging his feet slowly out of bed so he could stand up to look for Ruth. She was safely asleep in one bed, Zelig in the other. Jesse sat again on the edge of his bed and delicately felt his aching ribs with cautious fingers.

They were bruised and swollen, as if he had been kicked. In his dream, during that brief and confusing battle, the Other had kicked him. Injuries in dreams don't hurt, and they don't leave bruises. He started to lift the hem of his robe to peer at his ribs, but stopped when he noticed a streak of ground-in red dirt that had not been there when he put on the robe last night.

Forgetting his ribs, he brushed at the stain in mounting panic, as though by brushing it away he could brush away all the confusing implications that came with it. Neither the stain nor the implications disappeared.

"God, Jesse, what're you doing up so early?"

Startled, he stared at Ruth for a long moment before he said stupidly, "Woke up."

Her hair was tousled, her makeup smeared, and the side of her face crease-marked from her pillow. She was beautiful. "Go back to sleep," she said. "It's early."

"Can't." He felt like a small boy, defenseless and guilty. "I'm sorry."

She frowned at him, sat up, straightened her nightgown, and ran her fingers through her hair, studying him the whole time. "Will wonders never cease!"

"What?"

"You said you're sorry."

"Yeah." He stared at her, puzzled.

"You don't usually make polite noises like that."

"Wasn't a polite noise."

She blinked sleepily and used both hands to rumple her hair, thought about it, and asked incuriously, "Why can't you sleep?"

He shrugged. "I'm awake."

"I see that." The hint of a smile pulled at her lips. "Sometimes even people who are awake manage to go to sleep."

"Where are we?"

She hesitated, perhaps considering whether to pursue the topic of sleep. Then she shrugged and said in a resigned voice, "San Francisco, I hope. I don't suppose you want breakfast."

"Why not?"

"Because you never do."

"Oh. Well, maybe I could change."

"Change what?"

"My habits. I'm hungry."

"Me, too." She reached to turn on the overhead light, narrowed her eyes against the resultant glare, and stared at him. "Good God, what have you done to your face?"

He resisted the impulse to touch it. "Nothing. What's wrong with it?"

She climbed down from her bed without answering, bent to peer closely at his face, and lifted one hand to touch his cheekbone. "Turn more toward the light. Does that hurt? No wonder. You've got a bad bruise there." When he lifted a hand to feel for the bruise, she caught his wrist and stared at the knuckles, then reached for the other hand and looked at that, too. "Jesse, what have you done to yourself? You didn't get out somehow during the night, did you? You look like you've been in a fight."

He pulled away from her, scowling. "I haven't been out." He stirred impatiently. "We go out for breakfast, or what?"

"Jesse—" Whatever she intended to say, she thought better of it. Instead, she said dubiously, "You really are hungry?"

"Would I lie?"

"Yes, as a matter of fact."

"Oh. Well, that's another habit I gotta change. I thought you said you were hungry?"

"Always in the morning she is hungry," said Zelig.

"Oh, Doc, I didn't know you were awake. Morning. You hungry too?"

"Yes, indeed. How are you feeling this morning, Jesse?"

"Just fine. How 'bout you?"

"How I am feeling? You wish to know how I am feeling?"

"Sure, why not?" He glanced at Ruth. "S'pose that's another polite noise I don't make?"

"I feel quite well," Zelig said hastily. "What was it you were discussing with Ruth about a fight?"

"Nothing," said Jesse, at the same time as Ruth said, "He has a big bruise on his cheekbone, and his knuckles are a mess."

Zelig sat up, pushing back the bedclothes to reveal bright candy-striped pajamas. "Let me see."

Under Ruth's stern gaze Jesse, feeling very much like a recalcitrant child, displayed first his knuckles and then his cheekbone for Dr. Zelig's inspection. Zelig and Ruth both frowned over them and discussed possible causes as though Jesse were not there. After one or two half-hearted attempts to include himself in the conversation, Jesse lapsed into a sullen silence that lasted, in the end, through most of a very frustrating day.

No one knew about the bruise on his ribs, and Jesse was not inclined to display it. Ruth's attitude made him feel rather as though the injuries she knew about were something to be ashamed of, and there was no reason to think she would regard his bruised ribs any differently. Zelig seemed more sympathetic and puzzled, but even he was unlikely to be convinced, by the exposure of another bruise, that Jesse was the victim of some weird accident involving alternate universes. Jesse only half believed it himself.

He had expected to meet with the band to prepare for the evening's concert, but Ruth disabused him of that notion over breakfast. "Don't be silly," she said. "You don't have any new songs for them, do you?"

"Don't think so."

"You don't even know?"

"Guess I don't have any."

"Well, that's it, then. You know they won't spend any more time with you than they have to. You pay them to play, but you can't pay them enough to put up with you off-stage. You're rich, but you're not that rich."

"We aren't friends?"

She might not have heard him. "They'll practice new songs when you write them. And they'll go over the old ones at the beginning of a tour. For the rest, they practice together without you and hope for the best during performances. And they don't usually get it. But you know all that."

"Guess that means we aren't friends."

Ruth nearly choked on her coffee. "Friends! You and the band?" She controlled a fit of laughter with an obvious effort. "Jesse, my dear, you don't have any friends, least of all in the band!"

"What are you?" He regretted that the instant he had said it.

"What do you mean?"

There was no going back: "Aren't you a friend?" He didn't want to hear her answer to that.

"I am an employee, remember?" she said. "Physical therapist and general factotum. Strictly business."

"Guess I didn't," he said.

"You didn't what?"

"Remember." He pushed away his breakfast, no longer hungry. "Do I pay you enough?"

"For what?"

"For the time you gotta spend with me."

"Honey, there ain't that much money in the universe."

"Then why do you do it?"

She looked away from him for a moment, her expression puzzled. "You're in an odd mood this morning."

He shrugged. "Sounds like I usually am. If I'm such a bummer, why do you put up with me? I'd think you could get about any job you wanted."

She hesitated, and there was genuine regret in her voice when she said at last, "I liked you once, okay? I still respect the music you make, even though I don't much like it. I know it's good. And I guess—I guess old habits die hard."

Jesse looked away. The Jesse he was replacing was not a likable person. He wanted to dissociate himself from that Jesse, so he believed that this was a different world, and that the "other" Jesse was different from himself. But perhaps there really was no "other" Jesse, outside his imagination. Perhaps the knowledge of his own offensiveness had become too much for him to bear. Perhaps it was what had prompted him in the first place to decide this was a different world. It gave him an illusory chance to start over. And it was easier to believe in an alternate universe than it was to admit that for most of his life he must have behaved like the worst kind of self-destructive, egomaniacal nut case.

"I'm glad they do," he said.

Ruth looked at him in surprise. "You're glad who do what?"

"I'm glad old habits die hard, if that's why you haven't left me. Listen, you think—you think you could get the band to meet with me? For a practice session? Just an experiment?" he asked humbly. "They could walk if I—if I don't act right."

"Why?"

"Why what?"

"Why do you want a practice session?"

111

He shrugged. "Figure I need it."

She stared. "The great Jesse Farrell needs practice?"

He shrugged again, uncomfortable under her derisive gaze. "Yeah. Damn it, yes. Would you ask them?"

She sipped her coffee, watching him, thinking about it. "You'd better make it an order, or they won't show."

"See if they will. I don't wanta order them."

"That's new." At his look, she rolled her eyes and said, "Okay, okay," but her tone said how unlikely she thought it that the band would agree.

They did, though, if only because a request instead of an order from him was rare enough to pique their interest. And it turned out that he did have new songs to offer them. Even more surprising, they had new songs to offer him. There were a number of songs in their repertoire, supposedly written by him, that he had never heard before.

Fascination with the music went a long way toward overcoming the initial antipathy of the band members. They were all musicians first, and good ones. Darla Black was the only one who greeted him with any friendliness when they first met, but after only an hour with them Jesse had begun to win the others' tentative friendship. That improved the music they made together, which in turn improved their budding relationship.

Bob Lyle, who in his own world had been Jesse's best friend, was in this world wary and distrustful of him. But as in Jesse's own world, they had grown up together and had been friends once. It wasn't long till there were cautious signs of the old bonds still at work between the two of them: rapport over certain musical passages, shared jokes, unplanned harmonies. Lyle was obviously loath to trust him, but there were habits of friendship beneath the veneer of suspicion, and it comforted Jesse to find them.

With Darla responding to him with normal human kindness, and Lyle beginning to warm to him, it wasn't long till Mirabelle Kane was drawn into the musical togetherness with them. From there it was a small step to a sort of absent-minded camaraderie among the four of them as they traded musical ideas, anecdotes, and jokes. In his happy absorption, Jesse barely noticed that one member of the band was decidedly not being won over.

Bancroft Averill took to the new songs readily enough, but his suspicious hostility toward Jesse increased rather than decreased as the session went on. He was silent about it, but the looks he gave Jesse were murderous, especially when Ruth appeared after a time to encourage Jesse to rest before the concert.

"Come on, you need a nap," she said.

"I'm okay," said Jesse, so drunk on the music and hard-won companionship that he had all but forgotten alternate worlds and murdered Ruths. "Listen, what d'you think of this?" He launched into a newly-learned song the band told him he'd written, which had been wholly unfamiliar to him and which he had promptly begun to rewrite.

"You know I don't like rock music. Come on, Jesse, you're pale, and look at your hands. You'll have them so swollen you can't play at all tonight."

"I'm okay, really." He glanced at his swollen knuckles and gave her one of his mischievous, boyish grins. "They'll swell more if I stop."

"And your fingers? You haven't played guitar this long at one time in years. You'll wear right through the calluses, and then where will you be tonight?"

"No, they're fine, really." Surprised at her concern, he held out his left hand to show her the fingertip calluses. "See?"

113

She glanced at it, did a double-take, and took his hand in hers to feel the palm. "God, it's callused all over. How did it get this way?" She looked up at his face, still holding his hand. "You'd think you'd been helping to carry the equipment or something!"

"Would that be so weird?" It was a real question; he didn't know. But the looks the others gave him told him the answer, and plummeted him back into the dilemma of different worlds, alternate personalities, and probable insanity. "Okay," he said, "Guess I don't help. I dunno, then. But look, I don't need a rest now, okay?" He knew he sounded like a small boy begging his mother for a treat, but he couldn't stop now. "Give us another half hour anyway."

She looked at the other band members. This return from pure music to mundane realities had shaken their dawning confidence in him, but had not quite broken it. One by one they nodded silent agreement to the continued session, most of them obviously surprised by their own reluctance to quit. "Okay," she said. "Half an hour."

By the time of the concert that evening, everything had been going so well for so long that Jesse had managed to push to the back of his mind again the conundrum of worlds and doubles and drugs. The only drug he had ever needed was the music he played. That night he was stoned on it, ecstatic, and the band with him, and the audience responded to their mood.

When they broke for intermission, Jesse gave no thought at all to the fact that Ruth failed to meet him backstage. If he had, he might have been less stunned by the arrival of the police, at the end of the interval, to arrest him for her abduction.

12

The Other

I'd considered a lot of possible snags when I planned Ruth's kidnapping. Suli might get in the way, or maybe I'd get the time wrong, or any of a hundred things.

What I didn't think of was Ruth causing trouble herself. She was just a damn one-worlder: she didn't know from doppelgangers. To her, I'd look like the Jesse. I'd been growing my hair since I got out of Hell, so it was almost as long as his now. There wasn't any other major difference in the way we looked. I thought she'd accept me for him and give me no trouble, at least until I got her into the target world. Maybe she'd become a problem there, if she recognized any differences from her world, but time enough to deal with that when we came to it.

What I didn't take into account was that she had seen her Jesse go in minutes from a dying junkie to a healthy guy who didn't do drugs for fun. You'd need real determination to see that and not notice something was out of whack.

Most people would have that determination. They'd block out the evidence of their senses when what they sensed was too weird. It's a defense mechanism, and a good one, and it keeps a lot of people sane.

But Ruth, I guess, was too honest with herself, or at least too open-minded. She not only figured something was out of whack, she must've made a pretty damn good guess as to

115

what it was before I ever got there. When she saw me outside in the parking lot while the Jesse was onstage, she didn't waste any time about it. She said, "Who are you? Get away from me!" and she started screaming for help before I could even get close to her.

Well, I had to stop that in a hurry. I didn't need any locals messing with my business. The only way I could get out of that jail in the Jesse's world was by bringing them a living Ruth to take the place of the body I'd already dumped in the trolls' world. And this was the Ruth I wanted.

I could've gone to some other world and picked up another Ruth, but I guess I had some idea in the back of my mind about messing up as few worlds as possible. Maybe some of Suli's nattering on at me had stuck. Anyway, the monitors had already mucked with this world, putting the Jesse here when I doppeled him. It wouldn't make matters that much worse to take this world's Ruth back to the world where I needed her.

As to what it would do to that world to have her there . . . Suli'd been taught that one wrong footprint might destroy the universe, but I figured the gods would give us more leeway than that. Everybody at that Central of hers had probably been quivering in their boots since the Ages of Chaos, with no real notion what would cause trouble and what wouldn't. They were just making it up as they went along.

My guess was that when the boundaries were getting thin, they started making rules like crazy till the boundaries started thickening up again. And then instead of testing it out and finding out which rules they needed and which they didn't, they just taught the whole mass of them to new generations of world-walkers. Just to be on the safe side. Probably a good half to three-quarters of the rules they lived by weren't needed, and they'd never know it. That's the way these things usually work.

I figured I was maybe taking a small chance with world-walls or barriers or whatever, by taking over the Jesse's world and bringing another world's Ruth in to get me out of jail, but I didn't think it was near the big deal Suli would've thought it.

So when Ruth started screaming, I moved. I meant to just grab her and jump someplace where it wouldn't matter how much she screamed, but she fought like a wildcat. I wasn't ready for that. I lost my grip and had to chase her, and she didn't have a bum leg like mine to slow her down.

Plus, while that was going on we got witnesses, one of the band members and some little guy I didn't recognize. That could really screw things up. When I finally tagged her I didn't waste time being polite about it. I socked her, grabbed her when she fell, and jumped.

It wasn't till later I figured out she must've knocked my bracelet off in the struggle. I'd jumped without a god-damned stone. I'd jumped worlds and time both, and landed right where I planned to, and there wasn't a reason in any world why I should've. You can't jump without a stone. I mean, if you could, everybody would, right? What's to stop them? But I didn't have a stone, and I jumped, and I got where I was going.

I had more jumping to do before I was safe, and all I could do was stick to the plan and hope to Hell it kept working, stone or not. I'd jumped right into the hotel room I'd have been in if I weren't in jail. My luck held that far: there was nobody in there with us. I dumped Ruth on the bed and got out fast, figuring she'd let somebody know she was there soon enough. Meantime I had to get back in jail close enough to when I'd left that nobody would know I'd been gone.

That was the hard part. The jump to the hotel room had been an easy one because the time didn't matter too much. It's harder to jump time with precision than it is just to step between worlds any old whichtime, which was pretty much all I had to do going to the hotel. With the jail cell it mattered a lot. I wanted to arrive before anyone knew I was gone, and I *didn't* want to arrive before I left. I had no idea what would happen if I doppeled myself, and I didn't want to find out. And I didn't have the stone to help me out. I had to do it alone.

So I gave that jump everything I had. Which is probably why I finally, that time, for the first time, heard a gate. Goddamn. It was a goddamn symphony. It was soaring strings and crashing cymbals and bellowing drums and a bass section that moaned like eternity dying.

It was the thunder of battles, the greed of victory, and the twisted pride of defeat. It was heroes and harlots, monsters and myths, villains and victims, and under it all the slow pulse-beat of hope and hell and somebody's vision of heaven, and how I could have traveled through that as far and as long and as often as I had without hearing it the gods only know.

Because I was a part of it. I was the pan-pipes, a windy whisper of melody pulling and tumbling and tearing against the background of all that glory. I was the lonely echo of broken dreams at the edge of time. I was the beggar's curse and the liar's whisper and the hero's bark of laughter in the face of Death. I was both instrument and musician, and I played that gate the way the Jesses played their little guitars and violins and woodwinds, and for the first time I knew why they played: it was the only way they could taste that edge of eternity they all heard and yearned for. But I! I didn't just hear eternity, I played eternity! I was eternity!

And then I was just a normal guy again, back in that jail cell, shaking with reaction. I couldn't even think about what had happened. I didn't know how to think about it. So I thought about all the other problems I had.

I had enough of them: the fact that Ruth knew I'd kidnapped her, for instance, and might try to spoil the whole thing by telling the cops (which shouldn't matter, since they'd think she was crazy), and how soon Suli's Central would be sending some world-walker after me. Which was a worry I'd been trying not to think about for a while now.

They knew I'd doppeled the Jesse; they'd put him in a substitute world. So they knew I was in his. And that meant they'd be sending a world-walker to chase me out of it. And I didn't have a plan. I didn't have the foggiest notion how I was going to keep from getting hauled back to Hell or worse. I could dodge for a while, but damn it, I was sick of running. Or anyway, I was sick of being chased. I had as much right to a world as the next guy, and I didn't see why it had to be Hell.

If only I hadn't let myself get panicked into doppeling the target Jesse without a little preparation. The last world I'd been in, the people at Suli's Central had never known it, because I'd managed to doppel the Jesse there into yet another world, not Limbo. And I could've done the same to the Jesse I was replacing now, if I'd just had sense enough to take my time about it. I could've jumped into any old world—even Limbo—to escape the mob that was after me, and then gone after the world I wanted a little more carefully, if I'd been thinking.

If. Biggest little word in the universe, ladies and gentleman. Also the story of my life. If I hadn't been born in

Hell, if I'd had any normal human being for a father instead of the asshole I got, if the "accident" hadn't smashed my leg—Hell, if it had even just killed my father, that would have been a little something.

"If" never did a damn thing for nobody. It was a kid's game, and I should've outgrown it. I spent the rest of the morning sitting in that jail cell remembering the symphony of the gate, and wondering when Ruth would make her presence known in this world, and trying to decide what I was going to do when she did and they let me out of there.

I finally figured it out mostly because I was thinking about that symphony. I couldn't forget it, but I couldn't quite think about it, either. My thoughts kept skittering away from it, which led to general thoughts about walking worlds and why there were so many rules about who could do it, and a little time spent resenting the fact that Suli's Central didn't want to count me among the favored few. What had they expected me to do, just accept that and settle down to live out my life in Hell?

Maybe that's what they expected, but they shouldn't've been surprised at what they got instead. If any of them had been locked in Hell, they'd've stolen the way out if they'd found it, just like I did. They wouldn't've sat around fretting about what it would do to barriers between worlds they hadn't ever seen. Not when freedom had been waved under their noses and snatched away again, before they could grab it, because some sanctimonious son of a bitch in some world they'd never seen said they weren't fit to have it.

That's when I finally realized there was one sweet, simple way to make them let me stay where I wanted. What they were afraid of was somebody interfering too much with the different worlds, walking around where they weren't supposed to and causing too many changes. That was what hurt worlds, got new ones started that shouldn't've been, and weakened the barriers between the ones there already were.

If they stuck me back in Hell, I would not stay. The only way I could stay sane there would be if I killed my father, and I'd been over that a million times already. No matter how much I hated the son of a bitch, I couldn't kill him. I'd tried, before I met Suli. What I found out was, civilized people don't kill each other. In a fit of passion or a state of war, sure, but not in cool malice, not even if you wish to God you could. It's just not an option.

So I'd jump, and they'd catch me and put me back if they could, and I'd jump again. Which meant I'd never be free again. I'd be in Hell or running from it for the rest of my life.

But a running man can do a lot of damage. And in a case like that it wouldn't make a damn bit of difference to me what happened to worlds or to their barriers or to God It-self. The universe could blow itself up and I'd be just as happy. Especially if Hell went with it.

So, suppose I dropped the bastards at Central a little hint? They seemed to think I was just going to knuckle under to them no matter what it did to my life. Suppose I let them know I wasn't one of their brainwashed, obedient little world-walkers with the party line engraved on my soul? Suppose I just gave them a little warning about how smart it might not be to lock an innocent man in Hell?

Whatever I had done in my life, I did not deserve what had been done to me. I did not deserve what those self-satisfied bastards wanted to do to me. And the only way out that I could see was the one I finally took.

Maybe if I hadn't had that symphony still ringing in my ears I'd have thought about it a little longer, and maybe I'd have even come up with some other answer. But that symphony meant power, and when you're dealing with sanctimonious, self-satisfied bastards, power is always the answer. If you have it, you can beat them. If they have it, you're dead.

This time I had it. And I wasn't going to wait around to give them time to match it. I figured I better not take any more chances jumping out of that jail cell before I was let out legitimately, but the minute I got out I was going to do some heavy-duty music-making. Of the symphony variety. They would find out you don't mess with the music maker.

13

Jesse

Jesse bounced back out into the inferno of light on center stage and grinned into the audience, a sea of blank faces illuminated tonight by gel-diffused spots that picked out crowded circles of bodies in the featureless dark. He had just returned from a five-minute break that had, against his will, stretched to ten minutes.

His fans stopped hissing his name and stomping, but their impatience was still audible, their urgency for the concert to continue almost palpable. Facing them, Jesse stopped bouncing. The grin disappeared. For a long moment he simply stood, staring at nothing, his mind blank.

The police were waiting for him offstage, handcuffs ready, exactly as they had been the night before. The sense of *déjà vu* when they first arrived during the interval had shaken Jesse badly. All the questions that he had imagined resolved, if not to satisfaction then at least enough to live with, were back in the forefront of his mind, unanswered, echoing.

He lifted the microphone off its stand. The synthesized woodwinds whispered, with a hint of harpsichord sighing a tinny accompaniment. When Jesse began to sing, the unaccustomed gentleness of his voice blended almost perfectly with the synthesizer's sweet sorcery, provoking the audience to an even deeper stillness as it strained to make out the words:

She has a very fragile face
Like summer rain and old lace . . .

Had he imagined the Other, and the orange desert, and that alternate world in which he was sane and sober . . . and in which Ruth had been killed two nights ago? Or was he imagining this world, in which, according to the police, Ruth had been brutally abducted tonight but not, at least yet, killed?

If that other world was real, then he was insane to believe he was in this one. If this one was real, then he was insane to believe he had been in that one. If both were real, the universe was insane.

At least this time there had been no body, no photographs, no knife, no blood. At first sight of the police he had been momentarily paralyzed with anticipatory horror, imagining Ruth dead again. But this time she was only missing . . . so far.

The police said they had a witness who had seen Jesse attack and abduct her. That was all he knew; even if they had been willing to discuss it with him, there would have been no time. He was already late returning to the stage, and the thousands of fans out front had been roaring his name, drawing out the sibilants and keeping time with stomping feet so forcefully that the police, who had originally intended to arrest Jesse and take him away in the middle of the concert, were forced to change their plans.

Thousands of Jesse Farrell fans irate at being deprived of the second half of his concert would not have been easy to control. And it seemed self-evident even to the grim lieutenant in charge that Jesse could not escape unnoticed from the spot-lighted stage.

So for the second time in as many days Jesse had walked onstage to perform with the police waiting in the wings to arrest him. For the second time in as many days, reality had become a mire of unanswerable questions.

This time someone had seen Jesse attacking Ruth. Someone had seen him abduct her. He did not believe he had done it, but neither had he believed he had killed her when the police accused him of that, during last night's concert in his world. His conviction of his innocence carried no weight with the police. They stood waiting for him tonight as they had last night: in the wings, in the house, everywhere. He could see the gleam of the handcuffs dangling from the lieutenant's square-fingered, capable hands; and the glitter of his watching eyes like cold gems in the offstage darkness.

Maybe the Other had taken Ruth, as he had said he might, into that alternate world where the other Ruth, Jesse's own familiar Ruth, had been killed. If someone had seen him, it would be a natural enough mistake to think he was Jesse. The Other looked enough like Jesse to fool any witness, even Jesse himself.

"Jesse!" Bob Lyle performed a bit of fancy footwork that brought him to Jesse's side and, keeping out of range of the microphone, shouted in Jesse's ear, "Snap out of it, man! You stoned again, or what?"

The other band members had already been onstage when the police tried to stop Jesse from going on for the second half. Lyle had no way of knowing why Jesse was distracted now. And if he had known what Jesse was thinking, he would have been sure Jesse was stoned. Obviously, the Other looked like Jesse because he was Jesse. He existed as the Other, a separate entity, only in Jesse's mind.

He told Lyle, under the cover of the crowd's roar of approval at the end of the song, that he was okay. But he wasn't okay. The next song was harder and faster, and the drum beat pounded in his bones. He lost the thread of the lyrics. He groped for his place, found it, and couldn't keep his voice steady.

For the first time in his life, his music was a thing outside himself, separate from him. It had always come as naturally to him as breathing. He hardly knew how to think about it, to consciously perform it. He stumbled over the melody, forgetting the words. They seemed abstract and meaningless, the tune alien and strange, nothing of his. He could not become absorbed in it, as he usually did, and forget the world—or the worlds, if there were worlds.

With a sinking feeling that turned his blood to lead he realized that if Ruth was right about his drug use, the fans would know he was a druggie and would blame the mistakes he was making on that. But he didn't use drugs, damn it, and he had wanted to prove that to her, to the fans, to the band, and to himself.

Yet if he didn't use drugs, how could he be so out of touch with reality? How could he not know whether he had killed Ruth as the police accused last night, and not remember abducting her tonight, when they had a witness who saw him do it? (But he could hardly have done both; he couldn't abduct the living woman two nights after he killed her.)

How could he have imagined the police, when they weren't there, and Ruth's murder, when it hadn't happened? How could he have hallucinated whole bizarre worlds and a walking, talking copy of himself, if he were sane and sober? And if he had imagined the Other, what really did happen to Ruth? Had anything happened to her? Or had he imagined that, and the police, too? Was their existence in the wings only a drug-induced hallucination, and Ruth waiting safely offstage for him?

He looked again. The lieutenant's sour face looked back at him. Jesse looked away, shaken, and threw himself back into the music, trying to force his way into that exalted, unthinking state of oneness with it that had saved his life or at least his sanity so often in past. But although the drums thudded in his blood and the synthesizer's haunting cry ached in his bones like unrealized dreams, he could not escape the abyss of anxiety and doubt into which the presence of the police had plunged him.

If Ruth was missing, the police should be out looking for her, not wasting their time arresting Jesse. He didn't know where she was. They wouldn't do her any good by putting him in jail. He fumbled another chord and heard Lyle's bass guitar stutter as he tried to keep up with Jesse's erratic performance. This was killing the tentative alliance Jesse had formed with the band this afternoon. He was failing at his music, too, and that was as incomprehensible to him as if he had suddenly forgotten how to eat or sleep or breathe. It wasn't possible. The music was as much a part of him as his right arm was, or his nose; not something you had to think about to use. It was just there, or it always had been. He wouldn't suddenly lose the talent that was the most important thing to him in the universe . . . unless he really was either stoned or crazy.

He caught himself up short with an audible moan. He wasn't doing Ruth any good, either, wallowing in the self-pity and self-absorption that got him tangled in fretful examination of his mind, worrying about his sanity when he should have been getting through this performance so he could do something for Ruth. And the only possible way he could do anything useful was by accepting the evidence of his senses and acting on it. That meant believing that the Other was real, not just a figment of his imagination, and taking seriously the things the Other had said about different worlds. If the Other had somehow transported Ruth to that other world, there was probably nothing Jesse could do about it, but accepting the evidence of his senses was a place to start.

To his own surprise, that decision alone was enough to sustain him. Nothing had really changed, not even himself, but the simple determination to act instead of continuing only to react seemed to alter his perceptions and lower the alien, unseen barriers between himself and such familiarity as there was for him in this world.

Even the music seemed subtly altered after that; gentler and at the same time more piercing, more powerful, more painful. He did not lose himself in it as he had so often in the past. It seemed almost as though he found himself in it. He found his relation to it; found the rhythm of it; found the resonance of the heartache and the joy of it; found the wellspring of irrational, unreasoning, irresistible hope within it. He led the band into the next number with a fierce new sense of determination, and planned his next move.

The first step would be to avoid the police. That would have been simpler if he had been sure he could count on the assistance of the other band members as he could have in the world he came from. In this world, he barely knew them, though they thought they knew him. He had only begun to make their acquaintance this afternoon, and the fragile ties they had formed would not withstand any stress this soon, certainly not anything as damning as the police, with a witness who had seen Jesse attacking Ruth.

Various escape plans involving the assistance, witting or unwitting, of his fans came to mind, but none were really practical. In the end it seemed that the most straight-forward plan was also the best: when the penultimate song ended, the lights would go out, leaving the entire arena in total darkness for ten seconds. That should take the police by surprise; it was unlikely that any of them had attended any previous concert of his. Jesse could simply slip offstage and run while the lights were out.

Having decided on a course of action, he set the problem aside and gave himself up again to his music. He had nearly let it drown with him in the miasma of self-pity and self-absorption that had washed over him when the police had come for him again. But his relation to his music was simple and innocent and, ultimately, unshakable. Music was the one thing that had never betrayed him, and he believed it never would as long as he was true to it.

Even in this world, where Jesse Farrell was apparently a very unpleasant person, his music had the power to tran-scend that reality, so that people endured him and even ad-mired him for the music he made.

It had fascinated him to discover the differences between his songs and those of the man whose place he had taken in this world. The Jesse here had written desolate, distressing songs. Their sound was dark and dreary and forbidding, weighted with a terrible bitterness Jesse had never known. He recognized it, he could identify with it, but he could never have written the songs that harbored it. It was an-other proof, if he needed it, that he really was in a different world.

Trying not to look obvious about it, he studied the loca-tions of crew, equipment, and the waiting police, working out his escape route. When the band finally segued into the penultimate number, he had memorized a path between amplifiers, instruments, and people that should be possible to negotiate in the dark and leave him plenty of conceal- ment if he was not yet outside when the lights came back up.

After a concert was not the ideal time to start running, from the police or from anyone else. He was exhausted, physically and emotionally. He had just spent more than three hours singing, leaping, clowning, and dancing, all in the heat of lights that kept center stage at over a hundred degrees Fahrenheit. After more than six months of perfor- mances with very little time off and what there was of it seldom spent resting, he was approaching the limits of en- durance.

But his voice was as powerful as ever. Concentrating on the lyrics of this, the last song he would sing tonight (or, he thought sourly, perhaps ever, if things went really wrong), he forgot the escape route, forgot the police. The world nar- rowed until only the music mattered.

Mirabelle's synthesizer sobbed behind him, a forlorn voice crying alone in the wilderness. He sang as though his heart were breaking, and when the band brought their in- struments crashing across the aching silence he left behind, he paused and looked bleakly out into the crowd, gathering himself for next verse. The colored gels that illuminated the audience were sweeping back and forth across the front rows and up into and out of the balconies. The effect diz- zied him.

The drums were like thunder, the synthesizer shook the air with deep, resonant organ tones, the guitars were en- gaged in a war of convoluted melodies, and Jesse pressed close to the microphone to pour his soul into the lyrics.

Lyle harmonized softly in the background, a serene echo to Jesse's raw passion. It was a song of hope in the face of despair, and Jesse sang it as though he could, if he put enough of himself into it, force it to be true.

As the final verse sighed to a close in a mutter of bass guitar and a windy whisper of chimes, Jesse braced himself for the chorus. A moment of silence: then all the instruments screamed simultaneously and Jesse, clinging to the microphone stand and bawling out the chorus at top volume, was barely audible over their cacophony. The instruments quieted, their individual voices resolving out of chaos to become a pounding backdrop for the final notes of the vocal.

Jesse bellowed the words and held onto the final syllables, drawing them out into a soaring moan till the words were forgotten, till the sound faded to a broken sob and the pain in his voice was unendurable. Then he drew a breath and it came out in a howling scream, a roar, an inarticulate lamentation, as the drums rumbled and crashed and subsided in a deafening clash of cymbals. The guitars squealed like wounded animals. The synthesizer created a whole orchestra of reeds and woodwinds and great, resounding bells.

Jesse's voice emerged over all of them, a desolate cry rising above the winds and strings and even above the clangorous bells in a flat-out wail that held all the innocent anger, frustration, pain, and glory of life; of love; of his personal, naive vision of rock and roll.

And then it was over. The lights cut out, plunging the arena into black silence. The crowd roared. The sudden dark was so blessedly cool that for one long second Jesse just stood in it, head hanging, heart pounding, listening to his own labored breathing, and waiting numbly for the furnace blast of returning lights that would signal the beginning of the last number.

Even when consciousness returned and he realized he should be moving, he wasted another precious second locating his guitar stand because he was unwilling to drop his guitar on the stage floor or leave it precariously balanced against an amplifier.

There were barely eight seconds of darkness remaining when he left the stage.

14

Jesse

Eight seconds were not enough, not in that impenetrable darkness. Even with the path mapped out in his mind, Jesse could not get all the way out of the arena in only eight seconds. He barely had time to make his way offstage without bumping into the equipment, a crewmember, or worse, a cop, before the lights came up again.

Despite his aching leg he moved swiftly, with a feral grace that took him unerringly between and around the obstacles he had marked in his mind, with the sleek silence of a great cat closing in for the kill. But he was the hunted, not the hunter, and the path he had taken was really the only obvious way he could have gone. When the eight seconds ended and the lights came up, he crouched where he was and waited for seemingly inevitable discovery.

The searing white spotlight stabbed down onto the empty stage floor where Jesse should have been, wavered a moment in startled search for him, and was still. The other lights, barely cooler through their red, blue, and yellow gels, bathed the stage in a haze of brilliant color. Jesse's guitar, the wood stained and glistening with sweat, rested center stage in its chrome stand beside the drums. Band members, road crew, audience, and police stared at it in stunned confusion while Jesse, in the cluttered backstage area, quietly found a man-tall packing crate to hide behind while he figured out how to get the rest of the way out of the building.

The police were the first to break the silence, with enraged shouts and conflicting orders, and to challenge the seemingly universal paralysis by dashing half-hysterically in every direction. One even rushed headlong out onto the stage. Perhaps he hoped to find Jesse coyly concealed behind an amplifier or under the synthesizer. Probably he simply moved without thinking.

Once onstage, he looked nearly as dismayed to be there as the audience was to see him there. He stared frantically out into the house and turned in a slow circle, studying everything, his broad face comical in its distress. Blinded by the light, he couldn't see Jesse even though he was directly in Jesse's line of sight.

Before the onstage cop could remove himself, the dour-faced lieutenant who had lurked in the wings joined him, scowling savagely, his handgun drawn and his eyes wild. Jesse stood helplessly in the shadows and watched while the lieutenant braced his feet apart, as against a strong wind, and stood blinking in the spotlight, one hand holding his gun upraised and the other lifted to push his fellow officer offstage. Bancroft Averill backed away from them both and bumped into Bob Lyle, who held his ground, staring.

"He can't have gone far." The lieutenant was standing next to the microphone. It caught his words and hurled them toward the darkened rafters, but he seemed unaware of it. "You: organize a search backstage. Send Sergeant Burtness out front. Call for backup. Cover the doors." He turned to face the audience, raking them with his gaze as if he could see each of them clearly through the lights. "Stay in your seats. Nobody leaves till Farrell is caught."

That was a mistake. The audience, which had fallen silent in anticipation when the lights came up, and remained silent in shock when Jesse's absence was revealed, had been waiting to see what the police would do. The lieutenant's remarks revealed him as the enemy. They responded slowly, with a mutter that grew to a roar and then a sibilant howl as more and more of them grasped the fact that these armed policemen were actively searching for Jesse not to protect but to threaten him.

The band members were still sitting or standing onstage in attitudes of bewilderment, watching the police and glancing at each other in increasing bemusement. They understood what it meant when the audience began to howl, but there was nothing they could do to prevent the chaos that followed.

Why the first individual from the audience jumped up onto the stage with the police, or how he got past the security guards who ordinarily prevented such an occurrence, was never quite clear to Jesse. What was clear was that from then on the situation was totally out of control. Before anybody could react to the first civilian onstage, there were twenty, and the lieutenant was surrounded. The auditorium echoed with shouts and screams, drowning whatever further utterances the lieutenant might have made. The rainbowed air was tainted with the sour stink of fear and anger. The lieutenant fired his gun once, into the air; the report was drowned in the hissing roar of the crowd.

This was exactly what Jesse had feared would happen if the audience were involved in his escape. The fans on the stage were not the only ones converging on the police throughout the auditorium, and there was no telling what might come of it, except that in all probability someone was going to get hurt. Within minutes this could become a full-scale riot. Once it had gone that far, not even Jesse would be able to stop it.

Perhaps it was too late already, but he knew he had to try. Sighing, he stepped out from behind his packing crate. If he moved quickly enough, back onto the stage and into police custody without a struggle, he might be able to calm the audience and talk them back into their seats. His whole attention as he moved was on the mob onstage and on what he was going to do about it. He didn't notice Zelig until the doctor caught his arm to tug him toward the door. Even then he didn't consciously recognize who was trying to stop him. He tried to shake the hand off his arm and said impatiently, "Let me go, I have to stop them."

"Here you are at last." Zelig might not have heard him. "Come along."

"I gotta get to them before it's too late. They'll hurt each other," said Jesse.

"Too late is already, is it not?" asked Zelig. "Come along, I am looking for you. If you will observe, our path to the door is clear at the moment." The imminent riot had drawn the police from their guard duty toward the stage. None of them noticed Jesse and Zelig in the shadows as they passed.

Onstage, the first blow was struck, and a woman screamed. "Christ, they'll kill each other," said Jesse. He was relieved to see the band members snatch up what equipment they could and head for the backstage dressing rooms in hope of avoiding the worst of the riot.

"A sadness, but we must go," said Zelig. "You are wishing to help Ruth, yes?" Zelig nodded firmly in response to his own question. "So. You must avoid the police. Come along." He tugged at Jesse's arm again.

The riot was spilling off the stage in every direction. There was no hope of stopping it peaceably now. "Okay," said Jesse. "*Damn* it. Okay." He did not ask why Zelig was helping him. At the moment, such details seemed irrelevant. He simply followed, at the best speed he could manage on his aching leg, which had begun to stiffen with inaction since he left the stage. Together they crashed through the back door and out into the cold night air.

Sudden, misty silence enveloped them the moment the door swung shut. Jesse's wet clothes clung to his body, icy in the wind. His first thought was for a shower and dry clothes in the van, and he headed that way automatically, but he had not gone far before he realized that was the first place the police would look for him. Zelig's thoughts must have paralleled his. They both stopped at the same moment and looked at each other in confusion. "Now what?" asked Jesse.

"We are needing a car," said Zelig.

Jesse stifled hysteria. "We're surrounded by cars. Which one you want?" The parking lot was crowded with the cars of concert-goers.

"They will be locked, will they not?"

"Maybe." Jesse limped, shivering, to the nearest auto and tried its door. It was locked. He moved on to another. "Try a few. If we can get in one, I can get it started." He tried another door.

"Yes?" Zelig looked around with renewed enthusiasm. "This is good. I am choosing one." He hesitated a moment, then walked confidently to a small sports car parked between two gas-guzzling giants, opened its door without difficulty, and turned back to Jesse. "This one pleases me. What are you thinking?"

Jesse accepted Zelig's success without comment. "I'm thinking that one will be fine." He shambled over to it and climbed into the driver's seat, bent to reach under the dash, and fumbled for the wires. "Get in."

"But if you cannot start it?"

At that moment the engine caught and Jesse stepped on the gas. "Get in," he repeated, gesturing. To complete the accommodating good manners of the car, there was a woman's hair clip lying on the dash with which he secured the wires while Zelig got in. "Where to? You got anyplace special in mind, or are we just running?"

"At the moment, I am thinking that anywhere might be preferable to here, is it not?" Zelig was looking nervously back toward the auditorium, where the riot had begun to spill out the doors and into the parking lot.

"You're right." Jesse turned on the lights, revved the engine, released the emergency brake, and let out the clutch. The little car leapt eagerly out of its parking space. "Which way's the freeway?"

"How would I know? I am never driving in this place."

"Great." He steered expertly around a cluster of wildly gesticulating civilians. "If we can't get out of this parking lot pretty damned quick, we'll be trapped between the cops in the auditorium and the reinforcements they must've called in by now."

"I'm sorry. Perhaps if we follow the signs?" Zelig gestured diffidently toward an enormous purple sign that said FREEWAY with a broad yellow arrow pointing off to their right.

"Good idea." Jesse whipped the car into the turn between rows of parked cars. "Glad you thought of that."

"It was nothing." Zelig was pleased with himself. "I am glad to be of assistance."

"Which reminds me." Jesse swung the car into a sharp left turn as indicated by the arrows, and was promptly faced with a decision as to whether he wanted the freeway going north or the one going south. He took the nearest one, headed north. "Why are you helping me?"

"Because I was seeing you attack Ruth, of course."

"What?" The little car was very responsive to its steering. In turning to stare at Zelig, Jesse oversteered and very nearly lost control. Hastily facing front again, he wrestled the car back toward the center of the entry ramp. Water-filled barricades rushed narrowly past the windows. Tires squealed on grooved concrete. The engine whined, the car shook, gears clashed. When he had things under control again, Jesse looked at Zelig and said with labored amiability, "Would you mind going into a little detail on that?"

"Well, of course I was knowing it could not really be you," said Zelig. "I was thinking you would understand that, yes? Because of course you are in love with her, so you would not be so rough with her, is it not? But it was you. I was seeing that quite clearly, you understand. And that is when I knew at last that the explanation for the remarkable change in you is so. You are from Somewhere Else, of course." The capital letters were obvious in the way he said it. "You are not the Jesse we knew. You are Another. This is true?"

"I think it is," said Jesse. "But how the hell did you guess?"

"A simple matter. One is eliminating the impossible. What is left, however improbable, is the answer."

"Sherlock Holmes," said Jesse.

"A great man," said Zelig. "Although, like our Jesse, an abuser of substances. Who is the Other? He is your archenemy, yes?"

Jesse stared. "You know the Other?"

"I saw him. I was telling you that. He attacked Ruth and

abducted her from the world."

"Oh."

"You and he have been at odds all your lives, the one fighting for good and the Other for evil, is it?"

"Not exactly."

Undeterred, Zelig continued imaginatively, "He is stealing Ruth as a way to do you harm. He could not get at you. But with Ruth in his clutches, he is knowing you will give yourself over to his evil intentions." He looked at Jesse in sudden consternation. "You will not, yes? Instead, you will find some way to retrieve her?"

"I hope so."

Zelig settled back in his seat, comforted. "It is well. You are wishing to know more about the Jesse you are replacing here, yes? A matter of curiosity, I should imagine."

"I'm curious," Jesse admitted. "You're quite sure there is—was—another? I mean . . ."

"You are doubting your senses, not? It is hardly surprising, in the circumstance. But it is counterproductive, you understand. Best you should look for other explanations and trust yourself."

"Ruth says I do drugs."

"Indeed not," said Zelig. "She says our Jesse is using drugs. As he very much is, you know. Where do you suppose he is now, by the way? Are you knowing?"

"I think he's maybe dead. I'm sorry."

Zelig thought about that. The little car roared through darkness, its lights twin cones of reality in a void. Purple signs with yellow lettering lurched into existence by the side of the road, whipped past, and were gone. Green reflectors glittered between the lanes like electronic snakes guiding their path.

Zelig sighed, looked out a side window at nothing, and

shrugged. "Sad, but not surprising. He was not a pleasant person, you understand. One was spending one's life trying to keep him alive, against his best efforts, and it was really only for the music. For Ruth, who does not like rock music—perhaps she was doing it for what could have been, yes? Always I was surprised she did not leave him, but then, one did not, you see."

Jesse hesitated. "Did she love him?" He leaned into a curve and the little car skated through it with a muted roar.

"Oh, quite not," said Zelig, surprised. "Except perhaps as one loves an unruly and self-destructive child, yes? It is what he was."

"Why? What made him be like that?" Jesse's window was open a crack: salt-laden mist whipped through and tangled his hair.

"Insecurity only," said Zelig. "The which he was turning into self-pity."

"But he had it all," said Jesse. Shivering, he rolled up the window. "I mean, didn't he?" Beginning to relax at last, he let the car slow to the posted speed limit.

"He had everything," said Zelig, "except the things he really wanted."

"That's nothing to kill yourself over. It's not as if the things he couldn't have were things he couldn't live without."

"You are speaking as one who knows."

"Oh." Jesse made a wry face. "Yeah. Guess I figured I did. So what was it he wanted that he couldn't have?"

"A sound leg, a different career, and the woman he loved."

"In that order?"

"Very probably."

The car drifted up a slope and for just a moment the

lights stabbed out into space. Then they crested the hill and the lights washed down onto the stained concrete again with its twin green snakes for guidance. "He wanted to be a dancer?"

"Just so."

Jesse nodded. "Me, too. Before the accident smashed my leg." He blinked, scowling, at the amber tail lights of a car far ahead of them, the only sign of life on the deserted freeway. "I thought I wanted to die, too, when I found out it wouldn't ever heal right. I thought there wasn't anything else in the world I could care as much about or be as good at as dancing."

"You are speaking as though you had been mistaken."

He glanced at the doctor. His eyes were shadowed, unreadable. "I'd always loved rock music." He said it with palpable weariness, as one stating the obvious to an intentionally uncomprehending child. "It was what gave me the courage to try to be a dancer in the first place, when everybody laughed at me 'cause ballet wasn't macho. We were so poor sometimes it had to be a choice between food and ballet lessons. I chose the lessons." He hesitated, searching for words.

"Rock was like, I don't know, it was nothing exactly that I can figure out, there was just a message in it. Something that said a poor kid from the wrong side of town could make it if he tried, if he worked hard enough." He thought about it. "Maybe it was the lyrics. There was this song . . ." His voice trailed away. "Well, anyhow. Whatever. 'Course I know now that not everybody makes it. You can try all your life and still end up trapped. But I didn't know that then."

Zelig nodded. "So you tried. Just as our Jesse did."

"I was good, too. I was a good dancer." He knew he sounded defensive.

"I know," said Zelig. "You would be good at what you are choosing to do."

"Wasn't your Jesse good?"

"As a dancer? Oh, he was most quite good, I assure you. Most. It was expected that he would be the best. He was quite young still, you understand, when the accident—" He paused, glanced at Jesse, and began again. "And then the accident, and the bills for the medical services that kept him alive but could not restore his leg. And the father's illness, so that when Jesse was as much healed as he could be, he must make the money to pay the bills and to support his mother and sister." He was silent for a moment. "The ballet was gone, of course. I sometimes think he went into rock and roll out of a kind of spite, because it had told him he could have what he wanted if he worked hard enough, and that became a lie, and he wished to cause it to give him what it could. You understand?"

"Oh, yeah. You're right. It was a kind of spite." He had all but forgotten they were speaking of a different Jesse. "All the promises broken. All of them. All the work, and the sacrifices . . . and then the dream didn't come true after all. Rock and roll *owed* me." He smiled distantly. "And then I found out I was better at making music than I ever was at dancing."

"And so you could love it?"

"I couldn't have hated it so much in the first place if I hadn't loved it too. Rock and roll isn't like other kinds of music. There's no other kind of music that can save your life."

"There are those who might differ, but go on."

Jesse glanced at him. "Well, it saved my life." He looked back at the road. " 'Course I loved it. And when I found out I was good at it—" He shrugged, and said almost sheepishly, "I had to love it then, didn't I?" He didn't look at Zelig again. His face gleamed pale and still in the reflected light from the dash.

Zelig tilted his head, watching Jesse. "Because it gave you so much, or because one must love a thing to do it sincerely?" he asked curiously.

"Both, maybe. I dunno." He watched without comprehension as the headlights impaled another purple road sign in their brief glare, and passed on. "I read somewhere once that all art that has any vitality must have its basis in love," he said softly. "I think that's right." He glanced at Zelig. "Didn't your Jesse feel the same?"

"Quite not," said Zelig. "Sometimes I am thinking he hated all music as much as he hated himself. Sometimes I am thinking he hated the whole universe." He shifted in his seat and sighed. "And then I am thinking that he hated nothing at all except himself. He could not believe in himself. He was having only contempt for his fans, for example, because they were believing in him. He was thinking that they should be able to see through him, to see what he really was. Inept. Incompetent. Out of place." He shook his head. "He would have destroyed everything, if he could. Certainly he destroyed himself."

"Because he couldn't dance."

It wasn't quite a question, but Zelig answered it anyway. "Yes."

"We don't any of us get everything we want."

"Perhaps not. But Jesse was never seeing past his disappointment. And for him there was always the terrible fear: what if his fans were waking up one day to realize that this failed dancer was not a good musician? Always he was expecting it to be so. It was very sad."

15

Jud

Contrary to Suli Grail's supposition, her superior, Jud, the most senior world-walker in the worlds, did have a home. World-walkers Suli's age and at her level of experience were discouraged from visiting or even remembering their homes. Indeed, world-walkers of much greater age and experience were still discouraged from it, only not as forcefully.

The theory was that this enforced and artificial homelessness would foster objectivity. The fact was that it fostered a tendency, particularly among the older worldwalkers, to indulge in rebellious habits, such as visiting their homes or using, among themselves, their individual names again.

Still, it had been a serious slip for Jud to refer to Suli Grail by name, especially to someone as powerful and as rigidly conservative as the Lord High Monitor. Jud thought of that as he stepped from his bright little office at Central into the crowded darkness of the main hall of his ancestral residence in his home world. The Lord High Monitor had been crafty enough to do no more at the time than to demand that Jud correct himself, but he would remember the incident and use it if he could. He had doubtless been recording the conversation. As far as Jud knew, the Lord High Monitor had done nothing unrecorded in the last twenty years or more.

"Juddy!" Jud's father's voice—they were a very long-lived family—broke into his reverie before his eyes had fully adjusted to the dim light. "I thought you'd be home tonight. I fixed *peraq* for your dinner."

It was Jud's favorite dish. He smiled in the direction of his father's voice, yellowed eyes blinking owlishly in the dark. "Thank you, Papa," he said with real pleasure. "Is Mama home?"

"Always it's business first with you," his father grumbled, but Jud's eyes had adjusted enough now to note the twinkle of amusement in the older man's eyes. "She's in her study, waiting for you."

She was as massive as her son was frail, a mountain of wrinkles clothed in gold-threaded brocade and surmounted by a face whose incongruously pixyish smile diminished her eyes to half-moon sparkles buried in wattles of fat. "Juddy," she said, her voice as absurdly youthful as her smile. "I'm so glad you could make it home! Papa thought you would. He's made *peraq* for your dinner."

"So he said." Jud knelt stiffly before her and took her hands in his, ancient papery wrinkles holding more ancient papery wrinkles. "It's good to see you, Mama."

"Which means you need to talk," she said, still smiling. "Get up, Juddy. You're too old to kneel to me."

"Never," he said, "because that would mean you were too old to be knelt to."

"Well, I am," she said. "Get up."

He hesitated, crouched before her like a frail bundle of brittle bones, his expression sheepish. "I'm not sure I can," he admitted.

"Try," she said, "or I'll call the houseboy to haul you up, and you know how he complains of his back."

146

"Don't do that. We'd neither of us ever hear the end of it." He climbed, creaking, to his feet. "I'm feeling old, I guess. Mama, I'm worried."

"I know you are, love," she said. "Here, this chair is comfortable. Even for a geriatric case like you." Her pale eyes sparkled with amusement.

He eased himself into the chair with the air of one entering frigid water. "The Lord High Monitor was in my office today."

"Relax. The chair won't eat you. How is the Lord High Monitor, these days?"

"Terminally self-involved," said Jud. "He's terrified Suli won't kill the Other."

"And you're terrified she will."

"I suppose I am, though I told her to do it."

"Because you told her to do it, you mean," said his mother. "What did Ariel Greef have to say about that, by the way?"

"What could she say? I did what had to be done."

"Ariel didn't always see things in such simple terms."

"I wish you wouldn't talk about her in the past tense."

"Why not? She's dead, isn't she?"

He nodded, watery eyes blinking. "Certainly. For these three hundred years and more. But I still have to deal with her, and it makes me uncomfortable to think I'm dealing with a dead woman."

"You're not," said his mother, smiling beatifically. "She was alive when she visited you. And she was alive when she will visit you."

He scowled at her. "For a woman who's never walked worlds, much less time, you take to the paradoxes too comfortably."

She laughed at him, but kindly. "Would you rather I

147

didn't? Then you'd have no one with whom to discuss the ramifications of this particular paradox."

"It's not the ramifications of the paradox of Ariel's walk through time that bother me," he said slowly. "It's the ramifications of her reasons."

She tilted her ancient head to look at him, wattles of flesh wrinkling in new ways to accommodate the movement. "But I thought you agreed with her."

"That we're destroying the worlds with our overzealous rules? Yes, certainly. She must be right about that," he said, sounding not at all certain. "Though how she saw it in her time I don't know."

"I don't suppose she did," said his mother, teasing him. "She must only have postulated in her time, and had to Walk forward to find out. And then to mend the problem, when she saw she was right." But he didn't smile to hear her telling him what he already knew. He was feeling too uneasy to smile. "She was right, wasn't she?" she asked.

At that, Jud's gaze came up from studying the pattern in the carpet on the floor, to stare at her with rheumy intensity. "Mama," he said, "it was you who pointed out the evidence to me, in our own world."

"That the wrrsh are nearly all gone, faded in the mist of boundaries that shouldn't be, and gates that should not have been closed? Yes, and you told me about the ones in Ariel's world who've gone. What were they called? Elves? Faeries? Or was that another world? But son, what if that's as it should be? What if that's as the gods meant it to be?"

He shook his head certainly. "I can't believe that," he said. "Since time began the wrrsh shared this world with us at certain phases of the moon or conjunctions of the planets—" He sighed heavily, and waved a papery hand in the air impatiently, dismissing doubts. "No, Mama, it can't

148

be right. The worlds were never as discrete, the boundaries as rigid, as we have tried to keep them since the Ages of Chaos."

"I suppose you're right," she said. "It can't be right to make the worlds more separate than the gods made them. And yet . . ."

"There's no 'and yet,' Mama," he said, not unsympathetically. "By maintaining such rigid purity of worlds, Central destroys essential interactions and creates a situation that will ultimately be as harmful as indiscriminate walking was."

"You say that," said his mother, "but how can you know? How can you be so certain?"

He waved a frail arm in the air as though conducting a symphony. "By looking around us, by studying the legends and comparing them with the present, by thinking," he said, his voice impassioned. "Mama, you know the history of the worlds as well as I do, even though you've seen only ours in person. I've seen many of them, and I am sorry to tell you that in every one of them, I could see evidence of old conjunctions fading, of natural gates closing, of relationships dying. By maintaining the integrity of worlds we kill connections that were meant, that existed long before the Ages of Chaos."

A satisfied smile tugged at her lips, but she said dubiously, "Very well. Suppose you're right about that. And suppose Ariel's right in her idea that this Other is a Natural, an instinctive gate-crasher who, if he's chased long and hard enough, will learn to play the gates the way his doppelgangers play their musical instruments. What you may have forgotten is that you don't control him. You can't. That's the nature of a Natural, as I understand it.

"So what have you gained? A nasty little malcontent

who's spent his whole life blaming his failures on others, and whose primary goal in life is power, learns to play the gates and so acquires more power than any individual has ever held before. What makes anyone think he'll suddenly become an altruist at that point, and help you save the universe? It would be more in character for him to destroy it, if he can."

"Yes, I suppose it would," said Jud, studying her. "You've been playing devil's advocate, haven't you? You're not really uncertain about any of this."

She smiled merrily, her eyes bright half-moons in the fat of her face. "It always works to pull you out of your megrims," she said.

"Was I in megrims?"

"You were threatening them."

"You're not really worried about our megalomaniacal Other?" He was smiling too, but it was a frayed and uncertain thing.

"Why, no," she said, surprised. "I'd assumed, I suppose, that Ariel had foreseen the problem."

"And done something about it? How can she? What could she do, to turn an overgrown infant into a human being?"

"I don't know. But I'm not Ariel Greef." She studied him. "What is it, son? You've come this far on whatever understanding of her plan you have, or on faith in her, or belief. Last time you were home, you were uncomfortable about sending Suli Grail after the Other, but you certainly believed it was the only thing to do. Now you're questioning it. Why?"

His shoulders twitched. "I didn't really understand what the Other was, then."

"And you do, now?"

"I know now that he's more—and less—than I guessed. I knew Ariel's plan, and I guess I envisioned someone worthy of it. He's not. He's a spoiled brat."

"Oh, come! You said yourself he's in pain."

"I said that?"

She nodded, jowls wobbling. "When you first told me of him. You told me what Ariel had told you, and that included his history. That vicious father, and the terrible injury that caused the loss of his career dreams—"

He waved a frail hand impatiently. "All the Jesses in that sector suffered those things."

"And some of them died of it. Should the Other be so much stronger just because you want him to be?"

"Most of them are stronger than he."

"No. Most of them are more to your liking."

He shifted uneasily. "Perhaps. The point is, he's a blamer. He's spent his life blaming one thing and another, never accepting responsibility. Now Ariel is giving him responsibility for the universe."

"And you're afraid he won't cope?"

"I don't see how he can." He scowled, thinking of it. "Every world he's invaded, he's tried some scheme to acquire power, and every one has worked—to a point. He can manipulate, control, confuse—I don't know how he does what he does, but he's come close to ruling a world or two, and failed only because of miscalculations he can remedy on the next effort if he learns from his mistakes. And he does. Whatever his other flaws, he's no fool. He's been in better control, had greater power, in each successive world. And that's what he wants: control and power."

"Of course. In his place, wouldn't you want power? It's the only safety he knows."

"But the danger lies in the very fact that he's not a fool.

He does learn. Which means that eventually he's going to see through his own defenses. He's going to see that every world he's tried, including the one he's in now, is essentially like the one he left behind. He's going to realize, sooner or later, that the difference between his failure to make a life and the other Jesses' successes is that they tried, while he was busy blaming. He's going to have to see they didn't get special dispensation, they didn't get favors, they had as hard a life as his and they made their lives better. Which means he could have made his life better, in his home world. And that's something he really cannot bear to know."

"You're afraid of what will happen when he runs out of things to blame."

He smiled ruefully. "And if I'd known how to say it that briefly, I would have."

She shrugged massively. "I really wouldn't worry about it, Juddy. Ariel Greef will have seen the problem. She'll know what to do when the time comes. Your job is to keep the Lord High Monitor from interfering."

"Doesn't it worry you, even a little, that I'm putting the fate of the universe in the hands of a dead woman and a probable sociopath?"

"No," she said. "Should it?"

He smiled again, with real humor this time. "Yes."

16

Suli

World-Walker Suli Grail stepped through the gate into World V4G 7N7/4 with the expectation that simply finding the Other might be the most time-consuming part of her job. It was not. Having some acquaintance with newspapers from other worlds, she used coins the supply officer had provided her to purchase the first one she saw, intending primarily to familiarize herself with V4G 7N7/4, and found an article about the Other on page three, complete with photos.

He had brought Ruth Sutton from slash three to slash four. The monitors at Central had informed the world-walker of that, but she had not really believed it till she saw the headlines announcing that Ruth had been found alive in this world. Quite aside from anything else the Other might do in either world, Ruth's removal from one to another might alter the social history of both past mending. That the Other would take that chance with the integrity of worlds stunned her. She had known he wanted to keep Jesse's place in this world, but she had not guessed he would risk the universe to do it.

According to the experts, all the worlds began as one primordial world at the dawn of time. When life evolved, that world split into two: one where life evolved, and one where it did not. Thereafter, a new world split from the old when-

153

ever a pivotal event occurred on any world, until they were innumerable, all sharing the same theoretical "space" without any awareness of or contact with each other.

That was according to the plan of Nature or the gods. There was no problem as long as new worlds were created only from within, but when the use of gatestones became widespread, it was inevitable that visitors from one world would alter another sufficiently to create a new one, and that was not according to the plan of Nature or the gods.

No one had foreseen the chaos that followed: the boundaries between worlds became so weakened that breaks in them occurred without warning, stranding involuntary travelers in strange worlds or dumping them into Limbo when they met their doppelgangers.

Nor were humans the only beings so transported. Adjacent worlds had similar inhabitants and even doppelgangers, so the most bizarre results of interchanges between them were stories of disappearing persons. But where the worlds had diverged very long ago or very far apart, the inhabitants were very dissimilar. Between such worlds, involuntary interchanges produced much more bizarre events. In more than one world, visitors from another still lived on in legend, centuries after the Ages of Chaos, as myth or monster, magic or murderous or both.

The creation of Central with its corps of trained world-walkers had signaled the beginning of the end of the Ages of Chaos, but it had taken them generations to restore peace, order, and the integrity of the worlds. The Other was aware of that. She had told him, the night he came home with the bracelet she now wore on her arm. His world was rife with terrifying myths and legends of the things that had come through the boundaries during the Ages of Chaos, and she had told him where they came from. That he would risk

that again just to stay in the world of his choice was appalling. The world-walker had thought she knew him, but she had not known him capable of this.

The newspaper article left little room for doubt. "Rock star Jesse Farrell, arrested last night for the grisly murder of a woman member of his road crew, was released today when bewildered officials became aware that the 'victim' was alive and well and unaware of her alleged murder. A source in the police department said today there is still some confusion about the case, which sounds like something straight out of a TV movie, complete with a disappearing body and unassailable evidence of a crime that was never committed. However, Jesse's fans will be relieved to know that Jesse has been cleared of all charges and will be performing his scheduled concert at the Cow Palace tonight."

But it wasn't Jesse. It was the Other. He must have walked directly from his cell into slash three to pull the Ruth from that world into slash four, got rid of the body of the murdered Ruth, and returned to the same time as well as the same place from which he had started, inside a jail cell. He was a highly skilled walker by now if he could do all that without revealing himself by the smallest interval of apparent absence, which he seemed to have done.

The article went on at some length about the various confusing aspects of the murder case, but the world-walker had what she wanted: the Other's location. She was not much interested in the locals' reaction to the Other's machinations beyond noting with relief that they seemed, so far anyway, to be treating the entire affair with more amusement than distress. In this case, a sense of humor could literally save worlds. As long as they were laughing at it, they were unlikely to become sufficiently alarmed to turn this

into a pivotal and therefore disruptive event.

The newspaper pictured the Cow Palace where the Other was to perform his Jesse Farrell concert tonight. That made things simple for the world-walker. There were several ways to open a gate to the location of one's choice, but the easiest was by forming a mental picture of the place and adjusting the gatestone to scan and locate it. The world-walker did that and stepped through the resultant gate onto the mist-dampened surface of the Cow Palace parking lot.

Once there, she was near enough the Other to set her stone to find him. She had the power to bounce the two of them into Limbo, and used it. That was the first step on the way back to Central, but this was no ordinary renegade walker with an easily overpowered illicit stone. He would not stay where she put him. The dust of Limbo had barely settled around them when he was gone again, with a quick wry grin and an oddly defenseless shrug of his shoulders as if to say, "What else can I do?"

"Give it up." But he was no longer there to hear her. "Oh, Jesse," she said, because once that had been his name, too; then she remembered the monitors were listening. She squared her shoulders, set her stone, and followed him.

At first she thought the world into which she stepped after him was untenanted. Then she realized there was no weather to account for the mournful howl that filled her ears as though cold winds were whistling through the granite boulders around her. One of the boulders moved, and she realized they were not boulders at all. Dim light made it hard to pick out details, but all the boulders were moving now. They were the arms and legs of trolls disturbed in their nap by the arrival of aliens from another world.

Fortunately trolls moved slowly, and the Other had not

stayed long in their world. She set her stone and stepped after him just as a great sandstone hand reached awkwardly to touch her. That curious gesture would have crushed her. Most trolls were amiable, but they could not comprehend the fragility of soft creatures.

She had no time to dwell on their character. The next world was a human one, and she had stepped into the middle of a war. The earth trembled. The sky was lighted by unearthly fires. The air was sulfurous and foul. Automatic weapons chattered busily, death's messengers pleased with their work. Someone not far away began to scream in a thin, high, mindless wail like an injured animal until the world-walker found the next gate and stepped through. The sound was mercifully cut off, left in the wilderness of death behind her, but its memory tore at her heart.

She screamed the Other's name into a silent and sullen darkness. He did not respond. She never knew what world that was, or who dwelt there; she saw only darkness, heard only silence, and stepped out of it into a garden world strewn with vividly colored flowers, sweet and aromatic in the heat of a homey yellow morning sun.

The Other was gone from that world, too, before she arrived. She could follow him through a hundred worlds and he could keep always one world ahead of her, out of reach, till she lost him or tired of the chase. It was an exercise in futility; he was such a natural at gate-crashing that he could almost certainly return eventually to V4G 7N7/4 at exactly the time he had left it, no matter how long or how far she chased him, so she was not even protecting that world from him by keeping him occupied.

She sat abruptly on a tussock of mossy green in the petal-strewn shade of a willow-like tree that trailed its swaying branches almost to the ground, creating an ever-changing filigree of sun and shadow. Until now, she had been proceeding as if this were an ordinary case, impersonal and unremarkable in any way. But as she sat in the shifting sunlight, the image of the Other's wry little smile floated like an amiable ghost at the back of her mind. She could not forget that, or the blue of his eyes, or the gentleness of his hands.

He was such an odd mixture of child and man, devil and angel, hero and villain. She had loved him, she had shared dreams with him, and together they had built a home happier than either of them had known before. She had never known him. There had always been that small reserve between them. That invisible wall of his devising, which had made it possible for him to walk away; and impossible for her to see that he could, that he would, that apparently he must.

Now she remembered their time together in a golden haze of fantasy, like still photos out of someone else's life. Moments preserved in amber; the jeweled shards of an abandoned happiness. She shivered, though the temperature in this blossom-strewn world was warm. She closed her eyes against the riotous colors cascading around her. They were too joyous to endure. She hugged herself, as against a bitter wind, and heard herself whisper his name in the silence. No one answered. No one heard. When she opened her eyes, the world was still there. The flowers still nodded in the balmy breezes. Sunlight still filigreed the emerald moss at her feet. The Other would still have to be stopped from damaging worlds where he did not belong.

Unconsciously squaring her shoulders and setting her jaw, she set her stone to take her back to slash four. Now that she had been in such proximity to him with her stone set to follow, it could have taken her directly to the Other's side wherever he was. But he was too quick for her. He would run again when he saw her, and after a gate or two she would be as far behind him as she was now. It was a game to him, and he had made the rules when he fled Limbo without a word: no surrender, no discussion, no compromise. She would have to catch him or kill him.

He probably believed she could not catch him and would not kill him. If she walked to his side, prepared to kill the instant she saw him, she might succeed. But she might not, and then he would be warned. Better to save that method for if all else failed. He wasn't going to destroy the worlds in the next few hours. She had plenty of time to think of a better plan. When she reached slash four, she added a personal stereo and several Jesse Farrell tapes to her luggage and withdrew to a hotel room to consider her options.

17

Zelig

Zelig had fallen silent and Jesse had been driving aimlessly, with no goal other than to put distance between them and the concert hall. Now Zelig saw a rest area ahead, on the crest of a hill, and suggested they stop. Jesse signaled to take the exit. They were far enough from the concert hall now to be safe from the police for a while. There was no point in driving farther till they had some idea where they were going.

The view from the crest of the hill held both of them silent for several moments. They could see for miles. The San Francisco Bay was visible on one side, while sea-fog barely concealed the black expanse of the ocean on the other. The air over the bay was clear, and sparkled with the lights of distant cities and swooping bridges that arced up over the flat black mirror of the water in lacy splendor. The hills on their other side, toward the ocean, wore spilled jewel-boxes of light at their bases and white cotton crests of fog that cascaded up over ridges and down into valleys like misty waterfalls. San Francisco itself, with its bright tall buildings haloed in mist, was still hidden behind another line of hills to the north.

With a seemingly careless flick of his wrist, Jesse had steered the little car into a narrow parking space between two oversized campers, with its nose pointed toward the freeway on-ramp for quick escape if they needed it. When they had stared in awe at the view for a time, he said, without taking his eyes off it, "What'd you mean, when you said I'm from someplace else?"

"It is obvious, yes?" Zelig was concerned for this Jesse, who was so alone in a world not quite his own. "One Jesse is here, killing himself slowly. One Jesse is taking his place, who does not kill himself. Another Jesse is taking Ruth. Three Jesses cannot all come from this place. So. You come from another place. It is where, please?"

"I dunno. It's just like here, only—different. I thought I wouldn't be able to convince nobody. I mean, I'm not half convinced, myself. People'd be bound to think I was crazy. I did. How come you believe so easy?"

"I am a doctor." It surprised him that Jesse did not see that.

"So? I never heard doctors were real gullible."

"Ah, but I am knowing that Jesse is dying. He should have been hospitalized, but he would not go." He shook his head, thinking of that other, pitiable Jesse. "So odd, the strengths and weaknesses, yes?" When Jesse didn't respond, he went on, "To someone else it is perhaps simply a matter that Jesse looked unhealthy one moment and healthy the next. To me it is much more, much deeper than appearance.

"Also there is that the two of you have different gestures, expressions, ways of thinking and speaking. It is as if you were an actor without enough research or practice, trying to play the part of the Jesse I am knowing. Close, you understand, but not the same. Already I am wondering, and then I see a third Jesse who is like and yet not like either of you, and my guess is confirmed. Perhaps there are a great many Jesses somewhere, yes?"

"I have an idea there are a lot of worlds. With duplicate everybody in all of them. The one I'm from, I didn't know you, but that doesn't mean you weren't there. The band was there, and Ruth." Pain shadowed his eyes. "She was killed there." He fumbled with the front of his tee shirt, pulling it away from his body. Zelig remembered suddenly that it must still be wet and uncomfortable. "Wish I could've got a shower," Jesse said with childlike, uncomplicated regret. "And clean clothes. These smell. And they're too obvious. If we have to leave the car, I'll be spotted in a minute."

Zelig swiveled awkwardly in his seat to reach into the back for the cloth bag that was one reason he had selected this car. "I saw something back here. Perhaps it is useful." He dragged the bag off the back seat, between the front seats, and onto his lap. "Let us see, yes?" Unzipping it, he reached in and pulled out an oversized man's sweatshirt. "Ah. Perhaps this will please you."

Jesse accepted it gratefully, peeled off his shirt, and pulled the sweatshirt over his head. "That's great! Now all I need is a pair of dry blue jeans that aren't covered with studs and rhinestones." He grinned. "Got a pair of them in there?"

"I am looking. Tell me about the Ruth in your world. What of this murder?"

Jesse stared at the distant city lights. "The cops thought I did it." In a dull, lifeless voice, he told Zelig of Ruth's murder and the evidence against him. "So the cops were waiting in the wings for me last night, just like they were tonight. Only something happened last night. I had this kind of weird feeling while I was singing, and I closed my eyes, and when I opened them I was in a whole 'nother place. Like a desert, hot and red and empty. And I heard voices, but I didn't know what they were talking about and I couldn't see who was talking. And then before I could hardly even think about it, I was back onstage."

This was interesting. "But in our world, not yours," said Zelig. In his fascination with Jesse's story he had abandoned his search for blue jeans.

"Yeah, only I didn't know that. I just thought—I guess I thought I was crazy. I'd already been wondering about it, because they said I'd killed Ruth, and I couldn't remember what really happened. I was with Banny Averill that night, the night she died. And he said—" He was silent for a moment. "Anyhow, when I come offstage, there she was, when I'd seen the photographs and the blood and all. So I figured I'd flipped. Hoped I had, if it meant she wasn't dead after all."

Zelig frowned, thinking. "You said you had met this Other. When was that, please?"

"Oh, that was later. Last night. While I was sleeping. I thought it was just a dream, but hey, I got the bruises to show for it." His mouth twisted in a wry little grin. "I fought him. Don't know what I thought that would prove. But he threatened Ruth, and I guess I wasn't thinking real clearly."

Zelig stared. "He threatened Ruth how, exactly?"

Jesse shrugged. "I dunno exactly. He was talking about different worlds and stuff, and acting weird. Like I was hardly worth his notice. 'Cept he kept doing everything I did. Every move I made, he'd copy."

Zelig nodded, pleased to be able to explain. "Doubtless he is taking your place in your world, and has become aware of the need to imitate your mannerisms in order to provide a convincing performance."

"Damn, I bet you're right." Jesse looked thoughtful.

"Some of the stuff he said, that's what I thought he was gonna do to Ruth. Take her to some other world. My world. 'Cause the Ruth there's dead, and if he can get a live Ruth there, the cops can't bust him for killing her."

"And might she be in danger from the one who killed your Ruth?"

"Not if they're right and I killed her."

"Do you believe that?"

"I don't want to." Jesse's tone was dubious.

"Then don't," Zelig said simply. "Tell me again about the night she was killed. What was the evidence against you, please?"

"The killer used a knife of mine. I've never used it, dunno why I kept it. Somebody gave it to me. I have no use for it. But for some damn fool reason I kept it." He had opened his eyes again to stare sightlessly at the view before them. "And they found stuff of mine where she was killed. A button off my shirt, stuff like that. And there was blood on my clothes.

"And even though I remember starting out the evening with Banny, I don't remember the rest of the night. We were in his room having coffee, and I know we were s'posed to be talking business, but he says I wouldn't talk about anything but how mad I was at Ruth. He says I left his room early enough to kill her when they said she was killed. And I don't know. I don't remember. Dunno what happened at all. Woke up the next morning with the damnedest headache and sick as a dog, and I couldn't remember anything after I went into his room the night before." He rubbed his forehead hard with the back of one hand, as though the headache had recurred.

"You know," Zelig said thoughtfully, "I have never trusted Bancroft Averill."

"You think he made it up?" Jesse shook his head slowly. "But that doesn't explain why I don't remember. If I didn't kill her, I should remember what I did do."

"Not if you were drugged." Zelig looked at him. "He could have put something in your coffee, yes?"

"I s'pose." The distant lights twinkled under the edge of the encroaching fog and were extinguished, row by row. "But you're saying—" He frowned. "You mean Banny killed her? But why? Why would he?"

Zelig shrugged ineffably. "Why would you?" He paused, giving Jesse time to absorb the concept. "If you did kill her, would you not have had some reason?"

Jesse leaned his head back against the head rest. "Banny said I was mad at her." His voice was not quite steady. "He said I could have any woman I wanted except her, and she turned me down, so I killed her." He closed his eyes, opened them, and lifted his head again to stare wearily at the steering wheel.

"Is this true?" Zelig was sure none of it was, but he thought Jesse ought to say so, for his own good. He was worrying himself into fits over the wrong pieces of the puzzle. If he heard his own voice telling the truth, he might recognize it and be reassured.

"Which part? I didn't kill her." He frowned. "She never turned me down, either." He was silent for a long moment before he added, " 'Course I never asked her for anything. Never knew I wanted her till too late. Or—I guess I didn't want her. That her. I liked her okay, and I was sorry as hell when she died, but like a friend, you know? Not like the—" He stumbled over the words; the language had no adequate terminology for this. "The Ruth here. The one you know." He shivered.

"You are cold, yes? It is cold here."

"It's cold." Jesse hugged himself miserably. "Why would Banny kill her?"

Zelig delved into the cloth bag again, remembering his interrupted search for dry blue jeans. "Quite possibly for the very reason he ascribed to you. Because he wanted her, and he could not have her. It is done, you know. Dog in the manger, yes?" He brought out a pair of tennis shoes, tossed them in the back seat, and reached into the bag again.

"But, jeez, to kill her?" Jesse sounded bewildered. The concept was simple enough in Zelig's view, but he was beginning to realize that this Jesse, for all his apparently worldly experience and way of life, had really very little knowledge of the darker side of human nature. He could understand, empathize, and forgive where ordinary men could only hate, but he could not really imagine the thought processes that could lead to such a murder.

"He was having frustration? Wounded pride?" Zelig pulled out another oversized man's shirt, this one of warm flannel, wordlessly handed it to Jesse, then dug in the bag again.

Jesse accepted the shirt without comprehension. "That's crazy."

"Murder is crazy, yes?"

"Sure, but—"

"Further, my friend, Banny is jealous of you. Or at any rate, the Bancroft Averill here is jealous of you. Of the attention Ruth devotes to you, is it not? Put on the shirt. It may warm you."

Jesse looked stupidly at the shirt in his hands. "He's my friend."

Zelig rooted in the bag and emerged with a pair of colorful surfing shorts, which he pushed back down inside with a shake of his head. "Banny was with me when we saw the

Other abducting Ruth." He pulled out a pair of athletic socks, dropped them on the floor, and pulled out a dull olive tee shirt with one sleeve torn off. "We were the only witnesses." He dropped the tee shirt and rooted deeper, found a soiled towel, and tossed it over the back of the seat. "There are no blue jeans here. Perhaps no one will notice those you have on."

He looked at Jesse. "I did not inform the police that I saw you, because I knew it was not you. Also, I told Banny that it was not you, and of course he must have been knowing it was true, since he did know you were onstage at the time. He is the only one who comes on late, after the opening number, yes?"

"You're saying he told the police anyway, just to get me in trouble." Jesse struggled into the flannel shirt and buttoned it over the sweatshirt. "Okay, maybe this Banny. But the one where I'm from, he's my friend. He wouldn't do that." He bent awkwardly, struggling with small buttons between cold-numbed fingers, trying to fasten his cuffs. " 'Sides, if he saw me treating Ruth rough and he couldn't stop me any other way, it'd be right to tell the cops. He'd want to protect her."

"I told him the Other was not you," Zelig repeated patiently. "I reminded him you were onstage."

Jesse's mouth twisted. "In that case, Banny prob'ly figured you were crazy. Which, hell, maybe you are. You know what we're talking about here, just as if it were the most natural thing in the world? We're talking science fiction. People's doubles walking around doing things in alternate worlds. Anybody heard us, they'd be crazy not to think we were crazy." He shook his head. "Maybe we are."

"I, personally, have seen three different Jesses," said Zelig. "If it is crazy to believe they came from different worlds, it would be more crazy to think they did not. Unless you are one of identical triplets?"

"Not that I know of. But prove you saw three of us."

"I cannot, of course." Zelig was untroubled by that. "Do you doubt that I did?"

Jesse rubbed his eyes with the backs of his hands, an unselfconscious gesture, like a weary child. "I want to." He dropped his hands to look at Zelig. His eyes looked bruised in the darkness. "I really want to."

"Do you?" Zelig shook his head. "You would wish yourself insane?"

"It's that or the world's insane, and I don't like it either way." Jesse let his head fall back against the headrest again, his expression troubled. "Don't like any of this."

Zelig nodded. "It is natural to feel uncertainty when one's concept of reality is threatened," he said seriously. "I myself personally feel most dreadfully discomfited by all this, is it not?" He gave up on the bag of clothing and tossed it over his shoulder into the back seat. "Yet I cannot convince myself that it would be more the wise to dismiss the evidence of my senses simply because I see what I expect not to see."

They were silent a moment, watching the cascading fog on the far hills swallow whole housing subdivisions. "So if this is real," said Jesse, "what made me fall through whatever keeps the worlds apart? Why am I here?"

"Did the Other say nothing of that when you spoke with him? Did he not explain?"

"If he did, I don't remember."

"Unfortunate," said Zelig. "But the matter is irrelevant, is it not?"

"Not if he's taken Ruth to some other world, it isn't."

"A point well taken, that is."

"It isn't any use, is it?" Jesse crossed his arms on the steering wheel and leaned his head against them, eyes closed. "There's nothing we can do. No way we can stop him."

Zelig understood his despair, but knew, too, that sympathy would only deepen it. He therefore made his tone deliberately mocking. "Will we then not try?"

Jesse lifted his head to scowl at the doctor, who was looking over his shoulder and didn't notice. "I'm willing to try damn near anything that might help Ruth. But what the hell would it be?"

Zelig turned to face him, smiling beatifically. "The first thing is to escape the police, yes?"

"We did that already. For now, anyway."

"For then," corrected Zelig. He glanced over his shoulder again, out the back window. "For now, we are in danger again. There is a police car behind us."

Jesse looked up sharply, but the rearview mirror reflected only anonymous headlights approaching. "Sure it's cops?"

"I saw them turn off the freeway," said Zelig. "The lights on top were quite obvious."

"Turn around." Jesse's voice was tense. "Maybe they won't notice us."

"You are thinking my gaze might attract theirs?" Zelig turned obediently. "Or is that you are fearing they might recognize my face?"

"Thought they'd more likely ignore a car if the people in it were ignoring them."

Zelig nodded. "Quite possibly correct."

"No good," said Jesse, reaching for the wires to start the car. "They've seen us."

"You're quite sure?" Zelig restrained himself from turning around to look out the window again.

"They turned on the bubblegum machine. To stop us." He got the engine started, revved it once, and threw the car in gear. "Hang on. I don't know whether we can outrun them, but I'm sure as hell gonna try."

"You are thinking that wise?" Zelig braced himself.

"It's wiser'n sitting still."

18

Jesse

The little sports car was both faster and more maneuverable than the larger police car pursuing it, and Jesse was the better driver. "But I have watched car chases in the films," said Zelig. "I know how it is done. The policeman behind us will radio to others, to have them waiting where we are going."

"Then we'll go somewhere else," Jesse said cheerfully. Action—any action—was better than sitting still. If they weren't achieving anything else by running, at least they weren't just waiting to get caught.

"You know where they will be waiting?" Zelig asked in surprise.

"Somewhere ahead of us, right?" grinned Jesse.

Zelig clutched at the dash for support as Jesse whipped the little car around a curve. "Ahead of us, yes, certainly," he said dubiously.

"Then that's where we're not going." There was a paved turnaround across the median strip just ahead. Jesse fishtailed them across it and watched the rearview mirror with satisfaction. The police car's tail lights flared red as the driver overran the turn and had to back up.

"Most satisfactory," said Zelig. "But in a moment—"

"We'll be off the freeway." Jesse didn't wait for an exit ramp. For a half mile or so there was no fence between the freeway and the streets below. Jesse slowed the car just as the police car's headlights swept across the freeway behind them, wavering dangerously as the car fishtailed onto their side of the freeway. "He's after us now. Let's see if he can do this." He was watching the side of the road, choosing his moment.

When he found what he was looking for, he crimped the wheel and skidded the little car into a ninety-degree turn off the freeway and straight down the steep slope, bouncing precariously between looming oleander bushes and clumps of pampas grass to the foot of the embankment, where he turned onto a pot-holed access street, stepped on the gas, and skidded around the next available corner onto another street between darkened and deserted warehouses.

Zelig clutched at the dash with both hands, obviously trying not to look terrified. "Where did you learn to drive?"

Jesse grinned. "Doesn't matter: important part is, I learned. Hope for that cop's sake either he doesn't try that slope, or he knows enough to go straight down. He'll roll it if he takes it at an angle."

"I thought we would roll," said Zelig. "My goodness. Indeed. It is well to be alive, yes?"

"Did you think I'd kill us?"

Zelig nodded earnestly. "Oh, my, yes. I did indeed, yes. Are we all right now?"

"Yeah." There were no headlights visible in the rearview mirror. He whipped the car into an alley, found an inset loading dock halfway between streets, turned off his headlights, and backed into it. "Any luck, even if he gets down onto the streets he won't notice us."

"Ah," said Zelig.

"Trouble is, how'll we know when he's gone?"

"How is it certain he will go, I'm wondering?"

172

"It isn't," said Jesse. "I'm just hoping real hard."

"Ah. You are joking me, yes?"

Jesse shook his head. "He'll go. The question is, then what?"

"Then we also go, is it not?"

"It is not. At least, we don't go far. He'll broadcast a description of this car. Any cop that sees us'll stop us. You know where we are?"

"No," said Zelig.

"We'll have to abandon the car."

"We will buy another?"

"With what? You got pockets full of money?"

"No, but I am having credit cards. Have you none?"

Having learned from last night's experience, Jesse had his wallet—or rather, this world's Jesse's wallet in his work pants tonight. "Yeah, but they'd trace the transaction. It'd be a good way to tell them where we are and what we're driving."

Zelig looked at him in open admiration. "You, too, have watched films, is it not?"

"Something like that." He leaned his head against his hands on the steering wheel. "Damn it!"

"You regret the watching of films?"

Jesse ignored him. Outside in the darkness, a sudden gust of wind stirred crumpled papers on the littered roadway.

"I apologize," said Zelig. "Sometimes I am amusing, sometimes not. I think now is not, yes?"

"We're just running." Jesse's voice was muffled against his shirt sleeves. "We aren't helping Ruth. What the hell can we do to help her, anyhow? We gotta get her away from the Other."

"The policeman has gone past the end of the alley. I am

seeing him, you understand."

Jesse lifted his head. "Just now?"

"So." Zelig nodded. "You think perhaps we are leaving the car here?"

"Not here. Better get somewhere around more people before we start walking."

"Near here is, I think, a business district. I was seeing it from the freeway."

"Walking distance from here?"

Zelig shook his head. "Miles. But we can finding back roads, is it not?"

"Where'd you learn to speak English?"

Zelig smiled almost shyly. "I am speaking quite well now, yes?"

"Oh, yes." Jesse started the engine, let it idle a moment, then released the brake. The little car crept blindly out of its hiding place, into the alley. Torn papers swirled away from the wheels, caught on the wind, and bustled along the roadway like little animals. Jesse looked both ways. A black cat fled between buildings, a sleek, dark shadow against pale concrete. "Guess we'll have to chance it sometime." With the headlights still out, he turned the wheel and they rolled down the alley, back the way they had come.

The street was deserted. Jesse pulled the car out of the alley, turned onto the street, and flipped on the lights. They proceeded sedately between unkempt buildings, along criss-crossing railroad tracks, to the freeway underpass without seeing any sign of the police. The underpass took them out of the warehouse district, onto twisting residential streets through which they wended their way with difficulty, reversing direction at the occasional dead end, till they eventually found the business district Zelig had seen. On the way, they passed two or three cars and, as they neared the business district, increasing numbers of pedestrians, but no police.

Neither of them spoke as Jesse found a side-street parking place for the sports car and killed the engine. For a long moment after he had turned off the lights they sat where they were, Zelig watching passersby and Jesse leaning back with his eyes closed, his face pale and still in reflected light from streetlights. The adrenaline rush of chase and escape had faded, leaving him feeling oddly let down and helpless.

"Are you fine?" Zelig asked at last.

Jesse opened his eyes to find the doctor studying him with evident concern. "I'm fine," he said. But he wasn't fine. He was stiff and sore and weary to the bone, cold, hungry, dirty, and miserable. He sighed. "What now?" He could not remember whether they had formulated a plan or not. His mind felt as sluggish as his body. He had been going too long, too hard, and there was no rest in sight.

"Now we walk, yes?"

"Walk where?" The thought filled him with dread. He wasn't quite sure his bad leg would even support him.

Zelig shrugged ineffably. "It is what you said, that we would walk, is it not?"

"Did I? Wonder what I had in mind?" He rubbed his leg absently. "Well, I guess walking anywhere is prob'ly better than staying in this car. Let's go." His eyes slid closed.

After a moment, Zelig said cautiously, "Yes?"

"Oh, Lord." Jesse lifted his head, stared blindly through the windscreen for a moment, then put his hand on the door handle. "Okay. We gotta do something." He wrenched the door open and swung his legs out. "Come on, Doc. We'll think of something." He levered himself to his feet and stood swaying on legs that trembled with exhaustion.

"It is certain you are fine?" Zelig was coming around the car to Jesse's side.

Jesse braced himself and shut the door, looked at Zelig, and achieved a frayed smile. "Sure. Let's get outta here." He pushed himself away from the car, stumbled, and would have fallen if Zelig had not been there to catch him.

"It is the leg, yes? It pains you?"

"It's okay," he said too sharply. He straightened, his face set. "I'm fine. Come on." He led the way onto the sidewalk and away from the car. "We have to figure out some way to help Ruth. If he's taken her back where I'm from—" He broke off, staring wildly at nothing. "My God. You were right: what if whoever killed her does it again?"

Zelig steered him out of the path of a small group of people coming out of a restaurant. "If he has taken her there, I am thinking of nothing we can do for her from here."

"Then we have to get there. Somehow."

Pedestrian traffic increased as they turned onto the main street through the business section. A group of teenage girls stared at Jesse in growing excitement as he and Zelig neared them. Zelig eyed them nervously and steered Jesse toward a restaurant doorway. "First you need food. Then rest. Then is soon enough to worry about Ruth."

Jesse stared at the girls, who had made up their minds and were hurrying toward him, giggling. "First I need a rubber band. And a hat."

Zelig stared at him. "A rubber band? A hat?"

"Or glasses or something. Damn."

"Jesse! Jesse Farrell! Jesse!" The girls swarmed around him, giggling and pushing. "Oh, Jesse, it really is you! Jesse!" One of them thrust herself so hard against him that he nearly lost his balance.

He forced himself to grin at them amiably. "Hi, girls.

Ssshhh! Don't call attention to me, okay?" The girls giggled with delight and demanded autographs. Jesse supplied them, contriving somehow to look as though nothing could have pleased him more. "There you go. That's it, girls. Nice to meet you. Sorry I can't spend more time with you, but I gotta go now, okay?"

To Zelig's obvious amazement, the girls obediently said goodbye and backed away, clutching their autographs and staring at Jesse in unabashed adoration. "How did you do that?" Zelig stared from the girls to Jesse and back. "You, I mean our Jesse, could never get rid of them so easily. Not without rudeness, which unfortunately he was finding the simplest way. How did you do that?"

Jesse shrugged. "You treat 'em like people and some-times they treat you like people. Figured it was worth a try." He glanced at the nearby storefronts. "Gotta tie my hair back. And get a hat."

Zelig watched the girls disappear around a corner with a bright flounce of skirts and shy smiles at Jesse, who waved briefly and forgot them. "A hat," said Zelig.

"Yeah. Here's a drugstore."

The drugstore had rubber bands and sunglasses and baseball caps. Jesse bought those and aspirin and got change for bus fare. The sunglasses and baseball cap didn't do much to disguise his appearance, even with his hair dragged back and caught in a rubber band, but he decided the result was better than nothing and adjusted the hat be-fore he and Zelig stepped outside again.

The same group of girls was waiting on the sidewalk, twittering with excitement. They had brought friends to ask for autographs. The glasses, hat, and pulled-back hair con-fused them not at all. Jesse smiled and signed their scraps of paper and took off the sunglasses so he could see. Zelig danced with impatience and craned his neck, birdlike, to look up and down the street for signs of police or other hazards. He could see no police, but other pedestrians were beginning to notice the little cluster of girls in front of the drugstore and move toward them, curious to see what was going on.

"Jesse."

"I know," said Jesse. He glanced up the street. "There's a bus coming."

"Jesse, Jesse, sign mine, sign it to Cindy with love, please? Will you?"

"Sure I will." He wrote as requested, one eye on the approaching bus. "Gotta go, girls." They groaned with disappointment. "Sorry, but I really have to. Glad I got to meet you. See ya!" The bus pulled to the curb and Jesse leapt onto it the moment the door was open. "Come on, Doc!"

Zelig followed more sedately. "I am coming. Have you the fare?"

Jesse paid the fare for both of them and led the way down the narrow aisle to a back seat, into which he fell with a grunt as the bus started up again. "Jeez," he said. "Jeez." Opening the aspirin bottle, he ate several tablets with a grimace of distaste.

Zelig sat next to him and looked worried. "Where is it taking us?"

Jesse glanced at him, confused. "What? Oh, the bus? I dunno. Away from there."

"This is an adequate goal?"

"Jeez, I dunno. Seemed smart at the time."

"It was smart, Jesse. I just wonder whether it was adequate."

"I don't know what the hell to do." Jesse rubbed the

back of one hand across his eyes. "Guess we ought to go back to the concert hall. Where he took her from. Maybe we'd find something, a clue or something, that'd tell us where he took her to."

"Oh, my, no. I am reading detective fiction always, and I know." The bus was deserted but for them and the driver, who was too far away to hear their conversation, but Zelig lowered his voice conspiratorially anyway, and had to lean toward Jesse to make himself heard. "They would capture you there most certainly, my friend. Criminals always return to the scene of the crime. Most assuredly the police will be awaiting you there." He looked troubled. "Besides, are you not thinking that if there were these clues, the police would already have taken them up? Or whatever it is one does with clues, is it not?"

"They might've missed something." Jesse scowled out the window and tried not to think about how tired he was, or how much his leg hurt. "And they won't be looking for me there. They know we left the area, since they chased us on the freeway. They won't think I'd go back. Prob'ly the last place they'd look for me."

"Oh, no, no, I am telling you—"

"And they don't even know about the Other, and the other worlds. If there's anything that'd tell us something about that, you think it'd tell the police anything? Hell, they wouldn't even notice something like that."

Zelig looked interested. "What sort of something did you have in mind?"

"Dunno. How would I know?"

"Well." Zelig thought about it. "But think about it, is it not? Even though you guess of these other worlds, are you any better equipped than the police to be recognizing a clue about them?"

"Maybe not, but d'you have any better ideas?"

Zelig sighed, defeated. "I am having no ideas at all, I am very much afraid."

"Then we'll go back." Jesse stared blindly out the window. "We have to."

19

Suli

The tapes Suli Grail had bought were made by another Jesse Farrell, but his voice was very like the voice of the one now called the Other. A stranger would have said there was no difference. But Suli could hear the same difference in the voice that she could see in the photos on the covers of the tapes. This Jesse, ravaged by the same events that had scarred and embittered the Other, had somehow emerged with a child's sweet, guileless belief in the basic goodness of humankind, as though the only scars he bore were the outward ones.

And yet they were not. One had only to listen to his music to know they were not. The anguish, the confusion, the sense of loss and of isolation were there in his music as they were in the shadows of his eyes; he was as wounded as the Other, but the terrible harm done him had somehow not damaged his soul.

Suli lay on her stomach, fully clothed, on a hotel bed in World V4G 7N7/4, with a pillow under her stomach and her upper body braced on elbows dug deep into the threadbare bedspread. The Jesse's tapes lay in a tumbled heap beside her. Her personal stereo, with its earphones wrapped neatly around it, was beside them. She held a tape box in one hand and her gatestone bracelet in the other, but looked at neither. The Jesse's eyes were as blue as the

Other's: it hurt her to see them.

The gatestone bracelet had not been on the Other's arm when she chased him today. She was afraid to know all that might imply. She closed her eyes and let her head fall forward, thinking of the two of them, the Jesse with his pain so carefully contained, and the Other whose pain might destroy the universe. Why? What made the one able to live with what had been done to him, when the other could not? They were so like, and so unlike, and her head throbbed with the effort to understand either of them.

The one sure way to tell two doppelgangers apart, and to prove there was some essential difference between them however undetectable it might be by other means, was to bring them face to face in any world (other than Limbo) not belonging to either of them. The gates never made a mistake. Each was "bounced" to his home world every time.

But even in that, the Other broke the rules: from the first, he had never been bounced home. It was as though his revulsion for the world he called Hell was powerful enough to overcome the natural laws of the universe. Suli did not quite understand that, either.

She had returned to Hell after the Other had left her. She had studied his background, his environment, his world. It was just another world, no better but certainly no worse than most. If his life in it had been worse than many, so had the lives of the Jesses he now displaced, in worlds where he apparently expected to live quite happily. Could he really not see that he carried his pain with him, brought it lovingly from world to world, and used it, over and over again, to destroy his dreams?

Sighing, she lifted her head and opened heavy eyes to stare for a long moment at the photo on the tape box in her hand. The Jesse stared back at her, his sweet smile as defenseless as a child's. She put the box aside and turned her attention to the bracelet in her other hand.

The supply officer had been right, the communication device once detached from the bracelet was quite small and would be easy to lose. It was a chance she had to take. She would certainly lose it if she left it on the bracelet. She should have removed it before now.

Handling it carefully, she tucked it into the mesh bag in which she ordinarily carried her gatestone, then put the bracelet aside and closed her eyes again, rubbing them with the heels of her hands. There must be some solution to all this, short of the Other's death, if only she could find it.

Suppose the New Worlders were right? She stopped rubbing her eyes and stared blindly through the hazed darkness the rough treatment had left in them. If the New Worlders were right, then the Other certainly must not be killed. She let her head fall forward onto her propped hands again with an audible moan. She was grasping at straws, willing to accept even the outrageous and the ridiculous, if only it would save the Other's life.

The New Worlders were both outrageous and ridiculous: a political group with overtones of religion, they had believed since the Ages of Chaos that the trouble was caused, not by indiscriminate world-walking itself, but by the fact that it was not done by a Natural.

Ariel Greef had been a near-Natural, able to walk with an untreated stone, but unable to walk alone. The New Worlders maintained that, had she been a true Natural, her sojourns through worlds would actually have mended the damage done by any number of untrained others. They had long predicted the eventual emergence of a true Natural, whose existence would nullify the need for the corps of world-walkers that now policed the gates.

The Other could fulfill that prediction. By accidentally revealing the existence of worlds to him, by letting him know that her gatestone was the key to them, had Suli actually fulfilled some grand destiny, as New Worlders might believe? Or had she, as her superior must think if he knew, helped to damage the very boundaries she was sworn to protect? Was she an unwitting instrument of nature and the gods, or was she after all an instrument of chaos?

Either way, she was first an instrument of the corps of world-walkers, and her superior had instructed her to bring the Other back or kill him. As he said, it was her job. Had she been convinced of the New Worlders' beliefs, she could have turned down the assignment when it was given her. But she had not been: it was not her nature to ponder such grand-scale, and really very abstract, questions.

Nor did she did need the New Worlders to give her reasons not to want the Other dead. But how to save him? How, honorably, decline to kill him, if he would not come back with her alive? If only he would talk to her!

But they had talked, before, or she had, and he had seemed to listen, and then he had gone his way and done everything she had warned him against. If anything could get him to behave sensibly, it was obviously not talking to her. What, then?

Perhaps if he were more like the Jesse he was replacing, she could get through to him. That one, with his wary but willing belief in humankind, would surely listen to reason. But the Other could believe in no one but himself. So alike in so many ways, the two of them seemed in other ways to be almost exact opposites. She had never before encountered doppelgangers as different as they were alike.

Perhaps it was only that she had never known any two doppelgangers as well as she knew these two. But she thought it more likely that in this as in all else, the Other was breaking rules. He seemed to break them as often by accident as by design . . . which was saying a lot, since he broke them by design wherever he found them.

That, of course, was a consequence of the crushing rage that drove him, but she wondered about the ones he broke by accident. Perhaps it was an unforeseen consequence of being a Natural. No one knew, really, what made a Natural, or what he could do, or even really what he was. It was just a word, a name for a possibility that most people had never expected to see made manifest: a human gatestone.

What made him a gatestone? What, specifically, made the Other a Natural, but not his doppelgangers? Or—her eyes flew open in shocked speculation—were his doppelgangers Naturals, too? They could be. Her hands, which had slid into the hair at the sides of her head, curled into fists. They could very easily be, and no one, including they, would know. They didn't know worlds existed. They would hardly attempt to walk where there was, as far as they knew, no goal. The Other had never walked till he met Suli Grail. She realized abruptly that she was painfully pulling her hair, and released it.

How had Ariel Greef found out about worlds? How had she happened to walk with that first stone? And had her doppelgangers been near-Naturals, too? Had they walked worlds with primitive stones, as she had? Suli had never heard of them. Did that mean they hadn't Ariel's talent? Was it a talent? Or was it something genetic? Or something in a person's character?

The Jesse's photo caught her eye and she smiled in automatic, absent-minded response to the smile that was so like the Other's and yet so unlike any expression he had ever worn. There were too many questions she had no way of answering, too many problems she had no way of solving.

It all came down to only one question, one problem, really: could she find a way to save her lover, or must she kill him? With her elbows still braced on the bed, she folded her hands behind her head, pulling her neck down at an awkward angle till her aching forehead was pressed against the dust-scented bedspread. She was no nearer an answer than she had been when she first set out after him.

He had been the first real friend she had made since she left her home world for service in the corps of world-walkers that was supposed to replace her world, her family, and her friends, but never had. He was the only human being she had been really close to, touched by, made love with, since then. In what had become an eternity of bleak self-sufficiency, the memory of their time together was a brief spark of sheer bliss.

He had betrayed her, but only out of agony and ignorance, only because he really did not know what he did. How could she kill him?

If it was really a choice between him and whole worlds, if his walking destroyed boundaries and would cause the chaos Ariel Greef's had, how could she let him live?

Groaning, she let her elbows slide out from under her, pressed her face against the coarse fabric of the bedspread, and wondered without real interest whether she was going to be sick.

When the Other arrived from the past a short while later, she was in much the same position still. She had turned her head to breathe more freely when she fell asleep, and had curled one hand possessively around the nearest tape box. The remaining tapes, and the bracelet, were neither concealed nor protected.

20

Zelig

Night winds whipped silvery sea mist across abandoned acres of parking lot at the concert hall. The area lights were still on, creating barren wells of brilliance in the luminous air and geometric lakes of oily light on the glittering asphalt, through which long lines of departing vehicles swam and surfaced into darkness. The hall itself loomed, enormous and featureless, an ominous pale wall braced against the mist-dazzled night sky.

The nearest bus stop was half a mile from the building itself, across the street from a corner of the parking lot. Jesse and Zelig stepped down onto the sidewalk and the bus pulled away, bathing them briefly in a hot blast of exhaust fumes as they stood peering through skirling fog toward the concert hall.

The gate through which the long line of departing cars slowly left the parking lot was halfway across the lot from the bus stop and led straight onto the freeway, so that none of the cars ended on the same road with Jesse and Zelig. They walked toward the lot in silence, shoulders hunched and eyes narrowed against the wind. Jesse tried not to limp. Zelig tried not to notice.

It had been a very long day for both of them, fraught with peril and revelation. Zelig knew he was less physically exhausted than Jesse, but he was still exhausted. And however sanguine he tried to appear about it, the strain of accepting the evidence of his senses on this day of altered reality had taken its toll. He was dizzy, almost silly with the burden of outrageous belief. And he was uncomfortably aware that he might prove to be a very frail prop for Jesse to lean on.

That Jesse would need something to lean on was self-evident. Clearly this Jesse, unlike the Jesse Zelig had known before, had been in top physical condition when the tour began, but the nightly workouts coupled with the unsettled lifestyle on the road would wear on anyone. With all else that had happened to him, even without tonight's grueling performance onstage, it would be no wonder if he had collapsed of exhaustion. As things were, the wonder was that he managed to stay on his feet, however unsteadily.

They ought, Zelig knew, to have found some quiet little hotel where they could both have rested. Jesse might think he could keep going forever, but he couldn't. Nor could Zelig. He should have suggested a hotel, instead of going along with Jesse's foolish plan to come back out here. After all the trouble they had gone to, to get away from here, it was ridiculous to come back once they were safely away. The idea that they would find some clue to Ruth's disappearance was almost certainly wishful thinking.

Not that wishful thinking didn't have its merits, but Zelig preferred to indulge in it from comfort, not wearily, late at night, in dark and deserted streets under a fog-shrouded moon, with moisture collecting in his hair and dripping icily down the back of his neck.

It had seemed right and sensible to side with Jesse when they fled the hall after the concert, but out here in the echoing streets he was suddenly, newly aware that this Jesse was a stranger to him. He was aiding and abetting a wanted man, never mind whether the man had done anything wrong. Zelig didn't think that he had, but he didn't *know* that he hadn't, and the police wouldn't care one way or the other. Defiance seemed vastly less sensible now.

"Looks like the excitement's over," said Jesse. His voice was hoarse and sounded as uncertain as Zelig felt.

Zelig nodded without looking at him. "Your fans will have quit when they knew you were gone."

"The police are still there. Gate might be guarded. Can't tell from here, in this light. Can you?"

"No." Zelig eyed the fence, diverted. "We will climb over, to get in? In case of guards?"

Jesse grinned reluctantly. "You like doing things the hard way?"

"Oh," he said, deflated. "There will be an easy way?"

"I don't know, but it might be a good idea to look for one before we go climbing fences."

Zelig considered the problem. "If there is a guard, perhaps a good idea is that I create a diversion while you are going past him."

"Might work."

Zelig hesitated, surprised to realize how much he cared about this Jesse, whether he knew him or not. He could almost justify it to himself by remembering that Jesse was really the only hope, however feeble, that Ruth seemed to have; but the fact was that in the short time they had known each other he had become fond of this courageous, humorous, and altogether engaging young man. "But I would be left behind," he said anxiously.

"True." Jesse's face, taut with pain, was wholly unreadable, but there was a hint of a smile in his voice.

"I would prefer to climb the fence," Zelig said firmly.

"Maybe there won't be a guard." He still didn't quite

smile, but the humor was more visible now.

"Oh." Zelig smiled ruefully. "I was forgetting that."

There was no guard. When Jesse hesitated, Zelig took charge of the expedition, busily guiding Jesse through shifting shadows and fog-blurred distances. There were still numerous police vehicles near Jesse's van and the concert hall itself, but the kidnapping had taken place at some distance from either, where an equipment truck was still parked. There appeared to be no police near that.

Zelig, beginning to enjoy the role of fugitive from justice now that peril seemed less imminent, led the way toward it as through an impenetrable jungle, occasionally brandishing an invisible machete against mist-silvered air. "I will show you where I saw the other Jesse abduct our Ruth," he announced. "Though whether you will find anything of use to you there I cannot believe." His very strong wish that they would find something made him sound more certain than he was that they wouldn't.

"We'll see." Jesse kept pace with him, watching the distant snake of departing cars with feral alertness.

"There seem to be no nearby police, is it not?" That observation was comforting. In the stillness of the night, the whisper of the car-snake's tires against wet asphalt seemed near and loud. An occasional engine roar or clashing of gears broke the silence, and once a man's shout seemingly nearby froze Zelig to the asphalt for a long, heart-pounding instant before he sighed audibly and, scowling, moved on, with the coppery taste of fear in his mouth.

They avoided the pools of light cast by the streetlamps overhead, warily clinging to the swimming shadows between them even after they were near enough the equipment truck to be concealed by its bulk from the remaining police.

"Is this where you saw him?" Jesse asked when Zelig stopped.

"Ssshhh!" said Zelig, glancing around nervously. The taste of fear was still sharp in his mouth. "Here I saw the Other, yes."

"Okay." Jesse stood where he was, his gaze sweeping the equipment truck and surrounding asphalt. "Look for anything. Anything at all."

"The police will have found anything of importance."

"Maybe." Jesse glanced at him. "You got a better idea?"

Yes: let us go away from here, he thought. *It is no use, this seeking of clues like storybook detectives. We cannot help Ruth. Let us save ourselves.* Aloud, he said only, "No."

"Then humor me," said Jesse.

"Of course." Zelig made a show of searching the ground around him, though he was now convinced of the futility of the exercise. "What sort of thing did you have in mind?"

"I don't know, for God's sake!" Jesse pounced on a glittering object, found it to be only a gum wrapper, and threw it down again in disgust. "*Damn* it."

"Patience." As Jesse moved nearer the truck, Zelig followed, watching the ground without any hope. "You feel anxious for Ruth, is it not?"

"Yeah." Jesse stared at Zelig in absent-minded perplexity. "Yeah. I'm anxious about Ruth."

"I, too, am concerned for her. But we must be remembering that we may be unable to help her." He wandered away from Jesse, toward the truck, and bent to retrieve an object that had fallen into its shadow. "What's this?"

Jesse stared in sudden hope. "Well? What is it?"

Zelig shook his head. "Only costume jewelry." He held up a heavy silver bracelet that glinted dully in the light. "It is not Ruth's. I would know it."

"Let me see." Jesse limped toward him, stumbling in his haste.

"It cannot be of interest." Zelig studied it incuriously. It was heavier than he had expected when he saw it; a solid curve of silver set with roughly cut and polished ovals of veined turquoise, it felt cold and damp in his hand. "It is a nice piece, I suppose, but nothing to do with Ruth. Some roadie dropped it, perhaps. Do not excite yourself. You will do your leg more injury." The center stone seemed oddly translucent, a swirl of turquoise mist marbled with possibilities.

"I'm not excited. Let me see." He took the bracelet eagerly, and held it where they could both see it. "Doesn't seem like you'd lose this easy," he said. "I mean, you'd sure notice if it fell off."

"Someone comes."

"What? Who?" Jesse tried to stuff the bracelet into his pocket, but it wouldn't fit. "Damn. Police?"

There was no need for Zelig to respond; the approaching policemen, seeing him and Jesse, identified themselves. "Halt! Police! Stay where you are!"

Zelig glanced anxiously at Jesse. "What to do?"

Jesse forced the bracelet onto his wrist for safekeeping, caught Zelig's arm, and dragged him into concealment behind the truck. "We gotta run."

"Halt where you are!" A gunshot shattered the misty silence. "This is the police. Stay where you are." Leather soles echoed against wet asphalt.

"Possibly they might shoot us," Zelig said in surprise. He found he had not really quite believed in their fugitive status until now.

"They might. Maybe you better stay here; they won't hurt you if you're not with me." Jesse lurched away from the truck, running at an angle that kept it between him and the pursuing police.

"Jesse!" Zelig went after him. "Wait, Jesse!" His cry was nearly drowned by a sudden volley of gunfire.

Jesse glanced back at Zelig and opened his mouth to answer, but the words were transformed into a strangled scream as his foot came down on the edge of a speed bump and slipped, twisting his bad leg under him. He would have fallen if Zelig had not at that moment reached him and caught his arm to keep him upright. His face went so white so suddenly that Zelig thought he was fainting. Beads of sweat broke out on his forehead as the muscles of the crippled leg spasmed in agony. At that moment, the police could have brought forth tanks against them and Jesse would not even have noticed: he was, clearly, incapable of seeing past the blinding, immobilizing torment of torn ligaments and muscles.

"The police," Zelig said urgently.

With an obvious effort Jesse turned his attention away from the all-consuming pain to look behind them. The police had emerged from behind the truck. They approached at a dead run, weapons at the ready, as silent and swift as predators sure of their kill.

There was no shelter from them anywhere. The two fugitives stood alone in opalescent mist beneath a streetlamp, trapped and defenseless, supporting each other in helpless exhaustion, utterly defeated, waiting forlornly for the final, ignominious moment of capture. And then the approaching police disappeared.

21

Jesse

Jesse was looking directly at the police when they disappeared. He was becoming almost accustomed to improbabilities by now. Or perhaps pain had only dulled his sensitivity to wonder. "They're gone," he said quite calmly, and apprehensively shifted weight onto his bad leg. It felt as though a solid rod of white-hot steel had been substituted for the bones, but he found that he was able, if he did it very carefully, to balance on both legs.

"Where?" Zelig stared all around in confusion. "Where have they gone?"

"Dunno." Jesse pulled free of Zelig's absent-minded support and took a careful step forward. The leg supported him, but only just. "Disappeared," he said. "Poof." He moved toward the equipment truck. The leg buckled. He managed to stay both upright and silent, but it wasn't easy. After a moment he gathered his courage and tried again, more cautiously this time.

"Poof?" Zelig stood where he was, turning awkwardly in circles like a stunned dancer. "Poof?"

"Yeah. Poof." The leg held him if he moved carefully, and the pain had decreased from white-hot agony to mere throbbing torture. There was no hope of concealing his limp now. He snapped his fingers. "Poof. Magic trick. Now you see 'em, now you don't. Disappeared." He moved cautiously toward the equipment truck, watching for reappearing policemen. "They were right over here. And then they weren't."

"But where?" Zelig danced after him, still turning circles. "They went where, please?"

"Nowhere. They just went." He tried not to limp, and nearly lost his footing.

"But which way? They must go one way or another, is it not?"

"Doc, I was looking right at 'em, and they didn't go any way at all. They just went. Poof. Gone."

"Oh." Zelig stopped turning circles. He had begun to stumble dizzily. "They went poof. I see." He nodded wisely. "I am understanding now." He regained his balance and trotted busily after Jesse.

"Are you? Wish I was." They had reached the spot where Jesse had last seen the approaching police. There were none, nor any sign that they had been there. "This is weird."

"Yes," said Zelig, nodding. "Weird."

"Look, the cars aren't all gone yet. The audience's cars. Fact they aren't even started going, looks like. What the hell is going on?"

"Your concert, I would guess," said Zelig.

"What?" Jesse stared.

"Your concert," said Zelig. "You asked what is going on, yes? I think what is going on here is your concert. Inside there." He nodded toward the concert hall. "I think the police are not disturbing it, and so you are completing the final songs, the encores and whatnot, yes?"

"Oh, jeez." Jesse lurched toward the concert hall, stopped, stared for a moment at Zelig, then lifted his head in a curiously feral gesture, testing the air for scents. "You mean we're in another world." The air smelled of sea fog, damp asphalt, and auto exhaust, as it had in the world they came from.

"This seems most probably the case," Zelig said earnestly. "Because the police went poof, you understand."

"But how?" The air ought to have smelled different, or looked different, or sounded different. There should have been some obvious way to tell when one fell between worlds. "How'd we get here?"

Zelig shrugged ineffably. "How did you get there, I'm wondering? Most strange, all this, yes? Who can say?" He had begun to turn in circles again, more slowly this time, studying their surroundings. "But you see. The vehicles, the absence of police."

Jesse stared at the concert hall. "Guess we really are in a different world. And that means the Other—or an Other—is in there. Onstage. Pretending to be me."

"Not," said Zelig.

"What?" Jesse barely glanced at him.

"Not pretending," said Zelig. "As far as he is concerned, he must be Jesse Farrell, is it not?"

Jesse scowled at the concert hall and slowly, reluctantly, turned to look at Zelig. "I'm Jesse Farrell." The concert hall seemed to drag his attention back to it, so that he almost leaned toward it, balanced precariously on the fog-laden air.

Zelig shifted uncomfortably. "We must think, yes?"

Jesse took one awkward step toward the concert hall. "I want to see him performing. I want to go inside."

Zelig touched his arm. "I am uncertain it would be wise to look."

"Why?" He took another involuntary step as though drawn by an unseen force.

"Because you must think what might happen when two Jesses face one another, yes? Legends, stories of such happenings, all recommend against it. I have great fear of what might happen. Wait, Jesse!" This as Jesse took another step, stiff and puppet-like, toward the hall. "Wait, you really must consider! Have you knowledge of what is called a doppelganger?"

Jesse barely glanced at him. "The Other used that word. What is it?"

"A double, it is a person's double, in myth and fiction, you understand. And it is said that the two must not look upon each other, Jesse, they must not see each other."

"Or what? The world explodes? What could happen?" He took another step and closed his eyes as his weight came down too hard on his bad leg.

"It is said they can both exist in one world only as long as neither has seen the other."

"Who the hell could know that?" But he remembered the Other saying something like that, in his dream that was not a dream. Still he kept moving toward the hall, with Zelig trailing anxiously behind. The lure of that performance was too strong to be overcome by mere logic.

"How can I know who could know that?" asked Zelig. "But I have read it. It is said, Jesse." He said it as though those words made it a natural law.

Jesse faltered, but he did not, could not stop. "I need to see him," he said.

"Why? Jesse, listen to me, please. Why must you see him? Think of it. Is this really your desire, or some foul compulsion? Why need you to see him?"

"I don't know." He shrugged impatiently. "Jeez, Doc, what's it matter why? I just wanta see him, that's all. If there's a double of you here, don't you want to see him?"

Zelig nodded somberly. "I think I would be drawn to him. I think if we venture into the wrong world, we feel a need to seek out our doppelganger, and the sight of him is itself the force that thrusts us out of the world. Where will you go if that happens, Jesse? It is not safe! You must think, you must consider before you act!"

"I can't. I don't want to." They were almost at the stage door now, and Jesse was nearly running. Zelig caught at his arm, was shrugged aside, and followed doggedly, still arguing, till Jesse pulled open the door and stepped inside.

22

Zelig

The security guard at the door glanced at Jesse, did a double-take, and stared through the vaulted darkness toward the stage where Jesse could be heard performing with the band. While the guard stared in confusion, Jesse walked past him toward the wings where he would be able to see the stage.

Zelig trailed him helplessly, not even trying to discourage him now. It was obviously no use. Jesse was intent on seeing his doppelganger, and nothing short of a miracle would stop him. Zelig wished, desperately, for a miracle. Then he wondered why it mattered. And he wondered whether he would change worlds with Jesse when Jesse saw his doppelganger: and if not, what would happen to him. Then he thought it would be better not to think.

Several crew members stopped and stared at the sight of Jesse offstage, when they could clearly hear Jesse onstage. Jesse nodded absently to one or two of them, but most of his attention was on the unseen stage. He seemed to have forgotten Zelig's presence; he moved blindly, like a somnambulist, staring toward the unseen Other with eyes unreadable and shadowed.

Zelig knew exactly the moment when Jesse came in sight of his double. It was not difficult to tell. Jesse disappeared. He disappeared instantly and completely, just as the legends said he would. "Poof," to use Jesse's own term for it. Zelig was left alone in a strange world.

He wondered disconsolately whether it would be better to seek out his own doppelganger in the hope that when he disappeared from here he would reappear in his own world, or whether he ought simply to sit down where he was and cry.

23

Suli

She woke to a hotel room swimming with shadows, and a strong sense of another's presence. But before she could focus sleep-dazed eyes, the feeling was gone, the room oddly bleak in its clear emptiness of any presence but her own. She struggled up onto her elbows and sleepily rubbed her eyes, then remembered and reached blindly for the bracelet.

It was gone. That woke her, abruptly and completely. He had been there while she slept. He had taken the bracelet and gone back to the past, to the inevitable confrontation with her when she realized what he had done.

He must have thought then that she wouldn't know; that he could return her stone, keep the bracelet with its future stone, and she wouldn't be able to tell. He had known nothing of gatestones and very little of world-walkers. And indeed, despite the evidence, it had taken her a moment to understand, and still longer to believe.

When she had felt the stone in his keeping, and found it still in the little bag at her neck, she had accused him, but dubiously, and longing to hear the accusation honestly denied. Impossible, she'd thought, that he could have used her stone to steal its own future self, then carried both back together through gates that should not have let them pass. Yet it was the only answer, and to give him credit, he had

201

not even attempted to deny it.

She remembered the shock of realization: he had done the impossible. He had carried both stones through who knew how many gates, with no harm to the stones or to himself. She knew what it meant, even then. With that single defiant act, he had proved what he was, and signed his death warrant at Central.

She had not betrayed him. It would have served no purpose for her to match his perfidy. It would only have damaged her self-respect without helping him or the worlds. But neither did it help him that she kept silent. His acts betrayed themselves.

And now she must stop him. Sighing, she rose and collected her belongings, took a long, soothing shower, and then called Central to explain her predicament and ask for a replacement stone.

They recalled her to Central, of course, and sent her to her superior's office. For one wild moment she thought he might actually replace her on the job, but when she saw him she knew he would not. Only then did she realize that the emotion she had felt at the prospect was as much fear as relief.

She sat in the same ugly acrylic chair she had occupied before, and stared at him across his battered black desk, hoping her face was expressionless. He stared back at her with all the malignant interest of a dehydrated frog examining a captive fly. "They tell me you lost your stone," he said.

"Yes, sir," she said.

"And that you believe the Other took it?"

"Yes, sir."

He studied her dispassionately for a long moment. "You

knew this would happen?"

Not by the flicker of an eyelid did she betray her surprise. "Yes, sir."

"This was the pivotal moment you wanted to change?"

"Yes, sir." She hesitated. "From the other end, sir, since I didn't know what it would look like from this end."

He turned from her to look out the window at his patch of blue sky. "He used your stone to jump into his future, to steal your stone," he said.

"Yes, sir."

"And he carried them both back to you. Uninsulated."

"Yes, sir."

He sighed. "You've known, all along, what he is."

"Yes, sir." When he turned to look at her, she added almost humbly, "But I don't think he did, sir."

He blinked. "Past tense? He knows now what he is?"

She hesitated, choosing her words. "He wasn't wearing the bracelet the last time I saw him walking in the present."

He studied her. "Perhaps he had it in a pocket."

"It's large, sir. I think he would wear it."

"Yes." He looked at the information chips on his desk. "Well."

"Sir?"

He looked at her.

"You knew? When you sent me? You pretended not to be sure, but—you knew what he was?"

"I knew." He paused. "I told you to kill him."

"Yes, sir." She should have known that meant he knew. "You think I'll have to."

He turned his chair abruptly, putting his back to her. After a very long moment he said, "I have my orders, too, you know." She could not interpret his tone. "Have you met the Jesse?"

She stared. "The one he's replaced? No, sir."

"See that you do." He turned to face her again, but his eyes told her nothing. "If you can, see that he does."

"That the Other meets the Jesse? Why, sir?"

He might not have heard her. "I have a universal stone here somewhere." He was searching his desk drawers. "We don't like to have them scattered around, but no help for it. You need one to complete your assignment." He found it, and sat studying it for a moment. "It won't work as well as your own, of course, since you're not keyed to it, and the internal circuitry can't be changed."

"That's something I've been thinking about, sir. My stone isn't keyed to Jes—to the Other. Why would it work so well for him?"

He shrugged. "It doesn't. Didn't. He never really used it, you know. He didn't need it."

"Oh." Stupid. She should have seen that.

"Here, take it." He held out the stone to her. "Go do your work, child. It's all any of us can do."

She frowned at him, puzzled, but he turned away and ignored her. "Yes, sir," she said. She tucked the new stone safely into the little bag at her neck with the communication device she had taken from the bracelet, then hesitated. "Should I have a new bracelet made?"

"What?" He swivelled his chair to look at her with sky-dazzled eyes. "What? Oh." He waved a hand negligently. "No reason to."

Still she hesitated, frowning at him. "Then why—?"

"Figure it out, child." He looked back at the window.

"For me," she said, shocked. "You knew all along. You didn't just know he had taken it, you knew he would take it, long before he did. You wanted to be sure I'd know what he'd done. But why? Did you want me to know what he

204

was, when you sent me after him?"

"Go, child," he said, waving her away. "You weary me."

Clearly she would get no more answers from him. "Very well," she said reluctantly, and set out to attend a Jesse Farrell concert. It had been the next order of business before she lost her stone. Jud had given her much to think about, but no particular reason to change her plans, at least not yet.

Lack of a ticket was no problem, since she did not enter by way of the doors, and did not join the audience. She went backstage, and was within a few feet of Jesse when he caught sight of the Other and was thus bounced out of that world. But she did not see him come or go; she was watching the Other, listening to the music he made, fascinated by this new aspect of him that she had never seen before.

It was Jesse Farrell's music he played and sang, and Jesse's public persona that he imitated onstage, but he could not have done it as well if he had not had the same passionate connection with the music that all the other Jesses had. He did it very well indeed.

She could have killed him there and then, of course. But to do so would be as disruptive as anything he could do to this world, and it would leave the Jesse who belonged here with no place to come back to. It was not for the Other that she had come, this time. Turning away, she sought out the dressing room in which Ruth Sutton awaited the return from stage of this, the third Jesse Farrell she had known.

24
Ruth

What Ruth saw when she answered a knock at the dressing room door was an ordinary young woman, small and pretty and dressed like any other concert-goer. It was not wholly unheard-of for a fan to get through all the security guards and other obstacles to find Jesse's dressing room, but it was uncommon enough that Ruth was startled and, in her present state, not much inclined to patience.

"I'm sorry," she said automatically, "but you can't come in. If you want to see Jesse, look onstage. That's where he is. Now go, before I call a guard."

"I don't want to see the Jesse." She put a hand on the door in an apparently negligent grip that Ruth, though she instinctively leaned against it, could not counter. "I'm here to see you." The woman's clear amber gaze was calm and confident.

Ruth, already at her wit's end from trying to understand what had happened to her, found herself perilously near tears. The realization sent a surge of anger through her that did much to steady her voice as she said firmly, "It won't work. Give it up: I'm not going to let you in. Now let go of the door, or I will call a guard."

"I'm here to help you." The steadiness of the woman's gaze was unnerving.

"I don't need help." Ruth heard the petulant note in her

own voice and tried hard to meet the other woman's eyes, but something in their cold amber made her look away. She really didn't want to call a guard. She'd never had to call for help before to deal with a strayed Farrell fan. But she was not at her best just now, and this woman was clearly no ordinary fan.

"I think you do. May I come in?"

"No." She pushed uselessly against the door, looking beyond the woman for someone to help her. "Go away."

"I will," said the woman. "But first we have to talk about what's happened to you." At Ruth's quick, startled glance, she added gently, "And about the world where you belong. And the Jesse who belongs in this one." She spoke so earnestly that the dark curls framing her face bounced softly against the creamy tan of her skin, and the amber of her eyes looked warmer suddenly, like sunlight trapped under glass.

"You're crazy." But she was no longer leaning against the woman's grip on the door.

"Not unless you are, too. And I don't think you are."

She gave in then, overwhelmed by sudden despair. "I think I must be." She released the door and fumbled her way to a seat against the wall. The young woman entered and closed the door behind her. Ruth glanced at her and said too cheerfully, "Sit down." In a sudden maniacal fit of hospitality she added brightly, "Can I get you anything? Something to drink? Coffee?"

The woman selected a chair facing Ruth's and sat in one fluid motion, like a cat. "You're not crazy," she said, "and neither is the world around you. It's just that you don't belong here." She smiled kindly. "Let me help you."

Her voice was gentle, but the words were as crazy as anything else that had happened to Ruth since she woke alone in a strange hotel room with an aching head and no memory of how she got there. "Oh, God," she said, uncertain whether to laugh or cry. "Who are you? What do you want of me?"

"My name is—" The woman broke off, looked in confusion at the purse on her lap, started to open it, then looked at Ruth in dismay. After a moment's startled silence she said almost guiltily, "Suli Grail." She spoke as though the sound of it were as unfamiliar to her as it was to Ruth, and paused afterward as though uncertain how to proceed.

"Pleased to meet you, Sue Lee Grail," said Ruth. "Now, what do you want with me?" She felt stronger in the face of the woman's uncertainty.

"I told you, Ruth. I want to help you." Those amber eyes watched Ruth almost shyly now.

"What makes you think I need help? And how do you know my name? Who are you?"

"I know your name because I am a sort of peace officer assigned to your case."

"Oh, God, not something more about that dead woman they mistook for me." Ruth shuddered. "I just cannot handle that, I really can't. I don't want to talk about it. Must we go on and on about it?"

"No. We needn't discuss it at all, if it upsets you."

"But I thought . . ." Ruth scowled at her. "You said you were a cop. Why else would a cop be here? Unless—has Jesse done something? Is it drugs again? Is that it?"

"It may surprise you to know that the Jesse from this world has never used pharmaceuticals for recreational purposes." She smiled, and her dark curls shadowed her eyes. "Of course, that's not the Jesse onstage now. But the one out there hasn't, either."

"I beg your pardon?"

"The Jesse who belongs here does not use drugs for fun. And neither does the one who's onstage now." Suli's smile was kind, but her eyes were shallow pools of amber shadows, neither kind nor friendly. "Your Jesse did, because he could not stop counting his losses long enough to appreciate his gains. It happens to people sometimes. They think life should be all joy, and they imagine they cannot bear the reality that it is not." She stared briefly into some dark place where there was no joy at all; then she shook herself and achieved a fairly creditable smile again. "Sorry. I guess you know that well enough. Anyway, the Jesse who belongs in this world isn't like that."

"You keep saying things like that."

"Things like what?" Suli seemed genuinely puzzled.

" 'The Jesse who belongs in this world.' What is that supposed to mean? There's just one world, and one Jesse in it. Isn't there?"

"You know better than that."

"I do?"

"Come, now. In your world, your Jesse was dying of his drugs. You needed Dr. Zelig to help keep him alive and functioning. Where's Dr. Zelig, in this world? And what did he think of the Jesse you last saw in your own world? The one who came there just last night, who was healthy, and who probably could not understand why you thought he used drugs?"

Ruth shook her head, obscurely frightened. "I don't understand," she said uncertainly.

"And," said Suli, "what about that dead woman you didn't want to talk about? In your world, there was no dead woman that Jesse was thought to have killed, was there? Yet when he brought you to this world, what was happening here?"

She answered it automatically, too caught in the memory to maintain an insistence on ignorance of worlds. "They thought I'd been murdered. Jesse was in jail. I don't understand that. He wasn't—he couldn't have—oh God, it's all so complicated."

"I know. It's all right. You don't have to explain it to me. As far as you were concerned, everything was fine and Jesse had just gone onstage when suddenly he appeared in the parking lot and dragged you—where? To the van? To a phone? To a policeman?"

"Nowhere," said Ruth. "Or, or to a hotel. I don't know. He—I don't remember. He hit me."

Suli flinched as though she had been struck, but she didn't say anything, only nodded encouragingly and waited to hear the rest of the story.

"I'd let him know—I mean, I'd just seen Jesse go onstage, and he was so different from the Jesse I'd always known, and then this other one came up to me and—even if I hadn't known where Jesse was, this one's eyes are different. They're . . ." She searched for a word, didn't find it, and gave up with a little, helpless shrug. "Different."

"Yes," said Suli, her voice flat.

"So I asked him who he was," said Ruth. "And he hit me. And I woke up in this hotel room, all alone, and it was this afternoon again, not night, not time for the concert yet, and I found the band members, and they took me to a hospital, and the doctors said I had amnesia. I didn't argue. It was that or admit I was crazy. And then . . ." Her voice trailed off.

"And then the police, the reporters, and all that. Yes. And you found out Jesse was in jail."

"He had been in jail the whole time," said Ruth. "He had been arrested in the middle of his concert last night.

Only I saw him. Or I saw someone. Someone I thought was Jesse. I saw him come offstage after that concert, and I saw him all the time in between, and—"

"What you saw was your Jesse's doppelganger."

"His what?" She stared, confused.

"His doppelganger. There are different worlds, Ruth, and in each of them there is a different Jesse. And a different everyone else." The woman's smile was kind again, and her eyes like trapped sunshine.

Ruth stared, her thoughts uncomfortable. "Even a different me?"

"Yes." She watched Ruth patiently.

"Then the dead woman—" But she could not say it.

Suli said it for her. "The Ruth from this world was murdered."

"Oh, God." Her hands curled into fists in her lap. "That means I'm in a whole different world. I don't believe this. You're mad. Go away. I'll call the guards." But she made no move to call anyone.

"I'm sorry, Ruth. I know that doppelgangers and parallel worlds are difficult concepts when first encountered."

Ruth was silent for a moment, thinking about it. "I knew before you told me," she said. "It's the only explanation. But it's crazy." She looked up suddenly. "Who killed her? Did Jesse, this Jesse, did he kill her?"

"I don't know who killed her. But I'm confident it was not Jesse. Not any of the Jesses."

"But the evidence. They had all that evidence." Her voice was steady, her gaze expressionless.

Suli shrugged. "Evidence is not always an accurate path to the truth. You must choose what you will believe, of course."

"Whatever I choose, I've got to believe something crazy.

How could I be in a whole different world?"

"Jesse brought you here. A different Jesse. Not yours, and not the one from this world, who's in your world now. I suppose you could call him mine; I loved him once."

Ruth studied her dispassionately. "You love him now."

After a startled instant Suli shrugged, and her eyes were cold amber beads in a cold stone face. "Perhaps. And perhaps I have told you too much. But you will believe something easier than the truth, in the end. People always do. Come: you don't belong here." She rose and reached a hand toward Ruth.

"Come where?" Ruth looked uneasily at the extended hand and made no move to touch it.

"Back to your world, of course."

"And my Jesse?"

"Your Jesse is dead." She clearly regretted that the moment the words were out of her mouth, but it was too late to call them back. "Come along."

"Dead?" Ruth's voice was small and terrified.

"Yes." She let her hand drop to her side, but remained standing, looking down at Ruth with real sympathy. "I'm sorry," she said.

Ruth shook her head, staring up at the other woman. "How did he die?"

"He died of drugs. Last night, at the concert, when the Jesse from this world first came to you. That's why he could come to your world when the Other bounced him out of this one. Look, I can't explain everything to you. I've already said more than I should. Let me take you back to your world: it's where you belong." She extended her hand again.

Ruth hesitated for a long moment before she rose, reached reluctantly for Suli's hand and said cautiously,

"What do I have to do?"

Suli smiled, but her amber eyes were dark with shadows. "You've done it," she said. "Look around you."

It was true. And it should have been the final straw. She had taken Suli's hand in a backstage dressing room and now, seemingly without transition, released it in the familiar living quarters of the van. But bizarre as that was, it was, oddly, not unsettling. Perhaps because she recognized this world as hers, perhaps because this time she'd had an explanation and a reassuring hand to hold, perhaps because it was confirmation of something she had been afraid to believe. It didn't matter why. The important thing was that, far from being frightened all over again, she felt suddenly at ease, at peace. Safe. She was home.

25

Jesse

One moment Jesse was backstage in the concert hall, craning his neck to see his doppelganger performing on the stage. The next moment, having caught only a brief a glimpse of that Other, he was back outside in the parking lot. But not in the same world. Not only was the concert over, here, and the parking lot nearly deserted of cars, but the world where the Other was still performing did not have police in large numbers roaming the parking lot in search of him. This one had.

It also had the van in which he, Ruth, and Zelig had traveled from the last concert city. He noticed it because the police were converging on it, and because Ruth was there, holding its door open, her face clearly lit by the light outside the door. The mere sight of her, even without knowing which world he was in and which Ruth she was, lifted his spirits beyond all reason.

She was talking to a young woman who was evidently just leaving the van. Both of them looked up as the police approached. Nobody was looking at Jesse. He hesitated, aware that this was probably the world in which he had been accused of abducting her, and in which the police had been shooting at him when he left. In which case they might shoot first and ask questions later.

Or it might just possibly not be that world, in which case

he might be confronted by yet another Jesse if he approached Ruth. He was suddenly a lot less eager than he had been to meet other Jesses.

But the young woman was walking quickly away from the van, leaving Ruth alone to face the police, and she looked so forlorn that in the end it wasn't really even a conscious decision. She needed help. He could give it.

If this was the world in which he had spent the previous night, he would have liked to meet Ruth in less public circumstances. They had a lot to talk about, a lot of explanations to make and questions to ask and to answer. But that would take time and a certain amount of privacy, at least from officious police. The first thing to do was to get rid of them.

As he neared the van he could hear them arguing with her. They were confused because she insisted she hadn't been abducted. Which meant it was the right world, but . . . the Other *had* abducted her. Why would she deny it? How had she got back? How much did she know? More questions, and no chance of answers till the police were gone.

When they saw Jesse, they didn't shoot him, but some of them unbuttoned their holsters and two of them made a grab for him while Ruth insisted, with a strong hint of laughter in her voice, that as there had been no crime, they had no reason to arrest him. They were in no mood to listen to such an argument, and seemed to regard it as wholly irrelevant.

Ruth's exasperation, Jesse's controlled rage, and their combined logic had no effect. It began to seem as though the police would never leave them alone. But when they asked Ruth for the third or fourth time whether she would press charges against Jesse, something finally snapped. She glanced at Jesse, their eyes locked, and all at once they were both convulsed with laughter.

"What would I press charges against him for?" she asked finally, stifling a new outburst of giggles. "This is a farce, for God's sake, can't you see that? Jesse hasn't done anything to me. There's nothing to charge him with. If charges should be pressed against anybody, it's these so-called witnesses who told you they saw Jesse kidnap me."

That at least gave the police something new to think about. After only a few more arguments, easily countered, they left at last. Ruth and Jesse watched them for a long moment, both still grinning helplessly, before Ruth led Jesse into the van and collapsed on the nearest chair.

"Close the door," she said, resting her head against the chair's back and closing her eyes. "So you 'escaped custody,' did you?" She chuckled again and lifted a weary hand to wipe tears of laughter from her eyes. "What did you think you were doing?"

"Escaping custody," he said. "You okay?"

"I don't know." She opened her eyes, stared at the ceiling for a moment, then lifted her head to look at him in the chair opposite hers. Her eyes were cool and curious, all the laughter gone. "Which one are you?"

He hesitated. "Same one I've always been."

"Not the one who belongs here, in this world."

He frowned. "What do you know about that?"

She shook her head wearily. "More than I want to. How much do *you* know? Are you in control of any of this? Can you do this moving around between worlds at will? Why did you come here?"

"I dunno. I mean I came here, to the van, to see you. But I don't know how I got into this world in the first place, or why."

She studied him for a moment, and sighed. "He did

kidnap me, you know," she said. "A Jesse. There was a world where I'd been killed. Murdered. They thought he'd done it. He took me there so they'd have to let him out of jail." She eyed him curiously. "Your world?"

"Yes. *Damn* it. I was afraid he'd do that." Jesse rubbed his leg absently, trying to relieve the pain. "I'm sorry, Ruth."

"It's not your fault, is it?" She sounded surprised. "Why should you apologize?"

"I dunno. I feel like—I dunno." He shrugged helplessly. "He looks like me."

"And that makes you responsible?" Her tone was gently mocking.

"No, 'course not."

But she had lost interest. "Did you know he's dead? My Jesse?"

"Thought he must be. Drugs?"

She nodded. "Poor Jesse. I can't even mourn him, not really." She looked at him without lifting her head, and her eyes were pleading. "Well, how can I? We knew he was killing himself. It was only a matter of time. And besides . . . I know you're not he, and yet . . ."

He nodded, acknowledging the obvious. "And yet I'm here. In his place. And looking just like him."

That made her smile, very faintly. "Not quite like him. I don't know how I convinced myself at first that you were he, now that I look at you. He was sick, you know. He'd been abusing his health for a long, long time. He was swollen and soft and sick."

"But you cared for him." He didn't look at her. It wasn't really a question, but she might answer it.

"He was like a little brother to me. A wayward brother. I couldn't abandon him."

It was the right answer. "No, I s'pose you couldn't. No reason you should. Not when you still could maybe help him." He shifted, trying to ease his leg into a more comfortable position.

"It was your Ruth," she said suddenly, clearly realizing it for the first time. "The one who was killed."

He nodded, though she wasn't looking at him. "Yeah. My Ruth." A wry smile pulled at his lips. "She'd have cursed anybody who called her that."

"She didn't like you?"

He shrugged. "I don't know. She didn't dislike me. She was—" He shrugged again, helplessly. "I don't know."

She chuckled softly. "Articulate, aren't you?"

"Dammit, I—" He caught himself short and grinned sheepishly. "Yeah: not very. Or, only in my music."

She nodded. "You're that much like him, anyway."

"You aren't much like her." He realized after he'd said it that it was almost a challenge.

She studied him dispassionately. "I can't tell whether you're glad or sorry."

After a moment he said unhappily, "Glad, I think."

"Oh, Jesse." She moved as if to reach for him, thought better of it, and let her hand fall back onto the arm of the chair. "I'm sorry. I shouldn't have asked."

"No, it's okay." He used both hands to lift his aching leg and move it, still seeking a comfortable position. "We weren't close. I admired her. She worked for me." A rueful smile crinkled the corners of his eyes. "And that about defines both our roles."

"There's analgesic balm in the medicine cupboard."

"What?"

"For your leg," she said.

"It's okay," he said. "It doesn't need anything."

"Right. And I am Marie of Rumania."

"What?"

"It's a line from a poem. Means I don't believe you, that's all. Never mind. If you were my—if you were—" She made a face. "This is so awkward. How do we refer to all these identical twins?" She tried again. "The Jesse I knew, the one who belonged in this world, couldn't tend to his own needs. I'd have had to—" She drew a breath. "Well. You aren't that Jesse. And while a massage would do your leg good, I don't think I have the strength for it right now. So maybe you ought to just put some analgesic balm on it and see if that helps. Was it an auto accident in your world, too?"

"That's what they called it." He rose awkwardly, unable to support his weight on the bad leg and trying to conceal the difficulty. "Wasn't exactly an accident, though. My dad—" He paused, looking at her. "What's he like, in this world? My—Jesse's dad?"

She made a negative gesture without lifting her head. "Hell warmed over. A certifiable monster." She looked at him, her eyes clear and cold. "Mind you, he looks normal enough, pillar of the community and all that, but I've known Jesse a long time. He gets—got—talkative sometimes, on some drugs, or in some moods. I know too much. I think I'd like to tear his father apart with my bare hands."

She made a rueful face. "That sort of thing's frowned on, in polite society. I had to settle for just keeping him away from Jesse." She waved a hand toward the bathroom. "Go. You make me nervous, balancing like a stork and pretending nothing hurts you. We can talk when you've seen to that." She hesitated. "I think there's medication here somewhere, pills I mean, for the pain, if you—if it's bad."

"It isn't that bad." It was, but he couldn't afford to befuddle his mind with drugs. "I need a shower and clean clothes. You'll wait for me?"

"I'm not going anywhere."

When he returned from the bathroom, walking more easily now that a hot shower had eased his stiffening muscles and the analgesic balm had dulled the harsh edge of the pain in his leg, she was in the same position, utterly relaxed in the chair with her head back and her eyes closed. He thought for a moment she was sleeping, but she opened her eyes when he sat opposite her again. He said awkwardly, "You're worn out."

"I'm okay. It's been a very interesting day."

"It isn't over."

She nodded, watching him. "I haven't asked you: where's Dr. Zelig?"

"In another world. Mine, I think."

"You left him there?"

"Not by choice."

"No. You wouldn't." She sighed. "I'm not used to this yet. You're Jesse, and you aren't Jesse. I still tend to—" She shrugged helplessly.

"I know. I've had more time than you to get used to the idea, and I still—well, I don't exactly forget you aren't the Ruth I knew, but there's stuff I take for granted if I don't think about it, you know?"

"I know." She was silent for a moment. "Do you . . . do you know how to get him back? Dr. Zelig?"

"Not sure. How'd you get back?"

She told him. "She's trying to put everybody back in their proper worlds. But she doesn't know about Dr. Zelig, does she?"

"Dunno." He had been fingering the bracelet absently: now he held up his arm to show it to Ruth. "This thing's got something to do with my jumping worlds, before. I'm not sure, but it makes sense. Only . . . if it is this, I don't how to use it."

"Where did you get it?"

"In the parking lot. We were, Doc and me, we were looking for clues about your kidnapping. This is all we found before the cops came after us. Thing is, I had it, and Doc was hangin' onto me, and the cops were shooting at us, and I just kind of wished I was home, you know? In my own world. Doesn't make sense, considering the mess I was in there, but I guess I wasn't thinking of that right then. And what happened, we both ended up there. In my world.

"But he wasn't hanging onto my arm when I saw the Other. He'd said if I saw my . . . what he called doppelganger, one of us would disappear, you know. And I guess he was right, 'cause the minute I saw the Other I was right back here. Without the doc. So from his point of view, I guess I disappeared."

"You think if he'd been touching you . . . ?"

"Worked when we went there," he said.

"And all you do is wish you were somewhere else."

"That's all I did, anyhow. And it worked." He thought about it. "I s'pect you have to wish for some exact place else."

"Yes. It does make sense, Jesse. And I suppose it must be the bracelet." It was a small wonder in a sea of wonders. Neither of them thought to question what it was or where it came from. "It's the only new thing you have, isn't it? And God knows we've all wished, from time to time, that we were someplace else. You must've, ever, and not gone bouncing off to wherever it was, till you wished it with the bracelet."

"That's what I thought. 'Cept of course I never knew about worlds before, so I never wished for one till I knew this one wasn't mine, and the cops were shooting at us. And I had the bracelet, then."

She thought about it. "The times are different. In the different worlds. When Sue Lee Grail found me in your world, the concert was still on. But when she got me back here, it was well over. And you said you saw him, the other you, during his concert. But you got back here just now? When I saw you?"

"Just in time to see your Sue Lee leaving the van, and the cops coming toward you." He grinned ruefully. "Was a little nervous about that. If this was your world, I was in trouble with them for running away. And if it was some other world, I might run into another doppelganger and get bounced off somewhere else. But you looked kinda lonely, and I got all macho protective and came to your rescue. So I thought."

She chuckled. "I'm sorry I didn't need rescuing."

"I'm not. I'd've only got us in worse trouble."

"Are we in trouble?"

"Well, Doc is."

"Yes."

"And you know, it was Banny that went to the cops about you getting kidnapped. Which'd be okay, only Doc saw it happen too, and he knew it wasn't me. He told Banny so. And Banny called the cops anyhow."

"Well, if he saw it happen?" she said hesitantly.

"Yeah, but he knew I was onstage. And that isn't the only thing. He's been kinda weird in other ways."

"What ways?"

"Well, jealous, I guess. He ever make a pass at you or anything?"

"That's not a crime, surely."

"It's just that I've been thinkin'."

It took her a moment. "You mean about the other Ruth? Oh, Jesse. Banny?"

"Not this one," he said quickly, and then made a wry face. "Obviously. Jeez, this is hard. Hard to talk about, hard to think about." He shrugged. "Guess that's not really our problem, anyway. We aren't even in that world."

"But Dr. Zelig is."

"Well, Banny isn't gonna murder him."

She studied him. "You think the Banny here might— what? Harm me? Try to kill me?"

"If the Banny there did," he said reluctantly, "it's something to think about."

After a moment she said firmly, "I think it would do us a lot more good to think about how we're going to get Dr. Zelig back here."

"Gotta go after him, if I can." He did not look eager.

"I think I should go with you."

"What, and maybe get stranded there too? You just got back from there." He shook his head. "I don't want to take the chance."

"I don't exactly, either," she said, "but I think I ought to. I hated being in that other world. But I don't—I don't want to lose you, Jesse." She said it fiercely, daring him to comment.

"Right," he said, grinning. "That's settled."

"What's settled?"

"We'll go together," he said. "If we go at all. Which there isn't any assurance we will."

"We have to try," she said. "But what about the time difference? We don't know what it is, or when we'll end up there. If it does work."

"Maybe I should wish for a time, as well as a place. Just in case."

"That might work. What time?"

"If we're going after Doc, I guess it ought to be during tonight's concert, so we'll still know where he is. He'd prob'ly stay where he was till the concert ended, in case I could come back for him."

She nodded. "Okay. Let's try it." She held out her hand to him.

"You know," he said, taking it, "we'll feel awful silly sitting here holding hands if this doesn't work."

"Not really," she said, smiling.

The question was irrelevant. In this one matter, wishes worked.

26

The Other

I didn't see the Jesse when he showed up backstage at my concert, but I knew the moment he saw me. Since we were in his world, I just about got bounced out of it. But only because I was caught by surprise. I was good enough at playing the gates by then that as soon as I realized what was happening it was no problem to bounce him right back into his adoptive world. It was a simple trick of the mind, like recognizing Beethoven's *Fifth* from the first four notes, or memorizing a song on the first hearing. The audience never noticed a thing.

I knew it when Suli came to watch my concert for a while, too. I don't know why. I didn't have her stone anymore, so it can't have been the two of them (the two of it?) pulling at each other that alerted me. Anyway I knew she couldn't kill me right there in front of a concert audience in a world where the Jesse wouldn't die young without her help, so I wasn't worried what she'd do. It even added a little something to the concert, knowing she was there to hear it.

But she didn't stay long, and the weird thing was that right after she'd gone, the Jesse showed up again. That's when I realized he must've found the gatestone I'd lost in his adoptive world. Which meant he could make life interesting if he felt like it. That worried me.

But he must've actually made a real effort not to see me that time. Not an easy task, I knew. You get near your doppelganger and you just want to see him, so bad it's like a kind of pain almost. And then when you do see him you get bounced (or he does, if you know what you're doing), so it's an urge that never really gets satisfied. It's one of the very few bad things about world-walking that I know of.

And it isn't easy to resist, so that was another thing to worry me. Why would the Jesse come back into his world and then purposely avoid seeing me? Was he learning the rules of this walking business already? What was he planning? Was there any way he could bounce me out of his world even though I knew more about the gates than he did?

I couldn't see that there was, at least not permanently, but he sure as hell could make trouble. 'Specially if he happened to hook up with Suli Grail, which it would be just like her to do. I didn't like this. I didn't like it at all, but there was nothing I could do about it right at the moment, so I kept on with the concert and hoped for the best.

God had not usually granted me the best of anything. He wasn't going to start that night. I was allowed to finish the concert, but the minute I was offstage and out of the public eye Suli and her monitors got to work on their campaign to ruin my life. Together, they had the power to do it, or they thought they had. It was more power than I'd faced before: they had me out of that world and into Limbo before I knew what was happening.

Suli was there. And the first thing she said, before I'd even had time to realize where I was, was, "Jesse, please, listen to me. We've got to talk. For your own good, please—"

That's as far as she got. I've already said what I think of

that phrase. Maybe she didn't mean anything by it, or at least nothing worse than what a lot of innocent people seem to mean by it when they say it, but I can't hear that phrase without remembering my father. It was his excuse for some of the worst things he did to me. And that's all it will ever mean to me: deadly danger.

My reaction, when Suli said it, was automatic and stupid. I jumped back out of there and into the first of my preset situation worlds so fast I prob'ly made a thunderclap in Limbo. I hadn't meant to return to the situation worlds to set off the sabotage so early in the game, but neither had I expected to meet quite such a show of force as Suli had given me by dragging me into Limbo against my will.

There are worlds (Hell's one of them) where the people talk a lot about "turning the other cheek." That's not my way. I'm a survivor. I meet force with force when I can, and I run when I can't, and I don't trip myself up with the kind of high moral principles and self-destructive ideals that make people think it's a good idea, when somebody hits you, to calmly invite him to hit you again. I understand nonviolent resistance, but it's not for me. You can get dead that way, and I like living.

So I hit the first situation world and set off the first situation before Suli and her monitors could get me back to Limbo. Which they did, of course, as quick as they could. I responded by jumping into the second situation world and setting off the second preset situation. I'd laid my plans well: I didn't need a lot of time. When they dragged me back to Limbo the third time I had two worlds set to self-destruct within twenty-four hours, and nobody but me could stop them.

I figured it was the worlds' own faults for being so volatile in the first place. Too bad to risk so many people, but they should've thought of that before they kept the weapons and nation-states and political systems I was using against them. It's not enough to keep talking about nuclear disarmament and world peace and so forth if you don't do anything but talk.

That's the way it was in Hell ever since they used the first nuclear bombs against the Japanese in World War Two, and the situation I'd set up in Hell was one of the easiest political ones I set up anywhere. They'd been on the brink of nuclear disaster for some fifty years. It was just luck they'd made it as long as they had. I figured when I chose 'em, back when I first figured out this would be the best way to show Central you don't mess with the music maker, that I'd be lucky if they waited for my signal to self-destruct. As it happened, though, they did wait. Hell was the second of the situation worlds I jumped into out of Limbo that day.

When Suli and her monitors pulled me back into Limbo, then, I was ready for them. They may've tried to block my jumping again. I don't know. I didn't try. I just stood there and grinned at poor Suli and said as cheerfully as I was able, "What is it you want so bad to talk about for my own good, honey?"

"Jesse, please stay a minute." She looked miserable, but determined.

"I'm staying, already," I said.

"You can't keep walking like this," she said.

"You can't stop me," I said.

"I can," she said, "and I will, if I have to."

We both knew what she meant, but I pretended I didn't. "How you gonna do that, baby?" I put all the smug confidence I could into that. It was no good trying to sound mean with her; I never could do it.

"I'll kill you." Her voice was small, but steady.

"You do, and you'll be killing whole worlds with me." I meant to make that a threat, but my voice came out flat and lifeless. I didn't like what her damn Central had done to her by giving her this job. They should've known what it would do to her to think she'd have to kill me. That wasn't necessary. Plus it wasn't even smart. They should've given the job to some world-walker who didn't care one way or the other about my life; there was no way she could be as quick and efficient about it as somebody would who didn't know me from Adam.

I'd startled her with my threat, flat-voiced or not, and she was staring at me with real fear in her eyes. "What worlds?" she asked. "Why? How? What have you done?"

It was easy to grin into those big golden eyes. She was so damn cute. "Just a little push here and a shove there," I said. "No big deal. Nothing I can't fix—if I'm left free to go where I'm needed."

"What do you mean?"

"It's simplicity itself, honey. You're not paying attention. I've set up some worlds so they're gonna self-destruct if I don't get back to straighten things out."

"You're bluffing."

"You know I'm not."

"You'd really kill whole worlds just for your own freedom?" There was something in her eyes I didn't understand.

"Hey, a guy's gotta look out for himself. Ain't nobody else gonna do it."

"But to kill people?"

"You were gonna kill me."

"If I had to." She was always as honest as she could be. "But that's different."

"How, different? Because I'm not important, and somebody else is?"

"Because you're doing wrong, and all those people in those worlds aren't."

"Some of them are, I betcha." That drew the hint of a smile into her eyes, but it didn't really change anything. I shrugged. "Plus, who's judging? Who has the right to decide I got no right to live?"

"Who gave you the right to decide whole worlds don't deserve to live?"

"I couldn't kill a world that wasn't contemplating suicide in the first place. At least, not without a lot more work than the job would be worth."

"Even if they're contemplating suicide, as you put it, you have no right to make the final decision for them." That's what that strange look in her eyes was about: it was self-righteousness. That, I hadn't expected, not from her.

"Oh, but you have the right to make that final decision for me?"

"It's my job," she said, still looking wounded.

"Okay. Then it's my job to keep you from doing it. I mean, it's everybody's job to stay alive as long as he can, right? So all I'm doing is staying alive."

"By threatening worlds."

"Only because you're threatening me."

"Jesse, for the gods' sake, can't you see? It's different. There's only one of you, and millions, billions of people in a world."

"The one you love is worth a billion you don't."

She shook her head slowly. "Not to me," she said. "Or—not exactly." She looked serious and intent, trying to explain relativity to a child. How could she know I already understood it better than she ever would? "It would hurt me more for you to die than for a billion people I didn't know to die. I wouldn't know them. It would be horrible, but impersonal. Your death, like your life, would be a part of mine. But Jesse, I could live with the idea that I'd killed you. I couldn't live with the idea that I'd killed a billion people, billions of people, a whole world, whether I knew them or not. Can't you see that?"

I shrugged. "You can learn to live with damn near anything, if you have to." I knew. I'd had to, till I got out of Hell.

"Oh, Jesse," she said.

"Careful. That ain't my name anymore, is it?"

"Do you think I care so much about rules?"

"Yes, honey, I think you do."

She was like a little girl used to getting her own way, and having trouble getting it this once. She almost stamped her foot at me; I could see the muscles twitch. "Jesse, you're not being fair."

"So who told you life would be fair?"

She looked at me for a long moment, and then she straightened up and made her face all sober and serious and said very severely, "I think you'd better tell me exactly what you've done, Jesse."

"Done about what?"

"Done to those worlds you mentioned." She was all sober authority now, no jokes. "Which worlds? What did you do to them?"

"You know I can't tell you exactly what I did. You'd try to change it, and who knows, maybe you could even do it. I can't take that chance."

"Then I don't believe you've done anything."

"Oh, I have." It wasn't any problem sounding deadly serious about that, and I could see she believed me.

231

"Which worlds?" she asked again, almost wheedling this time. "Jesse, I have to at least know which worlds."

"Surely your monitors could tell you. I bet they keep a pretty close eye on me these days, don't they?"

"You must know they can't." She stared. "You didn't know, did you?"

This was better than I'd hoped. "They can't?"

She shook her head slowly, dark curls bobbing. "Not clearly, not accurately," she said reluctantly. "Not since you lost my gatestone and started walking on your own."

"Hot damn." I was grinning like an idiot. "For that, honey, I'll give you the name of a world. Check on Hell, why don't you? You know, my home world? Go ahead, check it out. I'll wait."

She didn't have to go anywhere. The monitors, silent till now, revealed themselves at last. After some garbled cursing that seemed to come from thin air, one of them said, "That was your doing?" He didn't sound happy about it.

I was still grinning. I knew they wouldn't like that. "What, the situation in Hell?" I asked the air. "Sure was."

There were a lot more curses. Somebody was becoming boring on the subject of my ancestry, but there was nothing they could say on that topic that would bother me. In fact, I'd said it all before them.

I finally had to ask them to cool it. "Look, we all know my background isn't what it might be," I said. "You can call me a son of whatever you want to all day, but I don't see that it's getting us anywhere. You wanta show off your vocabulary, or you wanta deal?"

"Deal?" said Suli, staring at me like she had no idea what I was talking about. "What do you want?" The monitors finally shut up.

"I told you what I want: freedom."

That got one of the monitors going again, but Suli shushed him with one imperious gesture. "And I told you," she said patiently, "that you can't have the freedom you're used to. You just can't. You're endangering the worlds, weakening the boundaries, strengthening chaos. Can't you understand that?"

"I understand that you believe it," I conceded.

"I believe it because it's true," she said.

"You believe it because you've been told it all your life," I said.

"His home world can't wait while you talk terms," said a monitor, sounding snotty and scared both at once.

"What would you have me do?" asked Suli.

"Go fix it," said the monitor.

"Try, and that world's gone for sure," I said. "I'm sorry, kid, but that's the way I set it up."

"You said maybe I could do it," she reminded me.

"So I did." I grinned. "I got a lot of respect for you; maybe you could. Wanta try?"

"It's a trap, isn't it?" she said.

I shrugged. "I hope so." I waited a minute, then added, maybe a little sheepishly, "And I hope you don't try me on it. I wouldn't like to lose you." It was a hell of a thing to say right then with everybody listening in, but I figured it was the best chance I had at keeping her out of Hell.

She thought about it. "Jesse, tell me what you did."

"Nothing much, really," I said. "They've got hundreds of little nation-states and a bunch of big ones, all at each other's throats all the time, right? So I just went to a bunch of different leaders and let 'em know what I could do: jumping time, disappearing, going through locked doors, that kind of thing. Made 'em think I was some kind of superman. Which naturally they saw as super-*weapon*.

"And I told 'em there was a whole world of people like me, able to do all that same stuff. I told 'em you guys were warlike monsters who were after me 'cause I was such a peaceable guy. I only wanted world peace with them in charge, but you guys wanted to rule the universe. I told 'em you'd go to their enemies, ally with them, attack the good guys. Convinced 'em they'd better strike first. Then convinced 'em not to strike yet: not till they saw some sign you were there, see what I mean?"

"Jesse, they might take anything as a sign we're there."

"And blow each other up." I nodded. "I give 'em twenty-four hours at best."

"And if I go, if I try to talk to them—"

I shrugged. "Maybe you can convince them I'm the bad guy. I told 'em you'd try."

She shook her head. "You have to go back, Jesse. You have to straighten this out."

"Why should I?"

"They'll die!"

"We'll all die," I said. "It's just a matter of timing. Nobody wants to do it now."

"Jesse, I can't promise you freedom. Even if I thought you should have it I couldn't. I could maybe, maybe, get you permission to stay in one single world that wasn't yours, but I can't get you permission to keep walking."

"I never much liked Hell, anyway," I said. "Rotten place. Might as well let it blow."

"It's just a world, Jesse. It's not that different from the one you've just been living in."

"It's different, all right."

She shook her head. "Not really. You just think it is, because you want it to be. So nothing that happened in Hell will be your fault."

234

I wasn't ready for that. I just about hit her. For a minute it was all I could do to hold still and wait for my vision to clear. Then I said, very carefully, but maybe not very convincingly, "It wasn't my fault."

"Oh, Jesse, I didn't mean what your father did to you. Of course that wasn't your fault. Don't you know that? He was sick, evil, what he did to you was vile. You didn't deserve it, not any of it. You were just a little boy, how could you deserve that?"

"I wasn't always a little boy." I don't know why I was arguing for my own guilt, except that on some level I knew I was guilty and now I was half-hoping she could prove me wrong. But of course she couldn't.

"Inside somewhere, you've always been a little boy, at least in relation to him," she said. It wasn't enough, and she knew it. "Jesse, it's natural you couldn't fight him, couldn't stop him. It's what he trained you to think, that you deserved what he did to you. But you didn't, Jesse. You didn't. It wasn't your fault!"

I wanted to believe her. "Right. It wasn't my fault, and Hell isn't just another world. If it was, I could've done something with my life. Like the Jesses in the other worlds. When Dad killed my dancing I could've made another life with some other kind of music. Like they did."

She knew I didn't mean it. "You could've, Jesse. They started with the same thing you did. Including your father."

"They didn't start in Hell."

"It wasn't the world, Jesse. It was you."

"You said it wasn't my fault." I sounded sullen.

"What happened to you, what was done to you, wasn't your fault. What you did with it, what you did afterward, that was your fault. You just gave up. You never accepted responsibility for your life. You just blamed your father,

235

your world, your God, and you never really tried."

"World-walker, be careful," said the air, in a voice he hadn't heard before. "Remember what you're dealing with, here. If you goad him into an adolescent rage he'll run away without even trying to save his home world."

Suli looked up suddenly, her expression startled. "Jud?" she said, and blushed. "I mean—"

"The monitors thought it best to call me," the voice said in a tone that meant she was right about who he was. I knew they weren't supposed to call each other by name, though she'd never said why, exactly. Something about spending their time in worlds where their names belonged to their doppelgangers.

"We don't need you, Jud," I said.

"Perhaps not," he said, "but it's my job to be here. Tell me, did you really imagine we'd barter with you for the safety of your home world?"

"Of course I did," I blurted, shocked. Everything I knew about people said they would. "Would you rather let them die?"

"Oh, I don't think that's the question, is it?" said Jud. "Obviously you can't save them now. You must have meant Hell as an example, only. But I'm curious, what did you hope to prove?"

"That you don't mess with the music maker," I said. "But you're wrong. I could save them."

"Naturally you'd want us to think so. You're supposed to be all-powerful, then? That's the meaning of this 'music maker' title you've given yourself?"

"I got it. You're trying to use reverse psychology. You think I'll save them just to prove I can."

"No." He sounded absolutely certain of that. "I don't think you can. I think you've bitten off more than you can

chew, my boy, and I don't quite know what we're going to
do about you, now."

"You really don't think I could save Hell if I wanted to?"
I was sure this was reverse psychology, and at the same time
I was falling for it. I wanted to prove I could do what he
said I couldn't.

"If you could," he said, "or rather, if you did, you'd be
in a better bargaining position than you are now."

"What'll you give me if I save 'em?"

He didn't hesitate. "I'll give you my consideration, my
boy. I'll hear your case."

"Big deal. You're hearing it now."

"Not with any intent to bargain, however."

"So it's a standoff. That's what you're saying?"

"Unless you save that world."

I thought about it. "It's not the only world I put in
danger," I said.

"I'm aware of that. But since we can't find any others, I
think they must not be in as imminent danger."

"Not quite," I said, "but you won't see it till it blows
up." I wished I could see his face. "You better believe it: if I
save Hell, you still need me to save the other."

"I'll grant you that, for the moment," he said. "Though I
make no guarantees if we find a way to do it ourselves."

"Try, and the world I targeted dies. It's not the same
setup as on Hell, but it's just as effective. You need me." It
wasn't easy, bargaining with a disembodied voice. I wanted
to see how he was reacting to things, but I could only guess
from the tone of his voice.

It wasn't much help. It was dry and papery and sounded
about a thousand years old. "Right now, yes," he said. "We
need you. Will you save your home world, boy?"

There wasn't really any choice after all, and I knew time

must be getting short. Besides, I was getting tired of Limbo. The dust hurt my throat. "Sure. Give me a minute," I said, and jumped back into Hell. The job wouldn't take long. I'd planned that part, too.

It was ironic, really. The simplest way to save that world from a terminal war was to unite its nation-states against an outside enemy they could all believe in: me. When I was finished with it, Hell would be politically healthier than it had ever been in its recorded history. It might not deserve the name Hell anymore.

And it wouldn't be a safe prison for me anymore, not if I was meant to have a chance to live. Even the tyrants at Central might think twice about trying to send me back to a world bent on killing me—unless they were bent on killing me themselves. If I could convince them they needed me alive (and on their heads be it, if they didn't believe that!), they'd have to think of something else to do with me. Like maybe let me walk where I wanted.

They might just as well agree to it. I'd do it, whether they liked it or not.

27

Ruth

Three Jesses, at intervals, seemed difficult and unlikely but just barely believable. Two Jesses, at once, proved wholly disorienting. When she took Jesse's hand, Ruth was prepared for the peculiarity of the sudden transition from van to backstage area, but she was not prepared for the shock of seeing another Jesse onstage, just finishing his concert, while she still held the hand of the one she had come with. She had known the Other would be there, of course. But it was an intellectual acceptance only; confronted with the reality, her emotions rebelled. It was simply not possible.

"Ruth! Jesse!" Dr. Zelig came hurtling out of the shadows, arms outstretched to embrace them both, nearly strangling Ruth in his excitement. "I was not knowing whether I would ever be seeing either of you again."

"We weren't quite sure of it ourselves," said Ruth. A roar of applause from the arena informed them that the concert was ending. "Jesse, we'd better get out of here." The band members were bounding offstage, coming toward them. Darla didn't notice them, Bob Lyle merely gazed at them in a bemused way, Mirabelle looked confused when she saw them, and Ruth never noticed where the Other was. She was mesmerized by the sheer malevolence of Banny Averill's stare.

Jesse was facing the other way and couldn't see any of

them. She wanted to beg him to get her away from there, away from Banny, but the words died in her throat. Banny moved toward them, his gaze as compelling as it was evil. Dr. Zelig said something, but Ruth couldn't hear him. There was a curious roaring in her ears that drowned everything: despite Zelig's and Jesse's arms around her, she felt as though she were alone with Banny, defenseless, unable even to protest, able only to stare into those demented eyes in patient horror.

"Ruth, you okay?" asked Jesse.

Banny had disappeared. For one long moment she was unable to comprehend that she had somehow, after all, been saved. Then consciousness returned, and she understood that the entire band was gone. The diminishing roar of the crowd was gone. They were no longer backstage at the arena; they were safely home in the van again, Zelig and Jesse and she in her own world, where Banny, the Banny she knew, would never look at her like that with death in his eyes.

"Oh, Jesse," she said, and sat down suddenly in the nearest chair. "You didn't see him." She glanced at Zelig. "Did you? Did you see Banny, just now? The Banny in that world, I mean?"

Zelig shook his head. "You are feeling alarmed by that Banny?" he asked.

She nodded emphatically. "Very much alarmed. If you'd seen the way he looked at me!"

Zelig and Jesse exchanged a knowing look. "He'd be real pissed to see us together again," said Jesse.

"He might be losing what little control he has left," said Zelig, "if after what he has done he is still seeing Ruth in your arms."

"Banny did kill her, then?" asked Ruth.

Jesse eased himself into the chair next to her, his bad leg awkwardly extended, one hand rubbing it absently. "Guess he must've." His face was pale and set, his eyes unforgiving.

"But why?" It was a frightened wail.

Jesse shrugged. "Hard to know why anybody'd do a thing like that." His voice was as cold and unforgiving as his eyes.

"You said jealousy," said Ruth. "But you don't just chop somebody up because they prefer somebody else to you."

"*You* don't," said Zelig.

"But it doesn't make sense," said Ruth.

"Murder don't ever make sense," said Jesse. He managed a reassuring smile, incongruous in the gaunt, bruised pallor of his face. "He can't hurt you here."

She shuddered. "I'll never look at Bancroft Averill the same way again. If you could have seen his eyes!"

"But that was the Banny from my world, not yours," said Jesse, still trying to reassure her.

"And you said this one's been acting strange," said Ruth. "We know he reported the Other to the cops as you, even after Dr. Zelig told him it wasn't you."

"That doesn't mean anything." Jesse achieved an almost convincing grin. "How the hell's he s'posed to believe it wasn't me when he saw me plain as day? He doesn't know anything about parallel worlds."

It was a valid point, but it wasn't enough. "He knows Dr. Zelig," she said stubbornly.

"Never have I been trusting him," said Zelig, his tone conversational. "Tell me, I am making coffee. I will make some for each of you?"

"Sure," said Jesse, never taking his gaze from Ruth. "I'll get rid of him, Ruth. Now. Tonight. There's got to be another rhythm guitarist in San Francisco who can take his place, at least temporarily."

For just a moment she relaxed in the heady relief of safety. But reality intruded. "You can't kick him out of the band because his doppelganger scares me." She sighed heavily, knowing there was no safety from such groundless fears. "No, I'm being silly, Jesse. I'm sorry. I'm just tired, and—I don't know. Tired." She shook her head wearily. "Forget it, okay? I'll be all right."

"Banny won't," he said certainly. "No, I'll get rid of him." At her look he added quickly, "Don't worry, I'll be polite as hell about it. I know he hasn't done anything really. But I don't like him, and I don't trust him, and I won't take a chance with your life. There's no real reason to keep him. There's other guitarists, and I don't owe him anything that can't be paid in money."

Dr. Zelig turned from his industrious fussing with hot water, instant coffee, and cups. "We are forgetting one thing, is it not?"

"Dunno," said Jesse, eyeing him warily. "What're we forgetting?"

"You don't belong here," said Zelig. "Will you be allowed to stay here?"

Jesse's chin lifted defiantly. "Who's to stop me?"

Ruth felt the blood leaving her face. "Sue Lee Grail," she said in a small, shocked voice. "Oh, Jesse. I hadn't thought of that." She stared at him, instinctively trying to memorize the lines and planes of his face, the pure blue of his eyes and gold of his hair, the odd little quirk of a smile at one corner of his mouth, because she suddenly felt as though he might disappear without warning at any moment.

"Who is this Sue Lee Grail, please?" asked Zelig.

Ruth told him, aware her voice sounded as hopeless as she felt. "She was trying to get everybody into the right worlds. When she's got the Other out of Jesse's world, she'll take Jesse there." It was a childlike wail of desolation. She couldn't help it: she could not bear this.

Jesse's hand closed over hers. "Then I'll come back," he said. "I won't leave you."

Ruth stared at him, wanting to believe him, knowing she couldn't. "She'll take the bracelet. She won't let you come back."

"She won't stop me." Those clear blue eyes made it a promise. "I won't leave you, now I've found you."

She managed a small, frail smile. "You make it sound like you'd been searching and searching for me forever," she said unsteadily.

"I think I was," he said.

"Here is the coffee," said Zelig, bringing a tray from the hotplate to the table next to them. "But you must telling me, Jesse, because I am not knowing whether you are like our other Jesse in this, or whether you are different. You will have it with cream and sugar, or without, please?"

28
Jud

He had not, of course, been called physically to the monitoring station. He had been alerted, and his window had been transformed into a monitoring screen, and he was able to watch the scene in Limbo and communicate with its participants from the comfortable chair behind his own massive black desk. Which was fortunate, because otherwise he might have missed the young Ariel's visit to his office.

It was the first time he had seen a youthful member of her race. They were all of them, invariably, stunningly beautiful through most of their lives, becoming as grotesque as the older Ariel he knew only in their declining years. He had heard that, of course, but he had never seen it before. He had no idea who she was when she arrived.

"You're Jud," she said, tripping lightly across his office and sitting gracefully in the hard acrylic guest chair. Her costume was similar in style to the witch-robes worn by her older self, but the fabric was soft and sheer and settled slowly around her like silken cobwebs, disturbed by the smallest breeze. Her raven hair cascaded about her shoulders with an oddly silvery sheen, as though trapped stars were hidden under the heavy tresses. Her face was perfect, transcendently beautiful, unhuman in its ineffable loveliness, radiant with mirth.

She suited her name: she was a sprite, a pixie, a creature

of mist and moonlight and magic. When she smiled at him it took his breath away. "I'm Ariel, don't you know me?" she said. "I thought I'd have been here a lot of times before."

He swallowed. "Ariel . . . Greef?"

She nodded, eyes dancing with merriment. "I must have been here only in my later years, is that it?"

"Yes." The one dry syllable rasped in his throat.

"Oh, Jud." Her laughter was the silvery tinkling of fairy bells. "If you could only see your face!"

"You've surprised me," he said. A glance at the window/screen showed him that the Other was still gone from Limbo, and Suli Grail still waiting patiently in the vast expanse of featureless sand. The Other would not take long; or, rather, if the job took long he would jump time to get back shortly after he left, but Suli would have to hold him somehow till Jud could attend to them. He touched a button to mute the volume and turned his chair to face the youthful Ariel. "What can I do for you?" His voice was not quite steady. He cleared his throat.

"I chose you, didn't I? Later? I mean, I have been here before, haven't I?" For just a moment the bright glow of her eyes was shadowed. "I'm not wrong about that?"

"You've been here before," he said.

"Oh, good. You seemed likeliest, but I wasn't sure. Time is so confusing, isn't it?" She smiled at him merrily. "It's very strange to meet someone for the first time when you know very well he first met you a long time before, when you were older." She laughed again, that joyous ripple of chimes as sweet and clear as starlight. "Has that happened to you?"

"Often." He waited, watching her.

"I haven't done it a lot, yet," she said confidingly. "But I expect I'll get used to it."

"You will," he said dryly.

She tilted her head to one side, studying him soberly. "I suppose I hadn't even the kindness to warn you this would happen?"

"I guessed," he said.

She nodded slowly. "Yes, I see you would. I apologize for my older self, Jud ut Snydof ipFrendle Massengwenta."

That surprised him. He hadn't imagined she had ever bothered to look up his full name, much less commit it to memory. "Your older self is—older," he said inadequately.

"Yes, I expect I will be." Another of those dazzling smiles lit her face. It should have been impossible to be austerely serene and so mirthfully joyous, both at once, but she was. "Well, I hope you've enjoyed working with me, even if I will be rude."

He permitted himself a small answering smile. "It has not been an unmixed blessing," he admitted. "But now—" He hesitated, glancing at the window/screen. The Other was still absent, but surely he would not remain so for much longer.

"You've work to do," she said cheerfully. "I know." She, too, glanced at the window/screen, and it seemed to him that in that moment all the light went out of her eyes. "Oh," she said. "Oh, that poor child."

"I beg your pardon?"

She stared at him blindly. "So young," she said.

"Ariel?" he said. "What is it?"

She blinked, and the light was back in her eyes as though it had never gone. She studied him, a humorous half-smile pulling at her lips. "What is what? Did I say something wrong?" She honestly didn't know.

He shook his head slowly. "No." He had dealt with her

race before, though never one so young. Doubtless she was not accustomed, yet, to the mild precognitive episodes they sometimes suffered. He wondered bleakly what she had seen ahead for Suli Grail, but it was no use asking. She would know no more than he. Whatever it was, it was gone now, into the future, irretrievable and probably unalterable, else she would have been able to give a clearer warning. "No, you said nothing wrong."

She studied him a moment longer. "Did I foresee something? Oh, dear, I am sorry. Was it clear, at all?"

He shifted his shoulders. "No."

"That usually means it's tied to personalities, you know. I mean, you can alter circumstances, but you can't alter how people will be, so—sometimes there's nothing you can do."

"I know." He moved his shoulders again, irritably this time. "Don't worry about it, child. Just tell me why you're here."

"Oh, that," she said, and smiled as gaily as though nothing untoward had happened. "Well, I wanted to warn you, you know. About me and the gates. I'll be spending a lot of time in them, and I'm not sure you realize how they affect my memory."

"I've noticed," he said dryly.

"I forget things, you know," she confided. "Probably I'll forget quite a lot more by the time you first meet me."

"Probably," he said.

"So you mustn't count on me too much, you see. I'll do what I can, but the search is going to take a long time, and we, my people I mean, are not meant for this kind of magic."

"The gates aren't magic," he said.

She laughed happily. "Semantics," she said. "What would you call them, technology?"

"No more than I would call the wind technology. Or the sun, or the stars."

"A natural phenomenon," she said, nodding brightly. "So's magic, didn't you know that?"

"My race does not indulge," he said.

"What, in magic? You've none at all?"

"None," he said.

"How sad," she said, and then brightened. "Or maybe not so sad, since you're a world-walker, because I suppose then you'd have the same problem I have, so maybe it's really lucky. People whose worlds have magic are only supposed to go through the seasonal gates, you know. Full of the moon and that sort of thing. It's very limiting." She sighed, but instantly smiled again, eyes dancing. "Oh, well. I expect I'll get it done, whatever it is I'm going to do, anyway."

"You don't know?" he asked, startled.

"Whether I'll get it done?" she asked.

"No, what it is," he said. "You said 'whatever it is,' as though you didn't know." He stared. "How can you know to come here if you don't even know what we're going to be doing?"

"Oh. That. No, I don't know. But I know I'll be looking for something for a very long time before we'll work together. And I must find it, or I don't think we would work together. So I'll get that much done, anyway, won't I? And then I'll have you to help with the rest."

"Whatever it is," he said, shoulders twitching.

"Exactly." She bestowed a blinding smile on him. "No wonder I chose you. You're so understanding."

"You're so young," he said in instant response.

Silver fairy bells again. "Yes, I am, aren't I? You know what? I'll bet it's vanity, more than anything."

"Vanity?" he asked, bewildered.

"Why I came here just now," she said. "You said you'd already noticed I forget things, so it must not have been that. I mean, you'd think I'd have realized you'd know that." She giggled, a silvery ripple of delight. "I'll bet I just didn't want you to have only seen me old. We're very vain in our early years, you know."

"I didn't know." A smile tugged at his lips. "I can see why."

"I'm so glad," she said. "I feel much better now. Look, there's another person on your screen now. Had you better get back to work, do you think?"

"Yes." He glanced at the screen; the Other had returned. There was not time until later to wonder whether it was the sight of his face, here in Jud's office, that had led Ariel to the Other in her search for a Natural. Now there was only time to turn up the screen's volume and say over his shoulder, "Thank you for coming. You'd best go." There was no response. He glanced at the empty chair across the desk from him, smiled to himself at the ways of children and witches, and turned back to the screen.

A quick glance at the monitors' notes typed out at the bottom of the screen showed that the Other had saved his home world from destruction, but his actions there had become pivotal. Odd: they'd had no indication this Jesse Farrell was pivotal. Yet instead of killing a world, he'd created one. Now there was a Hell on the verge of self-destruction as always, and a new Hell safe from that particular death indefinitely.

And the Jesse Farrell who was called the Other was grinning at Suli Grail and asking smugly, "Satisfied?"

On Jud's screen, Suli scowled at the Other and asked the air, "Did he do it?"

The Other didn't wait for an answer. "You know I did. Come on, bargain time. There are other worlds on the line. You gonna keep messing with the music maker, or you wanta see them go down?"

"I don't quite know what to say," said Jud, stunned.

"Hey! You said you'd talk terms if I saved Hell."

"Yes," said Jud. "I did say that."

"So? Let's talk." The Other scowled at the air around him, eyes blind with the effort to see what was not there.

"You didn't exactly do what you said you would."

"I stopped the bastards from blowing each other up."

"In a sense, you did," said Jud. He thought about it while the Other fumed. "Go back and take a look at Hell now," he said at last.

The Other's entire body went rigid with frustrated fury. "You son of a—"

"Hold it!" Jud's voice held command enough to keep the Other from jumping, at least for a moment. "You listen to me, young man. I meant what I said. You think you can't go back to Hell because you've set yourself up as that world's personal devil, right? But you're wrong. That's not Hell. Not any more so than any of the V4G worlds ever were. The world you call Hell is unchanged. Your actions have not affected it. You did not threaten it and you have not saved it. You never returned to it."

The Other wanted to fly into a fit of rage, but there was nothing to rebel against except a disembodied voice that held too much conviction to be readily disbelieved. Suli Grail, the only immediately available target, was listening with as much puzzlement as the Other. He clenched his fists, bit back his fury, and said very carefully, "That doesn't make sense. What are you talking about?"

"I'm talking about damage to the universe, son," Jud

said wearily. "It's as much a crime to create a world as it is to destroy one."

"To do what?" The Other didn't notice Suli's look of shock and disbelief; he was too intent on what Jud was saying. "To do what did you say?" Distrust and growing fury were evident in every tense, graceful line of his body. "I didn't create nothing."

"You created a world."

"The hell you say. What's your game, anyway?"

"It's no game," said Jud.

The Other thought about it, scowling at the sand. "You mean that, don't you?"

"I mean it," said Jud. "You can go look, if you want to. You'll find your home world unchanged."

"The Hell you say. That isn't possible. I set 'em up for war, and then I turned it into peace. I didn't create any new worlds, I just mucked with an old one."

"And thereby created a new one," said Jud. He sighed heavily. "Don't you understand, that's how the worlds are created: by the pivotal actions of their inhabitants. Your world has been on the brink of self-annihilation for years. Your actions haven't changed that. Instead, they've created a new world. Once you turned that brink-of-war into lasting peace, a new world split off at the point at which your meddling began. Oh, you could make a case for the fact that the new world is your world too, since the split occurred after you left and you've therefore created no new Jesse Farrell. But the fact remains that you did create a new world."

"If what I did made a new world, why didn't you tell me that when I was here before?"

"Because you hadn't made a new world then. It wasn't the threat of war that caused the split. It was the advent of peace."

251

The Other flung both arms out in manifest frustration. "But they wouldn't have peace if I hadn't done what I did."

"That is correct."

"Then, what you're saying, somehow the world, or God, or whatever, waited till I'd made peace, then went back and split off a new world at an earlier time? That's crazy."

"No, it's relative," said Jud. "Time is relative. Son, I can't explain the mechanics of the universe to you now. The point is, you've created a world that wasn't meant to be."

"If you say so." He shrugged, rolling his eyes. "So I made a new world. Big deal." After a moment, he smiled to himself. "Music maker. World builder. Hot damn." Sobering, he turned to Suli and said, "I'm sorry, babe. Seems like I break the rules even when I don't mean to."

"Don't go," she said quickly.

"She's right," said Jud. "We have to talk, and we will talk, sooner or later. For your own good—" He broke off: the Other was gone. Suli was alone again in that awful wasteland of glittering red sand, a curious smile playing at the corners of her mouth.

She tilted her head back, putting her face more clearly on the monitor screens. "I should've warned you," she said. "I found out that's the one thing you don't ever say to Jess—to the Other. Not if you want to continue the conversation."

"What is?" Jud asked irritably.

"For your own good," she said. "I don't know why, but he always jumps if you say that. Almost before you've finished saying it. It's as though it frightens him."

Jud, who had no knowledge of the Other's childhood, but wide knowledge of human nature in all its infinite and awful manifestations, said bleakly, "I suppose it does."

After a moment, Suli said tentatively, "Now what, sir?"

"Go after him," said Jud. "Bring him back."

She hesitated. "If I can't—" She cleared her throat. "If I can't bring him back . . ."

Jud, horribly conscious of the listening and recording monitors, gave her the only response he was authorized to give. "Kill him."

29

Jesse

When Jesse told Ruth he would get rid of Bancroft Averill that very night, he meant it; but when he tried to rise a few minutes later, realizing that if he delayed too long he would not have the strength or energy left to perform any more demanding task than to take himself to bed, it became clear that he had delayed too long already.

His muscles had stiffened till the least movement was agony. His bruised ribs made every breath a small misery when he wasn't exerting himself; when he was, as in the effort to haul himself out of the restful comfort of his chair, it was sheer torture. And when he had dragged himself up, precariously balanced on his good leg, and tried the strength of his crippled leg, it folded under his weight.

He was able to save himself from falling by sitting back down very suddenly, but it was not graceful, and the jar of landing was a painful shock to his already aching ribs. He had finally reached the limit of his endurance. For a long moment all he could do was sit in dazed silence, trying not to breathe.

Ruth smiled at him, heavy-eyed, from her own weary sprawl across the table and said mildly, "Even superheroes have to rest from time to time. You can deal with Banny in the morning. Let's lock up and get some sleep."

That it was phrased as a suggestion, not an order, was

acknowledgment of the change in their relationship. She spoke to him, not to the Jesse she had known before. And she was right: he could accomplish nothing useful in this condition. "Yeah, okay." He waved away Zelig's hastily offered support. "Move over, Doc. You're as tired as I am. I can lean on the furniture to get myself to bed."

"Of a certainty," said Zelig, looking dubious.

Jesse lurched out of his chair again, onto his good leg. Leaning over to grip a chair back in one hand, he put the other hand flat on the little kitchen counter and swung himself one long step toward the beds at the back of the van. "See? I can do it." His arms shook with the effort.

Zelig nodded earnestly. "It is only that I am expecting you might be too prideful to behave thus, you understand. Sometimes you—that is, he—" He paused, looking confused.

"I know he was," said Jesse. "Sometimes I am, too. But not tonight. Tonight I'm too damn beat for pride." He found another pair of supports and swung himself another step toward bed. "What the hell, so I look like a cripple. That's okay: I am a cripple." He grinned ruefully. "Come on, you guys. Quit staring at the freak show and get yourselves to bed. We got business to take care of in the morning."

He had barely fallen asleep when the touch of a hand on his arm woke him. Had he been less on edge about Banny, he might never have awakened enough to know what happened to him, but even in sleep he remembered that threat, and instinctively grabbed at the hand that touched him.

When he had pried his eyes open enough to see, it took him a moment to recognize her; he had seen her only once before, fleetingly, in the darkened parking area. Memory returned in a rush when he looked dizzily around the room and realized with a shock that they were not in the van. "What—?" His grip on her arm tightened. "Where are we? What have you done?"

"You're hurting me," she said mildly.

"You're Sue Lee Grail," he said stupidly. "The world-walker."

She nodded. "If you keep hurting me, I'll have to hurt you to get free." It wasn't a threat, just shared information.

He loosened his grip, but did not let her go; he knew she would disappear if he did, and he would be trapped wher-ever she had brought him. The bracelet was in her hand, not on his arm. He reached for it, but she held it away from him easily. "What've you done?" he repeated.

"I've brought you home," she said. "This is where you belong. Let me go, Jesse."

"No." He shook his head, more in an effort to clear it than in denial, and blearily indicated the bracelet. "That's mine," he said.

"No, it's mine. I need it, Jesse. I've sent the universal stone I was using back to Central. I need this one to chase the Other."

"The Other." He shook his head again, cursing the fa-tigue that made him so stupid. "I don't care about the Other. Where am I? Where's Ruth?"

"You're in your hotel room, in your home world," she said patiently. "Ruth is dead."

"No." He struggled to a sitting position without letting go of her arm. "No, not that Ruth. This isn't my world any-more." He scowled up at her, blinking against the fog of ex-haustion that blurred both vision and thoughts. If he lost the bracelet, he was trapped. Somehow he had to get it away from her. "Sue Lee, hey, look, I don't belong here anymore. Let the Other have this world, okay? Please." His voice sounded frail, like a frightened child's. He cleared his throat. "The Other wants it, I don't. Let me have the bracelet so I can get back to the world I was in."

"I can't do that." Her eyes were the color of topaz. "You do belong here, Jesse. And leaving you here puts one more complication in the Other's way." Her voice was cold steel. "Let go; I should be after him."

"Hunh-uh." He tightened his grip again automatically, thinking as fast as his sleep-dazed mind would permit. "He'll just come back and bounce me outa here," he said. "What if I bounce into Limbo or some damn place instead of Ruth's world? Come on, you can't leave me here, dammit!"

"I must," she said implacably. "I am sworn to uphold the order, peace, and integrity of the worlds, and that includes keeping people in the worlds they belong in." She hesitated. "I am sorry, Jesse," she said.

He didn't see the blow coming, but he knew what had happened when he woke alone in his hotel room the next morning with a sore jaw. Considering the state he'd been in the night before, it wouldn't have taken much to put him out, but it was still humiliating to know it had been done by a woman. A small one at that. And one he'd been holding to keep her from walking away.

That thought brought him fully awake and upright in the bed to stare at his bare left wrist. The realization hit him like a blow. She had walked away, and she had taken the magic bracelet with her. He was trapped in a single world. And while it might be the world he'd started from and therefore theoretically the one he belonged in, it was not the world where Ruth was.

He had known it would matter. He had even known it would hurt, if this happened. He had not realized it would make this awful, aching emptiness within him, as though some essential part of him had died. He had not known the loss of her would be the loss of eternity; would shatter the universe and leave him frail and futile among the fragments, trembling with rage and grief and bitter, desolate despair.

He did not scream. He did not howl, or cry, or shout for her, or impotently pound his fists against whatever they could reach. He even made it to the bathroom before he was sick. But only just.

Afterward, sitting on the cold tile floor with his back to the wall listening to the toilet flushing, all he could think was how ironic, what a cosmic joke it was, that after all the years of pushing away anyone who got too close to him, he should now find himself this hopelessly far from the one person he had not wanted to push away. But he should have known. He should have seen it coming. It was a lesson he ought to have learned a long time ago: everything he had ever really wanted had been taken from him. Only his music remained, the one thing they couldn't take away, and this time it wasn't enough.

He remembered the way Ruth had smiled at him last night, her eyes heavy with sleep, her sweet face dazed and innocent as a child's. The way the light played in her hair, and outlined the soft curve of her cheekbone against shadows. The way she had of tilting her head to listen to him, eyes dancing with laughter. The trusting curl of her hand in his. A strangled sound tore at his throat and he bent forward, arms folded protectively over his head as if in defense against intolerable pain.

She had known what would happen, if he hadn't. She had warned him. He remembered the way she had looked at him when she said it, eyes huge and dark in the pinched white oval of her face. He should have held her, then. He should have told her he loved her. It would have been little enough to leave her with, but better than empty promises he had no way to keep.

"Please," he said. "Please." But if he made any sound at all it was drowned in the echo of his father's laughter. "Did you think you were gonna get what you wanted, boy?" asked his father. "I told you, and I told you." The words were always punctuated by blows. "You. Don't. Get. Nothing." And the small, steady voice of the boy soldier inside whispered over and over again, "Never let them know what you want. Never let them know what you want. Never let them know . . ." But he spoke too late.

In some sane corner of his mind he knew that his father no longer ruled his life, and that whatever gods watched over worlds, they could almost certainly not be bothered keeping track of what he wanted just so they could take it away from him. But this hurt went too deep for logic. He was as defenseless against it as the battered boy he had been was against his father. The difference was that then he thought he would die. Now he wished he could.

"Hey, Jess! You awake?"

It was Bob Lyle, calling from the living room of their suite. Jesse became aware that he was huddled in a little ball on the bathroom floor, and sat up dizzily. His face was wet. He could still hear his father.

"Jess! Hey! You awake or what?"

His father wasn't there. He was in a bathroom in the wrong world in a hotel suite his father had never seen. He tried to answer Lyle, but his voice wouldn't work. It didn't matter; he didn't know what he had meant to say. He leaned his head against the wall and closed his eyes, then opened them suddenly and wide when what he saw in the dark of memory was Ruth's sweet, trusting smile. "Never let them know." Too late.

Gripping the edge of the sink above him with both hands, he hauled himself to his feet and turned on the faucet to splash cold water on his face. When Lyle yelled again he said, "Yeah, I'm awake." Then he looked down at the terrycloth pullover robe he was wearing, realized it wasn't right for this world, and added, "Just a minute."

His suitcase was in the bottom of the bathroom closet. Even as he tossed the robe into it and pulled on a shirt and pants more appropriate for this world, he wondered why he bothered. It was not as though world-walking were a guilty secret. There was hardly a need to hide it; no one would believe it if he announced it onstage.

"What's up?" he asked, emerging from his bedroom at last with only the smallest trace of a residual limp from muscles stiffened on a cold bathroom floor.

An enormous bear of a man, Lyle was sprawled on the couch in his underwear, a cigarette in one hand and a half-eaten doughnut in the other. His auburn hair was an unruly mass of tangles that shadowed the sparkling green of his eyes. For a long, still moment he stared at Jesse warily. Then a slow grin spread over his broad, homely face. "Hot damn," he said. "It's you again, isn't it?"

Jesse stared. "What, you were expecting somebody else with the same name?"

"Yes, as a matter of fact," said Lyle. "Jess, what the hell's going on? I didn't know you had a twin—and what's the idea of trying to fob him off on us as you? Izzat your idea of a joke, or what?"

Stunned, Jesse caught at the back of a chair for support. "You knew?" His voice cracked. "You saw he wasn't me?"

"Hell yes," Lyle said. "Don't tell me you really thought I wouldn't! Oh, don't worry, I didn't let on to the others, and your twin kept up his part just fine, but jeez, Jess! You coulda warned me."

"Couldn't." Jesse stared at him. "How the hell'd you know it wasn't me?"

Lyle shrugged massively. "I dunno. Just wasn't. Hey, you really thought you could fool somebody that's known you as long as I have, for God's sake? All we been through, and that?" He shook his head. "I dunno, Jess. But how come you never told me you had a twin? Where's he been all these years? Where'd he come from now, for that matter?

"He's damn near as good as you, did you know that? The kids out front never guessed, I'll tell you that. Hell, the guys in the band didn't, either. But except for Mirabelle they're not the most alert group in the world. And you know how Mirabelle is. I mean hey, she coulda guessed, and I wouldn't know. You can't tell what that woman's thinking." He stubbed out his cigarette and picked up a cup of coffee, glanced at it, and put it down again. "But dammit, Jesse, the point is, why the hell did you do it? What's the point?"

Jesse looked blindly around the room, gathering his wits. What could he say? The truth was preposterous, and he was too numb with grief to think beyond it. "Where're the others?" he asked distractedly.

"Oh, sleeping, out to breakfast, who knows?" Lyle waved his arms ambiguously. "Don't change the subject, Jess. Come on. Spill it. What's going on?"

"Long story," he said dismissively.

Lyle wasn't so easily dismissed. "Figured that," he said. "You in some kinda trouble, or what? I mean, besides the bizarre stuff about Ruth, which I guess is over now that she's showed up again?"

Jesse shook his head. "Not the kinda trouble you mean."

261

He eyed Lyle's doughnut, suddenly aware of ravening hunger. "You got any more of those?"

"Of what? Oh, doughnuts? Yeah, there's a whole box of 'em over on that table. Bring 'em over, why don't you? Or you want I should order breakfast? There's more coffee over there, too, but I didn't order any real food like you usually want." He watched Jesse cross the room to pour a cup of coffee. "You're tryin' to change the subject again."

"Not really." He hesitated, studying the box of doughnuts, his hunger briefly forgotten. "I just don't know what to tell you."

"Try the truth."

Jesse shrugged helplessly. "You won't believe it." But he couldn't think of a more convincing lie. Besides, Lyle always knew when he was lying.

"Try me."

There really was nothing for it but to try the truth and see what happened. Lyle wouldn't give up till he did. "Okay." His mouth twisted in a travesty of a grin. "Okay. See, there's this magic bracelet—"

"Yeah? What does it do, turn people into twins?"

"Something like that." The grin was rueful.

"You're right," said Lyle. "I don't believe you."

Jesse shrugged. "Best I can do." He brought the doughnuts to Lyle. "Sorry." He sat in a chair next to the couch, where he could reach the doughnuts.

Lyle ate the rest of the doughnut he already had, drank his coffee, looked into the doughnut box, and lit another cigarette. "Okay," he said at last, eyeing his smoke with assumed fascination. "Okay, I'm a nosey damn bastard and it's none of my business, right? Whyncha just say so?"

"You know damn well I would, if I meant it."

Lyle glanced at him. "So what you're saying, you're

telling me you're f'r real about this magic thing?"

Jesse shrugged.

"Come on, Jess!" When Jesse didn't say anything more, Lyle frowned at him and said with forced jocularity, "You been getting into the weird smokes, or what?"

"*Damn* it!" That was a little too familiar, after his time with Ruth and Zelig. "You know better."

"Okay, okay!" Lyle made a defensive gesture, only half-joking. "Sorry, buddy. I do know better, or I think I do. But what the hell you expect me to think when you start talking magic bracelets?"

"I dunno. Jeez, Bob. Don't ask me any questions and I won't tell you anything you can't believe." He took a fresh doughnut and scowled at it absently.

"Oh, great. That's just great." Lyle smoked and Jesse ate in silence. "So what's it look like, this bracelet?" Lyle said finally.

Jesse looked at him. "Don't humor me, dammit."

"No, I'm asking. I mean, hey, you never lied to me like you meant it, before. And you don't act flipped. So what's it look like?"

He shrugged, giving in. "Just a bracelet. Silver and turquoise, like Indian stuff."

"Oh, yeah." Lyle nodded, satisfied. "You—I mean your twin wore it to the concert night before last. So what, you're saying that that thing—what? What did it do? It turned you into him, or what?"

"It takes people—jeez. Look, it's just too weird. I can't explain it. Forget it, okay? You won't believe it anyhow."

"Try me," insisted Lyle. "It takes people where?"

"Into different worlds."

"You mean like parallel universes?" said Lyle, pleased.

"Sure, I've read about those."

"Yeah, in science fiction, right?"

"Well, sure. You don't exactly run into that kind of thing in your humdrum everyday kinda life, you know."

"I did."

"You did what? You mean you've been to some parallel world? That's where you were when he was here? Is that what you're saying?"

"That's what I'm saying." Jesse studied his coffee with great interest.

"Oh." Lyle thought about it. "Well, what was it like? That other world?"

"Pretty much like this one, I guess. Only it was the wrong year, and I—the me there was a druggie, and the Ruth there wasn't killed."

Lyle frowned. "I thought she wasn't here, either. The cops made some kind of bizarre mistake, or something."

"Wasn't a mistake." Jesse sighed. "She was killed, Bob."

"Nah, I saw her yesterday. She was kind of, you know, quiet, and she couldn't remember what'd happened to her, but hey, I'd've noticed if she was dead." He grinned.

"That wasn't the Ruth from this world, though."

"Oh, shit." The grin disappeared. "I was afraid you were gonna say somethin' like that. Jesse, how the hell am I supposed to believe this shit? What, this bracelet turned Ruth into twins too, or what?"

Jesse shook his head wearily. "There are worlds," he said. "Parallel worlds, where things are kind of the same, and there's the same people in all of them, or in a whole lot of them, or something. I dunno. Doppelgangers, Doc called 'em. The bracelet doesn't turn people into twins, it just takes people between worlds. And the Other—the Jesse that was here yesterday, I mean—he brought the Ruth from the world I was in to this world so the cops would think they'd made a mistake and let him out of jail."

"You know," Lyle said thoughtfully, "I didn't see her around after the concert last night."

"A world-walker took her home," said Jesse.

"Oh. Now we got world-walkers. Right."

"Well?" Jesse said helplessly. "You asked."

"I did ask." Lyle leaned over and picked up a guitar that was leaning against Jesse's chair. "Okay. So she's there, and you're here. Where's your twin? With Ruth?"

"No. I dunno. I don't think so. He doesn't belong in that world. The world-walker's chasing him, I think. It's like he's breaking the law, you know, running around putting people in the wrong worlds, and she's trying to get them all back in their right worlds. Including him, I guess."

Lyle laughed suddenly. "Jesse, for Christ sake."

"I swear to God," said Jesse.

Lyle strummed a chord, studying Jesse. "Okay. I believe you," he said easily. "So no problem, right? It's all worked out. You're back where you belong, she's back where she belongs, and I guess your twin will be back where he belongs pretty soon, so what's to worry?"

"There's a few things, like maybe a murderer running around scot-free because nobody knows Ruth really did get killed. And—" He hesitated, looked at Lyle, and managed a queer little smile. "I wanted to stay there." His voice cracked.

Lyle's fingers muted the guitar strings. He eyed Jesse, frowning. "You wanted to stay where?"

"Where I was. With Ruth."

"Oh, ho." Lyle picked out the melody to the Wedding

March on the guitar. "Like that, is it?" He sobered instantly when Jesse failed to respond. "You serious?"

" 'Fraid so."

"Goddamn."

"Yeah."

After a long moment Lyle said, "You got any idea who this murderer is, or what?"

"I have an idea. No proof."

"Hell, you can't even prove there was a murder done, as far as I can tell."

"No."

"Okay, that's that." He played the opening few bars of one of Jesse's slow songs. "Okay. Next order of business, you gotta go back, right? So where's this bracelet now?"

"She took it. The world-walker who brought me back." He lifted one shoulder in an oddly defensive shrug. "It was hers," he said.

"Right, it would be." Lyle played a complicated bass run, green eyes staring absently at a window across the room. "How'd you get it in the first place?"

"I just found it."

Lyle nodded. "That's how they always do it in the fairy tales," he said reasonably. "Unless some old witch or a fish or somebody gives it to 'em. I don't know any witches or fishes. So what do we do, go out and look for another one? Where would you look for a thing like that? Where did you?"

"This isn't a fairy tale, and I wasn't looking for a magic bracelet."

Lyle shrugged. "Point is, you found one. What, it was just lying around in the street, or where?"

"In a parking lot," said Jesse.

"There's a lot of parking lots in a city this size," said

Lyle. "We could be at this for weeks." He threw up a defensive arm. "Okay, okay! Hey, I think I like the other guy better. He's got a sense of humor."

"Ah, hell." Jesse grinned sheepishly. "You're an evil sumbitch, you know that? You got no damn heart."

Lyle nodded comfortably. "Yeah."

After a time Jesse said irritably, "Thought you were gonna order breakfast."

"Order your own damn breakfast. You know how to use the phone."

"Know how to fire subordinate sumbitches, too."

"Ordering breakfast isn't part of my job description. Don't bother me: I'm thinking." He closed his eyes and began a series of complicated bass runs.

"Thinking isn't part of your job description either, last time I looked."

Lyle opened his eyes. "How'd it work? That bracelet? You have to push buttons or twist dials or something?"

"No, you just kinda wish you were where you wanta be."

"Show me."

"What?"

Lyle scowled over the guitar at him. "What're you, retarded, or what? I know you. You give up too damn easy, some stuff. You haven't even tried, have you? Look, if all of a sudden magic comes true for you, what the hell makes you think you gotta have some damn bracelet?" Jesse stared at him, white-faced with sudden, searing hope. "We haven't got the damn bracelet," said Lyle, ignoring the look. "So try it without, why not? What's it cost? If it works, great. If it don't, then we start getting familiar with parking lots." He waved an arm encouragingly. "Go on, do whatever it is you do. See what happens." If he said anything more, he said it to an empty room.

* * * * *

Jesse had passed through the gates before without any sense of elapsed time or distance to the transition: one moment he was in one place and the next he was in another, and that was all there had been to it.

This time there was more. Perhaps because he was concentrating so hard without the help of the bracelet, or perhaps because on previous trips the bracelet itself had somehow dimmed his senses, this time the experience was wholly unlike any previous walk he had taken. He was not prepared. He knew it might be different, even difficult. He braced himself for pain, for strain, for violent resistance. He was ready to fight the universe and all its gods for the right to go where he wanted.

What he had not expected, and could not have been ready for, was that there was no resistance at all. More than that, there was acceptance, as if the gate itself reached out to him in welcome. For a timeless instant he stood at the juncture of worlds, caught up in a dazzle of swirling stars and skirling nebulae, and then he heard the music.

It was a concert of the gods, with strings that danced with drumroll thunder, brasses that sang of golden sunrise, kettle drums bellowing like mountains building, basses that sighed at the falling dark. It was everything he had ever dreamed of, translated into musical terms: heaven and hope and glory, thirst quenched and hunger satisfied, hurts healed and needs met. And it was all he had ever feared or suffered, all he had lost, all he had wanted. It was the promise and the pain of a life, of a lifetime: the essence of existence made manifest and magnificent, it filled the universe.

And he was a part of it. Against that background of singing splendor he was a woodwind whisper of wonderment that built to a shout of joy. He was the threaded melody that mended a broken string or a faltering reed or the birdwing rustle of tearing drumskins. Without thinking, without even conscious awareness of what he was doing, he reached out automatically to correct sour notes, to strengthen failing instruments, to encourage weary players. Like a benevolent tempest he stormed through the heart of the universe, tending, mending, lending strength, his voice upraised in chorus with angels. He was the orchestra. He was the chorus. He was the music itself. He was freedom.

And then it was over, and he was in a world again.

30

The Other

As a matter of fact I did go back and check on Hell, to see whether Suli's boss was lying. Not that it mattered. I mean, lying or not, he'd weaseled out of negotiating with me. He'd have to talk to me sooner or later, or he'd find his little universe of worlds coming apart at the seams, but I wasn't going to even try to deal with him while he thought he was in a position to say it was for my own good. Still, I had nothing better to do for the moment, so I took another look at Hell.

He was right. There was Hell just the same as it had always been, as if I'd never meddled. And there was a brand new world right next door that had been Hell till I meddled. Now it was just brimful of world-peace and harmony except for the part about how they'd give their right legs to see me dead. I got out of there fast. Funny: I hadn't even noticed Hell sitting right next door when I'd left this new world before, thinking it was still Hell.

This whole business about worlds popping into existence the way they did was kind of creepy. But it didn't really matter how it worked, as long as I knew how to make it happen, which now I did. I could use that. I wouldn't have to threaten to kill worlds, if creating them was just as much against the rules.

Not that I'd hesitate to kill whatever I had to, to keep my

freedom. But I got a kick out of thinking of myself as a world-maker. And it was going to sound great when old Suli or her monitors dragged me back into Limbo and I told them, "Set me free or I'll create a world!" Ultimatums were pretty much my stock in trade, and I'd never before had one I thought I'd have trouble voicing without a fit of giggles.

Meantime there was still one world I'd left in jeopardy. I thought about leaving it that way and letting it blow itself up to let Suli and her boss know I wasn't bluffing, but that would be wasteful. Better to save it now so I could use it again the next time I really needed to shake them up. Right now they were pissed because I'd created a world, and maybe the fear that I'd do it again would keep them off my back for a while, but they'd get over it. I mean, where's the harm? No way they could really be as upset over world-making as over world-breaking.

And no sense getting them too pissed, either, which they might be if I let a world die when I didn't need to. So I went back into it and set things right before they had a chance to get out of hand. If I couldn't use that one again, there were plenty of other worlds where I could set up another situation like that quick enough if I needed to, so I wasn't throwing away an option or anything.

And then, since I figured Suli'd be coming after me soon and I needed time to decide what to do next, I made myself scarce for a while. I'd found a way to get inside the gate system itself. There couldn't be a better hiding place.

It was really just an interrupted world-jump; I could get the gates to open without setting a goal, so I wouldn't go right through because you have to have a goal in mind or the system doesn't know where to let you out. Not that it really knows anything, any more than an automatic camera knows how much to expose a piece of film to get a good picture. It has sensors that control what it does, and I don't understand how they work any better than I understand how the gate system works. You don't have to know what it's doing inside, you just have to know which button to push.

I mean, that's like a cosmic truth, or something. Hey, it holds true for cameras, for cars, for computers, for people, for everything. It holds true for the gates. I was learning which button to push, and one interrupted jump was all it took to show me that was a button I was going to push a few more times. Because that was where the music was.

I felt like I could stay in there forever. Heaven couldn't be better. I wasn't just listening to music, and I wasn't just making music, I was music. The one thing I'd ever done that came even close to feeling that good was dancing, and even dancing was just a feeble, world-bound imitation of this.

But it didn't get me any closer to knowing how to solve my problem, which was how to get Central off my back for good. I couldn't really stay in the gates forever; there is such a thing as having too much fun. Besides, after a while I started noticing these sour notes every once in a while. I could fix them easy enough, but it spoiled the mood and got me to thinking about the worlds again.

I finally decided the only thing to do was just to wait and see what they did next. Suli'd probably find me quick enough no matter where I came out of the gates, since her stone must be set to find me by now. Unless she, like the monitors, couldn't track me since I'd lost the bracelet. But I couldn't count on that.

So I pulled out of the gate and walked back into the Jesse's world just like it was my own. Which I figured by now it ought to be. I didn't pay any attention to the time, but it seemed to be early in the day when I got there. Bob Lyle was still sitting around in his underwear, eating doughnuts. He gave me a really weird look when I came out of my room, but as far as I was concerned he was a really weird guy, so that didn't mean much.

"Where is everybody?" I asked.

"I dunno," he said. "Asleep or out to breakfast or something." He was watching me like he thought I was going to burst into flames or something. "All except Ruth. Who I haven't seen since the concert last night." He lit another cigarette, even though he already had one burning in the ashtray next to him.

"Me neither." If I knew Suli, she'd already snatched Ruth back into her home world before they even pulled me into Limbo. It shouldn't matter, though. She'd served her purpose. I couldn't see the police deciding she'd been killed again, unless somebody came up with a body. Which they wouldn't, since I'd gotten rid of it. I poured myself some coffee and got a doughnut out of the box in front of Lyle and sat in the chair at the end of the couch. He kept staring at me till I started to feel like a bug or something. It pissed me off. "What the hell's the matter with you?"

"Nothing," he said, all innocent like a great big stupid teddy bear. "You sure you dunno where Ruth is?"

"Yeah, I'm sure. Why, you think she might've got herself killed again?" I gave him a big old silly grin about that: ho ho ho didn't those cops look dumb with egg on their faces?

He didn't think it was funny. "Could've happened, you know," he said. "But I guess what you figured, since nobody killed her in the first place—what? Nobody wouldn't try it again, if he found out she was still alive?"

"I don't know what the hell you're talking about." I really didn't. He couldn't mean what it sounded like, because how the hell could he know the Ruth from this world really had been killed? But I couldn't figure out what he was getting at if that wasn't it.

He didn't push it. He just shrugged again and said, "Whatever you say," like it really didn't make any difference to him.

"Look, Ruth isn't my responsibility," I said. "She's my employee. And she won't be that if she doesn't quit causing trouble around here."

"Getting murdered is causing trouble?"

"She wasn't murdered, for God's sake. You saw her last night, didn't you?"

Before he could answer me, Bancroft Averill came wandering in from one of the bedrooms on the opposite side of the suite from mine, and we dropped it. Banny was a real conversation stopper. The one thing that little guy had going for him was his talent on the guitar. He was ugly, he was dirty, and he was just a hair this side of stupid—That, or a few cans short of a six-pack. But he played a mean second guitar. I guess the Jesse had been willing to put up with the rest of him in exchange for that.

First thing he said this morning was, "Where is she?"

"Who?" asked Lyle.

Banny was glaring at me. "That Ruth," he said. "I heard you talking about her. Where is she?" He did something with his mouth that might have been meant for a smile. "Did you chop her up in little bitty pieces to match the other one?"

"Goddamn." Lyle sat up slowly, staring at him like he'd just grown horns and a tail. "It was you. Wasn't it? You son of a bitch." He looked dangerous, for a man dressed only in doughnut crumbs and baby blue jockey shorts.

Banny giggled. "Nobody killed Ruth, if that's what you

mean. She was here just last night, all huggy-kissy with Jesse." He made the name sound like a dirty word. "She didn't look dead to me. Did she look dead to you, Jesse?"

Lyle stood up just as slowly and carefully as he had sat up, and you could tell he wasn't much short of doing a little killing himself. "Get him out of here." His voice was weird, not like him at all. "I mean it, Jesse, or whoever the hell you are. Get this piece of slime out of here or I swear to God I'll kill him."

It barely registered that he knew I wasn't the Jesse. "Banny killed Ruth?" I said. It hadn't occurred to me that the killer might be a member of the Jesse's band. I'd been thinking of it like a mugging, something that just happened to her. I wasn't sure how I felt about knowing it was Banny. I mean he didn't just kill her, he butchered her. My father couldn't have done it worse.

"Prove it." Banny giggled shrilly. "Find the body."

Lyle shook his head. "You got rid of it, didn't you, Jesse? What the hell is your name, anyway?" He didn't take his eyes off Banny.

"Jesse." My voice sounded weird, too.

"Shit," said Lyle, glancing at me.

"Sorry." I shrugged. I could feel my mouth grinning, but I was not amused. I couldn't think. I could hear my father laughing. It was like I'd helped him as well as Banny when I got rid of Ruth's body. I hadn't meant to help anyone but myself.

Banny looked back and forth between us, his little pig eyes puzzled and suspicious. "His name's Jesse, Bob. What's the matter with you? It's always been Jesse. Jesse Jesse Jesseeee." He drew it out the way the crowd did at a concert. "That's all anybody ever cares about, Jesse Jesse Jesse. That's all she ever cared about. Jesse."

The deviant little spit-worm was falling apart right there in front of us. You could see it in his eyes. He giggled again, and it sounded a lot like my father. "But I fixed him: I set him up." His voice was shrill. "I put downers in his coffee, and I put on his clothes, and I used his knife. And I told her we were meeting him. She was willing, oh, yes, because she wanted to sleep with him. She had to be shown the truth."

I said "Banny," very calmly, but I didn't feel calm.

Lyle didn't look calm. "Get rid of him." He looked sick. "I'm telling you, Jesse. Whoever. Jeez, I wish to hell you had a name of your own. Banny, you get the hell out of here before I kill you, you hear me? You go, and you keep on going. And you don't never come back. And you do it quick. Because I ain't gonna stand here and look at your piggy face much longer before I decide maybe somebody better show you the goddamn truth."

Banny looked at him in surprise and said, like a troubled child, "Did you want her too? I could've let you have a little piece if I'd known."

Lyle surged at him like he was going to take him apart right there. I got between them. I don't know why. "Lyle, hey," I said. Banny giggled at him from behind me. Lyle looked like maybe he'd try to take me apart too. "Lyle, he's crazy, okay? He isn't responsible." How many times had I made that same stupid excuse for my father? I never knew why I did it for him, either.

Lyle shook his head, glaring past me at Banny. "He isn't that crazy. He knows damn well you cleaned up the evidence for him, or he wouldn't be bragging now." His gaze shifted briefly to me, and there was pain as well as anger in his eyes. "Why did you do it, damn you? Didn't you know they couldn't prosecute him for a crime you made disappear?"

"They were trying to prosecute me." It sounded feeble, even to my ears, and I knew damn well it hadn't been feeble. It had been the quickest and easiest way to get myself out of a bind, and how was I to know I'd be helping out a psycho spit-worm while I was at it?

And what the hell difference did it make if I had? So he'd get away with murder. Big deal. I looked at Lyle and swallowed my anger and said almost patiently, "It didn't look to me like they were very damn interested in anybody but me. Story of my life: who cares if he didn't do it? He's handy. What would you've done in my place, sat still and got hanged or whatever they do to murderers here? You think that would have been a smarter way to act?"

"Yes. No. I don't know." At least he was trying to be honest with me. "There must've been a better way."

"No, you see, there wasn't, really," Banny told him earnestly. "I had to kill her. She had to be shown, see? I explained it to her real carefully. I told her it was for her own good. I think she understood, Bob, really. I had to do it."

Shades of my father. How the hell could killing somebody be for her own good? But I guess that makes as much sense as telling a little kid it's for his own good when you do the kind of sick things to him that my father did to me. If you think you know what's good for somebody, I guess logic doesn't always enter into it. Banny was still talking, but I couldn't hear him. My father's laughter got in the way.

And that's when Suli showed up, brandishing a handgun that she started shooting at me before she even had time to aim, which really wasn't very damn smart considering how close I was standing to Lyle and Banny both.

I wasn't ready for that. I really hadn't believed she'd do it. I don't mean I trusted her, or thought there was some mystical love-thing going on between us that would keep her from killing me even if her boss told her to. I don't know what I thought. I just didn't think she'd try to kill me.

She did. I guess the guys at Central must've fed her a heavy dose of the party line, and convinced her what a terrible thing it was that I wanted out of Hell so bad I'd create worlds to keep my freedom. She was sworn to uphold the order, peace, and integrity of the worlds, and hey, if that meant killing your lover, well, things are tough all over, right?

Who knows what they told her? You do what you have to do. I was ready to blow up a whole world to keep my freedom. I guess anybody's a killer if the price is right.

It was Banny saved my life, of all things. Like I said, Suli fired once without hardly even taking time to aim. I guess she figured she wasn't gonna get a lot of chances once I knew she was serious, and she was right about that: I'd have been out of there and walking before she could sneeze, if that first bullet hadn't hit me.

It only nicked my arm, but the surprise of it just about knocked me over. After that she could've shot me half a dozen times before I recovered from the goddamn shock, only Banny saw the gun and he freaked. He wanted it, don't ask me why. Maybe he had a bunch of other people lined up he wanted to kill for their own good. Anyway he went after it. And Lyle, who'd been waiting for an excuse to go after Banny, decided that was it.

I don't know what I was thinking. I mean, I was bleeding, for God's sake, and for all I knew my arm was broken, and if you'd asked me I'd've said there wasn't a damn thing in that world or any other that I wanted more than I wanted to walk away from the woman who'd just tried to kill me, and I didn't do it.

For one thing, that little spit-worm had gotten his hands on the gun. And even though Suli turned out to be one hell of a fighter, Lyle was getting in her way so much it looked like Banny might get to shoot them both. Not that that's much of a reason. Compared with freedom, what were the lives of a man I hardly knew and a woman who wanted me dead?

I guess I just wasn't in a very reasoning mood right then. What I wanted to do, I wanted to tear Banny into little bitty pieces like he'd done to the Ruth, and tell him it was for his own good. And then maybe I wanted to shoot Suli or at least tell her what I thought of people who killed each other for really stupid reasons. And then I could tell Lyle thanks for keeping quiet when he knew damn well I wasn't the Jesse, and then I could walk away.

I usually do what I want to do. Ain't nobody gonna do it for me. So I jumped into the fight and did my damnedest to shred the spit-worm. Only Lyle and Suli both got in my way. I s'pose I got in their way, too. Things got real tangled up, real fast. And with that gun waving around, things got a little scary. I don't know whether it was Suli or me did it, but one of us panicked and took a walk, and naturally the whole tangle of us went along since we were all hanging onto each other.

We landed, of all places, in the world they'd dumped the Jesse into when I bounced him out of the one I wanted. He and the Ruth were both there, and they weren't hanging onto each other. So when they saw me, the Jesse was the only one that bounced. Leaving the Ruth there with Suli and Lyle and me and the spit-worm, just when he finally got the gun away from the rest of us and stepped back to decide who to shoot first.

31

Suli

She had known killing him would not be easy. She had not known it would break her heart. But there seemed to be no other way to stop him, and she could not really believe she should side with the New Worlders against Central. It was ridiculous to imagine that she could know better than those in charge of the worlds. If they didn't believe the New Worlders, it must be because the New Worlders were wrong. Their claims must have been investigated, examined, and considered at every angle by the finest minds in the worlds. That was what Central did; the welfare of all the worlds was in their hands. They wouldn't be stupid enough to ignore the claims of a group like the New Worlders, who had such a wide following among people from all walks of life, and whose beliefs, if accurate, would affect all the worlds. There was too much at stake.

No, if the New Worlders were right, Central would know about it by now, and instead of being ordered to kill him she might have been sent to protect the Natural whose un-supervised walking would in that case be healing instead of damaging world barriers.

Having reasoned that out for perhaps the hundredth time, and having run out of delaying tactics like the trans-ference of the Jesse from his adoptive world to his home world (a move so obviously pointless, since the Other would probably doppelganger him almost at once, that she didn't really know why she had done it), she checked her handgun to make sure she knew how to use it, and resolutely began her search for the Other.

It took longer than she expected. The monitors couldn't track him, since his use of the gates no longer registered on any of their instruments. Her stone, when she set it to find him, took her into a gate and right back out again in the same time and place, a result she had no idea how to interpret. A random search of worlds he was known to favor turned up nothing.

It was the Jesse's escape from his home world that led her to the Other in the end. That registered on the monitors' consoles, one of which she had commandeered for her search. She assumed at first that the Other had returned and doppelgangered the Jesse. That should have sent the Jesse to Limbo, but since he had developed such an affinity for his adoptive world, and since as the Other's doppelganger he might have some instinctive knowledge of the Ways, it was not beyond the realm of possibility that, bounced out of his home world, he could land in the world of his choice.

But she couldn't find any sign of the Other in the Jesse's home world, and the Jesse's trip through the gates registered very strangely on the monitoring screens. She called that to the attention of the monitors and returned her attention his home world, convinced the Other must be there.

He showed up several minutes later. He had not doppelgangered the Jesse. Which meant the Jesse was a Natural, too. He had walked without a stone. And like the Other, he seemed determined not to stay in his home world. Would she be sent to kill him, too? Would all the Jesses turn out to be Naturals, and she be sent to kill them, one by one?

"You'd better notify the senior world-walker," said a monitor, studying the screens.

"You notify him," she said. "I have a job to do." If she waited, she really might be ordered to kill the Jesse too. Time enough for that when she had killed the one she loved. Maybe killing Jesses would get easier after the first one. It couldn't get harder.

Reluctance made her clumsy. She had her weapon ready to fire on the instant of arrival, which she meant to coincide with a moment when the Other was standing, Lyle was lying down, and Banny had not yet entered the room. That should give her a clear target. If her aim were accurate, it would be the work of seconds afterward to reach his body and jump with it into Limbo. It would be someone else's job to decide how to dispose of him then.

But she arrived at the wrong moment, and her aim was not accurate. She hurt him, but she did not kill him. Perhaps, even then, she could have killed him: he didn't walk away from her. He just stood there bleeding, waiting for her to shoot him again. She had never seen such a look of desolation in anyone's eyes. He had trusted her, against his will and his reason, and she had betrayed that trust. It was as though, in that moment, he would welcome death: as though he simply gave in at last to a universe he had always known to be hostile but which he had somehow hoped would serve him with kindness just this once.

She wanted to say she was sorry. She wanted to hold him, to banish that terrible grief from his eyes. She wanted to explain to him one more time, to tell him again that there was a choice, there was an option better than death if he would only take it. She wanted to say that she could not live without him, that if she had to kill him she would die, too. She wanted to touch him one last time, and to feel his touch. She raised the gun again. It was the only option he would accept. Death, or the freedom she could not grant him. Best get it over with.

She didn't really see Banny until he attacked her. She had been distantly aware that she and the Other were not alone in the room, but in the face of what she had to do, and the look in the Other's eyes, she had no thought for anyone but him. They could have been onstage in front of one of his concert audiences and she would not have known or cared. Banny's tackle caught her wholly by surprise.

She reacted instinctively, and could have fended him off successfully, had Bob Lyle not interfered. Banny was after the handgun, and Lyle was after Banny. Between them they knocked Suli to the floor and, in their continued struggles, managed inadvertently to protect each other from her best efforts to extricate herself from them both.

She was distracted, too, by continued awareness of the Other. For one long moment he just stood there, bleeding. She was horribly conscious of the way he looked at her. If she lived forever, she would never be free of the memory of that look. She did not want to live forever. How could she have imagined she could obey Jud's order and live with herself afterward?

It was almost a relief when he moved, though the look in his eyes had changed to murder and when he moved it was toward the struggling little group on the floor, not away. For a brief instant she wondered almost without interest whether he meant to kill her. It would hardly be unreasonable if he did.

Then Banny got both his hands on the gun, Lyle's elbow nearly knocked her unconscious while she was trying to wrest the gun from Banny's grip, and the Other crashed against her with force enough to knock the breath from her lungs. He seemed more intent on killing Banny than on killing her, but she no longer had time or attention to spare for anything but keeping the gun from going off in her face.

Just when she thought she had lost the battle, she felt a gate open and close around them. The Other, in a reflex action in response to the imminent threat of that waving gun, had walked without thinking. It was no surprise that they landed in the adoptive world of the one Jesse he knew. Given the whole universe of worlds to run to, he would naturally choose the only one where there was someone he must instinctively have known he could trust.

Unfortunately, that one and he couldn't inhabit the same world simultaneously. The Other automatically retained his position, so even though he looked at the Jesse, it was the Jesse who was doppelgangered, leaving a startled Ruth behind.

Suli was only peripherally aware of all that; Banny still had both his hands on her gun, and Lyle and the Other effectively prevented her from retrieving it. They were getting in each other's way as much as in hers. It was a matter of seconds till Banny was able to wrench himself free of the three of them, gun in hand, and scramble to his feet and out of her reach to choose a target.

She came to her feet after him, but he was too far away to tackle, and he waved the gun at her to keep her from approaching. If she went after him anyway, he would only kill her first, leaving no one to protect these others. They were in a large, empty room, concrete-floored and echoey: probably backstage at a concert hall. The Ruth and the Jesse had been alone there, so there were no witnesses, not even the rest of Jesse's band. There was no one but Suli to help these people. She dared not throw away her chance too soon. Especially since it was a crisis she had inspired, which could not have happened in the ordinary course of events.

Even if Banny chose Lyle for his target, who was the only one of them from his own world, the result could be pivotal since he would have had neither the weapon nor, probably, the inclination to commit that particular murder if she had not interfered. The only ones he could choose whose death might not matter were the Other, already marked for death by Central, and Suli herself, whose absence from her home world had been ascertained to be of no importance before she was allowed to join the corps of world-walkers.

He chose neither of them. The moment he saw the Ruth he aimed the gun at her. He had already killed the Ruth from his own world. Doubtless mistaking this Ruth for that one miraculously risen from the dead, he meant to kill her again.

It might not matter to the worlds: she was not known to be pivotal. But neither was the Other until he created a world. At the very least, the Ruth's death at the hands of a man from another world would strengthen chaos. And Suli could see only one way she could prevent it.

Somehow the Other guessed what she intended and tried to stop her, to shove her aside, to save her, but his bad leg crumpled under him and he did not reach her. She hurled herself in front of Banny just in time to be hit by the bullets meant for the Ruth.

The sound of the gun was deafening in that enclosed space. The sheer force of the bullets at such close range was stunning. She could not catch her breath. There was no pain, but she was conscious of a sense of outraged dignity as she collapsed bonelessly, watching the falling dark.

She never knew what happened to Banny. Her ears rang

from the noise of the gunshots. When she could breathe again, the air was heavy with the sharp scent of gunpowder and dust. She was aware of the Ruth bending over her, and of someone fussing with the front of her dress. A voice said, "It is most too bad, but I can doing nothing. I am sorry, Jesse." Then that person and the Ruth were gone. Only Jesse remained. Her Jesse; the Other.

He held her and whispered her name, and she relaxed gratefully into his arms. "Oh, Jesse." She smiled at him, embarrassed. "Now look what I've done."

"Hush, love." He held her closer for just a moment, his face pressed into her hair; then he pushed her away enough to look into her face. "Could they help you at Central? They must have the worlds' best doctors. Couldn't they do something for you?"

She knew what it cost him to offer that: he would be playing into Central's hands if he took her there. She also knew they couldn't help her. "Not this time," she said, and smiled again. "At least now I won't have to kill you."

"Oh, God," he said. And then, very quietly, as if against his will, "Oh, please—" It was nearer a prayer than she would have thought he could manage.

She reached one frail, feeble hand to touch his face. There were tears in his eyes. "It doesn't matter, Jesse." But it did matter. There was so much they could have had, and been, and done, if only . . . If only. Such helpless, useless words. "It doesn't matter," she said again. The repetition didn't make it true.

"I love you." His voice was full of wonder and anguish and despair. He knew now what they had lost: what he had thrown away.

And yet . . . neither of them could really have lived the only way Central would have let them live, tied to one

world, trapped in it, forbidden the freedom of the gates forever. They had known too much for that, walked too far,
dreamed too many dreams. One world might be enough for
ordinary mortals, but neither of them was an ordinary
mortal anymore. They had come of age in the gates and
walked like gods. They were not fit for just one world. They
could not endure it.

She wanted to tell him that, to reassure him, to soothe
away the tears he didn't even know he shed. But she was
very tired. Perhaps she would rest a moment first. Odd,
how quickly the light failed. She could barely make out his
face in the dusk.

But that didn't matter, either; the sweet, sad lines of it
were etched in her memory forever, and the music of his
voice, and the touch of his hands. When she had rested, she
must remember to say she loved him.

There were so many things she had meant to say, had
wanted to say, but now they were slipping away with the
fading light. Perhaps she would be able to think more
clearly in the morning.

She closed her eyes.

32
Jud

The pattern of the Jesse's first unassisted walk was fresh in Jud's mind when Ariel came into his office again. He did not know quite what to make of it. The implications were clear, but it was a pattern he had expected to see only in the Other's walks: the pattern of a Natural who was instinctively pushing back chaos. The Other's walks left no trace at all. The Jesse should not have been able to walk without a stone. Had Ariel initially selected the wrong Jesse? Had Suli, by trying to trap the Jesse in a world he didn't want and therefore driving him to walk alone, altered the course of destiny?

It didn't really matter, of course, which Jesse saved the universe. It was only that this was so unexpected, so unforeseen. What else might they have overlooked? Would all the Jesses prove to be Naturals? If pushed far enough, could any of them mend world-walls in the course of unassisted walks? What would that mean for future history?

What did it mean now? The Lord High Monitor had been informed of the new development. If he couldn't see that the Jesse's walk had been a healing thing, he would certainly see that the Jesse was just as much a Natural as the Other was. Would he order world-walkers sent out to kill this Jesse, too? All the Jesses?

But of course not. Even the Lord High Monitor couldn't

288

order the death of a man known to be pivotal, which this Jesse was. For the first time, it occurred to Jud to investigate the other Jesses, to see whether any of them were pivotal too. That was what he was doing when Ariel arrived in his office and took her customary seat in the acrylic chair across the battered desk from him.

She was old again, older than he had ever seen her before. Her hook-nosed, warty face was a mass of wrinkles, her hands gnarled claws, her flyaway hair under the ugly witch's hat a thinning mass of pure white tangles. Only her mischievous eyes were young. When he looked into them he could see the beauty of the sprite trapped in the body of the crone and laughing at him for his shock at the sight.

"You must finally have had a visit from my younger self," she said. "I wondered when I would show up."

Odd: now that he had seen the beauty of her youth, he could see it still, hidden among the wrinkles and warts and age-shaped jutting bones. "Ariel," he said stupidly. The office was utterly silent except for the soft, sibilant hum of his borrowed monitor's equipment searching the pivotal possibilities of Jesse Farrells.

"Quite a shock, isn't it?" She cackled suddenly, briefly, but her eyes were not entirely amused. "Ah, vanity, vanity, get thee behind me, vanity. I should have warned you, poor boy. But I had no idea you had such resistance to the natural order of things."

"You were very beautiful," he said.

She shrugged, amusement tugging at her lips. "To one of my race I am more beautiful now. It was only through association with you strangers from the outside worlds that I came to regard that unformed, characterless creature I was with any admiration at all, and the admiration did not outlast the youth. But I am not here to discuss my misspent adolescence. Am I, as usual, to approach the matter with discreet circumspection?"

"I've just debugged the office," he said. "Say whatever you like."

She smiled. "Thank you. But I've nothing very controversial to say, I think. I just wanted to tell you that you're doing something right: the future is opening up nicely. The barriers are mending, becoming properly flexible again. It's time to call off your world-walker; the one you call the Other must know by now what he is."

"He's known for some time," said Jud. "But I cannot call off the world-walker. The Lord High Monitor would have me involuntarily retired in an instant, and send her after him again. You know the political climate here."

She frowned, a massing of wrinkles over her glittering eyes. "So do you," she said. "I'd assumed you had a plan for this eventuality."

"Things are not working out quite as I had planned," he said wryly. "But perhaps it won't matter too much if we lose the Other. Did you know the Jesse is a Natural, too?"

She brightened. "No, is he?" she asked in delight. But her pleasure faded as quickly as it had come. She shook her head soberly. "But that doesn't matter," she said. "It's the Other we need. I don't know why. The Jesse will help, no doubt of that, but—"

"It's the Jesse's walking that has helped so far," he said. "The Other's walks do nothing for the worlds. He destroys by second nature. Even when he means to mend, he breaks things. The Jesse has walked unaided only once, and look at the patterns of it." He showed her the monitor's printout.

She waved it away without a glance, her eyes fixed on his face. "Worms' tracks on paper," she said impatiently. "I don't understand your technology any more than you understand my magic. The patterns I understand are the ones between worlds." She smiled distantly. "Did you never hear the worldsong, Jud? Are you totally deaf when you go through the gates?"

He studied her, puzzled. "Worldsong? What is that?"

"The song the universe sings in the gates." Her voice was gentle, her eyes alight with remembered ecstasy.

"There's nothing in the gates," he said certainly. "Not songs, not time, not distance. Nothing. You step in here and you come out there; that's all there is to it."

"For you, doubtless," she said, and her look was pitying. "For me there's more. And I'm only a near-Natural. For the Jesses, for your Other—Oh, the music, Jud! If you could even imagine—! I cannot hear what they hear, but I've heard the echoes, and I know." Her smile was sweet, serene with memory.

"All right," he said impatiently. "But what has that to do with whether we need the Other?" His shoulders twitched. "If music is so important, all the Jesses are equally qualified. They are talented musicians."

"I don't know." She transferred her distant gaze from his face to the blue square of window behind him. "I don't know," she repeated slowly. "Perhaps any of them could mend the music, then." She looked at him again. "But when I went in search of the Natural who could save the universe, it was the one you call the Other I found. Not just any Jesse Farrell. Only the Other."

He rubbed one finger thoughtfully across a ragged scar on the desktop. "How did you happen to find him?"

"It didn't just happen," she said sourly. "I dedicated my life to the search."

"But how did you search, exactly?" he insisted.

She shrugged. "You wouldn't understand. You've never

heard the worlds sing."

"It was something to do with this music you hear?"

"It was everything to do with this music I hear." She imitated his dubious tone mockingly. "There is a song in the gates, you know, whether you can hear it or not. And Jesse—your Other—is the only person in all the worlds who . . ." She hesitated, frowning. "I don't know quite how to put it. I listen to the music: he plays it. He is it."

"Since this other Jesse is a Natural too, presumably he can play—or be—this music," he said dryly. "You didn't know another of them would prove to be a Natural, did you?"

"No." She scowled at the window. "I'm not sure it's enough to be a Natural. I'm not even sure it's enough to be able to sing, or become, the worldsong."

"He's mending things already," Jud reminded her. "That's more than the Other has done."

She shrugged that away. "Tell me about him."

"Who, the Other?"

"No." She scowled at him. "The Jesse."

"What's to tell? He's just like the Other."

"He must not be, or he'd have been walking worlds long before now. As the Other did."

"He didn't meet Suli as the Other did. He didn't encounter a stone until the Other brought one to him."

She studied him, her eyes inquisitive, interested, amused. "And what did he use it for, when he found it?"

"To walk worlds," he said impatiently, shoulders twitching.

"At random? In exploration? As the Other did?"

"No, to mend mistakes, as a world-walker should. To retrieve people from worlds where they didn't belong. Which I think is more of a recommendation for world-mending than the Other's selfish, chaos-inducing rambles."

"Perhaps," she said, unconvinced. "Did he explore at all, for the pleasure of it? Or was he so involved in his good works that he didn't have time for fun?"

"I don't see why you'd refer to his 'good works' in such a mocking way. But it wasn't that, anyway, that kept him from walking more. He has an affinity for his adoptive world, and for the Ruth there. I think he just wasn't interested in walking for its own sake."

She nodded. "There's your answer, then."

"What answer? To what?" he said, exasperated.

"To whether your Jesse will save the universe if the Other is killed. He won't."

"But what he's already done—"

She cackled merrily. "Are you being deliberately dense, my friend? Oh, I admit it, certainly: your Jesse will do his little bit for the universe, whenever he's hard enough pressed to walk. But don't you see, if he won't walk unless he has somewhere to go, he won't spend enough time in the gates to be of much use at all."

The monitor's console on his desk whirred busily and spat out a new printout into his hands. He looked at it with growing amazement. "They're all pivotal," he said. "All the Jesse Farrells. My God, if every one of them creates a world, the universe will double in size! How can this happen?"

She shook her head. "You and your instruments," she said with fond amusement. "Is the impending creation of a world the only thing that would make your instruments mark them as pivotal?"

"I'm not sure," he admitted.

"And are they infallible, these instruments? Are our lives as predestined as that?"

"No, no," he said impatiently. "But don't you see that doesn't matter? The Lord High Monitor can't order them all killed. Not if they're pivotal."

"That won't matter if the Other is killed," she said gently. "They may hold back the onset of Chaos, but they can't save the universe. Only the Other can do that."

"You don't know that. You're guessing."

"Oh, Jud." She sighed, and smiled, and shook her head as at the unreasoning optimism of a child. "There's no use arguing. You'll do what's needed, or you won't. I'm tired, Jud. I've done what I can for the universe. Surely by now I've atoned for the damage my youthful, untutored walking did. I leave it in your hands now." Without another word she disappeared, leaving behind only the memory of her eyes dancing with merriment, and the scent of pungent herbs in the air.

He barely had time to comprehend her departure before the monitor console began to bleep at him with impressive urgency. Irritated, he punched the communicator button. "Yes? What is it?"

"The Jesse, sir." A monitor's anxious face appeared on the screen to reel off world-identification numbers, specifying which Jesse. "He's back in his adoptive world, with the Other!"

"You mean he's doppelgangered the Other."

"No, sir. They're both there. In the same world. At the same time. They're both staying there, sir."

He scowled at the screen. "And the world-walker? Where is she?"

The monitor swallowed audibly. "I think she's dead, sir. Her stone registers . . . well, death, I guess."

"You guess?"

"Sir, if she died, the stone ought to bring her back to

Central. They're all preprogrammed for that. It's the last thing they're supposed to do before the inner circuitry burns itself out so the stone can be reused."

"And her stone didn't bring her back? Then she isn't dead," he said firmly.

"But it burned itself out, sir."

"Without first bringing her back?"

"Yes, sir."

"That isn't possible," he said. "It can't happen."

"It did, sir."

He rubbed one papery palm against the other. "Do you know where the Other is? Was he with her?" It was the only explanation he could imagine.

"I don't know, sir." The monitor blinked. "Sir, the Lord High Monitor wants—" He swallowed. "He wants you in his office, sir. Right away."

Jud nodded heavily. "Very well," he said, not moving.

"Sir?"

"What is it?"

"Should we transport her to Limbo, sir? The world-walker? For debriefing or, or disposal?"

He nodded again. "You may as well," he said, and turned off the screen. For a moment he sat still, inhaling the fading fragrance of Ariel's pungent herbs. Then he turned to the window and said wearily, as though to himself, "You heard. Ready or not, I'm afraid it's time we made our move. Notify the Board, and alert the others." Then he rose slowly, sighed deeply, and walked.

33

Ruth

The sound of gunfire brought Zelig and the band rushing backstage to see what was happening. In the ringing silence their footsteps echoed eerily, and the sound of their voices raised in excitement and alarm seemed oddly out of place. Yet by their very prosaic and ordinary existence those normal voices, untouched by death and danger and despair, pushed back the boundaries of horror just enough to make the reality of what remained, grim as it was, endurable.

Ruth relinquished care of the dying world-walker into Zelig's hands and rose in time to see the band members arrive. It was almost comical. The Bob Lyle and Bancroft Averill who had come here with the Other were grappling in the center of the room. The Bob Lyle who belonged here arrived, stared at the struggling men, and blinked. The one from Jesse's world disappeared instantly, so that when the one from this world opened his eyes again, there was only Banny alone and off-balance in the center of the room with the gun still in his hand.

He was glaring at Ruth, and his eyes were demented, terrifying. For a fraction of a second she thought he would catch his balance, and if he did he would certainly kill her: then the Banny who belonged here arrived on Lyle's heels, and the mad Banny disappeared. The remaining Banny and Lyle stared in bewilderment, uncertain what they had seen.

Meanwhile the Other was struggling awkwardly across the room toward Suli, clearly unaware of the comings and goings of doppelgangers or of anything else but the dying world-walker and his own agonized effort to reach her. He must have strained his weak leg in the fight. Ruth had seen him fall when he tried to stop Suli, but she hadn't realized till now that he was injured. She instinctively put out a hand to help him, but he shoved her aside with a wordless snarl and she backed away to watch in helpless pity.

His bad leg would barely support his weight. Every step he took on it was such obvious torture it made Ruth's legs throb in sympathy. He was grunting with pain and effort, but he seemed as unaware of that as he was to the blood streaming from his wounded arm, or of the stunned audience of band members watching him.

Bob Lyle said, "Jesse?" and took one step toward him, then paused, looking confused.

Banny just watched, his expression unreadable. Darla and Mirabelle were staring in fascination at the dying world-walker with the impersonal absorption of witnesses at the scene of an accident. Mirabelle glanced once or twice at the Other with an odd little frown, and lifted her eyebrows at Ruth in inquiry, but receiving no answer she returned with a shrug to her study of the dying woman. There was nothing any of them could do but watch, but it annoyed Ruth just the same. She wished they would leave. It was an intrusion to watch Suli and the Other in such extremity. It didn't occur to her that she was watching, too.

The Other reached Suli's side just as Zelig, who had been examining her wounds, sat back on his heels and glanced up at him with a heartfelt sigh. "It is most too bad," he said, "but I can doing nothing. I am sorry, Jesse."

A shaft of watery sunlight from a distant window threw a

long streak of pale brilliance across dust-laden air and turned the Other's hair to pure gold as he collapsed at the world-walker's side and gathered her into his arms with a strangled moan. Zelig, silhouetted against the light, made some gesture of sympathy, but the Other snarled at him as he had at Ruth. He was like an animal in a trap, too hurt and frightened and enraged to accept any aid. Zelig, sighing again, rose to join the others. Suli and the Other might have been alone in the universe, crouched on that cold concrete floor with the dust of the battle still settling slowly through the still air around them.

Ruth moved instinctively to Zelig's side and he put a comforting arm around her. "That is your world-walker?" he asked her.

She nodded silently, her throat tight with unshed tears. She could not have said whether they were for Suli, for the Other, or for herself because Jesse was gone and she did not know when or how or whether he would return.

"I was thinking so," said Zelig. "It is most awfully too bad. And for that unfortunate Jesse as well, who cares so much for her."

She glanced at him. "I thought you thought he was our Jesse. You didn't see him arrive, and you called him Jesse."

Zelig shrugged. "I am thinking it must be his name," he said. "But one does not so easily mistake one for another once one has met several. It is like identical twins multiplied, yes? One learns an alertness to minute details of carriage and character. Not infallible, you understand. But in this case obvious: he is as much concerned for the world-walker as our Jesse is for you."

She glanced back at the sad little tableau side-lighted by dusty sun. "There was nothing you could do for her at all?"

she asked uselessly. Of course there was nothing, or he would have done it.

"We could having rushed her to hospital," he said. "But she would be DOA. I was thinking she might rather spend this last small time with her Jesse."

"I think you were right," she said, and then they were near enough the others to be bombarded with the inevitable questions: "Who is that?" "What happened?" "Who shot her?" "Aren't you going to do something about Jesse's arm, Zelly?" "Who shot him?"

It was not until then that Ruth realized this was going to be even more complicated than she had thought. Only she and Zelig even knew who the players were. She started automatically to say, "That isn't Jesse," realized how preposterous it would sound, and glanced at Zelig for help.

"Let them be," he said, glancing over his shoulder at the pair on the floor. The Other cradled the world-walker in his arms and rocked gently back and forth, crooning just audibly in a voice hoarse with anguish. "Let them be," Zelig repeated. "She is dying. They are wanting time to themselves." He might even have succeeded in shepherding the onlookers away if Jesse hadn't returned just then.

Ruth was facing the band, helping Zelig herd them back out of the room, so she didn't see his arrival. It was their shocked gasps and exclamations that made her turn to see that there were two Jesses here now: one on the floor with the world-walker in his arms, the other standing over the pair of them and staring at Ruth, his face twisted with remembered horror. "You're hurt," he said, his voice unsteady.

She moved toward him without conscious intent, stunned by joy even in the face of grief. For a moment she did not understand his concern: then she remembered the blood on her clothes and said, "No, it's not mine. It's Sue

Lee's. I'm all right." She knew he was thinking of the photos he had been shown of the other Ruth. She had seen them, too. "I'm all right, Jesse," she said. "It's okay."

He reached for her as for an anchor in a storm and enfolded her gratefully in his arms. "What happened?"

"Banny shot Sue Lee. He meant to shoot me, and she got in the way." Her voice shook. "She did it on purpose. To save me." She swallowed tears and took a steadying breath. "He—the other Jesse—tried to stop her, but his leg—he fell. I think he hurt himself pretty badly. He could hardly walk, afterward."

Jesse held her closer. "I was afraid he'd kill you," he said, meaning Banny.

"I was afraid you wouldn't be able to come back," she said, and realized abruptly that he had done more than just to come back: the Other was still here, and Jesse was looking right at him, and neither of them had disappeared. "But how can you?" she said. "Why doesn't one of you—I thought you couldn't both be . . ." Her voice trailed off helplessly.

"I was afraid he'd kill you," he repeated, as if it were an explanation. Perhaps it was.

"So was I," she admitted.

The Other crouched at their feet, cradling his dead love and keening. He was not crying. She thought he probably had never cried in his life. The sound he was making was more desolate than tears: an utterly hopeless, unconscious lamentation, almost irritating because it was unanswerable. He had been their enemy. Now he was only a human being in terrible pain.

Ruth could not see his face from where she stood, but the protective curve of his body around Suli's was as expressive as his face could have been. She shuddered: that was Jesse's familiar tangled mop of hair, Jesse's body, Jesse's voice. Jesse in mortal agony. She wanted to hold him, to soothe him, to try to silence that terrible wordless lament in Jesse's voice. But she dared not offer him the smallest comfort, because he was not Jesse at all.

"I have to help him, if I can," said Jesse.

"I know," she said. His arms were warm and reassuring around her. The front of his shirt was rough against her cheek. "I hope you can."

"He doesn't want it."

"I know." She managed a small, frayed smile, tilting her head back to look at him. His eyes were concealed from her behind a golden veil of curls. A muscle in his cheek twitched and was still. She said helplessly, almost desperately, "I love you, Jesse."

"I know." He hugged her one last time and let her go. "Better get back with the others. You've got some explaining to do, looks to me like. Wish you luck with it." He grinned at her almost mischievously. "Go on. I'll be okay."

She went. It was all she could do. But she stopped, with some vague idea of helping Jesse if the Other fought him, while she was still near enough to hear what they said.

Jesse knelt by the Other and looked at the world-walker for a long moment before he spoke. "She's dead, Jesse," he said finally. "Nothing more you can do for her. Come on, you better let the Doc take a look at that arm."

Without warning or provocation, the Other exploded in a fit of such demented fury Ruth thought for a moment he would kill Jesse with his bare hands. And after all, there was nothing she could do. She wasn't trained to fight as Suli had been. She could only watch as Jesse and the Other went tumbling across the floor, Suli's limp body forgotten behind them. But Jesse fought him off and managed to get free without assistance. They might have been evenly matched under ordinary circumstances, but Jesse was rested and healthy. The Other had recently injured his leg and been shot. He was not, by any means, at his best.

His crippled leg gave out when he tried to rise to go after Jesse again. He was left in a crumpled heap on the floor, white-faced and gasping, holding his hurt leg in both hands. "I'll kill him," he said. Ruth thought he meant Banny. "I'll go back and I'll kill the son of a bitch." His voice was cold and deadly and oddly unfamiliar.

"That won't solve anything," said Jesse. He crouched awkwardly on his good leg beside the Other, his crippled leg used only for balance. Pale sunlight gilded one side of his face and turned his hair to spun silver.

"Didn't you ever want to kill him?" the Other asked curiously. He didn't mean Banny. He meant his father.

Jesse shrugged. "Yeah. Thought I did sometimes. When it hurt the worst. But you can't always do what you want."

"I can give it a damn good try," the Other said, and disappeared.

With one troubled and apologetic glance at Ruth, Jesse went after him. It was inevitable. She had known he would have to follow the Other's lead if he could. She had not known it would leave her feeling so vulnerable and alone. She was an independent woman, accustomed to providing rather than accepting; to being leaned on rather than leaning. Now, as so often lately, there was nothing she could do, no way she could help. It was a situation in which she did not know how to behave.

The room echoed hollowly with the silence of their going. It was so sudden: they were just there, and then in the blink of an eye they were gone. She stood still for a long moment, watching dust motes drift aimlessly through still sunlight, before she turned to face the startled band members and the explanations she did not know how to make.

34

The Other

I knew she was dead. Hell, I knew that as soon as Banny shot her. You could tell by the way she fell, by the look of her eyes, even if you hadn't been able to see the wounds. I could see them, too. I don't know how many times he shot her, but it was sure as hell more than he needed to kill her.

I figured I could deal with him later. She didn't have a lot of time, and I kind of owed her. I mean, it was her stone that got me out of Hell in the first place. Besides, we'd had some good times together. And I knew what it was like to die in a lonely place: I'd thought I was doing it, times enough, when I was a little kid. So I figured I'd hold her, just so's it wouldn't be quite so bad for her. I owed her that much, anyway.

It took her a while to die, but it didn't seem to hurt her much. Funny thing was I went on holding her, even after I knew she was dead. I didn't want to put her down. It was like she'd trusted me, and if I let go of her that would be a betrayal. She'd said some things, dying things, stupid things about love that she probably believed at the time, but that wasn't what stopped me. It was the way she kind of curled up against me like a little kid going to sleep in my arms. I couldn't get that image out of my mind. I couldn't hold her forever, and it didn't make a damn bit of difference to her anymore, but I still couldn't put her down. So I just sat there and held her, and I don't know how long I would've gone on doing it if the Jesse hadn't interfered like he did.

In a way I guess he did me a favor. At the time I didn't think of it that way. But I was so pissed off at him that I forgot all about Suli while I was trying to kill him. Would've served him right if I'd done it, too; he'd messed with my life once too many times. But my damn leg gave out again before I'd done him any damage. I'd hurt it pretty bad when I was trying to keep Suli from throwing her life away. So it kept me from saving her, and it kept me from killing him. Incompetent cripple, thanks to my dad. It occurred to me it would be a good idea to kill the son of a bitch. I'd only tried twice before, and they say the third time's a charm.

The Jesse told me that wouldn't solve anything. Goody two-shoes Farrell, my spineless doppelganger. I couldn't remember what it was I'd admired about him. So he was at peace with himself, big deal. So's a turkey, but that doesn't make me want to be one.

I s'pose I wasn't thinking real clearly. Thing was, when Suli died I heard my dad laughing. Like an echo, almost subliminal, but I could hear him. He used to laugh like that when he did things to me. Or when he made me do things to him.

I think I went a little crazy. I went after my dad without any kind of plan at all. Or at least nothing beyond a very sincere intention to kill him. I figured I could do it, this time. I'd had enough. I'd thought before that he'd already broken everything breakable in me, but he hadn't. Not till now.

The music in the gates didn't even slow me down. God Itself could've been singing in there and I wouldn't've even noticed. I didn't realize I was jumping time till I came out the other side. It was night. I was standing in front of the house we'd lived in when I was a kid. The air smelled like summer: fresh-mown grass, someone's charcoal barbecue, and moisture from a recent thundershower. There was a child crying in the house: a high, thin, hopeless wail that went on and on and on until a door slammed somewhere, cutting it off.

That could not have been me. I'd learned almost in infancy that crying only made things worse. My sister, then? Had he tortured her, too? Odd: I'd never even wondered about that before. Where had she and my mom been all the times when he did what he did to me? What had he done to them?

I felt the Jesse's presence beside me before he spoke. I was aware of his shudder as he looked at that house, listened to that forlorn cry cut off. Hell wasn't his home world, but I guess there must've been a little house a lot like that where he came from. I studied it dispassionately, trying to see it through his eyes.

It was just a little wood frame house. It was painted white, with green shutters at the windows, but you couldn't see that very clearly in the dark. All the windows were lighted, spilling soft gold through drawn curtains onto the manicured lawn outside.

It looked like anybody's house, cozy and safe, with crickets chirping merrily all around. There wasn't anything weird or creepy about it. It wasn't even dilapidated or dirty or dark. It should have been a cobwebby Halloween mansion, to let people know it housed a monster.

"Jesse," he said. His voice was hushed, respectful, as if we were in the presence of the dead. I guess we were. But the dead was us: that little kid in there, at mercy of the man I had come to kill, who had no mercy.

"You better go," I said. I wouldn't fight him again. I was

in no shape for it, and no mood either. He just didn't matter enough.

"*We* better go," he said. "Look, you can hardly stand up without help."

I almost laughed. "I could kill him sitting down," I said. "I could kill him with my eyes closed."

"You've tried before, haven't you?" he said. "You couldn't kill him then."

"He hadn't killed Suli then." That wasn't what I meant to say. I don't know what I meant to say. But this wasn't about Suli. I wasn't the kind of guy to go off on a vengeance trip because somebody killed my lover.

"He didn't kill Suli. Banny did."

"And I could've stopped him if my dad hadn't smashed my leg and turned me into a goddamn cripple."

"A lot of things would've been different if they were different," he said.

"Jeez," I said. "Philosophy." I looked at him, but his face was only a pale oval in the reflected light from the house. "Go away, rock star."

"You can't save Suli by killing him," he said.

I did laugh, then. "You sure about that? We jumped time to get here. This is before the so-called accident. That little kid in there isn't a cripple. If I kill his dad now, he never will be. I never will be. I'll be fit to stop Banny later. Hell, maybe I won't even know Banny, because I'll still be a dancer and I won't have to take over your life."

"Then you won't know Suli, either."

I shrugged. "Suli's dead. And even if she weren't, I'd trade anybody for a sound leg. Besides, you haven't thought it through. If I never met Suli, I wouldn't know about the gates, so I couldn't come kill my dad before the accident."

That stumped him for a minute. But not for long; he was

more intent on moralizing than on logic. "It's a paradox," he said. "Maybe that means you can't do it. But Jesse, that isn't the point. Point is you can't kill everything that gets in your way. That isn't how to get free."

The kid in the house was crying again. "Listen," I said. It didn't sound like my sister. Maybe I hadn't learned not to cry as young as I thought I had. How could he hear that and still want to save the son of a bitch that did that to him? "Get out of here, rock star," I said. "I'm through talking." I moved toward the house.

He put his hand on my arm to stop me. The same arm Suli had shot. Maybe he couldn't tell, in the dark. Maybe he could: a hand on the other arm wouldn't've stopped me. But that one hurt so much I couldn't move for a minute; it was all I could do to stay on my feet.

Farrell Two-Shoes kept talking. I could just hear him through the ringing in my ears. "If you came here to lay blame, put it where it belongs," he said. "Sure, your dad hurt you. But he didn't ruin your life. You did that yourself, when you picked up that pain and started carrying it around with you everywhere you went like it was the only friend you had in the world."

He was beginning to annoy me. I didn't want to waste the energy to kill him, but I decided that as soon as my head cleared I'd do it anyway.

"All you and that sick old man have got between you is a piece of a life," he said. "Your past. And you can get free of it any time you want, just by letting it go. It's past, it can't hurt you anymore if you don't let it.

"But get a death between you and you won't be able to let go. That what you want? You could leave him behind. You could learn to live beyond what he did to you. You could make something of yourself, and you don't have to go stealing other people's lives to do it. You always had as much chance as any of us, only you were too busy nursing your hurt to take it."

"You talk too damn much." I slugged him. He let go of my arm. I started toward the house. He caught my arm again. I should've seen that coming, but I didn't. This time I didn't keep my feet.

I think he really didn't know it was my hurt arm he was grabbing, because he seemed surprised when my knees gave out. He even tried to catch me, so I didn't go all the way down. I tried to slug him again, but there wasn't any force in it. He just rocked his head with the blow and kept on holding onto me, which is probably the only thing that kept me from falling on my face. I must've lost more blood than I realized. I figured if I was gonna kill my dad I'd better get it done while I still could, so I hauled myself back onto my feet and started toward the house again.

He was still hanging onto me, and I think he was still talking. I ignored him. He tried to pull me into the gates, but it wasn't hard to stop that: he wasn't half as good with them as I was. I kept moving toward the house. He must've raised his voice, because my dad heard him. The back door opened and yellow light spilled out across the wooden porch and onto the lawn. My dad's shadow cut through the middle of it, dark against the light.

"What's going on out here?" My dad's voice was calm, reasonable, normal. All I could see of him was a tall, straight shape against the kitchen light. "Who's out there?"

The Jesse didn't move. His grip on my arm relaxed. I glanced at him. There was enough light now to see his face, and I wished I hadn't looked. I'd been thinking his dad must not've been as bad as mine: it was the only reason I could think why he'd forgive so easy, and lecture me on letting the past go. If the past wasn't quite so bad, maybe it'd be easy to let it go. But all it took was one look at his face to know his past wasn't any picnic.

And whether he knew it or not, he hadn't let it go. It was a lot like having hold of a live electric wire: you might want to let go, wish you could, know you should, but you can't. So unless something knocks you loose, you hang on till it kills you.

I didn't know what it would take to knock loose my dad's hold on me, but I figured killing him would be a good place to start. I know I said before I'd found out civilized people didn't kill. But if I was ever civilized, I lost it then, standing there looking at my dad and feeling, through the Jesse's grip on my arm, the fear that shook him just as it had always shaken me. We'd neither of us be free till that monster was dead.

My dad reached back inside the house to turn on the porch light. It turned him from looming shadow to ordinary middle-aged man with a paunch. The Jesse and I were out of the light, so he still couldn't see us, but we could see him clearly. His face was mild, even the eyes gentle. His thinning hair was a silver halo around his head. He was dressed for the office, his suit impeccably tailored, his shirt just wrinkled enough to hint at a hard day's work behind him. One of the most unnerving things about him had always been that he looked so kind. Even when he was doing his worst he never looked like the kind of person who would do what he did.

My mom came to the door behind him, a small woman with sad eyes whose smile always looked like she was apologizing for something. "What is it, Tom?" she said. Her voice was as frail as she was. There was a visible bruise on her jaw.

"Nothing, honey," he said. His voice was mild. "I thought I heard something."

"You did," I said, or tried to say. But my voice wouldn't work: no sound came out. Upstairs in the house I could still hear that child crying, a forlorn keening like wind in the night.

"Come back inside, Tom," my mom said. It was a cautious plea, as apologetic as her smile. She must have known what he did to me all those years, and she let him. She did nothing at all to stop him. She didn't even try to leave him. Maybe she pretended she didn't know, but she knew. You could tell by the way she looked at him.

"Why, Mama?" That was the Jesse, and his voice was as forlorn as the cry of that child upstairs. "Why did you let him do it?"

I don't think they heard him. It was hardly more than a whisper; I barely heard him myself. But I did, and it sent a surge of adrenaline through me that gave me the strength to pull free of him and take a step toward my parents. I think I meant to kill them both. She was as much to blame as he, even though she'd never raised a hand against me. She'd never raised a hand against him, either.

But I couldn't do it. I never wanted anything more in my life, and I couldn't do it. Not because I was afraid of him, or because the Jesse tried to stop me, or because I got a sudden revelation from God that murder is a bad thing. I don't know what stopped me. Maybe I was still too civilized, after all. Maybe I thought dying would be easier than killing. Maybe I was just tired.

35

Jesse

Jesse caught the Other when he fell, felt himself dragged
with him into the gates, and the music washed over him
with hurricane force. Raging winds battered his senses with
glory; strings nearly drowned him in their liquid tumble
through silken rainbows of hope and heartbreak and the
thunder of drums; the ceaseless, driving fury of a bass surf
pounded relentlessly in his blood.

Before, when he had passed through the gates, the time
spent within them had been dreamlike, a bodiless fantasy,
an adventure of the spirit only. This time he was aware of
his own body, and of the Other's still supported, sagging, in
his arms. They stood in a place of mist and magic made of
dazzling rainbows and roiling clouds of radiance, and the
passion of the music hurled bright autumn leaves of loss
like crackling confetti through the air around them.

The Other stirred and hauled himself unsteadily erect,
his expression dazed. His face was haggard and pale under
the bright tumbled curls, his eyes dark and smudged. For a
long moment he stared at Jesse without comprehension
while the strains of the symphony soared like wild birds before a storm; then he turned his gaze to the prismed glory
beyond. "I thought you'd be scared," he said. His body became briefly transparent, wavered, and solidified again,
shiny with sweat. "Don't you recognize this place? It's the

gate to death." As if to emphasize his words, the symphony swelled in resonant grandeur and the clouds around them blazed with light.

"I recognize it," said Jesse, and the music faded to whispering winds and distant bells. "You really gonna let him kill you?"

The Other shrugged, and winced when the gesture hurt his arm. "He did that a long time ago. I just didn't have sense enough to lie down." The clouds darkened ominously. The Other cradled his arm absently against his chest, blood seeping between his fingers.

"You could forgive him."

The Other studied him curiously. "How can you forgive what he did to you?"

A single flute played a liquid melody against the silvery cacophony of bells. Far in the distance, almost at the edge of hearing, a vast string section poured shimmering silken solace over the dangerously sparking, red-tinged clouds. " 'Cause I can understand he's sick. You couldn't do what he did if you weren't sick." At the Other's impatient gesture he said quickly, "It's no excuse, I don't mean that. It doesn't make it okay, what he did. Makes it understandable. And what you can understand, even a little, you can forgive. You gotta forgive him. 'Cause it doesn't hurt him if you don't. Only gives him more power over you. Power to kill you, this long after.

"He taught you to be a victim. You've been hanging on to that ever since, 'cause it's what you know. Growing up, letting go, accepting the past and starting on the future, that's hard. But swear to God it's the only real way to get free of him. He put you in a cage. Won't let you out of it. You have to do that for yourself. It isn't easy: you have a lot of hard lessons to unlearn. But freedom's worth it, Jesse.

And that's the only path to freedom there is."

"There's death." His voice was reasonable, mildly amused, his eyes serene in a face almost gray with pain.

"That isn't freedom. It's just another cage."

The Other smiled distantly. "You think you know a lot, don't you, rock star?" he said, eyes fixed on the glimmering clouds beyond. The words might have been angry, but his tone was indifferent.

Jesse studied the familiar, not-familiar face. "Guess I know what really bothers you."

The Other's body became transparent again, wavered, and solidified. Snare drums rattled against the whirlpool radiance of harps. "Nothin' bothers me," he said, hugging his hurt arm against him. The whole front of his shirt was smeared with blood.

"Wasn't your fault, Jesse," said Jesse. "You didn't ask for it. Doesn't matter what he told you. No way can you say that a little kid deserves what he did."

The Other laughed harshly. "You're just full of easy answers, aren't you?" He looked past Jesse into roiling stormclouds that glistened with gemstone prisms. "You believe that shit, or you just talking to hear yourself?" A solitary cello mourned unendurable loss. The Other, smiling, faded again, to a tenuous, man-shaped, rainbowed cloud with Jesse's face. Diamonds sparkled as the cloud paled to a tenuous mist, almost invisible.

Startled, Jesse reached for him, but his hand went through the man-shaped vapor as though the Other weren't there. The symphony subsided to a distant, tinny, harpsichord whisper of song. "Jesse," he said. "Jesse, no."

The Other laughed again, the sound as insubstantial as mist. It mingled with crystal chimes like Mirabelle's synthesizer and cascaded into the luminous distance like falling water caught on the edge of day. But all Jesse heard was the undertone: his father's voice, reverberant kettle drums of triumph, resonant with lies. The symphony was gone, and the rainbows, and the light. The death-gate drew him as his doppelganger had drawn him the first time he had gone through the gates: a mindless compulsion that he saw no real reason not to obey.

He did not want to die. But hearing his father's laughter at the edge of consciousness, he knew that on some level he had always wondered why he was not dead. How had he survived? How dare he survive, after what had been done to him, what he had been made to do?

The symphony built slow colors in the air. The Other was only a sparkling outline now, his laugh and their father's laugh mingled in brilliant prismed hues against soft, neutral clouds like mountain fog. He thought, "Ought to call him back. Meant to help him," but instead he took a step toward the gate.

"Oh, no you don't." It was a woman's voice, sudden and fierce. Something black swirled between him and the gate. A woman's slender hand, disembodied and vague, reached for the Other, gripped the glitter-outlined area where his arm should have been, and pulled. "Come back here." Her glitter-shrouded form appeared beside the Other, took substance from the swirling black that had blocked Jesse from the gate, and became an ancient, gnarled, and warty witch straight out of a children's story, even to the pointed black hat on her head. The symphony swelled to a crescendo. He blinked, and she was transformed with a ripple of harpstrings into the most beautiful young woman he had ever seen.

The Other solidified, sleepy-eyed and frowning, under her touch. The arm she held was his wounded arm in its blood-soaked shirtsleeve, but he didn't seem to notice that. She did. She looked at it, and her aristocratic eyebrows lifted. "You humans are such fools," she said conversationally. Taking her hand from his arm, she wiped it fastidiously on the hem of her black silk gown.

"Who are you?" said Jesse.

She scowled at him. "You have doctors. Why hasn't this been tended?"

He felt oddly defensive, like a schoolchild caught in mischief. "He's been busy."

She made a derisive sound. "Too busy to live?" She looked at the Other. "This needn't have been fatal. Why are you here?"

He returned her gaze with drowsy indifference. "I belong here," he said. His face was translucent, his eyes already dead.

"Oh, nonsense." She withdrew a tiny golden drawstring pouch from a fold in her garment, opened it, and took out a pinch of something colorless and bright. "Here, give me your arm."

To Jesse's surprise, the Other did as he was told. He moved with the slow, dreamy lassitude of a man drugged or terminally exhausted, and for the first time Jesse realized how very near death he really was. Concern made his voice harsh as he said again, "Who are you?"

The witch-woman carefully sprinkled her bright, colorless stuff on the Other's arm and muttered something unintelligible under her breath before she said in a normal tone, "I'm Ariel Greef, Jesse. Pleased to meet you, I'm sure." She glanced at the Other. "Give it a minute," she told him. "Spells work slowly within the gates."

"Spells?" said Jesse.

She smiled, and for just a moment he thought he saw the

316

gnarled hag she had been when she first appeared. Then she was young and beautiful again, eyes dancing with merriment as she said, "Never mind. You wouldn't understand."

The Other lifted his arm experimentally, color returning to his face. "It doesn't hurt anymore," he said, amazed.

"Of course not," said Ariel. "I've healed it." She looked briefly pensive. "Lucky there wasn't a bullet still in it; that's a much more difficult spell." She glanced at Jesse. "Takes longer," she said, and giggled.

"Who the hell are you?" he said.

"I told you: I'm Ariel Greef. What you really want to know is what I'm doing here, right?"

"Right," he said dubiously.

"I'll be going through the gate soon," she said. "I'm late already."

Jesse glanced inadvertently at the roiling clouds at the gate. "You're dying?"

"Certainly," she said. "Everyone does, you know. But you really shouldn't try to go through ahead of time. It's such a waste of possibilities, not to mention silly. It's not as if you'll miss your chance; the gate will always be here."

"Wasn't," he began, and realized he had been moving toward the gate.

"Oh, I know, it must have been the Other Jesse's idea." She turned to the Other. "Why?"

"Why what?" He was bemusedly examining his arm. The shirtsleeve was still sodden with blood, but when he pulled it aside there was no wound beneath it, only a small, angry scar.

"Pay attention, I don't have all day," said Ariel.

The Other looked at her in profoundly innocent surprise. "Got a hair up your ass?"

"How crude." She made a grimace of distaste. "Truly, I

shall never understand how doppelgangers can turn out as they do. Nature versus nurture has nothing on this. The two of you have identical genes, and survived identical childhoods, with absolutely no divergence until the accident that crippled you. After that, every single Jesse I've run across has been different. There are no two alike. How can that be?" She looked at them as though seriously expecting an answer.

The two Jesses looked at each other. "Excuse me?" said Jesse, at exactly the same instant as the Other said, "Say what?"

"You see?" said Ariel, triumphant, as though they had just proved an important point.

"No," they said simultaneously.

"Oh," said Ariel, crestfallen. "Well, never mind. We're not here to discuss non-pivotal doppelgangers' divergence theories. I'm sure God has Her reasons." She looked at them expectantly. "Now, Jesse. You were going to explain why you're here."

"I was following the Other," said Jesse.

"Not you," said Ariel.

"Me?" said the Other, examining his arm again. "I forget."

Ariel studied him pensively. "Has this Jesse been lecturing you about forgiveness? It's just the sort of thing he would do," she added, with a disparaging glance at Jesse.

The Other shrugged. "He was on about something like that. I wasn't paying much attention."

"How tiresome you are," said Ariel. The symphony, since she arrived, had fallen into the background: now it rumbled with distant thunder and flashes of light. "If there were anyone else who could save the universe, I'd push you through that gate." Lightning dazzled the air.

318

"Save the universe?" said Jesse.

"Oh, no," said the Other. "No way. Not me. You're crazy, lady."

"That's as may be," said Ariel, "but the fact is you're the only one who can."

"He can save the universe?" Jesse said incredulously. "From what?"

"Never mind," said the Other. "I won't."

"From insular atrophy," said Ariel. "And yes, you will, Jesse Farrell," she told the Other fiercely. "I spent my whole life finding you, and I won't have you wasting that!"

"What's insular atrophy?" said Jesse.

"It's what happens when the gates begin to close between worlds," said Ariel. "They get cut off from each other, and they can't survive that way. It's a long story, and not particularly interesting."

"So don't tell it," said the Other.

"The important thing is that this Jesse can prevent it, just by walking."

"By walking where?" asked Jesse.

"Between worlds, of course," said Ariel. "Try to use your intelligence, if you have any."

"Thanks," Jesse said dryly. "I will."

"If you die," Ariel told the Other, "the whole universe will die with you."

The Other grinned disingenuously. "Seems fair."

"You are repellent," said Ariel. A slow pulse-beat of deep bass rhythm began to build beneath the receding thunder. "Oh, bother, I really am late." Violins sang of dreams and distance. "I tell you what." Horns called out portents of peace and joy. "Let's see what a nice dose of reality does for you."

The clouds around them boiled with the brilliant pastels

319

of a glass harmonica playing Mozart. Lightning flashed again, filling the air with ozone. "I'll close this gate after me," said Ariel. "No sense in either one of you finding it again any time soon. Go on." She made a shooing gesture at them. "I'm late!" She disappeared.

The Other shook his head slowly. "Bizarre," he said. "You ever have hallucinations in the gates before?"

"Not like that," said Jesse. "Hear colors and see sounds, but I've never seen anybody in here till this time." He looked at the Other's arm. "Don't think she was a hallucination."

"Whatever," said the Other. Lightning flashed again. The clouds boiled. "See you." The Other disappeared.

It seemed pointless to follow him. Thunder boomed in the distance. Cymbals clashed. Darkness descended from the direction of the death-gate. Jesse walked instinctively toward Ruth's world. But he didn't reach it.

36

Ariel

Ariel Greef stepped to the gate. *At last*! But then she made the mistake of glancing back. *Damn*! Her work wasn't done.

Unseen by either Jesse, because she was gone and back in the blink of an eye, she performed one last necessary World-Walk. She knew what Suli Grail meant to the Other, even if he didn't. And her experience at Walking, time and worlds, was greater than his.

She divested the injured Suli of her gatestone first, because it might still work, circuit-burnt as it was, and it wouldn't do for her to Walk right back after the Other. Once that was done, Ariel collected Suli in time to whisk her to her home world and heal her wounds, leaving behind an inanimate changeling curled where Suli had been in the Other's arms, so that no one noticed her absence and no new worlds were formed.

Without her gatestone, Suli would be unable to find the Other: but he would find her. When he was ready, the mark of her lifeforce in the gates would sing him to her. And then he would be complete, as he had never been nor imagined.

Ariel returned to the final gate and glanced back. The two Jesses were still staring after her, unaware of her side-trip. She smiled with deep satisfaction and pride. Now she could go. Life had been good. She had done well. The worlds were safe, and the final mystery lay before her, free for the taking, *hers,* well-earned.

Turning away from the Jesses, she stepped lightly through the gate, pulled it firmly shut behind her, and went on.

37

Jud

The Lord High Monitor's office was stuffy despite its raftered vastness. As big as a ballroom, in keeping with the Lord High Monitor's lofty opinion of his own importance, the room might still contain the same musty air that was enclosed when the building was constructed at the end of the Ages of Chaos. There were several large windows, but Jud had never known the Lord High Monitor to open any of them.

"You took your time," said the Lord High Monitor. He was wearing a pink skirt and chartreuse leather vest with a collar that rose to a curved point behind his head. His eyes glittered with malice.

"Yes, lord." One did not apologize or make excuses to the Lord High Monitor. "You've seen the pattern of the Jesse Farrell's first unassisted walk?" Jud stood patiently before the Lord High Monitor's desk awaiting permission to be seated.

"Is that what you call it?" asked the Lord High Monitor. "An unassisted walk?"

Surprised, Jud admitted it. "Should I have called it something else, lord?"

"Yes," said the Lord High Monitor. "It's a plot. A New Worlder plot. You don't actually believe that little nobody walked, do you? The New Worlders did it." He rose to pace behind his desk, glaring at Jud. "They faked that pattern somehow. They wanted it to look like he walked. That's all it is. I want you to find out how they did it, do you understand me?"

"Yes, lord," Jud said automatically. Frowning, he added uncertainly, "You're saying the Jesse didn't walk at all? Or that he didn't walk unassisted?"

"For all I know," said the Lord High Monitor, "that Jesse doesn't even exist! It's a plot against me. They've wanted me out of office, and this is their way."

"No, lord," said Jud.

The Lord High Monitor froze in mid-motion to stare at him, eyes wild. "No? No? What do you mean, no?"

"It's not a plot against you, lord," said Jud.

The Lord High Monitor shook his head. "You can see it is. There can't be two Naturals out there, that's ridiculous. And we know the Other's a Natural. They've just faked this pattern for the other Jesse, that's all."

"It wasn't faked, lord. The Jesse is a Natural."

"How can that be?" The Lord High Monitor sat down heavily. "It's not possible."

"It's true."

"Then kill him." The Lord High Monitor nodded decisively. "Yes. At once. Tell your world-walker to kill both of them."

"She can't, lord. She's dead."

"Then send another, for pity's sake," said the Lord High Monitor.

"No, lord," said Jud.

The Lord High Monitor looked up from rubbing his face nervously with both hands. "I beg your pardon?"

"No, lord."

"You won't have him killed?"

"Will you have all the Jesse Farrells killed, lord?"

The Lord High Monitor stared. "You're telling me all the Jesse Farrells are Naturals?" He shook his head slowly. "No. It's not possible."

"Nevertheless, lord," said Jud.

"My holy windmill," said the Lord High Monitor. "What am I to do?"

"Join the New Worlders, lord," said Jud.

"Do what, did you say?"

"Join the New Worlders, lord," said Jud.

"Get out," said the Lord High Monitor. "I'll have you killed." He said it without force or conviction. "I'll have you all killed."

"They're right, lord," said Jud. "The worlds are dying of insular atrophy. Only these Naturals, particularly the Other, can save us."

"You've gone crazy," the Lord High Monitor said wonderingly.

Jud seated himself without being asked. "No, lord, I haven't," he said. "If you want to save your career, you can, but you must listen to me."

"Get out," said the Lord High Monitor.

"You'll be kicked out of office as soon as it's known you couldn't handle this situation," said Jud. "The New Worlders will riot. The Jesses will keep walking. You can't kill them all, not quickly enough to save yourself. And if you could—lord, you might as well kill yourself, and all the rest of us, too. Didn't you study that pattern? He's not only a Natural, dammit, but he obviously pushed back chaos on that one little walk. Think what he can do in a lifetime!"

The Lord High Monitor shook his head. "No. The New Worlders can't be right." He rubbed one hand across his face. "They can't be. I've based my career on the premise that they're wrong."

"But they're not wrong," said Jud. "You shouldn't have dismissed the impact studies and forbidden the theoretical research. When people find out—and they will find out, you can't hide something like this forever—when they find out that the worlds are in danger, and that you could have ended the threat if you'd listened to the New Worlders . . . well, you see, lord. Political suicide, that was."

"I don't believe you."

"You saw the pattern."

"I will not be thrust out of office by crackpot theorists."

"Who happen to be right."

"I don't care if they're gods," said the Lord High Monitor. "I will not lose my job. I will not."

"I agree, lord," said Jud.

"But you just said—"

"I can make it appear that you didn't ignore the New Worlders," said Jud. "I can make it appear that you joined us some time ago, but kept it quiet so as not to upset your constituents until we had the matter in hand."

"We," said the Lord High Monitor, staring. "You're one of them."

"Yes, lord."

"I'll have you killed," said the Lord High Monitor.

"I don't think so, lord," he said patiently. "By maintaining the integrity of worlds, we've been killing connections that were meant to be, that existed long before the Ages of Chaos. By our rigid rules and regulations we've been destroying the very thing we meant to protect. That has been going on for all the years since the Ages of Chaos. You could be the man who saves the worlds from the faulty thinking of the past. You could be our deliverer. If you do as I say. If you don't . . . Well, someone else will, that's all. The Jesses will be allowed to walk. There's no question of that."

"I won't have it," said the Lord High Monitor.

"Then we won't have you," said Jud.

"You threaten me?"

"Only because I'm in a position of power, and you're acting like a fool," said Jud.

The Lord High Monitor appeared to be in danger of an apoplectic fit. "Get out," he said. "Get out, get out, get out!"

"Are you quite sure that's what you want, lord?"

"Damn you!"

"Yes, lord." Jud smiled.

"Why would you do this for me?"

"Because we've got to have a figurehead of some sort. You're as good as any other. None of us wants the job."

The Lord High Monitor nodded thoughtfully, unoffended. "The pattern isn't enough," he said finally. "I can't be sure, from that." He eyed Jud craftily. "The New Worlders could still be wrong."

"Quite right," said Jud. "Did you realize the Other and the Jesse he displaced are now capable of sharing a world? That they've been in one world, together, without doppelgangering each other?"

"I know," said the Lord High Monitor, subdued.

"And that the Other prevented my world-walker's stone from returning her to Limbo before burning itself out on her death?"

"I was told that. I found it hard to believe."

"It's quite true," said Jud. "I haven't seen it myself, but I don't doubt it."

"I don't like this," said the Lord High Monitor.

"I know, lord," said Jud, with genuine sympathy.

"It means the New Worlders are right," said the Lord High Monitor.

"Yes, lord," said Jud.

"Figurehead," the Lord High Monitor said thoughtfully.

"It's just time to change streams, lord, that's all."

The Lord High Monitor made a sound that might have been meant for laughter. "It must look easy from where you stand."

"Not easy, lord," said Jud. "But advisable."

"Yes," said the Lord High Monitor. He studied his fingernails. "What are these Jesses doing now? You're quite certain you have the matter under control?"

"Oh, my, yes, lord," lied Jud.

"If I agree to go along with you . . ." said the Lord High Monitor, and paused.

"I have my people ready now, lord," Jud said gently. "Whatever your decision, they're prepared to run with it."

"If I decide against, they'll kill my career."

"I think they can, lord," said Jud. "A little matter of the hasty publication of some interesting data."

"Yes," said the Lord High Monitor. "I've been a fool."

"Doubtless it seemed necessary to oppose us," said Jud. "How could you know we did not oppose you?"

"You won't need a Lord High Monitor if these Jesses can do all you say," said the Lord High Monitor petulantly. "What do you expect me to monitor, tourists?"

"Among others," said Jud. "We'll not disband the corps of world-walkers straightaway, I think. They'll still be needed. As will the monitors we have in place already. Don't you see, lord, your job can actually be more powerful? You sneer at the idea of tourists, but they'll come, once the rules are relaxed—and the rules will be relaxed—

and we'll have to monitor and police them. And we'll still have to monitor the world-walkers, and the monitors themselves. The Jesses can push back chaos, but they can't govern the worlds. We need men like you for that."

"The Jesses won't live forever," said the Lord High Monitor.

"A good point," said Jud. "One of your first new projects might be to send world-walkers in search of Naturals with which to replace them, someday."

The Lord High Monitor rose and went to look out a window, his back to Jud. "One thing I don't understand," he said.

Jud smiled faintly. "Yes, lord?"

"This Other," said the Lord High Monitor. "You seem to hold him in considerable importance."

"He is crucial," said Jud.

"Why, if all the Jesses are Naturals?"

"Because there's not been a Natural loose in the gates since the Ages of Chaos. Under ordinary circumstances I expect a few Naturals taking the occasional walk in the ordinary way of things would be adequate to hold back chaos. We'll hope for that, anyway, because we're not likely to find an Other in every generation. But now, when we've pushed chaos back so far it's coming in from the other side (that's what's happening, you know, in case you hadn't thought it through), we need not just a Natural, but one who needs the gates as badly as we need him."

"You think the Other does?"

"I know he does."

"Why?"

"Because his soul is too big for one world. He needs room to stretch. He's the destroyer whose every act of destruction contains the seed of creation. And the other way

329

around, to his sorrow. He calls himself the Music Maker. And he's a world builder. He's tried living in just one world, a dozen times or more. He can't do it. He thinks it's because he makes mistakes, wastes opportunities, ruins chances. I know it's not. So far, he still imagines that if he can only find the right world he'll settle into it happily. I know he won't. He can't."

"Why not? Everyone else can. We can."

Jud smiled. "You and I are small men, lord. I walk only when I have to, and you, lucky man, haven't taken a step outside Central since you first arrived. We can fit into a world, make it ours, live our lives. The Other can't. Like the worlds, he's prey to insular atrophy. He not only can save us, he must save us, if he is to save himself."

"You make him sound, in a twisted way, like a messiah. I mean, not just a savior, but a Savior, if you see what I mean."

"That, too," Jud said amiably.

"I don't like it," said the Lord High Monitor.

"Nor do I, in fact," Jud said cheerfully. "Nobody asked us." He studied the Lord High Monitor. "Are you with us, lord?"

"I don't quite see that I have an option."

"There are always at least three options."

"Doubtless," said the Lord High Monitor indulgently. He was rapidly recovering from his earlier distress, shifting mind and body with little rustlings and sighs, adjusting to the new order of things and regaining his natural pomposity. "I'll need my speech writers," he said.

"Yes, lord," said Jud.

38

Lord High Monitor

He waited until Jud had been gone for several minutes before he picked up the transceiver on his desk and said, "Plan B. The Other first. Then Jud." He listened a moment to the voice at the other end, smiled to himself, and said, "I'll be with my speechwriters, drafting my State of the Worlds address. Let me know when it's done. We'll set the broadcast time accordingly." Still smiling, he put the transceiver down and rubbed his hands together. Jud had played into his hands at last. "I have you now," he said. The words echoed in the empty room.

39

The Other

So much for the easy path to peace. The witch closed that gate in my face. But once she'd done her little number on the hole in my arm I felt so much better I didn't much want to go through it anyway. The Jesse was right: no sense letting the old man kill me now. I wouldn't give him the satisfaction.

I didn't have anything special in mind to do instead. No place to go, no appointments to keep. Maybe the logical thing would've been to go back to the Jesse's world and take up where I'd left off when Suli decided to kill me, but who knew what would be happening there by now? Banny and Lyle might still be fighting over Suli's gun, or Banny might've shot the whole band by now, or something. I didn't feel like facing any more nasty little interpersonal politics. Maybe I'd never go back to that world. I didn't know. I figured a little time alone in the gates would give me the space to decide what to do next. So I walked away from him, but not out of the gates.

Or at least, that's what I meant to do. I landed back in the Jesse's world with a strong sense that I wasn't going anywhere else real soon. What's worse, the Jesse landed there right behind me. And he didn't look any happier about it than I was, so I guess it wasn't where he was aiming for.

Banny and Lyle were still fighting for the gun. And here's where it got really weird: Banny and Lyle were standing right there watching Banny and Lyle. So were Ruth and a little guy I later found out was called Zelig. At least four people who didn't belong in this world, plus me and the Jesse. Whatever the hell the witch-woman had done, I didn't think I was going to like it.

First things first: with Banny and Lyle waving that gun around none of us were safe, so that had to be stopped. As far as I was concerned they could shoot each other and good luck to them, but they might shoot me first and I was no longer in the mood to die. I guess the Jesse had the same idea I did, but he was real gentlemanly about it, wading right in and joining the fight like a proper hero should. I'm no hero. I picked up the nearest heavy object, a brass vase full of flowers that I dumped on the floor, and conked Banny on the head with it because he was the one who had the gun.

He let go of the gun. I grabbed it before Lyle could. He and the Jesse stood there looking at each other for a minute. For some reason the Lyle didn't even look silly, dressed only in his jockey shorts. They both turned around to look at the extra Banny and Lyle (that one fully dressed) who were standing up against one wall looking stupid. I slipped the gun in my pocket and looked at them, too.

This was going to get real hard to think about, real fast. I tried walking, since I didn't have any reason to get involved, but the witch-woman had done something to me. I don't know what. Some kind of magic spell, I guess, weird as that sounds. Anyway, when I tried to walk it made me so dizzy I damn near fell down. I had a feeling I could've got out of that world if I'd just been able to concentrate a little bit harder, but "if" won't buy rice. I held onto the back of a chair for balance till I could see straight again.

Meantime somebody picked up the Banny I'd knocked down and put him on the couch. Zelig looked at the bump on his head while everybody else just sat down all around him like it was an everyday thing to be all bunched up in one world together, and the wrong world for most of them at that.

The Jesse explained things to them, like about the gates and what'd just happened to us in them. I guess they had to be told something, and at least he left out the personal bits. The two Lyles weren't listening anyway. They just stared at each other. The Banny who was awake was listening, but he kept staring at the Ruth and his doppelganger. The Ruth had hold of the Jesse's hand like her life depended on it.

"Don't know what Ariel had in mind," said the Jesse. "She said something about a dose of reality, and when we walked from there we both landed here. And so did you."

"She must have wanted the . . ." said the Ruth, and hesitated, glancing at me. "Um, the other Jesse," she said. "She must have wanted him to meet with all of us. But why?"

"I don't see what's so real about that," said the Banny. "According to you, he's met most of us before, one way or another."

The Jesse shook his head. "Dunno. I do know you're an important part of this—or your doppelganger is. Banny, I know you've never much liked me—"

"Understatement," said the Banny, not unkindly. "But I think what I mostly didn't like was that other you." He shook his head. "You know, the one I always knew. The junkie. I didn't like him, and I didn't like the way he treated Ruth. She deserved better than that."

The Jesse made a wry face. "You prob'ly think she deserves better than me." He looked almost apologetic.

The Banny shrugged. "None of my business," he said curtly. "Get to the point."

"Dunno if there is a point," said Jesse. "I don't know what we're doing here, or what Ariel expected us to do. Just thought I ought to tell you what I did know."

"You said my, um, that other me had something to do with it," said the Banny.

"Oh. Yeah. He's, I'm sorry, Banny, he's pretty crazy. He—we were better friends than you and your Jesse, but he was always, well, jealous. He got real jealous about the Ruth here. Hell, she and I were just friends if that, but he thought—" He shrugged helplessly. "I don't know how to tell you. He killed her."

The Banny's eyes widened just perceptibly, but all he said was, "Sorry 'bout that. But it's nothing to do with me. I'm not him."

The Ruth was studying him. "No," she said. "No, you're not." She smiled uncertainly. "I'm scared of him. And you look—Oh, Banny, I'm sorry. Sometimes I'm scared of you."

"Because of him?" said the Banny, looking grim.

She nodded. "Mostly."

He took that in. "And?"

"Oh, and," she said helplessly. "Sometimes . . . you can look so angry, Banny, you know? Not about anything, just angry. I spent a little time in this world. With him. You haven't seen him when he's—"

"I saw him try to kill you," said the Banny. His face was pale, his eyes bleak. The little runt loved her. Had his doppelganger loved the other Ruth? Was that why he'd killed her? That didn't make any damn sense, but I was finding out things didn't, always. "I don't blame you," the Banny told the Ruth. "You want me to leave the band?"

"Oh, Banny," she said. Maybe she knew he loved her. There was sure something in her tone that meant more than just thanks for a generous offer. More than just pity, too.

"No sense talking about that till we get back to that world," the Jesse said abruptly. There was something in the way he looked at the Banny. Hell, he *liked* the obnoxious runt.

I decided it was time to put in my two bits' worth. "What makes you think you'll get back to that world?"

The Jesse looked at me. I knew my face real well, but I didn't know what the expression he wore on it meant. "We'll get there," he said. "Soon as we figure out what it is Ariel wanted you to learn from this. And you'll damn well learn it."

I grinned. "Thanks for the vote of confidence."

"Meant to be a threat," said the Lyle in jockey shorts. I hadn't realized they were listening. "Don't think Jesse has much confidence in you, you wanta know the truth."

I shrugged. "So he's smarter than he looks. That's probably a good thing."

The other Lyle burst out laughing. "Good comeback!" he said, and I grinned with him, not really meaning to.

"This one," said Zelig, "I am thinking his skull may be fractured." He glanced at me. "You are hitting him very hard, is it not?"

I was so relaxed that I didn't even hear the accusation in that. "I didn't like the way he was waving that gun around," I said.

The Jesse glanced up, suddenly alert. "What happened to that gun, by the way?"

"It's in my pocket," I said. "Why, you got somebody you want to shoot?"

He grinned reluctantly. "Maybe not," he said.

"Good," I said. "Me neither." Hell, maybe we could all be friends. The way they were looking at me I felt a kind of belonging, almost of brotherhood, as if I really were a member of this band. Maybe that was even what the witch-woman had wanted me to see: that reality wasn't all bad. That it could include moments like this, people you could take a chance on. That you didn't have to live your life alone behind enemy lines.

"We should be taking him to a hospital," said Zelig.

"Better call an ambulance," said the Jesse.

So much for friendship. I was standing nearest the phone. I didn't move. "Why?" I said. "The sumbitch killed a Ruth. Why save him?"

"He's a human being," said the Ruth. "We can't just let him die."

I let my confusion show a little. Maybe this was a joke; maybe if they saw I didn't know how to take it they'd lay off. "Why the hell not?"

She stared. "Because we can't. You just don't." It wasn't a joke.

"Maybe you don't," I said. "Or maybe usually you wouldn't." Maybe they just hadn't thought it through. I glanced at the rest of them. "Think about it: call an ambulance and you're going to get cops with it. The guy's been knocked over the head: they'll want to know who hit him, why, and so on. Well? You gonna tell 'em what happened? That I hit him? You gonna tell 'em why, and expect them to accept the whole story and let me go?"

"That's not important now," said the Ruth. "We can worry about explanations when we've seen to it he's being taken care of."

"He's been taken care of," I said, exasperated. "He got what he deserved. Let him be. You want us all to end up in jail, the crazy story we got to tell?"

"They wouldn't arrest us all," she said with clear contempt. I guess she figured they wouldn't arrest her, so why worry?

"No, I see that," I said, matching her contempt without any trouble at all. "I'm not nearly as dumb as you seem to hope." But I knew I had been pretty dumb indeed. I had almost trusted these people.

"Jesse," said the Lyle in jockey shorts, meaning me.

The Jesse looked at me. I couldn't tell what he was thinking. "Guess you figure you're the one who would get arrested, right?" he said.

"Well, hell, I'm the one who hit him. Yeah, I figure I'm the one who would get arrested." A few minutes ago I might've hoped they'd help me out, but not now.

"And since you can't walk out of this, you'd rather kill a man." He made it sound like any decent person would give up his life for that deranged creature on the couch, any day.

Damn it, I didn't see him offering up his life for the little toad. "Not a man. A goddamn murderer," I said, correcting him. For what it was worth.

It wasn't worth spit. "Murder's murder," said a Lyle.

I looked at him. "Meaning?"

"Meaning if you kill him, what's the difference between you and him?" He said it very gently, but his eyes were hard and cold.

I grinned at him. There wasn't much else I could do. If you don't laugh at your mistakes, even when they hurt like hell, you prob'ly won't live to make a lot more of them. "The difference is I'd be alive."

"More or less," said the Jesse, even more contemptuous than the Ruth had been.

I swallowed the hurt; it was my own damn fault. I knew

better than to fancy myself brothers with any man. "What the hell does that mean?" I was still off-balance; I'd let my guard down more than I knew, and I was having a little trouble rolling with the punches.

"Means you haven't ever been alive, so what the hell do you know about it?" He was madder than made any sense to me, but I didn't think much about it at the time.

"Jesse," said a Lyle, meaning the Jesse this time.

"Funny." I forced another grin. "I feel alive." Weak, but my taste for banter was gone.

"Maybe you meant to kill him," said the Banny I hadn't hit. I'd just about forgotten he was there. "You didn't have to hit him so hard."

I should have seen that coming. Next it'd be that I didn't have to hit him at all. I waited, wondering which of them would be the one to say it.

It was Ruth. "Jesse and Bob were trying to get the gun away from him," she said, obviously meaning I should've left it to them and stayed the hell out of it and never hit anybody. And the rest of them looked at her, considering it, judging me.

Story of my life: Farrell did something? Well hell, it must've been a crime, because that's all scum like him knows how to do. They were united; a band of decent, law-abiding people drawing together in a time of stress. And I was the odd man out. If this was the reality the witch-woman wanted me to see, she was behind the times. I'd seen this one often enough already.

"He is needing attention now," Zelig said quietly.

"Then get him attention," said the Jesse. "Jesse, move over. Let the Doc use the phone." He said it like you would to an obnoxiously stubborn child.

"No way." I put a protective hand on the phone.

"Jesse," said a Lyle, "let him make the call. You don't really want to kill anybody." Like he was talking to a juvenile delinquent.

"That's how much you know. For two bits I'd kill the whole damn lot of you." I meant it. But meant or not, it sounded like a goddamn kid's threat. I guess finding out you're stupid enough to've let your guard down with a bunch of people who turn out to want you dead just doesn't make you feel real mature.

"Maybe this is what Ariel wanted him to learn," said the Ruth.

That startled me. "What, that you'd all rather see me hang than let a spit-worm die?"

She stared, like I'd said something bizarre. "That life is precious," she said. "Anybody's life. And you wouldn't hang, Jesse. We'd tell them you did it in self-defense. Because of the gun. You'd be let go."

She almost sounded like she meant it. "Easy for you to say. You're not the one did it."

"Believe me, Jesse, I'd say the same if I were the one who'd done it," she said.

I almost believed her. "Why, for God's sake? Why would you risk your life for him? He tried to kill you. What the hell do you owe him, after that?"

"Common decency," she said without hesitation.

That was a joke. "Common decency is pretty damned uncommon from what I've ever seen. Plus it's a good way to get yourself dead. Come on, are you serious? The guy was your enemy."

"Not too long ago, so were you," said the Jesse.

"Right. So you'll let the cops have me." I was suddenly too weary of the whole thing to fight it anymore. They had it all figured out, and I wasn't going to change anything by talking to them.

"That wasn't what I meant," said the Jesse.

"No?" I felt behind me with one hand for the phone cord and ripped it out of the wall, made sure I'd broken the jack, and pulled the gun from my pocket. The time for playing games was over. "I know well enough what you meant, rock star. Hell, what's the loss, right? I ain't nothing to you. By the time the cops get here you'll have convinced each other the spit-worm didn't even have a gun, the way you're going. Plus I prob'ly hit him a good few times, what the hell. Makes sure they won't arrest any of you for it.

"Well, maybe I can't walk out of this world, but I can still take a walk, the ordinary kind, and I figure that's smarter than standing around waiting for you to get me hanged. You can get together on your stories about the no-good lowlife that hit the spit-worm. But don't get any ideas about calling the cops." I held up the ruined phone wire for them to see. "If one of you sticks his head outside this room while I'm still close enough to see it, I'll put some extra holes in it. Remember, I'm not one of your tame Jesse Farrells. I'm the piece of scum you're ready to throw to the hangman to save yourselves." I backed toward the door. "Give me, oh, fifteen minutes. Then you'd maybe be safe to go looking for cops. Maybe."

"Jesse," said a Lyle.

I didn't answer. I didn't even bother to look at him. Did he really think I was fool enough to fall for his fake friendship and listen to that big-brother tone, after all that had been said here?

"Jesse, don't do this," said the Ruth.

I didn't answer her, either. There was nothing to say.

The Jesse stood up and I paused, centering my aim on his chest. "Don't try anything."

He spread his hands helplessly. "Jesse, you're wrong about this."

"I don't think so." I wished to hell I was. "Sit down, rock star, and maybe I won't kill you."

That was when the first of the trained assassins from Central arrived, so I never found out whether he would've done what I told him or not. Good thing, because I don't think he would've, and I didn't want to kill him.

40

Jesse

When he suggested calling an ambulance and the Other reacted by blocking the phone, Jesse knew at once what was going on in his mind. He had seen the Other's slowly budding trust, his shy and tentative impulse toward friendship, and he knew too well from his own experience the unconscious recoil and instinctive expectation of betrayal that would inevitably follow.

For him as for the Other, intimacy had always been suspect, and the natural human tendency to trust was overbalanced by hard-learned early lessons in the value of protective hostility. Letting someone get too close spelled danger. It made one vulnerable. It gave the other guy weapons by letting him know one's weaknesses. The only safe response was to attack him before he could use them.

Jesse had long recognized and fought that pattern in his thinking, but the Other was probably not even aware of it in his. How often had he, in his perpetual struggle for the safe security of power, had occasion to test his reaction to intimacy? All he would see was that he had felt a fellowship with Jesse and the others, and that they had inexplicably turned against him. He would not believe it if Jesse told him that he had pushed them away.

He argued against calling an ambulance as if it were logical and wise to let a man die. Even Jesse, knowing how

343

threatened he felt, could not entirely control his disgust at
that. The rest of the group, with no idea what troubling
emotions drove the Other, were openly contemptuous,
which fed the Other's already great sense of outrage and betrayal.

He expected to be attacked, took the offensive in an effort to reduce the expected pain, and thus drove the others
to attack him. Where they did not actually attack, he imagined they had; he turned innocent observations into accusa-
tions and queries into threats. And all Jesse could do was
watch the process in mounting frustration. Once he lost his
temper in an impassioned effort to force the Other to see
what he was doing, and it ruined the effort and drove the
Other deeper into withdrawal.

And then, to as if crown the Other's suspicions with fact,
Banny made a genuine accusation. "Maybe you meant to
kill him all along," he said. "You didn't have to hit him so
hard."

Jesse would never know what made Banny draw such a
wild conclusion, but he could see the way it hit the Other.
The familiar face paled, for all his effort to keep it expressionless and bland, and his body jerked—almost imperceptibly, but the movement was there, a sharp recoil as from a
physical blow. There was a curious, waiting tension in him
afterward, but he didn't say anything.

Ruth tried to mend it. "Jesse and Bob were trying to get
the gun away from him," she said, reminding them the
Other had saved more than himself when he brought the
fight to such a timely end. Jesse and Lyle had not been succeeding in their efforts. They all knew it. They looked at the
Other, trying to fit the mantle of hero over the sullen
boy/man whose violent distrust so set him apart. It wasn't
an easy fit, but they knew that in some sense it did belong.

The Other returned their looks with a defiant little half-smile that said he had misinterpreted that, too. Jesse nearly groaned aloud in frustration. When Zelig reminded them of the need to get help for the injured Banny, and Jesse told the Other to let him make the call, he knew as soon as the words were out of his mouth that his tone was too impatient, too weary of needless argument. The Other would hear it as yet another sign of expected hostility.

The Lyle from Ruth's world, knowing nothing of the undercurrents, seeing only the Other's baffling resistance to helping Banny and recognizing in him the Jesse he knew whose personality was destroyed by drugs, spoke to him as to a recalcitrant child. That gave the Other fuel for his anger, and Ruth added to it with her suggestion that the value of life was what Ariel had wanted him to see. How could he believe that, when as far as he could see they valued the mad and murderous Banny but not him? He argued with her, but all he heard in her answers were threats she didn't mean to speak.

Even Jesse, knowing it was all but hopeless, knowing the Other's mind was so set on the expectation of rejection that anything any of them said would be interpreted in its distorting light, still tried. When the Other told Ruth that Banny was her enemy, Jesse reminded him that only recently the Other, too, had been their enemy. He thought surely the Other had enough empathy to see from that if not by instinct that even an enemy is human, deserving of life, perhaps not even bound eternally to enmity. But the Other heard it as another evidence of betrayal, and Jesse knew his trust was lost.

It was lost, really, before the argument began. It was lost long ago, in that unspeakable childhood they had both survived, and in the damage to their legs that the Other really had not survived at all. For whatever reason, because of luck or determination or fortunate stupidity, Jesse's outlook had made him capable of building a new life on the ruins of the old. The Other's had not.

And now, perhaps, it was too late. The Other drew Suli's gun and Jesse knew, better than any of them, that the threat he made was real. Yet he could not let it go, could not wholly give up on this sad, battered twin of his. He stood up, with no real thought in his mind beyond the wordless need to get through the Other's barricaded defenses somehow.

"Don't try anything," said the Other, aiming the gun at Jesse.

Jesse spread his arms helplessly. "Jesse, you're wrong about this." It wasn't enough, it wasn't even close, but what words would be? What could he say that the Other would not unconsciously twist into malice and threat?

"I don't think so." The Other's eyes were shadowed with pain and loss and terrible rage. "Sit down, rock star, and maybe I won't kill you."

Before Jesse could respond, three huge, muscle-bound men emerged from thin air in the center of the room, drawn weapons aimed at the Other: world-walkers, sent to kill him. They fired almost before they were fully materialized, and it was sheer luck that their first shots didn't kill him. A beam of sizzling green light just brushed the side of his head, leaving him stunned and bleeding but still on his feet. It punched a smoking hole in the wall behind him. Suli's gun dangled from his nerveless fingers, forgotten.

While everyone else was frozen in shock, Ruth moved. In a sudden access of pure fury she attacked them single-handed, screaming wordlessly. That broke the spell. Jesse saw the Other remember the gun in his hand and raise it to fire, but the hammer clicked home on an empty chamber. The mad Banny had used all the ammunition on Suli. The Other kept pulling the trigger with dazed incomprehension till the Lyle in jockey shorts dived to knock him to what cover they could find.

Jesse leapt to Ruth's aid, as did the Lyle from her world. Behind them Zelig hauled the injured Banny off the couch to the greater safety of the floor, while the other Banny stared in confusion and uncertainty, his mobile face twisted in dismay. "Walk, if you can," Jesse shouted at the Other, but he had no time to look back, to see whether he was able to do it. If he had, the intruders would surely have walked after him, and they didn't go. Either Ariel's spell still held him or the head wound stopped him.

Their only hope, then, was to stop the intruders. But the one Jesse had tackled knocked him aside almost negligently, as easily as if he were a child. One moment he was grappling with a massive, musky creature whose oiled muscles were as hard as banded steel, and the next he found himself sprawled on the dusty floor beside a sobbing Ruth. Her mouth was bleeding from a bruised cut at one corner. Before they could gather themselves to try again, a Lyle landed next to them and the intruders, free of interference, were headed for the Other.

But they held their fire when they found a Lyle between them and him. They could almost certainly have hurled him aside to get at the Other, but habit or training prevented them. Instead, with a wordless signal, they split up and spread out, each of them seeking a clear shot at the Other. Doubtless they would realize their mistake soon enough. Meantime it gave Jesse and the others a few more moments in which to try to stop them. He scrambled to his feet and leapt at one of them, only to find himself knocked aside again as easily as the first time. The soldier hadn't even glanced at him.

Ruth did a little better, hurling a wooden chair to trip one of them, but it slowed him only for a moment. The Lyle who had tackled one staggered to his feet and stood swaying, blood streaming from a cut on his forehead, dizzily choosing his next target. Jesse hauled himself upright and looked around for a weapon. There was clearly no point in tackling them bare-handed.

"They are not shooting us, only the Other," Zelig said suddenly, from his position of relative safety with the injured Banny on the floor by the couch. "Jesse, all of you, look! They are perhaps forbidden to be killing of us, is it not? We must be placing ourselves therefore as a shield for the Other, yes?" He threw himself with the Lyle between the Other and the intruders.

With a wordless glance at Jesse, Ruth grabbed the wavering Lyle and dragged him, unresisting, to join the others. He staggered dizzily against the Other. She stood defiant, arms spread, her body a frail shield between them and the intruders. Jesse crossed the room to join them, dodging soldiers. Oddly, that wasn't difficult. None of them made any effort to stop him. In fact they didn't seem to notice him, so intent were they on the Other behind his human barricade. When Jesse reached the group, the uninjured Banny moved slowly to join them, still studying the situation with an expression of stunned confusion.

The Other, still reeling from the blow to his head and perhaps from an unsuccessful effort to walk, tried dizzily to push them all aside. "These guys aren't kidding," he said, as if they might not have noticed that. "Come on, you don't know they won't kill you. What the hell do you think you're doing?" His tone was childishly impatient, and he shoved at them feebly, but none of them moved.

As Jesse took a stand beside her, Ruth glanced over her shoulder at the Other, a pitying look. "You really didn't understand, did you, Jesse?" she said. "I thought you were just being difficult."

"Understand what?" he asked, exasperated, watching the intruders warily. The room was not large enough to allow much maneuvering. It must have been as obvious to him as it was to Jesse that this temporary stalemate couldn't last.

"That we have no right to judge each other. That every life is precious," said Ruth. "Every life. Even yours."

"Oh, even mine." He managed a wry grin. "Well, that is saying something, isn't it?"

"They'll figure it out pretty quick. How to get past us," said a Lyle. "We gotta make a full circle around him."

He was right. Promptly obedient, they shifted till they stood shoulder-to-shoulder in a tight circle around the Other. He pushed at Jesse impatiently, disturbing them all. "Don't be dumb," he said helplessly.

"It just comes natural," grinned a Lyle. "Hold still."

"This is good," said the other Lyle. "But we can't stand here forever. What's our next move?"

"Depends on them," said Jesse, nodding toward the intruders. "Maybe they can't stand here forever, either."

Another intruder appeared, took in the situation at a glance, and moved toward the little group, a purposeful look in his eye.

"Looks like you're right," said a Lyle. "I don't think they're even gonna try."

"Link arms," said Ruth. They did it, quickly. "If we hang on, and brace each other, maybe—" The intruder reached them, took hold of her shoulder, and yanked. She very nearly lost her grip on Lyle and Jesse's arms. She did lose her temper. "*Damn* it, you stinking murderers! Leave him alone!" She kicked the intruder in the kneecap.

He was about to return the favor, a move that would almost certainly have done her a great deal more damage than her kick did him, when a new intruder appeared behind him and stopped him with a single, quiet word. The new one wasn't a soldier. He was a frail old man, ancient and gray, whose voice shook with the feebleness of age.

Three of the soldiers responded as to a minor god, halting in their tracks with stricken faces turned toward the old man and weapons automatically lowered. The fourth, who had just edged around the group till he faced Jesse and could shoot without endangering anyone but him and the Other, snapped off a shot before he realized what he had heard and, startled, turned meekly to face the old man.

If he had not been distracted by the old man's arrival, they would both have been dead. It had occurred to none of them that the intruders might shoot Jesse. The weapon's sizzling green bolt glanced off his ribs, and he would have fallen if the Lyle he had linked arms with hadn't caught him. He heard the Other grunt as the bolt struck him as well, but he couldn't turn to look. His entire universe was centered on the pain in his side.

"I said stop. Come here." Jesse heard the voice as from a great distance. It was the old man, his voice quavering and small, but nonetheless adequate. The soldiers moved toward him in almost comical haste.

Jesse concentrated on breathing. Behind him, the Other fell to his knees. "Get them out of here, Jud." His voice was barely more than a windy whisper. "If you don't, I swear to god I'll—" He broke off, giggling weakly. Jesse turned awkwardly, one hand over his injured ribs, to stare. The Other glanced up at him, eyes brimming with mirth in a blood-smeared face. "Get them out of here, Jud," he said again, "or I swear to God I'll create a goddamn world." He burst into gales of helpless laughter and disappeared.

41

Jud

He was almost as dismayed to see doppelgangers sharing a world without bouncing each other home as he was to see proof of the report that the Lord High Monitor had sent world-walkers to assassinate the Other. At least the world-walkers responded to orders. But not quite quickly enough: both Jesses were wounded, he could not tell how badly. Was the Lord High Monitor mad? Did he understand nothing of what Jud had told him? How dare he try to murder the worlds' one hope of survival?

As easily, perhaps, as he dared order the murder of the most senior world-walker in the worlds. It was that order that had been his undoing. The world-walkers might assassinate anyone else the Lord High Monitor asked, but not one of their own, and especially not the most senior of them. They held him in too much respect, almost reverence, for his experience if not for his character. The order, instead of being carried out, was brought to him in time for him to stop the world-walkers sent after the Other as well.

He did not expect to find them in the Jesse's world, and he did not know what to think of finding other pairs of doppelgangers there with them. Before he could ask how that had come about, the Other delivered his ultimatum and walked.

When he went, the others who did not belong in that

world went, too. And after them, before Jud could stop him, the Jesse. That left only one Bob Lyle and the injured Bancroft Averill in the battle-scarred hotel room with Jud and the world-walkers.

"What the hell?" said the Lyle.

Jud gestured toward the Banny. "You'd best call a doctor for him," he said.

The Lyle looked dazedly around the room. "Yeah," he said. "How the hell am I going to explain this mess?"

"You'll think of something," said Jud, knowing it wouldn't have to be much of an explanation. The authorities of a world such as this, where the universe of worlds was unknown, would be eager to dismiss the bewildering and bizarre with prosaic, if improbable, answers. Lyle or Averill would be accused of having destroyed the room themselves. Jud could check back later, to be sure neither came to any real harm over what the world-walkers had done. Meantime he had other things to see to.

He sent the world-walkers back to Central. Their fellows there would already have arrested the Lord High Monitor for trial by the Board, and the New Worlders would be quietly and efficiently taking over government offices as needed to protect order until the Board could meet. They would also distribute all the information available, including the scientific studies that had been undertaken despite the Lord High Monitor's ban, on the Other and his doppelgangers and their importance to the worlds. Now it was up to Jud to be sure the Jesses survived to fulfill their potential.

He paused in the gates, questing for the Other, but to him it was, as it has always been, only a barren emptiness where no voice answered his uncertain call. Defeated, he followed the Jesse to his Ruth's world, where he found Ruth and Zelig in a huddle with the Jesse's band. Though Jud didn't know it, they were in the same backstage room where Suli Grail had died. The Jesse was not there.

They all looked up and fell silent when Jud arrived. For a long moment they just stared at him while he, puzzled to find no Jesse there, looked vaguely around in search of him. "Where's the Jesse?" he said finally.

"Who wants to know?" one of the women asked belligerently.

"He's the one who called off the soldiers," said Lyle. This one, unlike the one Jud had just left in the Jesse's world, was fully clothed.

"Yeah, well, maybe he's also the one who sent them," said Banny, glaring fiercely at Jud.

"The Other knew him," said Ruth. "He called him Jud." She studied Jud impassively. "How did he happen to know you, Jud? Who are you?"

Unaccustomed to such impertinence, Jud smiled faintly. "I am the most senior of the world-walkers. The Other must have recognized my voice," he said. "We hadn't previously met, if that's what you wish to know."

"But you'd talked to each other?" she said, frowning.

"Yes," he said curtly, losing patience. "Where is the Jesse? It is imperative that I find him."

"So you can finish the work those soldiers started?" asked one of the women he didn't know.

"If I had wanted the world-walkers to finish that work," he said, "I'd have let them do it while they had the chance. The Other's survival is very important to me. I'd like to see that he's in no danger now."

"Oh, sure," said Banny. "That's real believable."

"Believable or not," began Jud, but Zelig interrupted him with an imperative wave of one hand.

"We are asking many questions. You will answer them," he announced. "Then perhaps, if we are liking your answers, we will see to the helping of you."

"What questions?" Jud asked reluctantly.

"These gates the Jesses speak of," said Zelig. "What are they, please? You understand, we are knowing they are the path between worlds. But what are they? How came they to be?"

Jud spread his hands. "I don't know. No, listen to me, I'm quite serious. Nobody knows. The gates are a natural phenomenon, but not an easy one to study. They've been in existence as long as the worlds have been. What you ask, I'm afraid, is rather like asking how the cosmos came to be. I can tell you theories for as long as you're willing to listen, but I cannot tell you certain truth. It is not known."

"Jesse says there's music in them," said Ruth, her eyes fixed on a distance none of them could see. "A concert of the gods."

Jud stared. "Does he? I've walked them a good many years, and never heard music."

She shook her head, smiling faintly. "I didn't, either. But I haven't been through them very often." Her eyes darkened, troubled by the memory. Few one-worlders were ever comfortable in worlds not their own. She turned her gaze to Jud and the distance died in her eyes as she studied him. "Why do you want to kill the Other?"

"I don't want to kill him," said Jud. "I didn't send those world-walkers after him."

"They obeyed you quick enough," said Lyle.

"Not quite quickly enough," he said. "The Jesses were injured. That's one reason I want to find them. I need to be sure they are well."

Ruth might not have heard him. "You sent Sue Lee

Grail," she said shrewdly. "She tried to kill him."

He hesitated, scowled, sighed. "Yes." His shoulders twitched. "I regret that. But I saw no way around it at the time."

"So you wanted him dead then, but you've changed your mind?" asked Lyle.

Jud shook his head. "I never wanted him dead. I wanted him awakened, aware of his abilities, and the quickest way to achieve that was to chase him through as many gates as we could. To make him feel close-pressed, hounded. Suli might not have chased him closely enough if she hadn't believed he was such a threat that he must be killed if she couldn't catch him."

"She might have killed him," said Ruth.

"Yes," he said.

"It would have killed her, too," she said.

"Yes."

"You risked both of them. For what?"

"For the universe," he said. "For the worlds." He glanced at the rest of them. "How much of this do you people understand? How much has the Jesse told you?"

"Enough," said Ruth.

He returned to the problem that had been puzzling him. "Did he tell you how it could be that in that other world, where the world-walkers came after the Other, some of you were there with your doppelgangers? How could that happen?"

"Ah." Zelig nodded comfortably. "Doppelgangers cannot share a world, is it not?"

"But they did," said Jud. "How?"

Ruth shrugged. "Jesse said someone named Ariel made that happen. But he didn't take time to tell us much: he had to go after the Other. To make sure he was all right."

"I might have known," said Jud, reluctantly amused. "Ariel always has to have her nose in everything." She couldn't have known what would happen in the Jesse's world. But perhaps it had been enough to know that something would happen: put enough of these people together with the Other and they were bound to do something that would shake his preconceptions, maybe enough to make him rethink his attitudes. She could have based the release of the spell on that. It would have been a gamble, but Ariel was always a gambler. He looked at Ruth again. "Did he say where they met her?"

"You're supposed to be answering questions, not asking them," said Banny.

"I don't think it matters," said Ruth. "I don't think he can hurt either Jesse now."

"What's more important," said Jud, "I don't want to hurt them. I want to help them."

"Why the sudden change?" asked Lyle.

"I always wanted to help them."

"You had an odd way of showing it."

"Yes." He sighed. "You can't tell me where they are, can you?"

Ruth studied him dispassionately. "I think they're both in the gates," she said at last.

"Ruth," said Lyle.

She shrugged. "I don't think he can find them, anyway. He's probably looked there already, right?"

Jud admitted it. He hesitated, scowling, hating his position as supplicant. But he had to know: "What are they going to do now, do you know?"

"Heal themselves," said Ruth. "And then I think they'll heal the worlds."

"Well, we'll do what we can," said Jesse's voice, "but

there's a limit. We're not gods, you know."

Jud whirled so sharply he nearly lost his balance. The two Jesses stood behind him, supporting each other, bloody and battered and triumphant. "Where have you been?" he demanded.

One of them shrugged ineffably. "Just in the gates, enjoyin' a little music, no big deal," he said easily.

"Hi, Jud," said the other. "It is Jud, isn't it?"

He nodded, staring. "And you. You're the Other?"

"I'm Farrell," he said with a child's clear certainty. Or a man's determination. "Jesse Farrell, human being. I have as much right to a name as anybody. Time you figured that out." His knees buckled, and the other Jesse caught him till he regained his balance. They leaned unsteadily against each other, grinning like idiots. Except for the blood and bruises they looked more like drunks than walking wounded.

Jud's shoulders twitched. "Time *you* figured it out," he said. "Tell me, what exactly did Ariel do to you?"

Farrell shrugged. "She showed me a little something."

"Yes," Jud said impatiently, "but what?"

"You wouldn't understand," said Jesse.

"Try me," said Jud.

"No, I'm serious," said Jesse. "You really wouldn't understand. Hey, you're the one tried to take his identity just because he wouldn't stay in Hell."

"It wasn't hell," said Jud, his tone impatient and dismissive. "It was just a world, like any other. He had the same chances any of you had, but—"

Farrell waved a hand negligently. "I know, I know. I made an ass of myself and a mess of my life. Hey, nobody's perfect."

Jud groped for support, found the back of a chair, and

leaned against it. "What the hell did she do to you?"

Farrell shrugged. "She showed me a little something I'd overlooked. Or at least, she made me stay in one place long enough to see it." He looked blearily at the others. "What you did, back there." He paused, looking confused. After a moment he swallowed hard and said with evident difficulty, "Well, thanks. You're a bunch of damn fools, but— Thanks."

"But what was it she showed you?" asked Jud.

He shrugged helplessly. "That being human isn't as bad as I thought it was, I guess," he said. "Or maybe just that I am human." He looked beyond Jud at the watching others. "I'm not much good at words without music. Let's just say I found out there's more than one music maker in the world. And more than one kind of power. Okay?" He grinned ruefully at Jud. "See? Jesse told you you wouldn't understand."

"No, I don't think I do, quite," said Jud. "But I can see I've misjudged you. I thought it would take a lot more time and trouble to turn you into—" He hesitated, at a loss for words.

"Into your kind of human?" Farrell's grin broadened. "You didn't misjudge me," he said. "I'm still not the kind of guy you'd think much of. Don't think I am. Maybe I figured out I'm not either the worst or the best person ever born, but hey, you gotta admit I'm still the most important right now, right? And I just might create a world or two for the hell of it if the mood happens to strike." He meant it. His gaze was a challenge. "Think you can stop me?"

Jud shook his head. "I know better than to try," he said weakly. "Which reminds me: I think I'd better get back to Central and see what I can do about preparing the worlds for your, um, advent."

Farrell emitted a burst of startled laughter. "My advent, is it?" he said. "Okay, whatever. Just don't go telling them I've turned into some kind of goddamned hero, or a model citizen, or something, okay? Because I haven't. I'm the same old Farrell, warts and all, and I haven't learned much about forgiveness yet, if I ever will. So if I see any of those muscle-bound world-walkers anyplace where I figure they hadn't ought to be—Hey. Next time the gun'll be loaded." He brandished it dizzily until Zelig came forward to take it gently from his hand, give it to Ruth, and help both Jesses to a seat where he could examine their wounds.

"I think you'd better go now," said Ruth, holding the gun in both hands as though prepared to defend her world with it.

"Yes," he said. "I think I had." He hesitated. "Take care of them." He gestured toward the Jesses.

"We'll do a better job than you did." It wasn't quite a challenge, but almost.

"I hope so," he said, and smiled. "You'll have your hands full."

She nodded seriously. "I know."